Cara's Call

Cara's Call

David S. Norris

Cara's Call
David S. Norris

ISBN # 978-0-9824032-2-8

Cover Design by Faithworks Image Consulting www.faithworks.us
Interior Design by Laura Jurek *laurajdesigns@gmail.com*

Audio-book produced by Brian Hord, directed by Shauna Hord, read by Kristina Wilson. Audio book may be downloaded and additional books and materials are available from carascall.com

All rights reserved. No portion of this publication may be reproduced, stored in an electronic system, or transmitted in any form or by any means, electronic, mechanical, photocopy, recording, or otherwise, without the prior permission of the author. Brief quotations may be used in literary reviews.

Printed in the United States of America.

Unless otherwise noted, Scriptures cited are taken from the New King James Version. Copyright © 1982 by Thomas Nelson, Inc. Used by permission. All rights reserved.

I Will Be Here
Words and music by Steven Curtis Chapman
© 1989, 1900 SPARROW SONG (BMI) GREG NELSON MUSIC (BMI) and UNIVERSAL MUSIC-CAREERS (BMI) SPARROW SONG and GREG NELSON MUSIC Admin. at EMICMGPUBLISHING.COM
All rights reserved   Used by permission
Reprinted by permission of Hal Leonard Corporation

ATR
Apostolic Teaching Resources LLC
Florissant, MO, USA
Copyright © 2011
By David S Norris

David S. Norris

A Word about *Cara's Call*

This narrative is an expansion of Cara's story, shared as a dramatic presentation at a 2010 UPCI General Conference. While the author is responsible for any errors in this book, Crystal Micko and Claudette Walker have been the two most significant influences on the direction and approach of my writing. Crystal's research serves as backdrop while Claudette's passion to empower a generation is its inspiration.

Cara's Call is a novel. To find out what elements of the narrative are true and what elements derive solely from the author's imagination, see the acknowledgments at the end of the book.

David S. Norris

David S. Norris

To Cara

Chapter 1

It was five past seven, less than thirty minutes until the meeting was supposed to start; not a meeting Pastor Jim Shepherd wanted but one that circumstances had forced. Driving north on I-57, he ignored the big tractors framed against the setting sun, tractors that turned over the best black dirt in the world. Jim loved to see it when Illinois turned green with new life. But not tonight. Tonight looked more like death than life; more like an ending than a beginning. Six years of pastoring, twelve years of preaching, and it all came down to this, one meeting that could well determine his future. Right now, that future did not look good.

Jim chided himself for the kind of father he was. Although his second oldest daughter was the catalyst and the cause for all of this, Jim still had no excuse. He himself had allowed it, embraced it, and had even promoted it. He breathed out, "Cara, Cara, Cara...how could I have ever let you get into this?"

Jim always cooperated with the district. He was straight as an arrow in his preaching, his finances were in order, and he was morally upright. A man well into his forties didn't take chances. Because this was his first pastorate, Jim had been especially careful and had never gone out on a limb.

Despite all this, in less than fifteen minutes he would be sitting on the wrong side of another pastor's desk; a man who wanted answers, answers that would be hard to come by. It hardly seemed possible that only eight months earlier everything had been so normal.

She hoped that he would not be angry, but clearly he was. The autumn sun had already set, yet it was still light enough to see the front door of the house slamming shut as he huffed and puffed his way to the car. The vehicle was still rolling to a stop when he jumped in the passenger side of the car. "I'm already ten minutes late—thanks to you!" he barked.

Cara was relieved when she discerned the tone of her brother's voice. This was not genuine anger; just junior-high-speak for "Hello, how was your day?" so instead of responding, she threw the car into reverse and backed out.

Cara's Call

"What are you looking at?" said Shay as he caught his sister sneaking glances at him.

"Nothing," she said.

"If you're staring at my hair, this is how everyone is wearing it." Shay had moved from sporting that slightly tussled faux-hawk to a much rowdier version.

"It's nice," Cara said quickly, which was older-sister speak for, "I like you no matter what." Shay didn't risk a smile, though he would have been disappointed with anything less than full approval. Not that he'd had any trouble attracting girls before this change in appearance. Tall for his age, he had the personality to charm.

"I might get a ride from Johnny tonight," Shay announced, attempting a bluff to freedom.

"Okay by me," Cara countered. "Just have Dad text me to let me know it's good." His face registered disappointment at being busted and stuck with Cara. He protested further by twenty minutes of silence. Oblivious to the corn that flanked the two-lane highway and now stood ready for harvest, Shay texted, played a couple of games, and then checked to see if the Yankees were beating the White Sox. There was no score yet. Shay didn't look up from the phone until he sensed that Cara had crunched to a stop on the overflow gravel area of the church parking lot. By the time she put the car into park, he was out the door, crunching his way to the blacktop and then into church.

Cara turned off the ignition, debating what to do. She decided not to go to church. It wasn't the fact that she had too much homework or even that events like these tended to be geared toward those who were about fourteen years old. It was something else. She didn't want to go in because of her problem.

Cara knew she couldn't just sit in the car so, with a long sigh, she unbuckled her seat belt and got out. Vans from several area churches were parked every which way in the overcrowded parking lot. She had known it would be like this, for tonight was "The Encounter," a widely advertised back-to-school rally. The praise band was amped up appropriately, for Cara could feel the bass guitar coming through the bottoms of her shoes the second she stepped into the vestibule. And when she opened the door to the auditorium she knew she could not stay.

Cara had almost flunked her college speech class because of her problem. Although her mom said, "Aw Cara" and hugged her when she knew about it, nobody in her family really understood her. They weren't like her. It would have been no big deal for any of them that the only seats open were in front and that in order to get there, one would have to parade in front of the whole church. This Cara simply could not do.

Yet, as she turned to leave, something stopped her in her tracks. Out of the corner of her eye Cara caught the look of desperation coming from her best friend, Amanda. She was the sole inhabitant of the empty row of chairs in the front. Amanda anxiously signaled Cara in an appeal that was not at all subtle.

Her friend's predicament was easy enough to see. There was a row of college guys behind her, and they would be staring at the back of her neck the whole service, leaving Amanda to feel like a leftover serving of meatloaf in the refrigerator—not actually good enough to eat, but too good to throw away. "Only for Amanda would I do this," mumbled Cara under her breath as she put one foot in front of the other on that long walk toward the front.

While there was, of course, some risk in walking down the center aisle, it was a calculated one. Teenagers were packed into the auditorium like sardines, swaying on their feet, lost in praise, and even though the chorus was ending, they always worshipped awhile after the song was over. So Cara kept walking. That's when catastrophe struck.

In a split-second change, the praise leader vanished from behind the pulpit to be replaced by Kyle. Kyle was the assistant pastor. He was a "no lingering in the afterglow, get the show moving" kind of service leader. Sure enough, "You may be seated" ricocheted inside Cara's head at the same moment Kyle spoke those deadly words. So there she was, traipsing down the middle aisle like a wannabe bride in all her glory. The college guys' heads swiveled to look at her when she passed them. One dark-haired guy was particularly striking. Either he had just stepped straight out of a fashion magazine or he was a Greek god. Perfect white teeth, bronze tan, and jet black hair.

If only Cara had had time to change after work, but her afternoon shift hadn't ended until just before it was time to pick up her brother. If only this powder blue jumper didn't make her look like she should be working at the concession stand instead of sitting in service. If only it was not the wrong color for her green eyes and not-so-fixed-up very long brown hair. And if only her three-year-old shoes matched the rest of her outfit.

Cara saw Fred sitting with the row of guys. Fred was her "always funny but more than a little sarcastic" cousin who spoke more words per minute than what was legal. She prayed that just this once he would be struck dumb. Yet, it was not to be. Fred announced for whoever cared to hear, "Nice you could make it to church, Cara." She would kill him later.

As Cara sat down in the chair next to her, Amanda gifted her with a thankful smile, which, unfortunately, Cara could not fully appreciate. *Funny,* thought

Cara's Call

Amanda, *she's so pretty and doesn't even know it. Wish I had her eyes and her chestnut hair—and her trim figure.*

Cara, who would have felt better had she known what Amanda was thinking, sat like a stone statue trying to calm her heart that was racing so furiously it would be a full fifteen minutes before she could even focus on her surroundings. Her grand entrance had so completely unnerved her that she was oblivious to the offering and the two incredibly long choir songs. And while the whole congregation stood on their feet, energized by the singing of the choir, it was all lost on Cara.

Finally, zoning back into the service toward the end of their second song, Cara poked Amanda and asked, "So who's the guy in the red tie?"

"Where?" asked Amanda.

"Standing on the platform behind the choir."

"Oh. He's the new youth leader from Bloomingtown."

"I've never seen him before."

"Just moved there a few months ago after Bible college."

"Is he doing something in the service?"

"You should keep up on things. He's the speaker."

"If you girls would stop chatting up there, maybe we could have a little church here tonight," came the words of Cousin Fred from the row behind her.

Someone nudged Cara from the aisle side, and Cara turned to see Stephanie motioning for her and Amanda to move over. "Just scoot in," she said, apparently needing the aisle seat for some reason. Stephanie had a clear complexion and except for a few freckles, she had a china-doll face. Her nose turned up cutely and her hair had a luster that women would die for.

Stephanie took control of the pew at once. She set her purse on the chair after retrieving her phone, checked her messages, sent a quick text, and then put her phone down next to her purse.

"Wow," said Cara, "I didn't see you coming in or I would have waited for you."

"Actually, I was already here," Stephanie said truthfully.

"So you came up to support me?"

"Uh…yeah."

Stephanie gave a kind of flirty look to the Greek god behind them, and this prompted another sarcastic remark from Fred. "So then, is this a contest to see who can be the latest to church?" But Stephanie was not Cara. It only took one quick look from her to freeze Fred in place. Fred was tall and lanky, never smiled when he delivered his one-liners. Sarcasm came easy and he simply never got embarrassed. Yet, Cara's glance revealed that he reddened under Stephanie's unrelenting glare.

Kyle was talking. "Let's remain standing to welcome our speaker, a great friend and best of all, a great Christian. We're honored to have the youth pastor from Bloomingtown speaking to us tonight: Josh Peeler. Come on young people, let's give him a big welcome."

Then, of course, there was that wild clapping and pleasantly insane cheering that always attends these sort of youth events, and after the speaker's perfunctory "Let's give that praise to Jesus!" the commotion went on for some time until Josh instructed the audience to be seated. The speaker then proceeded with the normal thanking of everybody and their kin, after which he offered a self-deprecating joke or two before finally getting down to preaching.

Cara studied him. Josh clearly wasn't "over the top handsome," nor was his face bronzed like the guy behind her, but his was a good and honest face, and he had a wholesome attractiveness about him. His hair was medium-tussled, tamer than her brother's. What she couldn't quite figure out was whether his eyes were hazel or brown.

Eleven minutes into the message, Cara whispered to Amanda, her trusted confidante: "His preaching is a bit much, don't ya think?"

"You wouldn't think so the way that Stephanie is 'amening' him," responded Amanda dryly. It did indeed seem that Stephanie was attempting to attract the attention of this youth leader who was quite single.

Cara continued, "Something about the way he says 'church-uh' and 'na-ow' reminds me of someone. Why doesn't he just say 'church' and 'now'? Do you think he is copying somebody?"

"Stephanie's getting louder on those amens," noted Amanda.

"I thought she was interested in that guy behind us," said Cara.

"Well, maybe she's keeping her options open."

"We're trying to listen back here," came Fred's voice.

Then things got better as Josh got into the rhythm of his message. And after another well-told story, he had the crowd in the palm of his hand. The musicians began to play in the background as he began closing the message with his own personal story. He was from a broken home. The Sunday school bus picked him up, and then he got in the youth group. He went to camp and got the Holy Ghost and felt his calling. Still, he was in and out of church in high school. After he earned a wrestling scholarship to college, he was at the altar one night when he finally fully dedicated his life to God. That's when he gave up his scholarship to go to Bible college to answer his call. The best thing he said, though, was that he was on an adventure, just taking the next step to live out God's purpose. He clearly meant it.

Cara's Call

"I like him better now," said Cara. "He seems a bit more real to me." Amanda nodded obligingly.

Josh closed with a final blood-and-guts story that played well for junior high kids. It was about a rebellious kid who had smashed up his motorcycle, and with his dying breath he wished he had just one more chance to dedicate his life to God. Cara couldn't help thinking it would have been better if Josh had enough confidence in himself just to finish with his own personal testimony. Teens quickly filled the altar area in prayer. Cara headed forward to pray with a teenager who was crying so intensely that her shoulders were shaking.

Cara put her arm around the junior high girl. After praying with her a few minutes, Cara stopped her and asked, "You doing all right?" The girl began explaining that her alcoholic dad had abandoned the family three years earlier and she had not seen him since. Cara nodded, listening with her heart, affirming her. After a bit, Cara prayed with her once again, yet it was clear that the girl had more to share. As Cara held the little girl's hands and shared in her brokenness, the girl continued to talk.

The service had its own rhythm, and the music became less reflective and more upbeat. Some began drifting back from the altar to visit with each other while others stayed to worship in time with the praise band. Cara's attention was distracted by a conversation going on behind her. It was Stephanie responding to questions from the Greek god.

"Oh, her. Well, that's Cara. She attends a little home missions church in a small town near here." Cara didn't know her whole life could be reduced to such a tiny sound byte, but she couldn't deny it either. Stephanie went on to talk about her own plans for schooling, her ideas for the future, and even where she believed the church should be headed.

Then Stephanie was suddenly cut short when out of nowhere appeared a beautiful girl with long blonde hair who came up to lay claim to the Greek god by simply whispering something into his ear and then whisking him off. Stephanie immediately recouped and headed to the platform to congratulate the preacher on his fine message.

"Hey, I'm heading to Denny's and was hoping you'd sit with me," said Amanda to Cara after the dismissal prayer.

"Sorry. I've got to get home."

"If you change your mind, text me," Amanda said over her shoulder, heading quickly toward the door.

Cara sought for and found Thomas, a young man she always tried to encourage. Thomas was talented, dedicated, and good looking, but she was hardly pursuing him as a boyfriend because Thomas was two years younger than she was. When it came to romance, the social chasm between a twenty-year-old college girl and an eighteen-year-old senior in high school is one that simply could not be spanned.

Shay interrupted his sister, insisting that they head out to the restaurant at once. "Cara, everybody's going to Denny's."

"Not everybody," she asserted, affirming that she was in charge.

"But I need to go," he insisted.

Cara checked her cell phone. "Look, it is almost ten now, so by the time we got there and ordered, it would be past eleven. It would be way after midnight by the time we got home. I have a couple of homework assignments that I need to keep working on, and I open the store tomorrow morning at seven."

Shay had not listened to a word she said; instead, he was planning his next line of attack.

"So, all you really care about is yourself." he said.

Cara, unfazed, turned from him and walked toward the auditorium exit. Shay caught up with her on the way to the car and tried a different strategy.

"Just because you don't like people…" This, too, had no effect.

By the time they reached the car, Shay had surrendered and was about to climb in when Cara offered, "I like individual people just fine. I'm just not fond of ninety people who are all trying to get the attention of the same three waitresses."

"Do it for me, Cara." Shay paused for a moment and then said, "There's this girl named Shiloh who said she would like to talk to me more. She's with the van from Pinckneyville."

"Just Facebook her."

"Cara…come on. I'll order right away, and you don't even have to eat. Just get a Coke or something. We can work it out. Please?" It was Shay at his most charming. He was even batting his long eyelashes. She started to soften a little.

Cara thought about Amanda's invitation to sit with her. It would be nice to catch up with her friend, and because Amanda would already be seated, Cara could probably shave some time off the whole Denny's expedition. It might even be possible to get home at a decent hour. "Okay. But when I say it's time to go, you'd better be ready."

"Yeah. Can do—but you don't have to rub it in just because you're older," quipped Shay, back to his usual teenage self.

Chapter 2

"Over there," said Shay pointing to the darker side of the parking lot. Cara dutifully parked in the spot Shay had indicated so he couldn't be seen getting out of her car. As soon as she parked, he ran from her twelve-year-old Mazda. What galled Shay the most about the car was not the two rumpled quarter-panels or the deep scratches on the doors. It was that he had to roll up his own window.

Unhappily, it was just as Cara had predicted: the flash mob had descended on Denny's. Teenage boys mostly sported messy hair; some wore ties while others were more casual. Similarly, teenage girls were dressed all different ways. Although some wore fashionable dresses and heels, jean skirts were more typical—so many that it could have been a uniform of some kind.

Shay quickly wove through the masses and found his place, a curved booth in the corner. While to the casual observer there was simply no room in the booth for him, his appearance facilitated a miracle akin to Moses' parting of the Red Sea. Space appeared suddenly in the midst of seven girls and two boys.

Cara scanned the crowd for Amanda but without result. Fishing her phone out of her purse, she typed, "where r u?" which was answered quickly by Amanda's "?"

Cara explained: "im @ dnys…u?"

"not comin."

"YYY?!"

"mergncy."

Peeved, Cara typed, "LIKE?" The answer surprised her: "youthgroup from Charlestown." As close to sanctified swearing as Cara would ever come, she angrily typed, "JRHIKIDS n4th row?!!!"

When Amanda texted yes, Cara took in a resigned breath to calm herself, finally texting "?" Amanda immediately responded, "2 busy @denys went2mcds."

Cara typed "?" holding back further capital letters.

"important invite," Amanda texted back, and Cara, with a poise she did not feel, once more inquired, "jrhikids?"

When Amanda replied "Greg," Cara responded "?"

The situation finally became came clear when Amanda announced, "vandrivr."

The entire exchange lasted forty-eight seconds, but in that brief time Cara's evening was totally ruined. Although she was happy for her friend, Cara stood alone in the middle of a big crowd, her phobia now beginning to attack. Her anxiety level rose like mercury in a thermometer plunged into boiling water.

She was on the brink of a full-fledged panic attack when a voice behind her asked, "Can't find someone?" Cara turned. It was the Greek god from church. He was surely Italian and had what Cara could only call a noble chin. If not noble, certainly striking. If he hadn't come from a fashion magazine, his clothes certainly had. Besides, that was no ten-dollar haircut.

"Yeah," said Cara. "Ah, no. I was just getting ready to leave."

"Come sit with us," he offered. "We're just about to be seated and one guy isn't showing up, so there's plenty of room." As if on cue, the hostess signaled him to follow.

"Justin's the name," he said, lightly touching her arm, guiding her along with him.

Then, as the group approached their table, the blonde girl Cara had seen with him earlier came rushing up to Justin and said, "I invited Jaime to sit with us since we have an extra chair." Her hair was beautiful, her tan golden, and she had on designer shoes.

Justin's eyes got wide. As did Cara's. Awkward. Cara didn't belong at that table anyway. She didn't belong anywhere. "You know what…I'll just find someplace else. No big deal," said Cara.

Cara quickly offered, "You know what, I should go anyway. Tons of stuff to do." She then made a beeline toward the exit, her heart pumping and her face coloring more with every step. She would go to McDonald's to find Amanda and then come back later for Shay.

But she didn't get far. A familiar voice called out, "Cara! Cara!" Turning to look, Cara saw Kyle, the assistant pastor from the church service. He was motioning for her to come sit by him. He was a great guy. A half dozen years earlier, when she was fourteen, he had invited her to join in with the youth group at Salem. Now, while Kyle's wife sat on one side of him there was, for whatever reason, an empty chair on the other side. Unfortunately, the table was forever long and situated smack-dab in the middle of the restaurant.

Under normal circumstances Cara would have waved him off, but she was so thoroughly defeated by this time that she no longer had the will to assert herself. Awkwardly she made her way over to the long table. As she sat down, it was clear to her

the table was populated primarily by platform people. Yet Kyle easily welcomed her, making her feel like she belonged. Cara was surprised to find she was sitting across from Stephanie and could only make sense of this when she realized that Stephanie sat next to Josh—who was himself sitting across from Kyle.

"And you are…" said the youth leader and visiting evangelist, a smile beaming across his face.

"Cara."

"That's a nice name," he said. Even his eyes were smiling as they captured her gaze. "Are you named after a relative?" he asked earnestly.

What happened next was totally unplanned. Cara rarely shared; some things were just too personal and precious. But she just blurted out, "My mother named me. Cara means 'dear one,' because, as she said, I was an answer to her prayer." And then Cara waited, feeling the beginning of a blush.

"Your mother is a wise woman. She couldn't have picked a more perfect name for you. I take it she was in church when she prayed for you." Cara saw that his eyes were in fact hazel, and they never left hers. His intent gaze made her want to say more.

"Yes. My name is Italian, and even though Mom named me Cara, she prayed that I would be like Ruth—resourceful, affirming, and helpful. Ruth is my favorite Bible character." Suddenly looking around, Cara became acutely aware that every eye along both sides of the table now seemed focused in her direction and that a hush had descended on the group.

Josh, sensing her discomfort, went in for a rescue. "I wish my mother or father would have put that much thought into my name. Neither were Christians when I was growing up, but I'm still praying for them."

"But Josh—short for Joshua—is a significant name," said Cara, briefly forgetting that she had an audience. "It's from the Hebrew."

"I do recall studying about this some in class," he said.

"Right," she said, continuing earnestly. "It means, 'The Lord saves' and it is the same name as--"

"My mom named me 'Stephanie' for my aunt," a voice chimed in from across the table. "Because my eyes are a brilliant hazel, just like my aunt's."

Josh then turned sideways to give his full attention to Stephanie's eyes and was no doubt about to affirm their incredible "hazelness" when Kyle interrupted the interruption.

"Speaking of names, why don't we get ready to *name* our orders? That waitress looks pretty tired, so let's not make it any harder on her than it has to be. And we'd better give her a good tip, guys," he said, purposely scanning the large group seated at the long table.

"So, Josh, what kind of schedule are you keeping over there in Bloomingtown?" continued Kyle, commanding the conversation and celebrating the evangelist. Stephanie, with her brilliant hazel eyes, leaned into the answer.

"Well, as you know, I'm only part-time at the church, and while that includes helping the pastor in whatever he is doing and occasionally preaching, it is mostly working with the youth. But I don't really consider myself part-time as far as ministry is concerned just because I work at Starbucks. Let me explain. First, I'm getting health insurance even though I only work a little over thirty hours. And second, it's a place where ministry happens organically."

As he said the word "organically," he once again turned his attention over to Cara and looked deeply into her eyes. So complete was his focus that Cara started wiping an imaginary speck off the water glass because she didn't know what else to do with such direct attention.

"I'm saving up for AIM—the Associates in Missions program," said Stephanie, recapturing the spotlight. And when enough focus was dispatched in her direction, she waded deeply into how profoundly she hurt for the wounded of this world.

It was during Stephanie's rather lengthy oration about her desire to become an Associate in Missions in some African country or another that Cara consciously worked at slowing her own racing heart rate. Stephanie's burden for the hurting had a different sound to it than it had an hour earlier when Cara had heard her tell Justin "the Italian Greek god" how she was about ready to start schooling for interior design. But that was then and this was now.

Josh turned back to Cara, and asked eagerly, "Are you called to ministry, too?"

The question was innocent enough.

Of course, Cara's family was in ministry. And of course, it had been way too stressful with way too many responsibilities. Cara started to say, "Not in this life" but as she said "Not…" she could see Stephanie smiling broadly. It irked her. After a long pause Cara finally offered, "Uh…not something I like to talk about publicly."

"I understand," said Josh appreciatively and turned back to ask Stephanie more about her upcoming plans for a short-term missions stint as an AIMer.

For Cara, the evening ended right then and there. She was absolutely horrified with herself, having skirted more closely to a lie than she ever cared to think about. While the conversation continued to go on around her, she tuned out, not able to excuse herself for her deceit. What kind of person was she becoming?

The ride home from Denny's did not lighten her mood. Shay didn't care one way or another as he was busy texting all of his newfound friends. But "foul" her mood was, and foul it remained.

The same conversation played over and over again in her head. She turned off the ignition, got out of the car and walked up to the house and through the front door. Of all the stupid things that had happened during the course of the evening, she felt responsible for the stupidest thing of all.

Then it occurred to her that the fault was not entirely hers. Much of it was Josh's fault. His lame question had prompted her lame response. What did he mean by, "So are you called to ministry?" Did he mean was she a preacher? Of course she wasn't. That was obvious. He knew that before he asked it.

Did he mean was she as spiritual as Stephanie? That wasn't a fair question. It required some sort of comparison. He had no right to create a "dedication contest" between two girls who were obviously both interested in him. It wasn't just unfair. It was stupid!

Did he mean, was she called to be a pastor's wife? If that is what he meant, then that was stupid too, because there was no such calling in the Bible. Cara's mom was a pastor's wife, and she wasn't called to anything. Her role was just a supportive one. Or was she called? No. Of course not. It was simply a ridiculous question for Josh to ask.

There was no other word for it. Josh was a stupid evangelist who asked very stupid questions. Well, one stupid question. Nonetheless, it was that very stupid question that was the cause for Cara only getting five hours of sleep, five fitful hours of tossing and turning in bed.

At ten o'clock the next morning, fifteen minutes before her break, Cara's cell phone vibrated. The text read: "CALL ME!" As soon as she was free, Cara dialed the number. "So what's the emergency?"

"Billy is taking me out tonight for our fifth anniversary!" said Cara's older sister.

"Make him take you to someplace fancy."

"One problem…"

"What's that?"

"My regular babysitter canceled."

"Really?" She already knew why—a teething baby and a very active toddler. She also knew where this conversation was leading.

"That's why I need you," said Sandra, her voice a bit more demanding now.

"Not in this life."

"Are you saying that there's something wrong with my kids?"

"They're great. I love to play with them in controlled situations. But I have to study. I have children's church tomorrow, and a chemistry test on Monday that I haven't studied for and—"

Cara's Call

"Cara, you know that you can ace that chemistry test. And really, you're not going to be doing any major prep for children's church tonight. It's just two or three hours and the kids will be just fine. The baby always sleeps and Sissy is totally awesome to play with so…"

Five minutes later, Cara texted Amanda: "y cnt I have backbone?" It brought a quick response from the other end: "?"
Cara responded: "barnboss conned me n2 bbysittng agn...so greg? good?"
Amanda: "hes texting now ☺."
Cara: "nice."
Amanda: "k g2g."

"Sissy goes to bed at eight-thirty, and Angel will get up from her nap and will get her bottle at seven-thirty. She'll conk out again immediately after she has the bottle. And we'll be back by nine-thirty."

Although Sandra, a.k.a. "Barn-Boss" confidently prophesied how the evening would go, Cara knew it to be more wishful thinking than reality. "Sounds easy enough," replied Cara, not believing a word of it.

"Angel may even sleep till she gets up for her bottle. And Sissy will just play in the living room. Everything good?"

"Great. Wonderful. Can do," Cara responded, although only her lips were smiling. Her eyes told the truth, if anyone had cared to read them.

"Great. You're the best."

Then as she walked out the door, Barn-Boss dropped the bombshell. "Oh, and by the way, tomorrow is Sunday."

"Yeah?"

"Well, while you're at it, can you give both kids a bath? Maybe when Angel gets up? It won't be much trouble. You've seen me do it lots of times. Love ya."

Cara let out a resigned breath as her sister fled. Then, opening her chemistry textbook to the review questions at the end of the chapter, she ignored Sissy who was emptying out one toy after another from the toy chest onto the living room floor. The only good news was that Angel was still asleep in the nursery.

Cara's phone buzzed. It was Fred: "hey cuz saw u sitting w/ bigwigs. 2 good 2 tlk 2 me nemore."

She knew this was Fred-talk for "I'm glad you found a place to sit last night." She returned, "jealous?gofish." It was how they bantered. Fred wasn't really her cousin, but had become "Cousin Fred" as the son of "Uncle Bob," her Dad's mentor. Uncle Bob sometimes brought little gifts over to the house and his family always came over for Christmas. Last year Fred and Cara had been charged with helping to keep the children occupied. Since then, Fred and Cara used the code word "gofish" to lightheartedly tell each other to take a hike.

Fred texted back a crazy face which was then immediately trumped by a text from Stephanie: "joshs bday is nov22 Im gettn anew pic 2give2him."

Cara had no time to respond to this as Amanda was texting in details on her McDonalds fellowshipping. This too was cut short when a toy doll whizzed over Cara's head and hit the wall behind her. It wasn't altogether unexpected.

Although they were called Sissy and Angel by their mother, Cara had other names for her two nieces: "Time for Terror," and "Baby Lungs," respectively. Cara was now required to divert her attention to Time for Terror, who apparently resented not being the center of the universe. And then, after only five minutes of playtime, Baby Lungs made her presence known very loudly from the other room.

Cara marched into the nursery to find that the red-faced crying machine was a bit damp and mushy on the bottom side. The prescription: one good clean diaper. Sadly, the change of diaper didn't yield a change of behavior. Baby Lungs simply would not quiet down.

She had to implement Plan B. A bottle and a burp later, the baby was supposed to be heading back toward La-La Land, but apparently, Baby Lungs hadn't gotten the memo. The creature went from crying to screaming, refusing to be comforted. Then, because Time for Terror was no longer getting all the attention she deserved, she demanded snacks that she wasn't supposed to have, which quickly led to a full-fledged tantrum on the living room floor.

More confusion resulted when it was not merely a text but an actual phone call that continued to vibrate Cara's phone. Clearly, this would be Barn-Boss checking in. With the bathwater running, a howling infant in one arm and whining toddler throwing toys across the coffee table, Cara pronounced to her phone, "We've got a sinking ship here!"

A guy's voice quipped, "Hey, I hope I'm not catching you in the middle of something."

Upset and confused, Cara barked, "Fred, I told you to go fish!"

"It's not Fred, it's Josh."

"Josh who?" she said, perturbed, as the baby screamed louder.

"Josh from last night."

She stopped short. "Oh. Can you call back in an hour? I have to go drown a couple of kids in the bathtub."

"Oh, well sure, I mean…if you have to."

Cara wasn't surprised when he didn't call back. Who would?

The bath didn't reduce the racket. Neither of the two hooligans wanted anything to do with their clean jammies. Even at nine-thirty, Baby Lungs was still exercising vocal chords while Time for Terror was bashing one toy against another to protest life.

Cara was not too surprised that Sandra did not return on time. Ironically, by the time Barn-Boss and Billy actually showed their faces an hour and a half later, Baby Lungs was angelically sleeping in her cute little crib while Time for Terror was sawing logs in clean Snow White pajamas. Cara had just cleaned up Armageddon from the living room when the key rattled in the door and Sandra and Billy happily entered.

"Looks like everything went really well here," said Sandra, handing Cara a generous wad of cash.

"Wonderful time," said Cara, and then more quietly, "More fun than a barrel of monkeys."

Chapter 3

The next afternoon they were eating at Ruby Tuesday, the same place they had eaten the previous Sunday and the Sunday before that. Everything seemed scripted with everyone playing their part. It was their Sunday afternoon ritual. Dad and Sandra were involved in their usual combat.

"Yes, we do need to spend more money on the military," said her father.

"And this from a Christian minister," replied Sandra with a hint of a smile, randomly looking for an opposing position to that of her father's.

"We can't be weak against this godless Chinese government who is trying to control the world and forcing us into so much debt that we'll be bankrupt. They're just trying to control the world economy."

"And we're not?"

"For democracy. Sandra, please. We are looking at the face of evil here."

"Dad, did you know there are probably more Spirit-filled people in China than in the United States? They're having a big revival. China can hardly be called godless."

"But the government is godless. They're corrupt!"

"So there is no corruption in our own government?"

As if knowing it was her cue to speak, Cara's mom broke in, "Well, if the Chinese are making so much money off of us, I'm glad it's going to Christians." Karen delivered the line perfectly, and everyone laughed. That was Mom's role: back-door peacekeeper. Settle things down with her dry wit so the waitress could begin passing out the entrées. If it wasn't the military or the Chinese, it would have been defining the right sort of music or the value of counseling or the price of gold. It was all as certain as clockwork; the Sunday afternoon roundtable that always accompanied the food.

"It wouldn't hurt you to join in with the family," said Jim to his son Shay, who apparently didn't have anything to add about the Chinese but was rather, as he explained, focusing on a kind of follow-up ministry with some needy young ladies from Pinckneyville. His Dad didn't buy it. Nor did his mother. But she was more amused than frustrated.

"Shay," asked his mother, "how many girls are you texting right now?"

"You mean, at this very minute?"

"That's how I define 'right now.'"

"Six or seven," he replied thoughtfully.

"Can't you just put it on hold until we finish dinner?" demanded his dad. "Really!"

"Okay, Dad," said Shay. "Just signing off."

"With who?" asked his mom, smiling.

"Samantha, for one."

"Is she the ditzy one?" asked Cara.

"No. Samantha has red hair."

"Who is the ditzy one?" asked Sandra, now interested.

Shay reveled in the attention. "I don't know who you mean. It could be you're thinking of Cally or Louellen."

"Is Louellen from Pinckneyville?" asked Mother, keeping the conversation going.

"Actually, I'm not certain about that. I don't really know who Louellen is."

"Shay," said his father, "just stop texting right now. I declare, these youth rally things should be more than just trying to find somebody to flirt with."

"Don't talk to *me*," said Shay. "It was Cara who was getting all googoo-gaggah over the evangelist."

Cara didn't defend herself from her brother's accusation. It wasn't her part to play in the family. And then, as if her little brother's words were prophetic, Cara's phone buzzed. She glanced inside her purse to see that it was a text from Josh. It read, "can u talk?" Cara took the phone from her purse and typed, "not now."

Whereupon another text asked when she *could* talk, but before she could specify, her father said, "Cara, if it isn't too much to ask, I wonder if you could join us here at our family dinner. Whoever that is, just ignore them."

"It'll just take two seconds—"

"Cara. I mean it. Now. Not another word on that phone while we are trying to have a decent family meal together. Now."

Her mom patted Cara's hand meaningfully. "Maybe you can text a little later."

Her mom was the buffer. The negotiator. Nothing seemed to ruffle her feathers. Cara's older sister could argue with her dad, her brother could talk around him, while her mother could make sense of him. Cara's phone vibrated impatiently again, requesting attention.

Cara's dad had once been an alcoholic. The oft-told story was how his marriage was on the skids. How one night at the lowest point of his life he decided to go to church. How things changed immediately. No more desire to drink. Family made whole. Hunger for the Lord, a burden to serve, and then after some time, his launch into ministry. And miracles. Cara's dad believed in miracles. And the church experienced them. Like he always said, "You get what you preach."

Her dad had a string of one-liners she could quote in her sleep: "We don't need no panty-waist-willy-nilly preaching. We need to preach truth. And we need to preach it straight and hard."

Cara was proud of her dad. There really was no other word for it. Yet it was not a word she could ever speak. He was her hero. It was just that in her family the words "hero" or "proud" didn't exist as usable words. She didn't know why—didn't even think about it. It's just the way her family was.

Cara's phone vibrated once more but then died for lack of interest.

Later that afternoon, when it was just Cara's mom and dad in the living room, her mom brought up something she had been thinking about for some time. "Jim, dear, I was wondering about Marta." Karen was sitting on the couch pretending to read the paper while her husband was in the recliner reading his Bible, jotting down a couple of notes in a spiral notebook for his sermon that evening.

"Hmmm..." came the voice from the recliner.

He was not yet focused. So she continued, "So what do you think?"

Twenty seconds went by before Jim remembered he was supposed to be in conversation with his wife. He looked across the room and noted that she still looked pretty, even at forty-five years of age. Even after twenty-seven years of marriage, Karen had kept her figure. Marrying her was one of the few right choices he had made as a teenager, although he had chosen her solely on her looks and didn't deserve too much credit. "I'm sorry, what did you say?"

"I was asking what you think about Marta."

"You mean, Marta—as in Cara's friend Marta?"

And then remembering that his wife had tried to talk to him about this the previous Sunday, he said, "Oh, that. Why can't Cara keep doing it by herself?"

"Well, she is one person, and she has all the three- to eleven-year-olds on Sunday mornings. She did okay when there were seven of them, but this morning, there were twelve, and sometimes she has even more now. And she has to keep them during the preaching, and sometimes that can get long."

"Careful, there...." Jim said with a smile.

"I'm just saying that she is stretched pretty thin to keep their attention that long."

"But Marta—why Marta? I mean, she isn't even in the church."

"Well, she has been coming on and off. And Cara is teaching her Bible studies. Marta wouldn't actually be teaching Sunday school. She would just be helping Cara in children's church, on a short-term basis, until we can figure something else out."

Cara's Call

"But that thing she does—that cutting thing with her arms—is she still doing that?"

"She hasn't done that for months now."

Karen hadn't signed up to be a preacher's wife, and she was still negotiating just how her role was supposed to work. Although her own father had pastored some while she was growing up, she was pretty sure that whatever he had done was probably not the way to do it. More than a dozen years earlier Jim had started formally speaking in church, and after another six years he quit his job in Texas to evangelize. That didn't last long because, after only four weeks of evangelizing in Illinois, a presbyter asked them to take over a struggling home missions work, and her husband consented.

Jim was clearly thinking through the implications of Karen's request. He said, "If we allow Marta to help, I am going to hear about this from several dear sisters in the congregation."

"Cara said that Marta could wear long sleeves."

"I don't know."

"Cara did ask me to find out about this six weeks ago."

"She's not getting a bad attitude about it, is she?"

"Not at all. She hasn't mentioned it since she spoke to me about it the first time. It's just that… well, I was passing by her classroom and saw how much she needs the help. I could help her some I suppose."

"You know I need you in the main service, and don't even suggest Shay or Sandra. Sandra has keyboard and Shay plays drums, and I need them both for altar call."

"Well, it appears you have run out of children to help."

"Well then," he teased, smiling, "I suppose we could have a few more."

Jim was a bit heavier than he once was but he stayed in shape. His sales job made him less active but he played racquetball to compensate. Karen still found him handsome, even though his salt-and-pepper hair now had more salt than pepper. But today she would not be charmed. When she continued to dead-pan him, he suddenly announced, "The Sunday school is important to be sure, but it is secondary to what is happening in the sanctuary. I don't want to give up anyone else to it at present, so you tell Cara we can try Marta helping out for a month. But Karen, I want you to keep a close watch on things and keep me informed about how it's working."

"I'm gonna flunk," said Marta. "I know it. I'm gonna flunk. And then my life will be ruined and—"

"Just wait a minute," said Cara, looking over her friend's flawed research paper. Marta was a very pretty girl with shoulder-length jet-black hair, almond eyes, long dark eyelashes, and no self-esteem. She had come to Cara for help in math toward the end of the previous school year, and then for help in another subject, and that had defined their relationship.

"It's really bad, isn't it!" complained Marta, ignoring the noise around them in the student commons. It was Tuesday morning, only 11 a.m., so it was not so packed that they couldn't have a conversation.

Cara marked something on the paper and said, "Okay, Marta, now here you credit John Adam's Christianity for his success, but then on the next page you blame his Christian outlook for his fights with Jefferson. You're obviously quoting sources in both places. And I'm not saying you're wrong, but there doesn't seem to be a point. Your last four pages are pretty random."

"I ran out of time, Cara. I just ran out of time." When Marta was happy, she could light up a room. But when Marta was sad, like today, she was a black hole that sucked the emotional life from anyone who gravitated near her. A tear escaped unbidden from the corner of her eye and rolled sadly down her cheek.

Cara tempered her words. "Well, again, you offer some good stuff. I see you've done a lot of research. Your sources are good. But this prof is a stickler for writing. He is pretty big on having a main point to your paper."

Cara's phone wouldn't stop buzzing, so she signaled to Marta that she was taking it. It had to be her mother. She was the only one who actually called her anymore.

"Hello."

"So you do exist," said the male voice.

Cara looked down at her phone. It was Josh. "Just a second, Josh."

She handed the paper across the table and said, "Marta, while I'm talking I want you to think about how to create a one sentence statement that tells what you really want to say. They call it a thesis statement—you know, what your paper is about, from English Comp."

"I don't know what you mean," said Marta, tears now welling up in her eyes. As she bit her lip, they coursed down her cheeks in earnest. She wasn't far from sobbing.

"It's okay," said Cara, and then to her phone, "Josh, my life seems to be one emergency after another."

"Hey, no problem. I'll catch you later."

Because Cara was usually at work on Saturday morning, her mom was surprised to see her walk into her kitchen where she was busy taking pies out of the oven for the bake sale. As she plopped the last pie on the table, Cara spoke without

Cara's Call

preamble. "Mom, if someone asked whether you had a call to ministry, what would you say?"

"Well, it depends what you mean," said her mom. "We're all called to serve."

"I appreciate that. But this is a serious question. I'm not talking about philosophy. My life is on the line here." Her mom's eyes widened.

"Mom, if someone specifically asked you if you were in ministry, what would you tell them?"

"Well, it depends who was asking, dear. Why are you so upset? I pretty much know who I am."

"Which is?"

"A minister's wife."

"So what does that mean?"

"I've never really needed a label."

"Okay, Mom, here's the deal. There's a boy who I think very seriously wants to know if I have a call to ministry, and I kind of think that whatever I answer will determine whether we have a future or not."

Her mom looked troubled for a second, and then conjured up some reconciling words. "Why don't you just wait to see what develops?"

"He's picking me up for dinner in ten hours and thirty-seven minutes."

"Oh, well, then. That's a different story." But her mom apparently had nothing more to say. Finally, she suggested, "Maybe it won't come up."

"I'm pretty sure it will. It already has."

"Oh."

"Okay, so are you in ministry with Dad?"

"Well, certainly I support his ministry…as do you."

"And if something happened to dad, if he died tonight, would you be in ministry?"

"Cara!"

"Just saying. No prophecy, Mom."

"Well, then, no. I wouldn't be."

"But you're a ministry couple."

"Yes."

"This is so confusing."

"Is he asking you to be a part of a ministry couple?"

"That's what's so strange. I've just met him one time. And it is a really awkward question for me. I don't know what to say. But he is so serious about this and I don't want to say something stupid."

"Just let the Lord guide you."

"Mom, forgive me for saying it, but I think that is very stupid."

"Well, I'm sure you've thought about this before. Have you prayed about what you want to do in life?"

"Yes. And, like I told Dad when he insisted on knowing, I'm going to be a lawyer."

"Okay. That's good then, isn't it? If this is what the Lord told you to do, then—"

"Mom! I don't need platitudes right now. It's not what the Lord told me, but it's what I told Him, and He hasn't told me no. I could make good money and I wouldn't have to live in tiny little towns and wouldn't have to scrape to make a living like you and Dad."

"We've always been blessed and you've never gone without," Cara's mom said with what seemed to be a pinched look of hurt.

"I'm not saying there is anything wrong with the way I was raised. I just want to do better."

Now her mother looked genuinely wounded. Cara tried again. "I mean, better financially. I'm so sorry, Mom. I don't want to be hurtful. But here's my question. Could I be a lawyer and still be called to be a part of a ministry family? I mean, could you be a lawyer?"

"I don't want to be a lawyer."

"I'm just saying."

"I don't even know if I like lawyers," her mom said, with the gleam returning to her eyes.

"You like me, don't you?"

"No, I love you!" she said, and embraced her.

Chapter 4

It was already Saturday afternoon when Cara realized her mistake. The last guy who came to pick her up at the house was grilled by her dad, ignored by her mother, and teased by her brother. Cara was still hearing about it. Her mother called him "that quiet boy"; her brother called him "the forehead" for reasons unknown; and her dad called him a loser. While Cara herself referred to him as "Gag Reflex," the name was one she kept private from her family for obvious reasons.

That was her last date. Almost a year ago. Unfortunately, because it was so late before Cara started panicking, she wasn't sure whether Josh got her text to meet him at the restaurant. He hadn't answered. As a result, she had only compounded the problem. Cara decided to wait until fifteen minutes after the original six o'clock pick-up time and then leave the house. That way, she wouldn't miss him, if by chance he did come to the house. Their reservations weren't until 6:45, so that left her plenty of time.

It was five minutes after six when Cara thought she heard a car in the driveway, and by the time she looked out her upstairs bedroom window, Josh was already walking toward the door. At least she could meet him outside. That way no real damage would be done. And she would have made it, too, except that when she was halfway down the stairs, she realized that she'd forgotten her purse, and when she went back to get it, she realized that the purse that matched her outfit was empty. It took a few seconds to remedy this, and as she hurriedly plopped the last random item into her purse, the doorbell rang. All was lost.

As Cara came down the stairs, her mom was opening the front door. "You must be Sister Shepherd. Cara's told me so much about you," said Josh. Cara noticed that Josh's total attention was focused on her mother. He continued, "It was you who gave Cara her name. It's Italian, isn't it? And you wanted Cara's character to be like Ruth."

Although Cara recognized a rehearsed line, she was thankful for it anyway. Still, this was only a small victory. Rumbling from the living room recliner came Jim Shepherd, clearly dismayed that he had not been informed about the present visitor at the door. He strode over to the front entrance with great authority, yet

Josh was not intimidated. "Ah, Brother Shepherd, Josh Peeler. I'm the youth pastor from Bloomingtown who spoke at the youth rally last Friday. I just want to tell you that I have always looked up to church planters."

At least he wasn't monosyllabic. Nor did he stutter. Good start. But she needed to get him out the door before her brother made an appearance. Chances were good because he was hibernating in the basement. He would not investigate a doorbell. But then the unthinkable happened. Dull thuds came up the basement stairs. Disaster had struck. But here too Josh was quick on his feet, challenging the intruder, "Cubs or Cardinals?"

Shay crossed his arms in defiance. "Yankees," he trumpeted.

"Those losers pay their way to the pennant and they still can't win."

"Yeah, so the Cubs are really incredible, aren't they? Let's see, they just recently won the World Series in…1924, wasn't it?"

"In 1908, actually, but next year is going to be a good year for them. Since the Yankees haven't been able to hit their way out of a paper bag this year, next year they don't even stand a chance to win their division."

Shay was incensed. "What are you smoking, because—"

"Now let's not be smoking in this house," said Cara's dad with a broad smile, asserting his authority over the conversation. Clearly, Josh had made a clean sweep.

"Josh, did you say the reservations were for 6:45?" Cara asked quietly, and he understood.

"Oh…yes. So nice to meet you Brother and Sister Shepherd. And Shay, let me tell you, I'll be praying for you that you can see the light on those Yankees. I think they're mostly atheists. You should be praying for a godly team like the Cubs!"

When Josh opened the car door for Cara, she could see that his six-year-old Ford Focus was spit shined and polished. Even though the evergreen deodorizer was a bit overpowering, the miles flowed easily to the restaurant. Josh worked his magic to keep the conversation light and the banter easy, all the while drawing out her feelings. "So you call her Baby Lungs, huh?" he said as he helped her out of the car.

"A rightly deserved name."

All the time they were waiting for a table, Josh kept it up. So much so, that he seemed more like someone trying to make a sale than a date. "Now, did your dad start the church himself?" he asked, but Cara suspected he already knew the answer to this and most of the questions he was asking.

She said, "We've been here six years. The church was about three years old and had dwindled down to nothing. There were a few churches that helped us a lot at the beginning. Pastor Jean's church in Salem was particularly helpful. They sent over a few families to help us in our Sunday afternoon service—"

"No, thank you—we won't be needing those wine glasses," Josh mentioned easily.

"Very good, sir!" said the fawning waiter.

By now Cara was a little bored and decided to move Josh off script. "So is this the place you bring all your dates?" asked Cara, surprising herself.

Just for a moment, Josh had nothing to say. But then he pulled off a quick recovery. "Well, I can't really date someone from my youth group. I don't think it would be ethical."

This surprised Cara. "What are you talking about?"

"Unequal power relationships and all that." Cara wasn't sure she agreed, but she let it go. How much power did a youth leader have, really?

"I had a casual girlfriend or two in Bible college," he continued, "but nothing really came of it." Then Josh quickly took control of the conversation. "So why did you tell me to 'go fish'?"

Cara let herself be diverted. "When you called me at Sandra's, I thought you were somebody else. I thought you were Fred. It's something I say to him when I catch him saying stupid things."

"Stupid things?"

"Yes. Fred specializes in trying to see how gullible people are."

"I don't understand how this relates to fishing."

"Let me tell you a story of what happened to me a month ago. I got a call from the president of my school. He congratulated me that I had been selected as a representative of our school for an all-expense-paid trip to a summit on Asian-American economic relations in Bangkok, China."

"That's wonderful," said Josh.

Cara laughed. "One problem. Bangkok is the capital of Thailand. It's not even in China. Right then, I knew it was a hoax. I said, 'Fred, go fish!' He thought it was hilarious that I believed him as long as I did."

"And this is your cousin? He's good."

"Actually, all my real cousins are in Texas. But since the first time we met Brother Samuelson, he told us to call him Uncle Bob. He comes over a lot and plays racquetball with my father. That's how Fred and I got close; hence Cousin Fred. But he can be a bother. Last week I got this call from a crack-cocaine addict. He was on his way to the top of the Gateway Arch to jump.

"But it's impossible to jump from the top of the arch,'" said Josh, and then they both laughed. "So, I take it you told him to go fish? So Cara, were those your real nieces you were drowning?"

"Unfortunately, yes. They belong to my sister Sandra. She's four years older than I am. I wasn't really close to her growing up, but she's almost talking to me like an adult now."

"And she goes to your church?"

"Yeah, she's the music director, although I'm not sure how much that title means in a home missions church."

"It must be neat having a family in ministry together."

"To tell the truth, up until a few years ago, things were really rocky between Sandra and Dad. Lots of drama. But somehow it got turned around."

"So, do you sing?"

"Is this a part of the thirty-page application process for you to go out with someone?"

"Actually, I have a six-page questionnaire for you to fill out but I forgot it in the car. I can probably get most of it by memory."

"Is it true or false, multiple choice, or essay questions?"

At that point, inspiration seemed to hit Josh. He stated, "Actually it is called 'either/or.' You pick one response or another."

"Sounds like something I can do. Fire away."

"Okay, hip/hop or reggae?"

"This is ridiculous. You have to give me realistic choices."

"Station wagon or Mini Cooper."

"Mini Cooper."

"Yellow or Green?"

"Yellow."

"City or small town?"

"City."

"Do you want one kid or five?"

"Five."

"Listen to a concert or go to an art exhibit?"

"What kind of concert? What artist?"

"You've just gotta pick."

"Concert."

"Would you write or draw?"

"Write."

"Novel or textbook?"

"Novel."

"Fume at people or just get even?"

"Definitely fume."

"Suburbs or farm?"
"Suburbs."
"Preaching or teaching?"
"Depends on who—"
"Just pick."
"Teaching."
"One pet or lots of pets?"
"Lots of pets."
"Dogs or cats?"
"Cats."
"Brown house or white?"
"White."
"All right then. That concludes our exam for this evening," said Josh. "They're bringing our salads."

"So, did I pass?" asked Cara after the waiter had sprinkled ground pepper on her salad and they had said grace.

"Pass what?"

"Your exam."

"Oh, it wasn't really an—"

"Did it tell you what you wanted to know?"

Josh had a twinkle in his eye. "Yeah, sure. Okay, so you want to live in a white house in the suburbs but actually in the city, have five kids in a Mini Cooper. All while writing novels with lots of cats."

"So how's that work for you?" said Cara.

"Those were exactly the answers I was looking for."

"Sounds pretty crazy, doesn't it?"

"Actually it sounds pretty…special." At that mesmerizing moment Cara had a sudden inspiration that this could be the one; that maybe this was a man she could love.

But then, as the waiter placed the chicken entrée in front of her, she was suddenly suspicious. Maybe that last interchange wasn't as spontaneous as it seemed. Just as he had planned what he would say to her mom, her dad, and to Shay, perhaps Josh had really planned that whole interview all along. Either way, he was good.

As their meal progressed, Josh seemed to come to the end of his prepared script. She guessed this was the case now that he was working harder at the conversation. She wondered about the way he said, "In my experience…" or by his strongly asserting, "It seems to me…." It smacked of a false certainty. But maybe not. Maybe he was just nervous.

Cara's Call

"Wouldn't you agree?" Josh said, and Cara realized she was so concerned about discovering the real Josh that she was no longer present. "Um…so, well, I'm not sure. Could you say that again?" And despite herself she blushed just a little bit.

"Okay. This is important," Josh said with finality. "I was saying that as great as the heroes from the past are, young people today don't really want to be compared to them. They don't want to be like G. T. Haywood or Billy Cole or Nona Freeman. They just want to be the best at whoever they are and the best at whatever God calls them to do."

It wasn't a question. It was a statement. And the scary thing about it was that Cara had no opinion. She didn't know these people, and he assumed that everyone must know them. She was just a girl trying to finish college. She lamely offered, "I'm not sure."

Josh turned the conversation. "The real problem is that young people lack direction. While a young person can say they want to live a passionate existence, they don't really know what that means because they have no dreams."

"I have some dreams," said Cara, determined to break into the conversation to talk about the fact that she would be a lawyer.

"So there you go," said Josh. "Most young people don't. In my experience…" The moment passed where it might have been possible for her to share.

When they pulled up into the driveway and Josh opened the door for her, he leaned in. He said, "You have the most beautiful eyes. Did you know your eyes are more than one shade of green?"

She didn't. He continued, "See, there's this really dark, forest green around the edges, but then you have different hues of green throughout the iris. It takes your breath away. They're beautiful. And they change colors depending on what you wear. Take that dress you've got on now. It makes your eyes a more subtle green."

And then Cara knew. Josh was just setting her up so he could kiss her goodnight. But he didn't. He just waited for her to turn the key in the lock and turn off the porch light, then he thanked her for the nice evening and left. As Cara went up the stairs she knew he had planned that last set of lines. It was just too smooth. Still, she went straight to the bathroom mirror and looked deeply, examining the different shades of green. It turned out Josh was right.

The racquetball zinged into the corner with absolutely no bounce on the return. Jim ran to front court but to no avail. The ball was dead in the corner. Bob had gotten him again. "Well, that's the game," said Bob, smiling, "and I think someone is out there waiting for the court."

The YMCA wasn't exactly the top-of-the-line racquetball club, but it was good enough for Jim and Bob, who had been close since Jim moved to Illinois. Bob had been pastoring for twenty-two years now and had kind of taken Jim under his wing. "Tell me, who's getting your vote for presbyter?" he asked.

"I hadn't thought about it," said Jim. "What's wrong with voting for Broadberry again?"

"Term limits are gonna get him. That's why. He'll never get the two-thirds he needs to get in."

"He's been in eight years?" asked Jim.

"Yep."

"I wonder if Smith will get it then. People always seem to vote for the guy with the biggest church."

"Don't even think about it," said Bob. "I'm telling you he doesn't believe fat is greasy. Vote for Vance. He's solid and believes the doctrine. And he's tough on sin."

"Okay. Will do," said Jim.

"What's this I hear about Cara?" asked Bob. "Word on the street is that she's dating that Josh guy from Bloomingtown."

"Man, Bob. It was one date. And it was four days ago. How do you keep up with everything?"

"I just know what's important to know. Let me give you a heads-up about this Josh. He's solid. You need to jump on this thing and make it happen."

"Bob, I hate to break it to you, but the days of arranged marriages are over. The only people who can make it happen are the ones—"

"Do you want another situation like the one you had with Sandra?"

"Look, I did what you told me and confronted her about that earring guy, and that turned ugly very quickly. But she got over him."

"Okay then. That's where you missed it. Train up a child in the way she should go. You started too late. Now with Cara, if you start a little earlier, this thing could really be good."

"I don't know, Bob. I think I'll just—"

"Listen to me. You've got to act now. And I know just exactly how you can do it."

Chapter 5

It was thirty seconds after the dismissal prayer that Karen smelled trouble coming her direction, for a white-haired lady shuffled straight toward her. "Sister Shepherd, we need to talk," complained the big-bunned, self-described "mother-in-Israel." Because this elderly lady deemed herself important enough to advise the church on any subject, she never held back an opinion.

"Certainly, Sister Pridgitt. I'd be glad to talk," said Karen, to the lady who was about to transition from feasting on the Word to gnawing on other things.

"I've been talking to a few ladies, you know, sharing important prayer requests," began the mother in Israel.

"We can always use more prayer," agreed Karen.

"The ladies are all concerned about the backslidden condition of the Sunday school."

"Oh?"

"I couldn't help noticing there was a juvenile delinquent teaching with Cara. You know, a lot of the ladies are upset by this. They've told me so. We figured Cara probably just slipped one by you."

"Sister Pridgitt, my husband is certainly aware that Marta is helping Cara."

"Hmmph. Then, in that case, I would like to know what in the world is going on. How can that girl be teaching? She isn't even converted!"

"Thank you for your concern. I appreciate it. Cara is the teacher in the class. Marta is just helping her with a few things."

"But to have that ungodly influence!"

Karen smiled warmly. "Oh, you didn't hear?"

"Hear what?"

"Marta is getting baptized this Sunday night. I guess she's got some friends who are coming to watch."

Sister Pridgitt harrumphed that it was wonderful, though the way she said it didn't make it sound wonderful at all.

Cara's Call

On Thursday night, because the college library was open late, Cara camped out behind two stacks of books. Marta was at the same table anxiously looking over Cara's shoulder. "This is much better, Marta," said Cara. "I think this third revision is just about perfect. The only suggestion that I would make is where on the second to the last page you should maybe think about—"

Glancing down at an incoming text, Cara suddenly lost her train of thought. The incoming message read: "which lady did u call the wicked witch of the west?" Only two people knew of Sister Pridgitt's nickname, and the one texting her was not Amanda. "y?" she typed back. Josh's response came, "im gonna meet her Sun nite."

"how?" Cara asked.

"ur dad called my pastor."

"&?"

"Im preaching @ ur church nxt Sun nite."

"Great!" Cara texted back, not sure if that was quite true.

"I'm telling you, Amanda, something is very, very wrong with someone if he requires another someone's whole family to make the sale. See what I mean?" said Cara.

Amanda nodded, keeping her eye on the road. She had patiently listened for over an hour to the same rambling before finally countering, "But it's good, isn't it? Not like that last guy, Ricky 'what's his name.'"

"I told you not to bring him up. Amanda, help me out here. You're supposed to be on my side. How did this happen? Do my parents even know the real Josh? 'Sister Shepherd, it's sooooo nice to meet you' he says as he's staring into her eyes. I'm telling you, something is clearly wrong here.'"

"It's a gift Josh has with people," said Amanda, "and I don't think you can fault him for being gifted. Really, Cara."

Cara would have started in again except they had arrived at Pizza Hut. They got out of the car and walked toward the restaurant entrance.

Up until now Cara had forgotten that her ride over to Charlestown with Amanda would ultimately place her in the middle of a crowd of strangers, but seeing the twenty-five kids at two long tables and a booth did it for her. "Hey, Amanda, loan me your car keys."

"Why?"

"I'm not going in there. I'll just run up to Wal-Mart and come back for you when they all leave."

"Cara. I promise you that none of those kids will even notice you."

"Not good enough."

"Come on! They'll only be in there another twenty minutes before Greg drives them home."

"Fine. I can spend that time in the Wal-Mart."

"Do it for me...Cara. Please?" And of course, that is what got Cara in the door and down the middle of the restaurant. What Amanda said proved to be true. None of the kids even looked up from their pizza. They were loud and laughing and Cara was not even a blip on their radar screens. Amanda led the way to a couple of empty chairs waiting for them and sat down across from a guy with startling red hair who sat a head taller than everyone else at the table. This was Amanda's Greg—van driver for junior high chaos.

Before they ever settled in their chairs, Cara made quick calculations. If a 5'9" Amanda married this giant, their children would comprise a ready-made basketball team—her own starting five. But then Cara corrected herself. Greg was not just tall—he was big. Not fat, either. He looked like he lived in a gym. Huge biceps. Okay, recalculate. Blue-eyed Amanda and blue-eyed Greg would produce blue-eyed running backs and—

"This is Cara," Amanda said easily.

"Hey," said Greg, standing to his feet and reaching out with a hand that swallowed hers. Not one speck of pretense. He smiled easily and had an athletic chin. And no neck. One giant muscle.

"Greg's an EMT," explained Amanda, for no apparent reason.

"And you're their youth leader?" confirmed Cara as a boy at the other end of the table threw mushrooms into the air. Greg merely leaned in and raised his eyebrows. The offending boy was appropriately rebuked, apparently not wanting further discipline from the Jolly Red Giant.

Having taken care of the disturbance, Greg replied, "No, I'm not the youth leader. That would be my brother." Immediately Cara scanned the area for another tall red head. Only then did she notice the blond across the table from her reach over to shake her hand. "My name's Kevin," he said, with a shy smile. He was maybe 5' 8", an inch shorter than Cara. His boyish face made him look like a teenager.

Then Cara got the joke. "You are not brothers!" she laughed, refusing to be taken in by the same sort of scam that Fred would pull. Yet, both merely looked at her and smiled. In the exact same way!

Then Cara looked closer. True, they had different hair color, but they both had fair skin and their eyes were the same blue. Although Kevin's face wasn't nearly as athletic and imposing as his brother's, he actually had stronger features than Greg.

Cara's Call

"My big brother, actually," said Greg with a wink as he poured Coca-Cola from a pitcher into their glasses.

"No way!" responded Cara. "Kevin can't be a day older than nineteen!" But as Greg walked over to palm four more slices of pizza, Cara studied Kevin's face noting that he was probably older than he looked at first glance. Greg dropped two large slices of pepperoni onto her plate and then announced to the group, "Van leaves in ten minutes." The kids groaned in reply.

Kevin was gone now, visiting first one table and then another. Greg and Amanda were talking. Cara ate, happy to be alone, mulling over her own "guy issues." She thought to herself, *Nothing soothes a worried heart like pepperoni pizza.*

Ten minutes later, Kevin reappeared. "You good, then?" he asked Greg, apparently brother shorthand for a much longer conversation.

Greg nodded, and then yelled, "Load her up." The girls, at least, immediately popped up from the table.

Kevin then got a bit more verbal, informing Greg, "Make sure everyone who drove has the people that came with them." Greg nodded, whereupon Kevin grabbed the check for the pizza and headed to the cash register. Strange. That one interchange said it all. Kevin wore his authority easily.

Amanda whispered into Cara's ear. "Hey, I'm thinking about riding along on the van. The whole route is only a half an hour."

"I don't mind staying here waiting for you," Cara said. "After all, it was ninety minutes getting here to see this guy. Better make it worth your while. But I will not ride in that van."

"You're the greatest!" said Amanda. "Let me see if Kevin can hang around a little while longer." Before Cara could protest, it was all arranged. Cara was left with Kevin at Pizza Hut.

"So how long have you been the youth pastor?" Cara said.

"I don't know that I am the youth pastor," he said with a twinkle in his eye.

"But your brother said—"

"All of this was his idea. He just got me into it. A couple years ago, he went to the pastor and asked if we could start this youth outreach on Friday nights. The pastor said yes, and so we've been doing it ever since. But I'm not sure we've actually settled on titles."

"So you don't sit on the platform or anything like that?"

"I'm not even here except for weekends."

"How come?"

"I go to Northern Illinois University, and all week long I'm doing student teaching. I've got the same deal next semester."

"What grade are you teaching?"

"Fourth grade this fall semester and first grade in the spring semester, but I'm hoping to teach second grade once I graduate."

"Really. That sounds pretty specific."

"Blame it on Mrs. Bleahardt."

Cara could smell a story coming and sure enough, Kevin obliged. "My kindergarten teacher didn't like me. My first grade teacher didn't like me. Don't ask me how I knew, but I just did. It wasn't anything that they said; it was just a feeling. Well, anyway, my second grade teacher really liked me. I don't know for sure exactly what she said or did, but I liked her, too. Her name was Mrs. Bleahardt."

"So one teacher liking you changed everything?"

"Let me back up a little. I was six when my parents got a divorce. I don't really know my father very well, but I know that the brokenness in our home really affected me. Anyway, it was in Mrs. Bleahardt's class where I started feeling like I belonged. I can't point to any one incident, just the feeling of being loved and belonging. A teacher who can do that has a rare gift. Don't you think?"

Cara had never had such a conversation. "I can't believe you remember who liked you and who didn't."

"Well, then," he said, "do something for me." Cara nodded, so he continued. "Close your eyes for a second." Cara obeyed. "Okay, now name your fourth grade teacher," he requested.

"Mrs. Hanson."

"Did she like you?"

"Yes."

"Why?"

"Because I did good work," is what came to Cara immediately.

"Okay, now open your eyes." Cara did. He said, "Here's the thing, Cara. I didn't do good work. I'm not sure how I know it…whether I was in the lowest reading group or if it was because I was categorized some other way, but I know that I was not anyone's prize pupil. And that's the amazing thing: my teacher liked me despite myself. And the fact that she did is what changed my life. So that's why I'm going to teach second grade—because of her."

"Wow," was all Cara could say. Kevin had trusted her with his life story.

"What about you? You're going to school then?"

After he had been so vulnerable, it was easy for Cara to open up. "I'm just going to a small college near my home, and I might be transferring to Southern Illinois University next fall."

"What will your major be?"

"Prelaw."

"You say you might be going to SIU?"

"Not sure. I had a full scholarship to Saint Louis University that I didn't utilize, and I am in the midst of checking to see what scholarships will be available in different places when I transfer in as a junior. I'm trying to stay away from student loans."

"You had a free ride to SLU and you turned it down? That borders on bizarre. If you don't mind my asking, why in the world aren't you there?"

"Long story."

"We've got nothing but time."

It wasn't something she talked about. Neither her mother nor her father really understood the implications of her choice. But when it appeared Kevin was not going to settle for less, she had no option but to share. "Well, my dad is starting a church, and he could really use the help, so I just thought it would be better to, you know, hang around a bit more. Even after I transfer somewhere else, I'll come home on weekends."

Kevin nodded but made no further comment about her choice. Instead he said, "So you'll be a lawyer then?"

He didn't seem to be judging her. But she wanted to be sure. "What? You don't approve?"

"Well, if that's what you want to do, go for it."

"What, no lawyer jokes? Or no asking me about my sense of calling or asking me what I'm really going to do to save the world?"

His smile said it all. She was okay just like she was.

"You set me up," said Cara to Amanda as they were driving back home.

"Cara, would I do such a thing?" said Amanda, but the dashboard lights betrayed her sly smile.

"Was Kevin in on this little deal?"

"Cara, there is no conspiracy. I didn't even decide to come over here until this afternoon, and Kevin has never even heard of you."

"Oh. Well, I guess I'm just getting a little paranoid about things."

"I should say so."

CHAPTER 6

As Jim stood at the pulpit, weaving a story into his morning message, children in Cara's classroom listened to another kind of story. Cara and Marta had set up the puppet stage in their classroom, and now, assorted ages of children hooted and howled during the performance. When they recognized a familiar song, they enthusiastically sang along.

When Jim became pastor, he and another man put their carpentry skills to work and added those two small classrooms on either side of the entranceway. Although the addition made for less seating in the auditorium, this was hardly a problem, and it gifted the church with a prayer room and a Sunday school class. Still, it wasn't ideal. Both rooms exited into the auditorium and there really was no vestibule, just a wide hallway between the classrooms where the auditorium extended to the double-door entrance of the church.

Nobody who leads children's church should ever describe it as "easy." Behind the curtain of the puppet stage that morning, props and puppets were being used and discarded as the song progressed. Marta struggled to coordinate the Muppets' movements with the music.

"You're drooping again!" complained Cara as the song marched along. Marta shrugged but didn't seem to know how to fix things. "Your guy needs vitamins!" Cara urged but to no effect, as Marta's Muppet sagged lower and lower over the PVC pipe that supported the curtain.

"How long is this song, anyway?" said Marta, laughing. "My arm is killing me."

Cheers from in front of the curtain confirmed that at last the song was done, and now Marta could interact with the children one on one. Marta was a natural at keeping order with the children during Cara's teaching, and the children loved the memory verse game. Several girls hugged her on their way out the door.

As they were cleaning up, Marta asked, "Am I supposed to wear something special?"

"When?"

"Tonight. When I get baptized. I was wondering if I was supposed to wear something special."

"No, we have robes. Just bring a change of clothes. And there's nothing magical about what you wear in the water or even about the water itself. Like we talked about, what is special is that you've committed your life to Christ and that—"

"Johnny is coming too."

Cara frowned at the news. "Are you sure you want Johnny here?"

"Yeah. I think I can handle it. He really needs God. He might be a little spaced out, but don't you think it would be good?"

"Only if you do. And we'll meet this afternoon to—"

"Is everything all right in here? I just thought I should check." Both Marta and Cara looked up from where they were wiping down the table to see the source of the voice that had imposed itself on them.

"Everything's fine," said Cara to the white-haired, big-bun lady who was now attempting to enter their space.

"And this one..." she pointed to Marta as if the girl were a side of beef in a butcher shop, "She is acceptable to you as an example of holiness to the children?"

Pure anger now motivated Cara. She stood up straight and walked toward the door. "No, she's more than just acceptable. She's wonderful. Now if you will excuse us, Sister Pridgitt." Cara moved into the personal space of the lady at the door, backing her out into the hallway. "We're just getting everything cleaned up so we can train these children in the way that they should go so that when they're really old they can—"

A demanding yell came from the front of the church. The voice commanded, "Cara, come up here right now." When Cara suddenly stepped out of their classroom into the church auditorium she had become visible and now fell prey to her older sister's whims. Another five minutes passed before Cara finished cleaning the classroom and hurried to the platform where she was soundly rebuked by Barn-Boss for her slothfulness. "I haven't got all day."

"I was protecting Marta from the Wicked Witch of the West. What did you want?"

Sandra ignored her sister's tone and got down to business. "You've got the alto on these three praise choruses."

"What are you talking about?" argued Cara. "I don't praise sing Sunday nights. I'm on PowerPoint; you know that."

Sandra continued, nonplussed. "I think you should sing. We need an extra singer."

"Mom sings alto. That's good enough Sandra. I've got maybe a half-dozen kids coming for this baptism, and I need to sit with them."

"But I need your help," continued Sandra, losing steam.

"Not this week."

"Cara, Dad said you are supposed to praise sing."

Only then did Cara understand. "What! So I'm on display as a candidate for Preacher Josh Peeler? Oh...this is just way too much!"

"Do it for me. I already had one argument with Dad about this. I'm on your side. I told him you shouldn't have to do it. He told me that if I could somehow get you to praise sing, he would spot me for that new keyboard I want. Come on, Cara. I really need that keyboard."

"You've got to be kidding!" fumed Cara.

Her father surveyed the congregation as the little sanctuary filled with worship. Josh stood next to him. The music was perfect; all was right with the world.

Cara sang dutifully into her microphone but winced because Shay's drums were too loud again and Sandra was overpowering everything with her lead soprano, plus her keyboard was way too loud. Cara didn't want to be so nervous in her home church, but the whole performance idea added to her anxiety and she felt weak in the knees.

After the obligatory three praise songs, Cara fled the platform, musing to herself, *This is worth a few 'get out of babysitting free cards.'* She positioned herself between Marta and Marta's stepbrother Johnny. Johnny was thin as a rail, greasy as a gearshift, and high as a kite. As her dad reiterated how special it was that Marta was being baptized, Johnny whispered something sarcastic to Marta and was only slightly discouraged when Cara signaled Marta to ignore him. Cara wished Johnny had chosen not to come. Not after what he had done. Not tonight. And not with the malicious way he was acting.

Marta made friends easily as evidenced by the three girls in the second row and the tall shaggy kid next to them, plus one more additional guy and girl on the front row. Indeed, these visitors and Marta made up almost a third of the Sunday night attendance.

Pastor Shepherd now introduced the special speaker, indulging in exorbitant praise for the visiting evangelist. Her dad finally sat down, no thanks to Cara's continual wishing for him to do so.

Josh announced he would be reading from the Book of Habakkuk. His scripture text was way too long and too hard to understand. Cara could see at once that most of her visitors had checked out long before he was finished reading.

Come on, Josh, reach these kids, Cara wished silently, but Josh, of course, would be no more affected by her wishing than her father had been.

This kid knows his Bible, thought Pastor Shepherd as Josh worked through several types and shadows from the Minor Prophets. Cara kept praying, willing Josh to move into different territory. "We're dying out here..." she mumbled. Then

Josh worked in a well-placed story and got back everyone's attention. Cara started breathing easier but then, for whatever reason, Josh started hacking away at how sinful and awful people were these days. "Amen," came the voice of the pastor who evidently thought this a good strategy.

"Help us, God," mumbled Cara, who was now convinced that the service would end in absolute disaster. She closed her eyes and thought, *No, Josh. Everyone in the first two rows already feels like a failure, and they know they've messed up. This is not news.* Yet, Josh kept hammering away at it until, mercifully, Sandra stepped to the keyboard and began playing for the altar call.

Asking everyone to stand, Josh began telling the story of the prodigal son. "This is good," affirmed the pastor's voice from the platform.

No, shrieked the silent protest inside of Cara. *Don't do this, Josh!* It was now a certainty that the service was going to bomb, and this perception prompted Cara to do the most unusual thing she'd ever done.

Cara never knew why she did it, but as she looked back to the second row, she had an inspiration. Though her heart was racing and her knees were weak, it was as if she couldn't help herself. She moved to that row as Josh was talking and said to the shaggy-haired guy, "What's your name?"

"Ron."

"What if I told you that you could change the world?"

"Yeah," was all he said, but that was enough.

"What if I told you it was no accident you came tonight and that—that God has an incredibly special plan for your life?"

He nodded again as if she had asked him if he wanted to order a hamburger or hotdog. But he was clearly interested. "Yeah?" he asked. "How?"

"Okay. Just walk with me up to the front and stand. Just stand there, and keep your eyes closed. Then I'm going to get these girls, and when we pray for you, good things will start happening."

"Like what?"

Cara did not know where the words were coming from, but she kept talking. "God is going to do a miracle in your life." Ron's eyes got big, but he was buying into what she was saying. He nodded, ever so slightly.

"Are you ready?" she asked.

"Okay," he said. Before she could think about how she might be embarrassing herself, Cara took Ron's hand and walked him up to the altar. He stood there, his eyes closed in expectancy.

"And in the hog pen," the voice intoned from platform, "he realized that his father's servants were not starving but were eating very well."

The music played softly. Cara ignored the story and went to the three girls, focusing more on the first one because she looked like the strongest leader. She spoke to them with the same sort of unexplained rush that overcame her as she approached Ron. She said, "Ron believes that God will use him to change the world, but he needs us to pray for him. I told him we would." They didn't hesitate, understanding that Cara was asking them to do something very important. Together, they marched up to Ron, and together, they laid their hands on him.

Pastor Shepherd watched his daughter in absolute disbelief. First Cara brought one and then three more to the altar. And then Jim's eyes popped as Cara did something even more out of character. She moved to Marta's stepbrother whom Jim noticed had been mocking the entire service. She got in his face and started speaking sternly and forcefully while pointing to the door. At first Johnny hesitated but then threw her a dirty look and walked down the aisle toward the exit. He was leaving. Probably for the best. *One thing is certain*, Jim thought. *Her actions are a confirmation of Josh's ministry.*

Having dispensed with Marta's stepbrother, Cara signaled to her mother to come over to Marta. Her mother didn't act surprised, though clearly she was. Cara whispered to her friend, "Marta, Mom is going to help you change into your baptismal robe. I can't come right now because I am going to pray with Ron, okay?" Marta nodded.

"And the prodigal knelt before his father and said, 'I have sinned against you.'" said Josh dramatically as Cara moved to pray with Ron. Tears began to trickle down Ron's face as all three girls laid their hands on his back and prayed. Pastor Jim Shepherd could only stare.

Cara rose on her tiptoes to speak into his ear. "Ron, I know something that will really help you do what God is calling you to do."

"What's that?" he said.

"Jesus died on the cross so you wouldn't have to carry around all the junk that we usually carry. All the guilt for wrong stuff, all the anger and hate. Would you like to get rid of all that right now?"

"Yeah…sure…how?"

"Okay, just tell Jesus that you're sorry, and ask Him to forgive you, and you're going to feel that junk lift from you, okay?"

Ron nodded and began to say simply, "God, I'm messed up…but not too messed up for you…"

The girls continued to pray while Josh came to a close: "So, if there is someone here tonight who has wandered from home, this is your night."

A couple minutes passed while Ron prayed earnestly, then Cara stopped him again. "Ron, did you ask the Lord to forgive you?" Ron smiled his relief. No, he was beaming. "Okay, then Ron, you can thank Him. Tell Jesus you're going to live for Him and that you want Him to live inside of you and take control. And when you do, something very special is going to happen to you. Don't be afraid of it. Okay?"

Ron obeyed, and the girls never stopped praying. Cara had no idea why she didn't talk to the girls or why she was focusing on Ron. It was like she was obeying a voice, although she was still trying to understand whether this was God's voice.

Now the altar was full, the whole congregation at the front. Cara looked up and saw her mom signaling for her to come back to the baptismal changing room. Cara headed in that direction as Josh walked over to lay his hands on Ron.

When Cara reached her mom, Karen asked, "Should we wait till everyone is through praying before baptizing Marta?"

"I'll ask Dad what he thinks," said Cara, but quickly realized it would be unnecessary, for Jim Shepherd was already tucking his tie into his shirt and putting his wristwatch into his pocket. While rolling up his sleeves, Jim signaled his wife to bring the girl to the baptistery and then to Marta to walk down the steps into the water.

At the same time, praise erupted from the altar area where Ron was praying. Jim said, "Marta Rodriguez, I now baptize you in the name of Jesus Christ—" just as another eruption of praise sounded and continued while Jim pronounced, "—for the remission of sins, and you shall receive the gift of the Holy Ghost."

In any other circumstance, Cara would either have wished to be in the audience watching the baptism or behind the baptistery praying quietly for the person who was being baptized, but tonight nothing mattered. Nobody was even watching the baptism, so she just began praying for Marta, not worrying what anyone said or thought. For the next half hour, Cara remained oblivious to the crowd around her.

"So how'd last night go?" asked Bob, as he bounced the ball off the ceiling of the racquetball court, one of his trick shots that landed the ball tight into the back corner with no possibility of fishing it out.

But Jim had seen that blooper enough times not to be fooled. Before the ball could die he caught it just right and easily returned it. "Two got the Holy Ghost. One baptized. The service was incredible."

"That's what I said would happen. Listen to me, Jim. Kids just need a little encouragement."

Jim continued, "But afterward was not so good."

"Why not?"

"Well, the wife and I took Cara and Josh out to eat and I told them what a great ministry couple they made."

"And that didn't go well?"

"Bob, I don't know what happened. Everyone looked at me like I had leprosy."

Bob shook his head in disbelief. "If that don't beat all. You just can't understand kids these days, can you?"

"Okay, keep spilling the beans," said Amanda, sitting next to Cara in the library. Cara had offered an edited version of the service, downplaying her own part in it, but Amanda was an expert on "Cara-speak" and squeezed almost everything out of her, amazed by the tale.

"Cara, this sounds more than mildly bizarre. Are you sure that this was the Cara I know who was holding hands with a stranger, telling unknown girls what to do, and kicking someone out of the building? Maybe it was just someone who looked like her, because the Cara I know would never do those things."

"I know. And I still can't explain what happened, and though it turned out well in the end, I keep reliving it, and my heart starts racing all over again."

"I'm just sorry I missed the show. I would have come, but we were doing a stick drama for the service in Salem and I couldn't miss. Next time you plan this kind of performance, let me in on it. I'll be there in a heartbeat."

Cara smiled in spite of herself and said, "Ron was really affected by what happened to him. After the service, he told me he wanted to meet me for breakfast. We talked for two hours. He has all kinds of questions. He wants to know what receiving the Holy Ghost actually means and what he should do next. We're meeting again tomorrow with Marta and two friends. In fact, he wants to meet everyday this week."

"Uh Cara, he's not, uh, like interested in you, is he?"

"No. He's just excited about changing the world and figures he should start sooner rather than later."

"I'm not sure what that means."

"Well, it was something I said to him…something I'm sure I was supposed to say. I just didn't know he would want to start so soon."

"What does Josh think of your antics in service?"

"We didn't talk about it. And I'm not going to talk to him about it."

"Why not?"

"Because if he would have been a little more spiritually sensitive, then—"

"Cara, uh…does the word judgmental come to mind?"

"He's a preacher, Amanda. And he ought to act like one. He should at least be able to figure out who he's preaching to."

"Oh, Miss Huffy Puffy," said Amanda with a teasing smile. "The new expert on spiritual things."

Cara laughed at her own silliness. Then quickly losing the smile, she said. "I'm still upset, but mainly about what happened afterward."

"Did you get in a fight with him?"

"No. That would have been easier to fix."

"Oh. You mean going out to eat with your parents. How bad was it?"

"Pure disaster. Made the sinking of the Titanic look like nothing more than dunking a plastic boat in a bathtub."

Chapter 7

Tonight's date—dinner at Chili's—was a lot less formal than their first one. More importantly, it started with lower expectations. "So, how are your Bible studies with Ron and Marta?" asked Josh.

"They're not Bible studies."

"You're teaching them the Bible, aren't you?"

"Well, sure. We talk. The Bible comes up. So do other things."

"This has been going on for, what? Three weeks now?"

"Yeah. It's pretty intense at times."

"It's just you three?"

"Sometimes. But usually not."

"What do you mean?"

"Who would have ever thought Ron would be such a recruiter? He always has someone in tow. And Marta has a million friends."

"How often do you meet?"

"Whenever."

"But how often, like once a week?"

"No. More."

"Three times, what? Once a day?"

"Sometimes we don't meet. And sometimes we get together more than once a day. We'll do like a breakfast deal, and then maybe we'll get together late at night. That's when Ron gets bigger groups together."

"Like four or five?"

"Usually. But last night there were fifteen, at least for part of the time. Still, that was way more than usual."

"Cara. I am so proud of you having this outreach! It's so—"

"It's not outreach; it's friends. And I don't invite anyone. Ron is great—"

"Say, you're not dumping me for Ron."

"Ron and I are friends," she said, and then, as a kind of challenge, added, "Just like you and I are friends." The fact was that Josh had made no real commitment to her. She wasn't going to just let him slip in a comment like that without making him pay for it. Besides, he was so sure of himself he obviously wasn't threatened by Ron.

"But when something comes up about the Bible, who do they ask?" continued Josh, choosing not to comment about their relationship.

"Josh…Ron and Marta don't know anything. They can't be expected to have answers. But it's not teaching."

"Well, are things getting any better?" asked Bob.

"Not sure," said Jim. "I think Cara and Josh are seeing more of each other than what they let on. But the funny thing is that he never comes over to the house. It's probably that texting thing. Young people live their whole lives on their phones. It's not right. I don't think it's a real relationship."

"How can you be sure they're even seeing each other then?"

"The wife told me. They went to Chili's a few weeks back. And this week she's going with him to that big youth rally."

"And she won't talk to you about Josh? Strange isn't it?"

"Kids these days. They're just hard to figure."

"I get to sit in back, then?" said Cara as they pulled up to the church in Herrin.

"About that—" said Josh.

"But you promised I could just sneak in and—"

"And that was my intention, but Jennifer made a special appeal for you to sit with her."

"And Jennifer is?"

"The youth pastor's wife."

Cara tensed and asked, "She's not sitting in front, is she?"

When Josh did not answer, Cara knew she'd better reconfirm the rest. "And you are going to keep your promise not to acknowledge me, and you won't call on me or have me testify?" Her words had a threatening tone.

"I will not," he said. But the response was less certain than what Cara would have liked.

Instead of Josh calling on Cara, the local youth pastor did. Further, he called her to the platform to speak. "Cara Shepherd," he said. "Let's welcome her as she comes!" And because this was Friday night, and because the audience was composed of mostly junior high kids, and because there were several hundred of them, the crowd went wild as Cara made her weak-kneed way to lean on the pulpit. She was obedient. But she was blank. She had nothing. After a few seconds of silence,

Cara finally turned and scowled threateningly toward Josh who was staring innocently at the audience. "What do you want me to say?" she mouthed to him angrily.

He came up to her and whispered, "Tell them about Marta." And in so doing, he laid claim to her, made her a public object, and used her as an extension of his sermon.

Cara began and soon got lost in the story. She didn't think it right to use Marta's name, but told the story of a girl from a terrible home, who had been abused by those closest to her, and how she and Cara had become friends. She told about how, because Cara simply made room for her in her life, Marta started coming to church. And how, six weeks ago, she was baptized in Jesus' name and received the Holy Ghost. Again, the crowd went wild.

"Tell about your Bible studies," mouthed Josh, but she ignored him and walked off the platform and into the audience. Still, because it was a youth rally, the roar of applause continued as she made her way to her seat. The congregation was standing and clapping and cheering as if she were Moses descending from Mount Sinai. She wanted to go home. Cara felt very, very stupid.

Instead of listening to Josh preach, Cara relived the trauma of facing that crowd. She rehearsed to herself how small and uncertain her voice sounded, how it was so unfair to use her friend as a sound byte, and how she had been tricked into the whole episode. Her feelings were so intense toward Josh that they bordered on hatred.

Josh launched into the same sermon she'd heard at the previous youth rally. Same examples. Same jokes. It was only when he told his testimony that Cara started to melt a little, because it was an honest testimony. And then, amazingly, he skipped the story about the kid on the motorcycle who only wished he had one more chance and let the whole altar call hang on his personal testimony. And that's when Cara knew she really did like him despite his trickery.

Cara prayed for some girls and then asked Josh for his keys, quickly slipping to his car while he fellowshipped. She had enjoyed twenty minutes of peaceful silence when Josh showed up, turning the keys in the ignition and saying, "We're heading to TGIF at the mall."

"Okay," Cara said. But that was enough. She said nothing the rest of the way to the restaurant, even though she sensed that her silence was totally inappropriate. She was supposed to say, "Good sermon," and Josh was supposed to reply, "Good testimony." Only then would they make the ideal couple. But things were considerably less than ideal. Josh filled the car with chatter, working hard to keep things together on their way.

"So Bryce is from Ohio, and his wife Lydia is originally from the same church in Ohio where I grew up. They met at Bible college when…" But she wasn't listening. It was only when he got to the third friend she realized what she had missed, for she heard him say, "They'll all be at the restaurant."

Cara pulled herself together. "Very nice," she said, forcing a smile. Suddenly, she felt stupid. Josh was inviting her into his life, and she was making a mess of things. She was just being selfish.

"Good sermon," she said.

"Good testimony," Josh replied.

As she had suspected, everyone decided to eat at the same place. This made her wonder about the other thing: whether it was mandatory that the platform table be set in a prominent place. Apparently it was. Unhappily, it sat in the middle of all the booths. She could see it through the window.

Josh opened the door to the restaurant for her, leading her by the arm like a Barbie doll. It was surreal. Little junior high girls stared at her like she was the Queen of Sheba. Boys looked at her as if she were Princess Polly from the wannabe Planet Pluto! So, to avoid a panic attack, Cara visualized herself in the starring role of her own drama. Ignoring any spike in blood pressure, Cara knew, in fact, she really was the Queen of Sheba from Planet Pluto.

To the first table of staring girls, Cara envisioned herself laying hands on them, pronouncing, "May the powers of Pluto be upon you." And to that fifteen-year-old boy who was gawking at her—yes, a boy actually gawking at her—she would say, "Rub the saltshaker, turn it in a counter-clockwise direction, and I will grant you half the wealth of Sheba!" Yet, even with all the mental gymnastics, her heart was not fooled. Nor could she wish away the hundreds and thousands and millions of eyes that were fixed upon her.

Her hands visibly shook as Josh pulled out her chair. He must have sensed she would either pass out or start screaming like a crazed lunatic, for he quickly went into action, morphing into his overwhelmingly charming self. He stared deeply into people's eyes; he fielded the hardball questions heading her direction, leaving only the softballs for her to handle.

"Yes," she said, "our family has been in Munson Heights for six years."

"Yes, that's my Dad. Originally from Texas. Yes, that's right."

"My major," she repeated when someone asked. "Oh, you mean, what am I majoring in at school?" Her eyes looked for a way of escape but there seemed to be none. She could not say "Pre-Law." She simply could not say that. "Well, right now, I'm, uh…just doing my gen. eds. There will be plenty of time for majors in the next couple of years."

Before the food was served, a group of four ladies rose and headed for the washroom. It was hard to say who started the migration, but Cara was casually swallowed up by the group and found herself added to their number.

Unfortunately, she was just as much an outsider with this smaller group as she had been at the long table. They all seemed to know each other and were far enough into marriages that all talk revolved around sharing pictures and stories about babies and such. Unnamed Minister's Wife asked her, "How long have you and Josh been together? He seems to be really smitten with you."

"Smitten" was really such a funny word. Cara imagined herself in medieval garb, challenging Josh to a duel. *I smite thee on thy cheek as a matter of honor*, she pronounced in her mind, which quickly led to thoughts of her and Josh dueling and him trying to smite her on the cheek with a sword, and she fending off getting smitten. "We're just friends," is what came out of Cara's mouth.

"Well, he would be a good friend to have," returned Unknown Minister's Wife, who was just, after all, trying to be polite. And because she smiled and demanded nothing more, Cara relaxed just a little. "I met Josh a couple of months ago, and he's taken me out a couple of times. We text and talk some on the phone. That sort of thing."

Unknown Minister's Wife seemed to appreciate her willingness to share. She returned, "I hope I get to see you again." And because Josh wasn't included in the exchange, Cara took her words as an invitation to friendship.

"You know, I never learned your name. I'm so sorry," Cara said. And that's when it turned out that Unknown Minister's Wife wasn't even married and that her name was Julie and that she had just finished college and that she was really nice. Cara really liked this girl.

Still, Cara felt trapped by the dating game people were required to play. "Just friends," she had told Julie. "Just friends" was what she was required to say. It was all so stupid; as if Josh's name wasn't at the top of her prayer list; as if he hadn't been a major part of every devotional she'd had for the last forty days.

The rest of the women were already long gone before Cara started making her way back to the table with Julie. That's when the "incident" happened. At least that was what Josh called it later. A girl from across the restaurant signaled frantically for Cara to come over to her table. There was something pretty desperate in the girl's eyes, as if she were calling for an EMT.

As Cara walked in her direction, the girl hopped up from the booth where she had been sitting and met Cara in an open space between tables. Although the middle of the restaurant was an odd place to have a private conversation, the girl began without preliminaries. "Do you ever have trouble with doctrine?"

Cara guessed the girl was about her own age. She had no clue what the girl was even talking about, so she did what she always did in this sort of situation. She echoed what had been said to her. "So...you're wondering if I'm having trouble with doctrine."

"Yes," said the girl, "because I am."

"You're having trouble with doctrine."

"Exactly," said the girl, excited that Cara was hearing what she was telling her. "I am not sure whether or not to believe the Bible."

"You're questioning whether to believe the Bible."

"You see, there's this Muslim guy at school, and he says the Bible is full of errors and that only the Koran can be trusted and—"

"Okay, you're in conversation with a Muslim guy. He's a student where you go to school?"

"Actually, he's my boyfriend." Thus began the story of a girl in crisis, and it took some time to tell. But the girl was earnest. Further, she was absolutely in need. Why she picked her out, Cara did not know, but she listened as they stood there, forgetting she was the center of attention in the middle of a big crowd. She had not one flutter of anxiety.

How much time had elapsed she could not say, but after a while she felt a tap on her arm. It was Josh. Cara had already gotten the girl's number and promised to text her with some good resources and to be in prayer with her about the whole situation, so it was easy enough for Cara to let herself be led back to the table where most of the group had already made a good dent in their entrées.

Josh was more than a little irritated with her, and although she said she was sorry, in truth she was not sorry at all that she had talked to the girl. Indeed, she preferred it to some sort of artificial social interchange. But she had upset Josh, and she was certainly sorry for that.

When they were going out the door of the restaurant, someone who looked to be in charge gave Josh an envelope that was no doubt an honorarium. He tucked it into his suit pocket, opened the car door for Cara, walked around to the other side, got into the driver's seat and headed home. It was already well after midnight and would be approaching two o'clock in the morning by the time Josh dropped her off. After that, he would have another forty-five minutes to travel back to Bloomingtown.

Josh filled the conversational vacuum in the car with one-sided monologue, sensing that Cara was pretty spent emotionally. "Peter Tilkin is from Indiana originally," he added to some other story he was telling. "He came over after he got married. And James is from Texas. He's going to marry Julie."

Finally, Cara had something to talk about. "Yes, I talked to Julie for a long time. She's really nice, and we're going to try to stay in touch."

"I was hoping you'd get to know her. And about that other thing," he said, a bit more sternly.

"What other thing?"

"The incident with the girl on the other side of the restaurant."

The girl whom Cara was trying to help was now reduced to an incident. Josh continued, "I just need to share this with you. There is a time and place to help people. You know I believe in ministry. I live for it. But kids always have needs. You could still be there talking to that girl right now if I hadn't rescued you, and even though you might be helping her, you also have to know something else."

"What is that?" Cara asked evenly.

"Boundaries."

"Boundaries?"

"Yes. There is protocol. Speakers are obligated to spend time with those who invited them, as are their...ur, uh, those who are with them."

"So you are saying that I was violating protocol?"

"No, the girl was. She should have let those in ministry have time for fellowship."

"She wasn't allowed to talk to me?"

"Not to dominate you. That was wrong!"

"You are angry that I can't take care of myself and that I let myself be dominated? Is that it?"

"Cara, you didn't do anything wrong."

"Well, it sure feels like you think so."

"I'm just trying to help."

"Well, it feels more like I have been smitten," Cara said, although she had no idea why she said it. Josh had no response. He didn't even know what she meant. And because he was just now pulling into her driveway, he had a feeling there might not be any further sort of elaboration. But Cara was not finished yet. "You know Josh, you have this whole restaurant full of girls with googly eyes for you. They adore you. And you know what? You could choose any one of them who would love to plop themselves in the front pew, who would be tickled to death to have you call them up to the platform, who would gladly listen to you explain how it is they are supposed to behave in restaurants."

"But Cara, I was just trying to—"

"Josh, I don't think we have the commitment level to sustain this sort of conversation."

"But I want to have—"

"Have a good life, Josh Peeler." Cara marched alone to the front door, went inside, and turned out the porch light.

Chapter 8

Unfortunately, Cara did not feel as certain as she had sounded. In fact, she cried herself to sleep. Still, there was something inherently wrong with what had happened to her in that car. She knew it. Josh must have known it too. She ignored seven texts from Josh on Saturday and Sunday.

Ron, who was still sporadic at church, showed up Sunday morning with three kids in tow. "Can we come to class with you?" he asked. Cara smiled and told him they had better stay out in the sanctuary. But Ron, ever the free spirit, went back with Cara and Marta once the song service was over—as did the rest of his friends.

After church, when the Shepherd family had settled around a table at the restaurant, the subject of children's church was the first item of conversation. "Sister Pridgitt told me there were several sinners back there teaching our children," Cara's dad said sternly.

"Sorry, Dad. I tried to get them to stay in the sanctuary. I don't know why they came back. But they obviously weren't teaching. They just sat and listened. They liked the Muppet show Marta and I did. And I would hardly call Ron a sinner. He and Peter have both been baptized. And the other guy is coming along, too."

"Well at least they were in church," said Cara's mom. Yet, despite her efforts, her husband's jaw remained clenched.

Sandra then remarked, "But what I really want to know is whether they put anything in the offering plate. Because if not, then why bother?" Barn-Boss's sarcasm did the trick of disarming Cara's pastor-father. Despite himself, his face relaxed into a smile, and nothing more was said about children's church.

Cara was at work on the following Saturday when her mom phoned. She called her back during her break. Karen asked, "Did you and Josh have a fight?"

"I wouldn't call it a fight," said Cara, though she wasn't sure why she said that. Probably because, as she was journaling about it, she referred to it as "the incident about the incident."

"Cara, I was just wondering if it was Josh who sent you a dozen roses with the little note that says, 'Still thinking about you'?"

Cara's Call

"Okay, we're having a few problems, Mom, but I don't want to talk about it."

On Sunday afternoon, Karen was sitting on the couch pretending to read the paper while her husband was going over notes in the recliner and flipping the pages back and forth in his Bible. She said, "You know, I wonder how we could get some more of these kids from college to come to church."

"Yeah, good point," said Jim. "That's kind of got me scratching my head. I mean, they'll go to Cara's Bible studies; they'll even go watch her teach Sunday school, but only a few of them ever darken the doors of the church."

"I wonder if it would be good if they got to know us better?"

"How are we going to do that? We'd stick out like sore thumbs on that campus."

"Say, what do you think would happen if we invited them to the house for some activity or another?"

"I don't know. All that racket. And who knows what they are into? It might not be a good idea."

"Of course, dear. You're right. We're not thinking about something on an on-going basis, certainly. But then again, I wonder what would happen if they came over for just one thing? Maybe like a Christmas social? If they got to meet us, they might even like us."

"Hmmph. I'll have to think about it."

Another week went by before Josh just showed up at Cara's work. How he knew her schedule she wasn't sure, but he asked if she wanted to go for coffee after her shift, and she couldn't say no.

Josh started acting pretty serious over coffee. "I believe that everyone has gifts," he said. "And that everyone brings gifts to a relationship. Dreams too," he said.

Cara was happy that he was opening the door to find out about her plans. She decided to walk through. "I know what you mean," she said. "Because I've got some dreams that I'm working on. They're not all thought through or anything, but they are important to me."

Josh looked deeply into her eyes, and she felt that for the first time it was safe to open up to him. She said, "I know I've been part of a ministry family, and I've done my part. And I still want to. And yet, I have some other things I want to do with my life, Josh."

"I know what you mean," he said, "and I want you to know that I believe in you."

"You do?" she asked in surprise.

She realized that she'd better clarify. "But Josh, I think you need to know that I'm thinking about doing something other than—"

David S. Norris

"Right," he said. "Thank God you've been helping in a little home missions work, but I think God has something different. Something more for you!" Cara's eyes brightened, but he did not let her speak. "Cara, someday, I believe it is quite possible— sooner more likely than later—that I will be voted in as the sectional youth leader. And then, you know, Anthony is not getting any younger, and if I play my cards right, it is quite possible I could be the youth president for Illinois. I know I could do a good job if I just got the chance."

Cara pictured Josh in a poker tournament wearing sunglasses, making sure to play his cards just right. She replied, "Good enough, Josh. And I'm happy for you. But I—"

"Cara, remember when you said that all the girls in the restaurant were all googly eyed over me?"

"I was being stupid, Josh."

"I just brought it up to say that if there were a thousand googly-eyed girls, it wouldn't make any difference. I only want to commit to one girl, Cara, and that's you."

"What are you saying, Josh?"

"Just what it sounds like. I don't date just to date. I am looking for the one who can complete me, Cara."

"I'm not sure I can complete anyone."

"I've really been miserable since that rally. I need you in my life."

"Josh, do you remember what you asked me the first time we met?"

"Who named you?"

"I'm talking about calling. You asked me if I had a call."

Josh looked defensive. "I was probably just making conversation. Okay, Cara, let's not talk about this too much here. We'll just hit the reset button, start from the beginning, and figure out the details as we go."

"But Josh—" she began again, but he put his finger to her lips to sweetly shush her. Then, he did that thing where he gave her his total attention, gazing into her eyes and telling her what she meant to him, and by the time it was over, they had decided they were going to keep working on figuring out if they had a future together. They wouldn't see anyone else. Not that Cara had anyone in mind.

"Okay, so are you coming with me tonight or what?" asked Amanda.

"I already texted you my answer," said Cara.

"'eek' is not really an answer."

"Amanda, I need to get caught up with my reading on the European Renaissance."

"It will be fun. The church in Mattoon is hosting it. It's a bunch of single adults who—"

Cara's Call

"I am so not going."

"And why not?"

"Amanda, please! I've gone to one singles event and it was populated by middle- aged people, divorcees, some little old ladies, and a few single guys where there was no mystery at all as to why they were single."

"They're not all like that!"

"No. And that's final."

"Cara, it's called Hyphen and it's for single people from 18-30 years of age."

"Amanda, maybe if Josh would come, I would go, but I already know he has a deal tonight that he has to do. I won't know anybody, and you know I don't do crowds."

"Look, go with Greg and me. You know us. Someone told me they're just doing small-group stuff. It won't be like a big crowd. And I think Fred will be there. He told me it would be really fun."

"Fred being there is supposed to sway me?"

"Do it for me, Cara. Please!"

Cara picked up Amanda in her rumpled Mazda from Salem. Greg drove over from Charlestown and met them at the church at Mattoon, his brother Kevin in tow. When they arrived together at the door, Cara was surprised to see Fred more than merely attending the event; he was welcoming people at the door. He asked Greg in an official-sounding voice, "So did you bring your embossed invitation? You'll need it for entrance."

Greg responded, "I didn't know that—"

"And your tuxedo. Where's your tuxedo?" demanded Fred.

"What? I didn't know that—"

"Don't pay any attention to him," said Cara, shaking her head as she led them past her pseudo cousin.

"Ah yes, then," said Fred as they breezed by him. "I suppose we'll make an exception in your case."

They walked into the fellowship hall where everyone was sitting around tables. Fred's tuxedo talk was full of beans; everyone was casually dressed. Fred hollered after them, "There's no assigned seating, but the rule is we have to fill every table before people can be seated at the next one."

"Over here," called an annoyingly loud girl, as she pointed to five empty chairs at her table. Given the way she was carrying on, Cara wasn't surprised there had been no takers. Yet, because there didn't seem to be another option, she and Amanda seated themselves at the table, followed by Greg and Kevin. In the middle of the table was a large number "9."

"So, my name is Sue," said the girl who had recruited them. "And I suppose I should know your names." Then, instead of waiting for everyone to introduce themselves, she continued without pause. "Sitting next to me is a girl named Lee Ann whom I just met, and I forget this guy's name. He just sort of wandered over to the table from places unknown." It would be a long night.

"Cara! Cara!" yelled Stephanie from the table next to them. "It's great to see you!" Cara smiled in return, wondering about her sudden enthusiasm. Stephanie continued, "I just finished my last final, and I am so ready for a vacation!"

"Wow, that's great," Cara said noncommittally. Then, the empty seat next to Stephanie was suddenly filled by Justin, the Greek-Italian fashion model. Stephanie was apparently anxious to show him off.

"Hey," said Sue, who had been keeping score on these things, "you weren't supposed to save seats. You're required to fill in all the seats at each table before—"

"Looks like they're all filled in then," interrupted Stephanie, laying claim on the new arrival while bulldozing the objection.

Kevin worked at smoothing things over by saying, "Sue, thank you for having us at your table. You were saying we should introduce ourselves?" Sue agreed. It annoyed Cara that Sue felt compelled to comment after each person gave their name.

Fred, the event host, introduced himself and formally welcomed the group. After a not-so-fun crowd breaker, the host then said, "We are so glad to have Stuart Greene, a licensed counselor from Columbus, Ohio. Let's offer a warm welcome for Stuart." The clapping was more subdued than the sort of pandemonium that broke out at youth rallies. Cara was not disappointed.

"All right," said Stuart after the appropriate opening remarks, "I need a guy and a girl to help me out up here."

Stephanie was waving and pointing to Justin. "Here! Justin is willing to volunteer."

"All right," said Stuart, "and since you are so willing to volunteer your friend, why don't you come up and play the second part."

Stephanie did not seem at all disappointed to be heading up front. Stuart handed both of them several sheets of paper, saying, "I have a script for both of you, so you don't have to worry about any lines." Stephanie and Justin each took the script. "Now this is 'Cinderella' and 'Prince Charming,'" continued the speaker. "But the scene we are about to see is set fifteen years after their royal wedding."

It seemed appropriate for both Stephanie and Justin to play the parts. While it was true they each wore casual clothing, it was such expensive casual clothing that it wasn't a hard sell for them to play the part of royalty.

Stephanie, who now beamed as Cinderella, was introduced as "Cinders," the pet name her husband had given her. It turned out Cinders had her own pet name for her husband: "Charms." Stephanie immediately rose to the part, assuming the appropriate regal bearing as she said, "Anything, Charms…you know that I aim to please."

Stephanie became less enamored with the skit when Charms volleyed a few criticisms at her character. It seemed that, in his opinion, Cinders wasn't choosing the right clothes for the royal ball and besides, she had put on some weight since their royal wedding.

Cinders had a few criticisms of her own. For example, she didn't think much of the royal decorating—the drapes in her bedroom were horrid. The prince didn't take kindly to criticism. He replied, "Cinders, dear, the Queen Mother picked out those drapes that you are now calling ghastly."

"Oh, I don't mean to be critical," said Cinders. "I really don't. And your mother has wonderful taste. But perhaps we could do some updating around here."

Justin, a.k.a. Charms, retorted, "Well, this castle has been just fine for royalty for two-hundred years. I would think now that you are royalty you would see how nice things really are." And so it went. Their fight escalated until the script called for them to request help from the royal marriage counselor.

"Way to ruin a good story," announced Sue to their table. "I drove forty-five miles to see Cinderella trashed."

But Stuart proceeded to make a point: "The borrower is servant to the lender." Cara's ears perked up, for he had tricked her into investing herself emotionally. Stuart continued, "You see, unless a person marries someone who is their equal—with both partners believing they've gotten a good deal—then one will always be in emotional debt to the other."

Sue was not impressed. "I didn't know we came tonight for marriage counseling," she complained. Stuart then stressed application. He insisted that every relationship must begin with how a person actually feels about their own self. Sue kept offering asides, unable to stop herself from a running commentary and critique.

"All right, some group work," said Stuart. "I need you to pick a leader for the table. Someone who will make sure that everyone gets to share, and then I have a case study for you to work on."

"I pick Kevin," said Sue, and since no one objected, he was the leader.

Kevin read the paper that held their case study. "One of your friends gets the following email from a girl named Samantha. It reads: 'I need some advice. Could you please give a generic answer as to why someone would constantly attract a partner that uses them, and plays with their mind, or could you tell me why someone attracts obsessive and controlling partners? How does one get from dysfunctional to functional? Can it happen? Is there hope?'"

Kevin continued to read. In the case study, they were asked about the following situation: "Your friend has come to you for suggestions he could give to Samantha. You don't have to solve the whole problem; just point him in the right direction." Finished with his reading of the case study, Kevin began, "Okay, we have ten minutes. Anyone have any suggestions?"

Sue was quick to reply. "Obviously, this Samantha is a loser. Losers attract losers. So there you have it."

"You may have a point, Sue," Kevin said with a smile. "At least Samantha feels like a loser. But maybe there is something more going on here. Maybe she has something in her background that makes her feel bad about herself."

"Like zits?" said Sue.

"Well, I was thinking of something a bit more severe. We all struggle with self-esteem to some extent. I have dealt with a couple of girls who sounded like this, and one had been abused."

Cara immediately disagreed. "Kevin, that's a little unfair. A person can struggle with all kinds of issues and still come from a decent background. Maybe it's their personality or birth order or whatever." Then Cara blushed, feeling certain that everyone guessed she was talking about herself.

Then a very surprising thing happened. Kevin said, "You're right, Cara. I was being a little judgmental, especially considering that this is a hypothetical situation." Cara sighed in relief.

Kevin continued, "So what do you think, Amanda? Do you think there is something we can say to help her?"

While Amanda was surprised to be called on for an answer, she didn't lack for ideas. She said, "I think Samantha needs to step back from relationships for a bit; maybe work some things out in her own life."

"Fair enough," said Kevin. "That might be a good choice. Now, let's suppose she does that. How will that help?"

"It probably won't," said Sue.

"Thanks for sharing," said Kevin. "Anyone else?"

"You know what I think?" said Greg. "Some people don't have self-esteem, because they've never done anything to get self-esteem. I'm not saying football is something people should do, but when I was in high school, I played varsity football, and I was good. My accomplishments in football actually helped me do better in my English class. Don't ask me to explain how that worked. I just know that it gave me confidence to accomplish something in a totally unrelated area. In fact, now that I think about it, I would have to say that, at least in part, it translated into the confidence I have in church. I felt good enough about myself to go to the pastor and convince him that we could help teenagers."

"I still say the girl is a loser," said Sue.

"Okay, thanks for that. Do you want to explain why, Sue?"

"She just wants a boyfriend."

"Okay, that's an interesting point," said Kevin. "Now, Sue and Greg's comments bring to my mind an interesting question. How do you encourage people to accomplish things?"

Greg, who apparently felt himself to be in home territory, added something else. "Kevin and I let kids know that we're sincere, and then we listen to them. And when they talk about an interest they have, we jump on that and encourage them to give things a try."

"What if it is not God's will?" asked Sue.

Undaunted, Greg said, "Something is almost always better than nothing. If kids aren't motivated to do anything, then they don't have any chance of heading in the right direction. Kevin says, 'It's pretty hard for God to steer a parked car.' So if kids are actually going after a goal—if they're accomplishing something—then they might have enough self-confidence to believe that they can actually do something that will make a difference in the world. And in a roundabout way, just doing something worthwhile really can help them find God's purpose."

Cara was shocked. She had no idea Greg thought so deeply. She was embarrassed that she had stereotyped him in her mind.

Kevin then asked, "If you were to prompt Samantha and perhaps suggest something she could accomplish, what suggestions come to mind?"

"Maybe we don't have enough information," said the fellow named Ralph who had not spoken a word until now and whom Sue seemed not to appreciate at all.

"Good," said Kevin. "I like that you didn't prescribe what dreams Samantha should have. So, maybe you could help by sharing something that you have as a dream. Ralph, what dream of yours do you feel would be safe to share? You know, kind of priming the pump?"

Ralph said, "I really want to be a computer programmer, but I just need to save a little more money."

Sue noted without being prompted, "If she's a church girl, she should probably try to work on her music. I don't think girls should shoot too high."

The girl who hadn't yet spoken said offhandedly, "Hey, I have a dream to be a physical therapist."

"And I would like to be a lawyer," said Cara, in an attempt to affirm the girl who had just spoken.

Out of the corner of her eye, Cara suddenly noticed Stephanie at the neighboring table, eavesdropping on Kevin's group, her lips curved upward in a knowing smile. Cara wished now, more than ever, that she had stayed home.

Chapter 9

Cara looked up from her cash register into a familiar face. He said, "Hey, what time do you get off? I wanted to use my discount at Starbucks." When Cara told him, Josh promised he'd be back. She steeled herself against what was likely to be a confrontation.

"I heard about the other night," began Josh with no preamble, taking a sip of his latte.

"From Stephanie, I suppose," she said flatly. If Josh was not beating around the bush, neither would she.

"Let's just say word gets around," he said, but the guilt washing across his face indicated that Cara had correctly pegged his source.

"I know you had obligations, but I wish you could have been there," said Cara.

"Yeah, me too." There was a pause, and then Josh intoned, "Now, about this lawyer thing..."

The pause was deliberate. Then Cara calmly responded, "Yes."

"I've got to say, that this really pulled the rug out from under me."

"That's an odd choice of words," said Cara, working to keep her emotions in check.

"Well, it's just that of all the dreams we talked about, this never seemed to come up."

"So...whose dreams have we been talking about?"

"I'm not sure I understand the question."

"Josh, I've got to admit that since I met you, I have been reevaluating a lot of my future goals. I've been trying to ride your roller coaster. I'm still not entirely sure of my plans. But I was hoping you would ride a little way on my roller coaster with me. I'm just saying."

"Cara, you're making no sense."

"Because you have your own ride, your own plans, your own future."

"Cara, I'm not really sure what you mean. You've never talked like this before."

"I am talking this way now because I want to make sure the borrower is not servant to the lender." He had no clue what she meant, but recently she had been journaling about finding a partner who was her equal, and she became convinced that she didn't want to be in any sort of emotional debt to Josh. Not for anything.

"Cara, have I done anything wrong in wanting to include you in my future?"

"No."

"On a scale of one to ten, how important is this lawyer thing to you?"

"Is that a fair question?"

"I'm thinking it is."

"How long am I allowed before I assign a number to my life and hope it meets your approval? Before I see if I have been placed on the scale and found wanting?"

"Cara you know it's not like that. If I want a lawyer, I can hire one. But if I want a partner in ministry, I have to love one, and she has to love me."

Cara thought that the line sounded rehearsed. She responded, "And if two people do love one other, then one won't coerce the other into giving up something just because they say so, would they?"

Cara knew those were dangerous words—threatening, relationship-ending words. They were an accusation. At that moment, Josh would have to decide whether or not he wanted to escalate the fight or back down.

"Have you heard from the Lord on this thing?" he asked evenly.

"On what thing?"

"On the…uh…lawyer thing."

Cara was silent. They were at an impasse. Josh chose to break it. "Cara, I'm sorry for coming on so strong here. I shouldn't have, but it's just that I was surprised at everything that happened. And the way it happened."

"And I'm sorry for not sharing that information with you first before it became a matter of public discussion by others."

Josh continued, "Look, maybe we're not supposed to be together. Or maybe God's got someone else for you and someone else for me. But Cara, like I've told you, when I am with you, I feel so complete, and I don't want to lose what we have."

Cara smiled. Josh was being very real. Very vulnerable. And very caring. It's what she'd been waiting for. And if Josh would be real with her, there was nothing they couldn't work through together.

Cara's realization took them both by surprise. Because the hug she gave him was so unexpected, a big slosh of latte wound up on the floor. He made a dash for the napkins and quickly sopped it up and when he looked up, there were large tears rolling down Cara's cheeks.

First, he was only fumbling with the napkins. But as he wiped up the spill, he fumbled with his words. "So, uh, um, let's just take it one day at a time and we'll see where it all goes, okay?" Cara nodded.

An hour later she was with Amanda, telling her the whole story, right down to the spilled latte. Amanda listened but didn't like the ending. "What happens next?"

"Well, he didn't say I should give up what he's calling 'the lawyer thing,' but I get the feeling that he is waiting for me to get more, I don't know, spiritual? Or maybe pliable? Or submissive? Yes, that is probably the right word. The 'submissive' preacher's wife."

"Cara, are you sure you're reading this right?"

"Amanda, I don't know. But I've got to say, I just don't know if I can fit into the mold of a preacher's wife."

"There's a mold, then?"

"You know good and well there is, Amanda."

"Well, Cara, do you know what I think?"

"What?"

"I'm thinking that if you marry a preacher then you're a preacher's wife. And whatever you do or do not do, you're still a preacher's wife. And that's all there is to it."

"Unless of course people need you to change."

Amanda paused and then asked, "Do you love Josh?"

"Yes. I like him a lot. I think I love him, yes."

"And does he love you? Be honest."

"Yes, I'm pretty sure, but--"

"But what?"

"Oh, Amanda, I just wonder if he can love the real Cara."

"Maybe he already does," affirmed Amanda.

"Amanda, I don't think he's even looking for her. I think he loves an ideal Cara that lives in his head, or maybe he loves the person he thinks he can get me to be. Maybe I'm artificially supposed to be that person he wants—you know, a kind of fake Cara."

"You know that isn't right," said Amanda.

Cara let out a defeated sigh, offering, "Most likely, the real Cara needs to change."

"I like the real Cara just the way she is."

A dusting of snow gave the fellowship meeting at the Shepherd house a holiday feel. Karen hid her nervousness by staying busy all afternoon. Jim did not attempt to hide his nervousness, but he came across a bit differently than his wife. He did a lot of pacing and looking out the window. It was when people started arriving that he got more vocal.

"When is that guy going to get a haircut?" her dad asked Cara. It was true Ron's hair had that look that comes from having little friendship with a comb. Yet, Cara suspected the real offense was that Ron was playing host in the Shepherd home. Jim Shepherd could hardly complain directly, for he had given his consent for the event.

"So cool of you to come," said Ron, hugging a girl with black fingernails and who to Jim looked like a Halloween figure sporting extra jewelry. Ron pointed, "Head on downstairs. Pizza's coming in about an hour."

Cara's mother was doing something with cookies in the kitchen, while Cara's role consisted of continuing to distract her dad to keep him calm. Shay, who had been sampling cookies all afternoon, swooped in to grab a few more and then headed back to his bedroom to avoid the crowd.

"Very cool of you to come—glad you're here," continued Ron, hugging a young lady who didn't seem to have the Illinois winter in mind when she dressed in a mini skirt, thin jacket, and very tall boots that may or may not have been good against the snow. Jim thought she looked like a hooker and told Cara so and then asked, "Does that guy hug everyone?" Cara didn't have time to answer before Marta appeared.

"Pastor Shepherd, your basement is so fantastic. I love the nativity scene and the lights. It feels like chestnuts roasting on an open fire—the whole bit." Marta's eyes were shining and her smile was wide.

"Dad, hug her," whispered Cara. "She has no father." Jim went over, awkwardly shook Marta's hand and then leaned his cheek against hers. It was clear from the kiss that she gave him on his cheek that Marta felt loved.

Jim blushed and sought out his wife. "Do you need anything from the store?" he asked, looking for an escape. She thought of something, and he quickly made his exit.

Karen was suddenly concerned. She asked Cara, "Is there a delivery man that I should be waiting for with the pizzas?"

"No, Amanda said she would pick up the pizzas on her way over."

They kept coming—ten, twelve, and then close to twenty before it was all said and done. Ron had promoted Sister Shepherd's sugar cookies to his friends and that had apparently boosted attendance. And of course, "Pizza and the gospel always go together," Karen had quipped more than once.

The question as to who was going to pay for the pizza was no small bone of contention at the Shepherd home. Pastor Shepherd didn't want to support freeloaders. Karen had brokered a compromise of sorts, which included Cara collecting a donation from whoever had anything they wanted to give and from Karen's secret stash of money. It was the only way she could have sold the event to her husband. Otherwise, the fellowship never would have happened.

In the basement, Marta quickly tuned her guitar and began singing, "O, come, all ye faithful…" and others gradually joined in with her.

"She has a beautiful voice," said Cara's mom as she plopped down another tray of cookies. Three Christmas carols and two crowd-breakers later, the papa and the mama of the Shepherd household introduced themselves and said they were glad that everyone could come. Karen said that they should come back again but Jim didn't say any such thing. Karen decided that she would have to think of a way to get Jim to continue Cara's Friday night fellowship after Christmas.

Because Josh was the most recent employee to be hired at Starbucks, others were able to get more time off than he was. Consequently, he would not be going back to Ohio for the holidays since it would be his responsibility to open at Starbucks both the day before and the day after Christmas. So Karen invited him to share their Christmas dinner. He arrived without a coat, because the weather had warmed considerably. In fact, it was so warm that they had more Christmas decorations than snow.

"Josh, will you bless the food?" Jim asked.

There were three extra tables of them—Uncle Bob and his family, Bob's extended family with their kids, Sandra and Billy along their two girls, Sissy and Baby Lungs. The miracle of Christmas was that even Baby Lungs remained quiet during Josh's exceedingly long prayer, blessing the very wonderful family and the very wonderful food and the all hands that prepared it. The meal was followed by the expected Christmas celebration—food, laughter, presents and fun.

After the wrapping paper was cleaned up and the kids were all playing in the basement with their new toys, Sandra corralled as many adults as would play one of those table games where people guessed one another's preferences. During the game, new revelations abounded. Fred really wanted to be a dentist. Karen's perfect vacation was on a remote beach in Tahiti, and Sandra's favorite sport was skydiving, despite the fact that she had never tried it as yet. When Josh's turn came, his question was, "What do you wish for most?" Cara was sure that he would be

Cara's Call

able to spin some funny answer, but he didn't. Treating the question seriously, he stated, "I want to fulfill my calling and do the ministry the Lord called me to do."

A brief silence followed his remark, and then the game moved on. At least, it did for everyone else. Cara was troubled by his answer, though she wasn't sure why. Then, when the game was over, Shay appeared from the basement, inviting Josh to play some kind of baseball game where they got to pick this or that player.

"I'd hate to beat a poor innocent teenager in his own house!" declared Josh, clearly interested.

"And I'd hate to wipe the floor with someone who doesn't know a good player from a bad one," countered Shay.

They quickly disappeared into the basement where shortly afterward Cara heard muffled laughing and joking and shouts and yells, as well as loud charges from Shay that there might be some sort of cheating going on. But that was to be expected. An hour later the two emerged into the kitchen where Cara was helping her mom with the dishes. When her dad saw Josh, he told the young man he wanted to show him his book on prayer.

The two quickly headed downstairs to Jim's office. While putting a plate into the cupboard her mother said, "You know, Cara, I think Josh is like your dad."

"Do you really think so?" asked Cara curiously.

Cara's mom obviously had something to say. She was just trying to find a way to say it. "Well, in a lot of ways, he's quite a bit different. But he's like Dad in one very specific way. He is pretty certain about what ought to be done for the Lord and how it ought to be done."

Cara heard her dad and Josh laughing loudly about something and felt left out. She could never remember her dad laughing loudly with her. Then, she felt stupid for feeling jealous. She turned back to her mother. "So, would that be a good thing?" she asked.

Her mother didn't answer the question directly. In fact, she didn't say anything for a long time. Then, with no emotion attached, she simply said, "Josh is a good boy."

Later that night, after her dad himself said goodbye to Josh at the door, he turned to Cara and said, "Now, there's a young man who has it together."

With all the overtime at work, Cara didn't have time to clean the church until Saturday night, but she was actually glad for the alone time. The parking lot was still slushy from what was left of the previous night's snow, but it would likely be fully melted by the time church started the next morning.

Although the building had once been a warehouse, the complete refurbishing of the inside and the brick facing surrounding the doorway offered a friendly, if only a somewhat churchy, welcome. Cara hung up her coat and went straight to the sound booth. She took a CD from the stack of worship music, plunked it in the player and cranked it up loud enough to be heard over the vacuuming.

As she vacuumed the vestibule, she said, "Lord, I'm not going to make a good minister's wife." The vacuum swept back and forth, offering no consolation. "Why do I always feel so disqualified around Josh?" she said to the chairs as she straightened them back into place. "I love him. At least that's how I feel when we're together."

She sprayed Windex on the clear plastic pulpit, trying to work out an ugly blemish. Something had been spilled on it and simply would not come out. She channeled her anger and attacked the stain.

"He is so controlling, Lord! He pretends not to be. But here's the deal. He has created this little box for me to live in, one that You didn't design."

Cara continued rubbing angrily, "I know what his problem is; he's not listening to You. He's already determined what he wants to do and asks only for Your blessing. It's just plain wrong."

Just as the stubborn spot finally yielded to her efforts, Cara realized for the first time that the very thing she was accusing Josh of could also be applied to her. Hadn't she announced to God that she was going to be a lawyer? How was that any different than what Josh was doing?

Cara started vacuuming again. "Lord, I know I told You that I am going to be a lawyer, and I haven't done a whole lot of asking as to what You want. So I guess I'm pretty hypocritical here, though I still think Josh is wrong."

All of that was easy enough to say. Cara didn't mind owning up to her own shortcomings. It was the next thing she was going to have to say that would be the hardest. She let the vacuum run in place as she walked over to the altar.

"Lord, I thought I gave You my life. I still want to be a lawyer. I think I'd be good at it. But I release that dream to you. I give You my life. No limits. Whatever You ask, whatever little thing I can do, I promise, I will do whatever it is that You ask me."

She wasn't sure what she expected to happen after that, but the fact is, not one thing did. No emotional release. Nothing. She just felt empty. Her dreams had just crashed and she had nothing to show for it. A tear escaped down her cheek followed by another. Once they started, they didn't stop. One Kleenex after another wound up on the altar. Cara was not sobbing in sweet communion with God. She was grieving for her loss.

Then Cara did something really silly, but which, intuitively, she knew was the next step. She said, "I praise You, God. I praise You even though I just gave away my dream and even though I don't have anything left. I praise You." As stupid as she felt in uttering those words, she knew they were right. Only then did Cara feel something.

"Explosion" was the word that came to her later when she thought about it. Whereas the moment before she had felt nothing, God was suddenly present in an eruption of love and comfort. It felt like she was a small girl in her father's arms or an infant in her mother's embrace. And just as unexpectedly, something else happened.

It may have been a vision, though she didn't call it that later when she spoke of it. What Cara saw looked like a view from one of those professional cameras used in filming a church service. The camera zoomed in from its perch on top of a balcony in one of those mega-churches. The audience included people from all different nationalities who were listening attentively to the person behind the pulpit. Cara sensed that this person was directing them, shepherding their lives. As the camera zoomed in closer, she saw it was a woman. When the woman became recognizable, Cara saw that she was looking at herself. She was preaching, and she wasn't afraid.

At once Cara protested, "No!"

And then there was nothing. It was as if none of it had ever happened. As if a light switch turned off. As if she had made up the whole thing. Then she thought that perhaps she had.

But she couldn't so easily dismiss what had happened. It was as real—as real as any experience she had ever had. She tried to visualize herself telling her father about it. As she thought of him, he grew from six feet to maybe ten feet tall—or was it that she was becoming younger, fourteen or ten or even five years old? Dad stood with his arms crossed, shaking his head in disgust. Then she visualized herself telling Josh, but she could not see how he reacted. Suddenly Stephanie appeared and said with a guffaw, "You? You've got to be kidding!"

Why Cara thought of those things in that exact sequence or what all this actually might mean she could not say, but the reality was clear enough. She spoke once more with finality. "You know I can't do this, Lord! They would crucify me!"

Nothing. No sound. No condemnation. No voice. It was over. She had failed. Something had been offered to her, and she had turned it down. While Cara was disappointed that she hadn't been up to the task, she also felt incredibly relieved. "I just couldn't, Lord," she said quietly. "I know you understand. They would have crucified me."

That was the end of it, she thought. Except that it wasn't. Suddenly, she heard a voice, not an audible voice, but a voice in her head, so gentle and caring that she would never ever forget. "Cara, they crucified Me," it said. "Will you hear My voice?"

Chapter 10

Ron showed up at their Saturday night puppet practice. Marta had improved considerably, and even though it was only their second time through, their number went off without a hitch. Ron was so impressed that he stood to his feet and gave them a one-man standing ovation. While Marta and Cara changed out their props to practice their second number, Ron asked an off-the-wall question. "Say, Cara, what do we believe about capital punishment?"

"Why are you asking me?"

"Don't be silly. I'm asking you for the same reason I ask you every other thing from the Bible. Because God gives you answers so you can give them to me."

If he had said the same thing eight days earlier, it wouldn't have meant anything, but Cara now took offense. "Listen, Ron. This is not how this works. See, I'm just helping you get started. Then, other people will help oversee your spiritual progress. Once you get the basics down, you are good to go."

"I'm good to go as long as you're in my life," he said. And Marta was nodding like a puppy dog. But they were wrong. She was not in charge of other people. Her father was. Ministers were. Others with great gifts. As Marta started the music and Cara made her entrance with her Muppet, she felt absolutely miserable.

Cara had a hard time concentrating on her new classes. She liked psychology in general but hated her Monday afternoon class. Mr. Big-Shot-Talk-Down-at-You was making some convoluted point about how the textbook was wrong and he was right. Although Cara believed neither the teacher nor the text, this sounded like something that he might ask on the final exam, so dutifully, she took down everything he was saying.

Cara had enjoyed her previous psychology professors better than this one. Though they were still only three weeks into the new semester, she knew she would dread every class period with this pompous man. Maybe he'd had a bad childhood or a Sunday school teacher who offended him. By definition, the university had little use for God, but when teachers were so overtly biased, her "strainer" was to doubt everything the prof said and to think about it more when she had more time.

Cara's Call

Then Cara realized she not only hated this class, she actually didn't like any of her classes this semester. She also realized that she no longer liked going to work. Further, she was even getting a little bored with children's church. The more she considered things, the worse she felt.

She knew why though. A month ago her life had been filled with purpose. But now she wasn't sure who she was or where she was headed. She had no idea what she was going to do next semester. She had to do something. She just wasn't sure what.

Josh was pumped for any number of reasons. "I've been invited to do a youth revival in Iowa in three weeks," he was saying.

"That's great!" said Cara.

"It's a Friday and Sunday, but the Friday night they're inviting the whole section."

"That's great," she said. "I'm glad for you."

"And the Saturday night is a banquet and I'm supposed to come up with a skit."

"I'm sure you'll come up with something good," she said with as much enthusiasm as she could muster.

"I've been working on it but—hey, Cara, are you mad at me?"

"Of course not. Why?"

"Well, the last three times I've talked to you..."

"Oh. I am so sorry, Josh," said Cara not knowing what she was sorry for. "If I haven't been supportive—"

"It's not that, Cara. Quite the opposite! You support me alright. But it's...I don't know...overdone. I don't feel like I'm really talking to my Cara."

"Hmm," she sighed, not wanting to lie. "Well, I'll try to do better," she offered evenly.

"There you go again," he said. And indeed she did go, hastily explaining that she'd better get to her homework. He had nailed her, but since right now she was walking in a haze, he was simply one more thing she could not define anymore.

Then, two weeks later, things really started falling apart. Cara's motivation was all but gone. She no longer enjoyed college. In fact, she wasn't enjoying much of anything. For the first time in her early morning class, she took absolutely no notes. She doodled during the entire lecture. When the bell rang, she found herself in the library, struggling to finish her reading for psychology.

An hour passed when two things suddenly occurred to Cara. First, she hadn't read a single page. Second, she was late for class. Stuffing her things into her bag, she crossed over to another building and climbed the stairs to the classroom. But as she got close enough to the door to hear her professor spouting forth out of his pompous ego, Cara could go no further.

She didn't know why, but she spun around and went back down those same stairs that she had just climbed. As she descended, she called Amanda who picked up on the first ring. Cara didn't even say hello, but abruptly insisted, "Don't ask why, but I need you to do the fellowship group meeting tonight. I can email you the notes."

There was a pause on the other end of the line, and then a hesitant, "Okay, if you really want me to then—"

"You're the best," replied Cara, and then quickly punched in another number. "Gary, I know I'm supposed to close the store tomorrow, but something's come up. I won't be in."

"No problem, Cara. You came in for me three times last month on short notice. The least that I can do is cover for you one time."

When Cara got home, the house was empty. She grabbed extra cash, threw a couple of overnight things into a travel bag, and left a note for her mom. Cara said simply she would be staying with a friend.

Backing out of the driveway, Cara grabbed the rumpled note with the telephone number. She punched it in on her way to the gas station. When a friendly voice answered, Cara responded, "Hello, Sadie."

"Cara, it's good to hear from you! I sure wished you could have come to Indiana for a visit after Christmas. But I understand you had work and all."

"About that," Cara said. "I decided to take you up on your offer."

"Great! When can you come?"

"Um, well, about that . . . I'm actually on my way right now. I am so sorry for the short notice. I just had this sudden need to get away, and you were the first person to come to mind"

"Cara, you never have to apologize to me. I'll be so glad to see you. There's just one issue. Mark and I have a prior engagement tonight so we won't be home until ten o'clock, but like I said, we've got that extra bedroom. And the forest is just down the road. You'll love it. Maybe we can check that out tomorrow."

Because she had left Munson Heights before noon, she neared her destination way too soon. Even though Bloomington, Indiana, had seemed a long way away on her map, it was clear to Cara that she would be in her car sitting in front of her friend's house for hours.

That would never do. Scanning her map, Cara found McCormick Creek State Park, and on impulse decided to take in the scenery. Certain it would lift her spirits, she wove her way down this and that road. She had to acknowledge that it was

Cara's Call

beautiful. The evergreens and firs reached toward the heavens. Here and there along the shoulder of the road, small patches of snow refused to go away.

Still, she would have appreciated it more if she had been in a better mood. Further, it would have been prettier on a clear day. The temperature hung just above freezing. It must have been humid out, for the road seemed to disappear into a haze. Then, because she had nothing better to do, Cara pulled the car over and killed the engine. There in the forest she was expected to feel peace. But she did not. Despite the beauty of the woods, what she began to experience was a gnawing loneliness.

Twenty-five minutes past before Cara started talking to God. It's not that she hadn't been talking to Him in the last month. It's just that since she wasn't prepared to listen too much, those talks had been pretty one-sided. But Cara knew she just couldn't continue this way. She opened her mouth in honest conversation.

"Lord, I know how to live when I'm following You one-hundred percent," she began. "I'm just not really good at following You half-way. The truth is that I've run out of gas trying to follow my own plan."

If Cara had been expecting some divine response, she was mildly disappointed, for she felt none. As she gazed out at the haze in front of her, she felt no comforting hand. Still, she knew that she was at least saying the right things. Cara closed her eyes, recalling the night the Lord called her and that simple question: "Will you hear my voice?"

In response, Cara fumbled her way into words of submission. "God, I know what You asked, but I just can't do this. If I were a bird, then I could fly, and if I were a preacher, then I could preach. But I can't fly. And I can't preach...yet, I heard Your voice, so, at least I could flap my wings a little...open my mouth to say a few things. You've got to show me the way. But if You do, then I'll follow."

Cara couldn't have had her eyes closed for more than two minutes. But when she opened them, the scenery looked amazingly different. A few moments before, the narrow road had disappeared into a gray haze, but now that mist was lifting. Where the road had once faded away into the fog, it was now splashed by the bright rays of sunlight filtering through the trees, and for all the world it looked to her like a path she could follow.

Cara's mom heard the front door open and then saw a light suddenly turn on in her daughter's bedroom. Puzzled, she went to investigate.

"I thought that you were staying with a friend tonight? That didn't work out?"
"No. I decided to come home."
"Cara, you've been acting a little strange lately. Is everything okay?"

"I'm just working through some things, Mom."

"Are you having issues with Josh? "

"Not that, exactly. It's something that happened."

"School?"

"No."

"At your fellowship meeting? Don't you like having them at the house now? I thought it would be better, but we can change it back. We don't have to—"

"Mom, I have to say something now!"

"Yes," said Karen, who now seemed genuinely frightened.

"Mom, God called me to preach." There—she had said it.

Her mother's expression didn't change. She just looked at her blankly as if Cara had told her that she'd decided to take organic chemistry instead of another math class. Her mom sat down beside her, nodding as if she understood the whole thing but saying nothing. Finally breaking the silence, her mother said lamely, "This may pass, Cara."

"It's been four weeks."

"Oh." And they both just looked at each other.

"What should I do?" asked Cara. "At first I told God no, but then, today, I told Him I'd walk through a door if He opened it. And now, I'm thinking I don't even know where a door is!"

"Well, have you thought about what your father would say if you told him?"

"I've thought about nothing but that."

"Oh. Maybe it would be good not to tell him right away."

"That's what I've been thinking."

"Yeah. We'll talk more," Karen said blandly.

With that remark, Cara's mother simply walked out of the room. Simply walked out. Cara had never known her mother to be without a soothing word or a good thought. This was not a good sign. Then just as quickly as her mother had left, she suddenly poked her head back in the room. "Cara," she said.

"Yes, Mom?"

"For now, let's just wait." Then she turned and disappeared once again.

The grass had already begun to turn green, thanks to a few warm days in the beginning of March. On one of those warm days Cara and her mother talked some more about her calling. And then, based on the advice her mother gave her, Cara did something that, up until this time, she would have never considered doing. She challenged one of the cardinal rules of the house: Don't interrupt Dad when he's studying.

Cara's Call

Cara stood at his door and knocked, peering through the crack allowed by the door being left slightly ajar.

Jim looked up and made eye contact with his normally submissive daughter. Thinking she was asking if he had a minute, which he didn't, Jim simply frowned and waved her away. "Not now, Cara. I've only got a couple of hours to get ready for Sunday because Saturday I've got to—"

"I don't think this can wait, Dad." Like Esther, Cara pushed through the door unbidden.

Jim Shepherd knew then that something was terribly wrong with his second daughter. Cara continued, "Dad," she began, "I have to tell you something…something about me."

Jim's face blanched and his eyes widened. He leaned forward in his chair. She knew in a moment he would come out from behind the desk and signal for her to sit in the loveseat while he sat in the chair across from it. He did that sort of thing at church when he wanted to disarm someone, look less pastoral, to make it seem as if he were not an enemy. But in doing so, it also seemed to Cara somehow false, though she would never tell him that.

When he had time, Cara's dad wrote out his sermons by hand. Consequently, there were loose papers all over his desk. He really shouldn't be doing it that way. Some preachers can read and never sound like they are reading. He couldn't. He was better as an extemporaneous speaker. She would never say so. Her mom hinted at it. But only just hinted.

Sure enough, her dad signaled for her to sit. But instead of taking the chair across from her, he sat next to her in the loveseat. "Dad, I don't want you to be mad, okay?" she began.

This was the same look his older daughter had given him right before her life spun completely out of control. He had missed all the clues. Though it had worked out all right in the end, he never wanted to go through that again. Intuitively, he put an arm of concern around her.

And when he thought of Josh—Jim knew. "Cara, honey, you can tell me anything, and I'm going to be there for you." Cara was in big trouble and it was all Jim's fault. He had encouraged that whole relationship. Of course, they would keep the baby, after he got rid of Josh. Jim was trying to remember if he had any shells for his gun in the hall closet.

Cara tried to speak but couldn't seem to get any words out. Tears started to flow down her cheeks. "God spoke to me," came the soft voice.

Now Jim was confused, totally disoriented. Finally, he asked, blandly, "What about?"

"About ministry."

Relief came to him quickly. "Thank God," he said. "I knew you were hesitant about Josh and you're really not an upfront person, but then, neither is Mom. So, you're thinking that Josh is the one?"

"Dad, listen to me. God called me to preach."

Her words took his breath away. Jim had a line that he had learned from one of his favorite preachers. It was a good one, one that he repeated often. "The only woman who ever carried the Word was Mary." It was a zinger if you really thought about it. Jim had preached that the presence of women preachers in denominational churches was actually a sign that these were the last days, proof that women were no longer women, and God's order was all out of whack. Jim had laughingly quoted, "I suffer not a woman to teach" a couple of times when he heard about some woman on the general conference floor who was promoting women for leadership. He hadn't been there, but he had heard about it from Bob. Bob said that she'd made a fool of herself.

"Oh, Cara," was all Jim could say, as if she had just told him she had been struck with leprosy or had contracted bubonic plague or was now a cannibal. "Oh Cara," he repeated. "Who's putting these thoughts into your head? It's not Josh, is it?"

"No."

"Some of those classes you're taking in college?"

Cara just looked at him blankly.

Jim tried to think of how to help her. He started saying whatever came into his head. It didn't totally make sense, but afterward, he wondered if it was just as well. "You know, Cara, the biggest problem that I find among women is a lack of submission."

He was encouraged when she nodded her head, not seeming to be in disagreement. He went on, "When a woman is not in submission, then it is difficult, hard... well, God simply cannot use her."

Cara continued to nod her head and so he decided to test her understanding. "So you see what I mean, then, don't you?"

"I do, Dad. And that's why I won't do anything about this without your approval." Jim's face broke into a smile.

Later that night, Jim was reading a book on prayer while his wife Karen perused a magazine. "You'll never guess what happened today," Jim said.

"I already know," came the rather cool response from the other side of the bed.

"Did Cara talk to you?" he asked.

Cara's Call

"Not after you spoke to her. But Jim, I sent her to see you in the first place."

"Good, then," he said, turning a page in his book. He wanted to teach a series on prayer, and while some principles offered by the book were helpful, it leaned way too much toward "speak the word—nab it and grab it." For almost ten minutes Jim continued highlighting important passages until he gradually became aware that the atmosphere in the bedroom had gone from cool to frozen. Ice cubes were coming from the other side of the bed.

"Something wrong?" he said.

"I don't know," came the monotone from behind the magazine. "Is there?"

Jim looked to see if he had left his socks on the floor. They were in the hamper. And then, as impossible as it seemed, he realized his wife was somehow invested in this deal with Cara. After thirty seconds of silence, he stated with firmness, "She said she would submit to me."

Another lengthy silence hung ominously over the room until a voice from behind the magazine tolled with an unfamiliar finality. "Jim, if you crush our daughter, I will never speak to you again."

Chapter 11

What upset Bob the most was not that he was losing the game; it was the way he was losing. Jim was doing all the things that old guys in a friendly game are not supposed to do: lunging, slamming, and running up on the racquetball.

Finally, Bob asked, "What is wrong with you?"

"Nothing," Jim repeated for the third time.

After he finished walloping him, Jim finally said, "I've got trouble, Bob."

"Bro...if there's anything I can do to help...if you need anything, just say the word. Are you okay for your Bible study tomorrow, because I'll come in a heartbeat."

Jim was winded now, paying for his frustrated show of adrenaline. He had no one to blame but himself. "Thanks for the offer, but I'll be fine for my Bible study," Jim said then sighed.

"Problems with the saints of the Most High?" asked Bob, thinking he had nailed the issue. But Jim shook his head.

"No. Problems with my wife."

"She sick?"

"Bob, she's stopped being submissive."

"Whoa. Are you sure you didn't mistake Karen for someone else's wife? Because if there's anyone whose middle name is submissive, it's her. Bro! What's the issue?

"My daughter."

"Sandra, huh? Well, you've got to expect that I suppose."

"No. Cara."

"Sweet Cara? I am not hearing this. Please! Jim, if your wife and Cara are causing you problems, then I'm going to quit the ministry and become a hermit. Who then can be saved?"

"This is not funny."

"So what's Cara doing? Did she dump Josh for some loser?"

"No."

"She's not pregnant, is she?"

"I wish that was all that was wrong."

Totally bewildered, Bob asked, "Drugs?" He was half-joking.

"No."

"Shot or robbed someone?" he quipped.

"You're not going to believe this. She says she's called to preach."

Bob burst out laughing. "Hey, Jim, you had me going for a minute there. I really fell for the whole thing! So really, what's going on?"

"I'm totally serious! This is really happening."

Bob was more curious than troubled, as if someone had just told him Cara had just learned how to speak Swahili. He had no knowledge base to process any of this. More soberly he asked, "What does this have to do with your wife?"

"It seems that my wife is supporting her."

Bob wiped sweat from his forehead and thought a moment before saying, "Jim, could it be you're making a mountain out of a molehill? You know how young people are. They want to be an astronaut one day and a fireman the next. Cara will drop this when she figures out it won't work."

"Maybe. If we were talking about other young people, I would say it didn't mean that much. But Cara has had a concrete plan for her life since she was five years old."

"Maybe so. But not the same plan. I mean, she could change, couldn't she?"

"I suppose, but I can't figure out how she even got this idea in the first place."

"Maybe you haven't preached on it enough," said Bob, but he quickly took it back as Jim simply stared at him. "Yeah, I guess that was a stupid thing to say."

Jim complained, "If she hasn't gotten the biblical perspective by now, she never will."

"Well, that's your answer," Bob said.

"What?"

"It's one thing to hear something preached, but Cara is one of those girls who needs to study things out. You should teach her a Bible study. Show her how things work scripturally."

"Bob, that's not how I interact with my daughter."

"How do you interact?"

"I'm not sure what you mean."

"How do you communicate?"

Jim paused and then said, "Well, up until now I've always told her what to do. And she does it."

"Look. You're a pastor. You teach Bible studies. Just tell her that you want to share together."

"And what? I'm just supposed to open up the Word to 'I suffer not a woman to teach' and explain to her that she is flat wrong? I'm afraid this might do more damage to her than good."

"No. I'm serious. Get some books. Cara really likes books. Study them together. That way, you'll be showing your wife that you are listening to her concerns, and at the same time you'll show Cara you're concerned for her, and then you can gradually help them both."

"I don't have a good feeling about this, Bob."

"Do you have a better alternative?"

"Cara, I want to talk to you," said Jim.

"Yes?"

"I've been praying about what you talked to me about. I thought that maybe we could study this out some."

"Okay…" said Cara, but, because her dad seemed unable to use the words "called to preach," she was now cautious. "How would we do it?" she asked tentatively. "I mean, how are you thinking of studying it out?"

"I'm not really sure how to proceed. I thought maybe we could decide together."

"All right. So…what are the choices?"

"Well, maybe we could use a book or something."

"Okay. Which book?"

"I don't know. I've got to admit I might need your help. But we can't be the first people who've wondered about this subject. Maybe contact a Bible college or the graduate school. If you can, get a list of books and then we can decide what books to use. If they offer more than one, then we'll just order them all and go from there. I'll pay for everything. You just do the legwork."

"You're serious about this?"

"Yeah," Jim said.

"Oh, Dad, I love you," she said spontaneously and hugged him. He was surprised and happy and now felt a little guilty.

"You remember Julie from the rally, don't you?" Josh asked.

"Of course I do," said Cara.

"Well she gets married in three weeks."

"I know. I've been friends with her on Facebook since the rally, and I'm really happy for her. She's a cool girl."

"It's about a two-hour drive. It's a Saturday afternoon wedding." He expected her maybe to balk a little about the crowd but she did not. No protests whatsoever.

Cara's Call

Cara decided to turn the conversation. She had been planning how to approach him for a week and began by saying, "My dad and I are going to be starting Bible studies together."

"With your fellowship group?"

"No. Just the two of us."

She expected Josh to ask what she and her dad were studying about, but he said nothing. After enough time had gone by to demonstrate that he wasn't going to follow her lead, Cara added, "We're studying about ministry."

She expected Josh to say, "What do you mean?" whereupon he would then be able to tease out what was happening in her life. It would be his discovery. Unfortunately, Josh wasn't cooperating with Cara's script.

"It's an afternoon wedding," he said, "so if we leave about ten in the morning, that will give us time to stop for lunch somewhere."

"See, Dad? I attached them as Word files to your email."

"I don't see them."

Stepping behind Jim's desk, she said, "Let me print them out for you."

On the floor were six books, and on his desk were a half dozen more. Cara printed the first document.

"What's an annotated bibliography?" Jim asked, reading the title on the first page.

"Books listed in alphabetical order by the author. It includes a little summary of what is right and wrong about each book."

"You mean they recommend books where things are wrong with them?"

"Yes."

"Now, who would do such a thing? Recommend these books?"

"It's from the seminary."

"But why would they recommend them?"

"The books aren't entirely wrong. In fact, they no doubt have some very good information in them. See, the idea is to take the good things—what is true—and then leave the stuff that is not as good."

"Hmm," he said as he started reading through the several pages of bibliography in an attempt to make sense of it.

"I ordered all the books," Cara stated, "but only half of them have come in so far. There's maybe another dozen or so more that are on the way." Pointing at the computer screen, Cara added, "I will also print out these papers."

Jim looked where she was pointing but wasn't sure what he was supposed to see. He was getting a sinking feeling that he was in way over his head.

"These attached files are actually papers written by faculty and students at the graduate school," she continued.

"Why don't we just go with what they decide at the graduate school, then?"

"Well, that would be your choice, Dad. We certainly could. I haven't read the papers yet. Still, it's my understanding that the papers pull significant research from the same books we have. So in a way, it might be good for us to go back to those original academic sources and look at it for ourselves."

The phrase 'academic sources' started Jim down the road to full-blown panic. "I'll tell you what, Cara," said Jim, trying to stall for time so he could work out a plan of attack, "Why don't you give me a week or two to look through everything, and then we can decide where to go from there."

"I've got issues, Bob."

"Jim, I'm here for you."

"This is going to be harder than I thought."

"What?"

Jim explained the problem. While there were a few books that in part were against women in ministry, the vast majority of them suggested the concept had clear biblical support.

"I can't even get through chapter one of some of those books," Jim said. "And the papers from the seminary are no help at all."

"What do you mean?"

"As far as I can tell, there may be one guy there who is so-so on women in ministry, but pretty much everybody else is gung-ho."

"Do all these papers say the same thing?"

"No. They seem to argue with each other a lot. But here's the bottom line. While they may not interpret every scripture in the same way, they all seem to be cut out of the same bolt of cloth as far as women in ministry is concerned."

"This is just wrong, Jim. And to think I supported that school one time with an offering."

"I'm just saying—"

"I wonder if Brother Bernard knows about the confusion in the school."

"He's the president."

"Oh."

"So, he's not straightening them out?"

"I've got a paper he wrote, Bob. His paper pretty much sinks me. There's no way I want to start a Bible study with Cara by using that paper."

"Bro, you are fried. But let's not give up yet. So you're saying the books offer all different opinions?"

"Well, some are written by feminists; so, they have a bias. Some are written by historians who don't seem to believe in the Bible but will argue for women in ministry historically; and some are written by people who only kind of believe in the Bible."

"But there's got to be somebody who believes the Bible and writes against women in ministry, isn't there?"

"Well, yes. There are one or two Fundamentalist types who are pretty strong into submission for women. They won't let a woman near a pulpit."

"Well, there you go. Pick one of those books."

"Bob, you think Cara wouldn't know that I was stacking the deck? Picking that and not another book?"

"Okay, I see your point. Well, why don't you use two books? One kind of for it, and one definitely against it."

"That might work."

"You'll have to make it work."

Chapter 12

"I've been thinking about not being a lawyer, now that I have a call to ministry," Cara told her mother.

Karen's eyes flashed confusion or perhaps something else--Cara wasn't quite sure.

"How are those Bible studies going with your dad?" Karen asked.

"Oh, Dad is great. We picked two books, one for and one against women in ministry. And I'm supposed to give him a report on a couple of chapters from each book. Of course, I started studying all the books and papers at once."

"Sounds good," said her mom, "but you actually haven't had your first meeting with Dad then, have you?"

"Not yet. In a couple days."

"Oh. Well then…"

"So what do you think about me not being a lawyer?" Cara asked.

Karen was anxious. "But what would you do then? Even Paul was a tentmaker, so it's important to have something to fall back on whether or not you're in ministry."

"I really don't know what to do. Maybe I could major in English or history. I once thought about psychology, but after this semester, I think I'll leave that one alone. I've got a really creepy psychology teacher."

"That's nice, dear," said her mom, clearly disconnected. She paused but then suggested, "Cara, maybe you could talk to someone about the best choice to make."

"I am. I'm talking to you."

"Well, yes. But I mean, is there someone who understands what's important in education that could—"

"How about Josh?" said Cara.

"Well, he may be good. And he might have good advice. But would you call him unbiased when it comes to your education?"

"I see what you mean."

"How about a counselor from school?"

"I'm a little hesitant to do that because I was hoping to get a spiritual perspective."

"Amanda?"

Cara's Call

"Great idea!"

"Don't make too many plans for sure until you see how this Bible study progresses."

"Right, Mom," said Cara, in a voice that sounded to Karen like a sheep happily headed for the slaughter.

Cara was pleased. Jim conceded that there was a place for women to speak, because the prophecy to the church age was that "daughters will prophesy." Cara took twenty minutes to share her typed summary of the first couple chapters of one book that was for women in ministry and another book that was against it. Jim listened closely and noted that she had a good attitude.

"Cara," he responded, "you certainly have done a lot of work. I commend you." Cara rewarded her father with a big smile.

"We can talk more about the scriptural principles related to women in ministry. But I want to go into a few of the cultural hurdles involved."

"Okay," she said meekly.

He began, "Cara, when you step onto the platform, you assume a certain place. You put yourself on a plane of leadership. You become God's voice in people's lives."

"Yes," she said, nodding in agreement.

"Can you see why this would be difficult?"

"I'm trying to follow you."

"Just think about the characteristics, naturally and biblically, of those who lead."

"All right."

"There are times when an individual in leadership has to be strong, resolute, and sometimes confrontational."

"You mean, confrontational, like when I told Johnny that he needed to stop mocking the church service or leave the night that Ron got the Holy Ghost?"

"Well, no. Not like that at all. I'm talking about pulpit ministry. I've seen women behind the pulpit. They just get up and tell everyone what to do. It's unseemly. Just isn't right. It's not a woman's place."

The ambush surprised Cara. She hadn't in any way expected it. She was absolutely aghast, and for a few moments said nothing. Then, in a very meek voice, she repeated what she thought was his position. "So, what you are saying is that being a leader requires a person to take on masculine characteristics, and if a woman takes on masculine characteristics, then she is biblically and culturally out of order."

"That's exactly right."

"So by definition, then, women shouldn't be leaders?"

"I think you're seeing my position correctly."

If this conversation had taken place several weeks earlier, it would have ended right there. But, because Cara had been given a chance to study and had been invited to talk about it, she was ready to take it a step further.

"Can a woman be over children's church?" she asked.

"Entirely different matter."

"Or over music like Sandra?"

"Different category."

"Have we ever had women missionaries?"

"Certainly."

"And have there been women missionaries who have opened up fields, even overseen pastors from the country where they raised them up?"

"Yes."

"Is what they were doing unbiblical?"

"Well…it worked, so it is difficult to fault, but you can't always say it is the best. Further, once things are established, then a man should take over."

"Are you saying that women should start churches and then turn them over to men to pastor?"

"Well, that's in another country, too. I mean, culturally things might be different here in America."

"If it were another culture or race, it would be okay for an American woman to be over them?"

"Well, on a short-term basis, I suppose."

"But not in America."

"I don't think it works. No."

"Dad, if we wind up saying that American women can oversee men of other races or cultures but they are not sufficient to do the same in North America, do you think someone might call us racist?"

"I think you're missing my point, Cara."

"I'm trying to understand it. What I'm hearing is that a woman could be a missionary and be over men so long as it was in another part of the world."

"Cara, I'm not talking about another part of the world. I'm talking about right here, right now."

Cara did not cry. She did not raise her voice. What she did say, though, let Jim know he had made a significant tactical error. "Dad, I've done everything you told me to do. Always. I love the Lord, and I will still do what you say. If this is your position, then I think we're done, and there's no reason to do any more study. Probably, we shouldn't have started in the first place."

Cara's Call

Cara then offered an invitation. "Dad, maybe there's something you're trying to say that I'm not quite understanding. Why don't you think about what you've said to me for a week or so. Then, if you want to clarify it, or if you want to talk to me about what you believe it means that the Lord spoke to me, then we could talk more. If it turns out you have nothing more to say, then I accept that as well. Okay?"

Only when her dad said okay did the tears cloud Cara's eyes. Jim wanted to embrace her but he didn't. For Cara's part, she didn't feel like being hugged anyway. She turned and silently left the room.

"It didn't go well, Bob."

"No."

"Why not?"

Jim offered a synopsis of the conversation. "Well, Bob, she pretty much called me a racist."

"Now, Jim, you know I'm not in favor of women in ministry. But you made a stupid argument."

"What should I have said?"

"You probably should have just told her no and let that be the end of it. Women should keep silent in the church. No more study, end of discussion." Bob paused, and then offered, "Actually, I'm not really sure what you should have said, but I will say you've pretty much made a mess of things."

"Amanda, what do you think I should do for a major?" Cara asked but Amanda just shook her head.

"Look, Cara, I'm studying to be an RN. I have no idea what choices you even have or which ones are better than others. If you want someone who knows more about this stuff, then Kevin's your guy. I've heard him counsel a number of kids on this. He knows education, and he has an uncanny ability to sort through what people really want and need."

The hour and a half drive was worth it. Though she left out the specifics as to why, Cara explained to Kevin, "I'm going to be making a change. I'm not going to be a lawyer, but I'm not sure what direction to take. What would you suggest as a career that would more directly help people? Do I need to study education like you?"

"Don't know," said Kevin, "though I've got to say you strike me as someone who would make a really good teacher. If you did go into teaching, would you prefer teaching children or teenagers?"

"The older the better."

"Let's back up. Do you prefer speaking or writing?"

"Writing."

"Are you good?"

It was not a tease, and she felt comfortable enough with him not to joke. "Yes. It's one of my strengths."

"So, do you prefer to talk or listen?"

"Listen."

"You have good discernment, like maybe a counselor or something like that."

"I took some psychology classes because I was trying to untangle a lot of things. I've enjoyed most of the classes, but I'm still trying to figure out why I don't fit."

"Maybe you're not supposed to fit."

"Thanks."

"I mean, maybe you are meant to live out a unique role."

"Now you sound radical."

"Not at all. I'm just trying to be practical—help you figure out what works for you."

"Okay. Well, there's no pressure, but I have four weeks to figure out what to do with my life."

"Why?"

"Scholarship opportunities. I have to accept by April 1st."

"Does someone else have a stake in what you do?"

"You mean like a boyfriend or something like that?"

Kevin smiled.

"I was kind of waiting until I had more direction to discuss it with him," she said.

On the way to the wedding, Cara talked to Josh. "I've really been thinking and praying about where the church is. There is so much need," she said.

"Absolutely," agreed Josh. "I was talking to Stephanie the other night, and she had read this article on postmodernism, and what it said was—"

"Josh, I'm not going to be a lawyer."

He only stared. And then a faint smile formed along the edge of his lips. "Well, if that's how you're feeling…" he said, and then just sort of let it hang.

Cara described her visit with Kevin. She said, "Right now I'm leaning toward either a degree in English or perhaps one in psychology. I would be open to other things as well. So, what do you think?"

Josh may have been still smoldering about the lawyer thing; maybe he had something else on his mind, or maybe he just didn't care, but what he said next puzzled Cara. "You know what, Cara? I don't have an opinion on this. You've been deciding things all along here, and I guess that's good. So here's another opportunity."

His words felt like a slap in the face.

At the reception, Stephanie came in on Justin's arm. Soon, though, one of the groomsmen captured her attention. And later, she spent a considerable amount of time talking to Josh. Cara was sitting alone at a table when Justin appeared from seemingly out of nowhere. "Well, another friend bites the dust," he said with a wink.

"I didn't meet Julie until that rally last fall," she said, "but we got together on Facebook and now actually we've become pretty close. Are you friends of the bride or the groom?"

"I don't know either one," said Justin, smiling.

"Oh?"

"They're both Stephanie's friends. She knows everyone."

"So you came with Stephanie then?"

"We've been going together almost two weeks." Then he darkened his voice, "It carries certain responsibilities."

"I see," Cara said, for she saw more than he supposed. Behind him, Stephanie had moved from Josh to where she cornered one of the groomsmen. Stephanie seemed to be making a very good impression on him.

On the way home, Cara explained how her whole worldview had changed. "I was praying, Josh. It was the most incredible experience I've ever had."

"Wow," he said, appropriately but then said nothing more.

"Yeah," said Cara. "It occurred to me that I hadn't been asking God what to do. I'd been telling Him what I wanted to do."

"That's true," he said, less appropriately than his first remark, yet still somehow disconnected from the conversation.

"And then," Cara said, now more tentative, "I realized I had to offer my total commitment to the Lord. I'm not yet sure what it means." Cara paused to make sure Josh was with her.

He said, "I was just talking to Stephanie about commitment. She said that she was reading this youth journal on how to challenge young people to gain purpose in their lives. And I think that..."

The next ten minutes were filled with Josh's exhortation on how the current generation needed to be challenged in new ways. Not surprisingly, that's all the further Cara got in telling him about what happened to her.

Chapter 13

Because her father had said no more, Cara tried to reflect about what that meant for her. She couldn't get any resolution. Journaling didn't help. When she prayed, she couldn't sense any sort of answer.

Three weeks after their talk, everything changed. As Pastor Shepherd stood to read his text, Ron waltzed into the sanctuary with six other college kids. Although one or two were familiar to him, the rest were new.

Consequently, Jim stuffed his notes underneath his Bible and began with his testimony. Then he talked about miracles he had seen. Only then did he read a scripture about faith and offer a brief explanation. Then, with no further ado, he gave an altar call. "If you need a miracle, come on up front." It was a very simple invitation, but every last young person immediately came forward.

When Pastor Shepherd laid hands on the first girl, Cara mirrored him, praying for the girl as well, both praying in Jesus' name for her to receive her miracle. As he moved to the boy, Cara moved along with him, praying with intensity and faith. When he moved on from the third girl, Cara didn't move but kept praying with her. It wasn't long before Jill—that turned out to be her name—received the baptism of the Holy Ghost.

While praying continued throughout the sanctuary, Cara counseled Jill, explaining what had happened to her. When she stepped away from the girl, her father signaled Cara to come up to him on the platform. She came at once.

It wasn't a long or flowery speech. He simply said, "Cara, I trust your integrity. And I trust your call." The praying was still pretty loud, so she had to lean in to hear him.

"Thank you for saying that, Dad," Cara said. But by now too many negative things had been said, and too long had passed. She needed more. She asked, "What are you actually telling me, Dad?"

He bit his lip, then said, "I'm telling you that I know less than I thought I did."

"Which means?"

"Cara, I believe God spoke to you about something. And I believe it has to do with ministry. So, I want you to know I'm on board. Beyond that, I'm confused.

Cara's Call

Look, I know you're pretty busy right now, so I'll tell you what. When school is over, we'll do a bit more studying together, and I promise you I will not surprise you again."

That night Cara tried to work through what had happened. She simply stared at a blank page for a long time. Then she wrote, "Was that an apology?" Since her dad never apologized, if he had really apologized, it would be a big deal. Then she wrote, "Was he saying yes to me being in ministry?" The more she thought about his words, it was clear that he was, even though his affirmation was tentative. While he might not promote her, he would not stand against her either. Then she wrote, "Is this enough?"

As she reflected back to that night God spoke to her, things were now clear. She wrote, "It is not a man but it is God who calls." The Lord was with her. He would somehow make a way for her. Then she wrote, "What next?" What came to her was that she needed to include people who were closest to her. She wrote: "(1) Talk to Josh; (2) Talk to Amanda." Since Amanda was one of her roommates at the Illinois Youth Convention, there might be opportunity. Maybe she could talk to Josh at the convention as well.

April showers were not merely making May flowers, they were soaking the hundreds of kids exiting the convention center after the first night's service. Chaos and laughter ensued as happy teenagers looked for buses or vans, or made connections with friends. Marta ran up to Cara and Amanda.

"I won't need a ride to the motel after all."

"Why not?" said Cara. "Are you riding back to the room with Stephanie?"

"No, but I did see her. She's going with a group of guys someplace. She told me to tell you not to wait up."

"Okay, why aren't you going back to the room with us?"

"Cara, I met this guy."

Cara was suspicious. "Does this guy have a name?"

"Yeah, his name is Denzel, and he really likes me."

"What's his last name?"

"I didn't catch it."

"Let me guess: this guy is short, has brown hair, his dad's a preacher, and he kind of acts like a big shot?"

"Yes," said Marta innocently, not catching Cara's implication. "He wants to go out."

"With a group?" asked Cara, a worried look on her face.

"No, just the two of us. But he's okay. He has a heart toward ministry and is going to be a missionary, and he says I have incredible potential as well. He thinks I would be good on the mission field."

"Marta, how long have you known this guy?"

"Ten minutes."

"Alright. You can go. But tell him that you have to call me at 12:30 if you're not back in the room."

"Okay."

That left Amanda and Cara in the car. As Cara put the key in the ignition, she couldn't wait any longer. She announced, "Amanda, there's something really big that I have to say. I've been waiting to tell you this face to face."

"Okay, so you're engaged."

"No."

"All right then, you got back your full scholarship to SLU. They awarded you the full deal!"

"No."

Amanda, now frustrated, complained, "Cara, I've always thought I knew stuff about you before you knew it about yourself, but now I am, like, totally clueless."

"Okay, but this requires your total concentration."

"Got it. What's going on?"

"I feel like God is calling me to do something."

"Do something like what?

"Well, I'll just say it. He's calling me to preach."

Amanda said nothing. She wasn't disbelieving. She was just processing Cara's words. Finally, Amanda said, "Wow…are you sure?

"Amanda, I can tell you where I was, what time of day it was, everything. It's as real as anything I've ever experienced."

"I don't know what to say. I've never met a female minister, and I really can't even picture one. That would be kind of hard, wouldn't it?"

Disappointment washed across Cara's face. If there was one person who was always in her corner, it was Amanda.

Because of her best friend's hesitation, Cara stated defensively, "That doesn't mean it can't be done. I mean, after all, God used a donkey, didn't He?"

"Well, sure He did. I believe in you, Cara. Sometimes I think I believe in you more than you believe in yourself. But I'm concerned what would happen if you told people that you're called to preach. Think about this for a while. In the meantime, if I were you, I just wouldn't talk about it."

At one o'clock in the morning, Marta called once again to say she would still be out awhile. "Fine," said Cara, but now, I've got a new rule for you. Now, instead of you calling every half hour, I want you to call every fifteen minutes." Marta said she would.

"Cara, what does your dad think about your calling?" Amanda asked, cautiously.

"Well, I've got to tell you, Amanda. It has been a crazy ride. The last two months—"

They hadn't heard the key slip in the door and Stephanie walk in. It caught them both by surprise when she was suddenly there, in for the night. "What's been a crazy ride?" she asked. "You didn't break up with Josh, did you?"

"No, no, nothing like that."

"Okay, what's going on then?"

Cara offered, "Look Stephanie, it's just something that is going on right now. I don't want to talk about it."

"You can talk to Amanda but not to me? Come on."

"It's just very personal, and so I am not sharing it with a lot of people."

"Come on. I won't say anything about it. Really." When Cara still said nothing, Stephanie continued, "Oh, come on…it can't be that big a deal. It's not like you're called to preach or something?"

Had they known what random charge would be made, they could have prepared, planned, or at least not have reacted, but instead both girls paled at Stephanie's remark. Stephanie, dissecting like a knife, delighted at her discovery. "Wait. You can't be serious. You really think that God is calling you to preach?"

Cara tried to temper it. "I don't know everything about what God wants me to do. But Stephanie, I'm trying to follow God one step at a time."

"Oh yeah, I can see it now: you'll say, 'Honey, can you come to the organ for my altar call?'"

"Stephanie, we're friends, right?"

"Of course."

"And you were the one who texted Josh about me wanting to be a lawyer."

"I didn't mean anything by it. You said it for everyone to hear, didn't you?"

"Okay, well, I need you to promise me something."

"What?"

"I want you to promise me that I'm going to be the one to tell Josh about this."

Stephanie did not hesitate. "Well, sure, yeah. That's only right. When are you going to tell him?"

"Sooner rather than later, I'm sure."

The waitress asked, "So, what can I get you girls for breakfast?"

"Just coffee," said Cara. "We have one more coming." Ten minutes later Josh appeared. As he sat down, he said, "Hey, Cara, Stephanie said you have something to tell me."

"She did, did she? That figures."

"Yeah. Hey, is my tie straight? I'm praise leader for the devotional." Josh moved his tie first one way and then another, complaining, "As if anyone will even get up this early." Now, clearly distracted, he asked, "Say, Cara, I have to meet the musicians in a half hour. Do you think I can get something to eat really fast?"

"We'll call our waitress over now. Eggs don't take long at all," said Cara. "By the way, I really like the red tie. It's nice."

"It's my power tie," he said, whatever that meant. But when the waitress came over, he ignored her. Instead, he simply stood up and wandered from the table. When he got over to the counter, he hailed another waitress. "Hey ma'am," he said, "coffee to go, please."

While the waitress was adding cream to the Styrofoam cup, Josh wandered back over and asked, "You think the matching red handkerchief is too much?"

"Perfect," said Cara.

"Thanks." And he was off.

"Okay," said Amanda after he left the restaurant. "Do I detect a few issues here?"

Cara was about to defend Josh when she heard a familiar voice announce, "Hey, look who's here!" It was Justin. "I'm supposed to play drums with the praise band, but they're not meeting for a few minutes. Mind if I catch breakfast with you?"

"Not at all," said Amanda, clearly pleased with herself for saying so.

Cara was less pleased, saying, "I thought you might be having breakfast with Stephanie."

"Not since she met that physical therapist at the wedding and dropped me like a moldy piece of bread."

"Sorry to hear that," said Cara.

"I should have expected it. While it's true that you can't ever be bored with Stephanie, she can certainly get tired of you quick enough. I'm thinking I should be focusing my attention on someone who is a bit more serious about life." He then smiled a flirty smile in Cara's direction.

"You must be meeting Josh over there for the practice then?" Cara noted. "He's leading worship."

Justin ignored the implications of her comment. "Yeah. But those practices never start on time. So, Stephanie told me that things aren't going so great between you and Josh after the whole lawyer thing."

"Stephanie knows a lot, doesn't she?" said Cara.

Then he turned his attention to Amanda and said, "You know, Amanda, I'm in this undergraduate program that slides right into an MBA. My dad says he might bring me in at executive pay."

"Sounds like a great opportunity," responded Amanda.

Turning toward Cara, he said, "As a businessman, I've been thinking of getting some legal advice. I've been trying to secure the services of a good-looking lawyer."

Cara thought his remark was corny. Amanda thought it was cute. Neither said so until later. What Cara did say, though, was that she was no longer pursuing law. She would be majoring in English, hoping that would put an end to it.

Justin was not so easily put off. As he fiddled with the collar of his designer shirt, he said easily, "And another thing. I always get confused between participles and gerunds. You don't know where I could get any help, do you?" The smile that followed the remark could have sold any toothpaste in the country.

After he finally meandered off to practice, Cara pronounced, "He's pure country club, Amanda. I could never measure up."

"You'd find fault with anyone," Amanda countered.

"And I don't like that flirty thing he does with his eyes," said Cara, "as if everything he says is supposed to melt me like butter."

Amanda shrugged. "Maybe it wouldn't work out at all. But somehow I'm getting the feeling you'd better not put all of your eggs in Josh's basket. I'll grant you that Justin is a bit odd. But you know, it wouldn't be too hard to look beyond his mannerisms. Not too hard at all. I think I'll do some homework for you and try to find out a little more about him."

"Don't bother."

The second night at the youth convention was even more powerful than the first. With a couple thousand worshipping kids, top-notch music, and good preaching, how could it be otherwise?

Everything in the service led up to the altar call. The preacher proclaimed, "It is God's purpose that this generation possesses the land; that it brings in the kind of revival that God intends for us. Yet, I am concerned. I am concerned that sometimes we are so worried about making ends meet, about advancing our careers, about fulfilling our plans, that when God speaks, we do not listen. Some of us are called to a full-time focus on ministry. That's not saying you won't have to work. But your life, your focus, and your purpose must be wrapped up in giving your whole self to Him."

Cara was buying the message. She was ready to walk in front of the entire youth convention. All he had to do is ask. And he did ask—sort of. He ended with the appeal, "I want all the young men who feel God has called you and who are willing to answer that nudging in the Spirit that you're feeling right now…young men…I want you to come to the front and pray."

Amanda didn't say a word, but her eyes kept glancing toward Cara. Cara was not moving. Amanda whispered, "Well?"

"He didn't want me. He said 'young men.' I wasn't invited."

The music played. Young men began moving out of their chairs and streaming toward the front of the auditorium. After about seventy-five or maybe even a hundred young men had gathered together, the preacher continued, "Now, I want all the ministers and their wives who are here to come in behind these young men and lay hands on them. I believe God wants to use them to change the world. Come on, people, let's make this a banner night for Jesus," he said, whatever that meant.

Amanda glanced again at her friend. Tears were streaming down Cara's cheeks. "He wants ministers and their wives to come," Cara said. "Amanda, there is no place in the church for me. None."

Chapter 14

Amanda and Cara traveled by themselves to McDonald's. Marta was with Denzel. Stephanie had disappeared to places unknown. Josh had said he would meet them at the restaurant, but then texted that he could not come because the youth president asked him to eat with the youth committee to help them plan youth camp.

Cara and Amanda were confused. The van from Charlestown left before they did so when they arrived they expected the place to be full of kids. Yet, the place was empty. Amanda texted Greg to see what happened. He replied, "busy."

Ten minutes later their van finally showed up. Greg walked in first but offered no instructions to the kids. They needed none. They flocked to order. Meanwhile, Greg walked over to Amanda, leaned down, and kissed her on the forehead. It was so genuine and sweet that Cara felt a flash of jealousy.

"Hey, where's your brother?" Amanda asked.

Greg pointed toward the door. Kevin was walking in with a high school girl. From the redness of her eyes, it was clear she had been crying. Kevin ignored the others and steered her into a booth. Fifteen or twenty minutes passed while he counseled her.

When he finally did come over, Greg slid a tray in Kevin's direction, pronouncing to his delinquent brother, "I was going to get you a Happy Meal, but they were out. You're stuck with the grilled chicken and some cold French fries. I think they got salted twice."

"Is she going to be okay?" Cara asked intuitively.

"I hope so. Kids were really teasing her."

"That is just so wrong. What about?"

"Elizabeth senses the call of God on her life. They just tore her up."

"How'd that get started?"

"They saw her go to the front at the altar call."

Cara willed herself to be expressionless. "So, were you able to help her?"

"Don't know."

"What did you tell her?"

"Well, I told her to be careful."

Cara blurted out angrily, "Because…you don't believe in her? Because you think God didn't really talk to her…because she's just a girl?"

Kevin either didn't notice the tone or chose to ignore it. He offered easily, "I'm absolutely sure that God called her."

"But you said—"

"She needs to be cautious who she tells. That's all."

The girl sat alone sipping a drink. Cara asked, "You mind if I talk to her?"

"Maybe you'll have better luck than I did."

That's all Cara needed before quickly crossing over to the booth where the girl sat alone. "Hey," she said scooting in opposite her.

"Did Kevin send you over here to keep me from sitting by myself?" she asked.

"Nope. I wanted to come. My name's Cara."

"Elizabeth," was her tentative response.

Cara said gently, "If I tell you a secret that is very important to me, would you promise not to share it?"

The girl nodded. She had beautiful long, naturally wavy hair. Her blue eyes, dulled from tears brightened just a little. Cara wasted no time on preliminaries. "I should have been standing down there next to you tonight."

"You mean…you have a call?" she began, and Cara nodded.

Elizabeth continued, "Well, why didn't you come? I was the only girl."

Cara coughed guiltily. "I thought about it," she said. "But then I decided it wasn't safe."

"Hmmm. Guess you were right."

"Elizabeth, four months ago God spoke to me. I was praying at the altar. Tell me about your call."

"Junior camp. The last night. I'll never forget it. Five years ago. I never told anyone. Not even my mom or dad. But then tonight..." Elizabeth paused, not sure how to finish her sentence.

"You are a great gift to me," said Cara. "I think God brought us into each other's lives for a reason."

As Cara was driving back to the room, she abruptly said, "Amanda, I was good."

While Amanda wasn't sure what Cara was talking about, she did know enough about Cara to know she wasn't bragging. Cara was trying to say something that was meaningful to her, yet Amanda could not decipher it. "Come again?" she said.

"With Elizabeth, I mean. I can't explain it, but it was like I knew the right thing to say. Like somehow God was helping me. Like I wasn't even the one doing the talking. She and I are going to get together this summer. I think I can help her."

"I'm glad."

"No. Amanda, listen." Amanda still could not grasp what pronouncement her friend was trying to make. Cara continued, "Here's what I think. I think that maybe God wants me to help girls who struggle with their calling."

"Hmmm…it's not that I doubt you. I don't. But don't you think it's pretty early on to be thinking about this sort of thing?"

"And that's why it's only safe to tell something this crazy to someone who is my best friend." Amanda nodded as Cara continued. "But who does Elizabeth get to talk to? Who can she tell her dreams to as they begin to unfold?"

Amanda changed the subject. "Kevin really appreciated you spending time with her."

"I'm glad I could," said Cara, lost in thought.

"Kevin said for you to feel free to counsel her; that you should stay in touch with her. So I guess you were both on the same page."

Cara panicked, "You didn't tell Kevin about my—"

"Cara! You know me better than that."

"Thanks."

As she drove, Cara's mood noticeably brightened. Amanda made what seemed to be a random observation saying, "He was engaged. His girlfriend broke it off a month ago."

"Who?" asked Cara, as if she were not thinking similar thoughts, but her attempts at ignorance were not too convincing.

"He's available just in case anyone wants to know."

"Nobody's asking any questions about anyone."

"Yeah, but your eyes were asking."

In the beginning, there had been no rules for the fellowship meetings on Fridays. But eventually a few rules did accumulate, partly because they were now meeting in her parent's home and partly because of some things that had happened. The fact that rules were few and far between didn't work to Cara's advantage when Marta approached her.

"He wants to come to the fellowship on Friday," said Marta.

"I don't know," replied Cara. "We've been using the fellowship as an outreach. Denzel is already in the church."

Cara's Call

"Well, six of the kids here have been baptized now, and Peter comes regularly with Ron and me to church. So we're all in the church. Amanda comes sometimes, and she's in the church."

"Who thought of all this? You or him?" Cara asked. Marta didn't have to say any more—she was guilty.

"All right, Marta. But if Denzel causes the first bit of trouble, anything at all—and I need you to back me up on this—I won't let him come again."

Cara should have trusted her initial instincts. Denzel was hanging all over Marta, and it was really distracting. Cara tried talking to him about it, but he did not receive it well. She needed some advice. There was still a car or two in the driveway when she found her dad in the kitchen. "Dad, can I talk to you about something?" she asked.

"Not now, honey. Maybe some other time. I need to drive Shay to the lock-in over at Salem."

Shay rushed back and forth making demands of his mother, who was also standing in the kitchen, "So my shirt is...?"

"In the laundry room. I took it from the dryer even though it was a little damp. I didn't want it wrinkled. But that was a few hours ago, so it should be dry on the hanger by now."

Shay bounded down the staircase taking two steps at a time, but when he got to the basement and tried to get into the laundry room it was locked. Although that was a bit odd, he knew just how to jiggle the door so it would pop open. When he swung it open, he exclaimed, "Oh boy!" in a voice loud enough for everyone upstairs to hear. Then, as white as a sheet, Shay pounded up the stairs, ran by everyone and fled into his bedroom. Less than a minute later, Denzel came up looking rather disheveled. Then Marta came up, and one after another they both got into their cars and took off.

The next day, Jim found out more about what had happened. When the phone rang, Jim answered and greeted the minister by name. "Brother Gulliver, it's good to hear from you."

Jim paused while Brother Gulliver talked, and then said, "I'm not sure what you're saying. What do you mean, 'what happened last night?'...No, it was a kind of college-age Bible study Cara's been running." Another pause. "Yes, it was at the house." Another pause. "And you're saying that...what? Some loose girl seduced him in my house?"

Karen, who had been working on supper, turned to face her husband, her eyes filled with worry. "Well no, I'm not calling your son a liar, but I think we should just—" apparently the speaker on the other end was not in the listening mood. "Uh huh. Okay. All right then." Jim hung up.

"What is it Jim?"

"I'm meeting Brother Gulliver at his office tonight."

That afternoon Jim talked on the phone with Bob, received counsel from his wife, and also heard Shay's version of what happened. Whom he did not speak with was Cara. Consequently, when Cara got home from work and found out from her mother what had happened, she asked, "So why didn't he talk to me?"

"About what?"

"About Marta. About Denzel. There are things he ought to know."

"I'm not sure, honey. I think he believes that he knows all the essential facts."

Jim looked at the time as he sat in Pastor Gulliver's church parking lot trying to figure out how this could have happened. He had a couple of minutes before their scheduled meeting time. He thought of Marta...how he'd let Cara talk him into letting her teach Sunday school, or whatever it was she was doing back there. Worse, he remembered that Marta led in singing for the fellowship group. He remembered Marta joking with Shay at the Christmas fellowship. He was sure of it now that he thought about it. Who was Marta going to seduce next? His own son?

Jim had read the manual when he got his ministerial license. There were pages and pages on judicial procedure—about what would happen when something went wrong. He hadn't paid much attention to it. To him it was unnecessary legalese. He had read some of it again that afternoon but couldn't make sense of it. When he called Bob, Bob told him not to worry about it. Jim would be able to ride it out just fine.

One thing was certain: whether or not Jim was liable for anything as far as his license was concerned, he was probably ruined in the district. Brother Gulliver was a popular fellow, and he would no doubt see to it that Jim's reputation was finished.

"Was this under your supervision, or was it under Cara's supervision?" asked Brother Gulliver.

Jim had covered this ground twice before, and he had been patient. Still, he went over it once more. "Cara was certainly in charge of the meeting, but none of this happened during the meeting. It did happen in my house, and I take full responsibility."

"You'd better take full responsibility. So what are you going to do?"

Here's the crux of it, Jim thought. *Brother Gulliver wants blood. He intends to see heads roll.* Rather than be baited, Jim responded, "About what?"

"About the girl?"

"Do you mean, Marta? Are you asking what I'm going to do about Marta?" Jim said her name so that Brother Gulliver would know that Marta meant something to him. That he cared for her just as he cared for his own daughter.

"Yes. What I'm asking is how will she be disciplined?"

Some sort of line was being crossed, although Jim wasn't sure how or in what way. He had been in the man's office for forty-five minutes and had been patient. He had not rocked the boat and was humble, but now the man was asking for more. On one level he couldn't blame him. Certainly, if it had been Jim's son, he might have asked the same sort of question. But Jim had nothing more to give.

"Look," he said. "I have listened closely to your concerns, and I have already apologized. So why don't we end it in this way: I will deal with things at my church, and I think it would be best if Denzel didn't come over to the fellowship meetings."

"Here's what I think," said Brother Gulliver menacingly. "You should stop these meetings immediately, given that they have turned into some kind of a loosey-goosey free for all!" He was leaning into Jim's personal space, challenging him, almost asking for some kind of physical altercation.

"I think we're done here," said Jim, angry enough to ignore whatever consequences might result for not doing more. "Thank you for your time." And then, Jim simply stood up, walked out the door, and left.

Driving home felt a whole lot different than driving to meet with that pastor. All the way there, Jim had worried about his standing in the district. Now, that was the farthest thing from his mind. Indeed, not everything going through his mind was altogether Christian.

In high school, Jim had gotten into a few scraps. One time when the high school bully came after him, Jim flattened him with one swing. He could still visualize it: the bully on the ground, face up, his eyes absently looking into the sky. Of course, that was a long time ago, before Jim knew Jesus.

Still, because Jim couldn't stop dwelling on how that pastor had verbally tarred and feathered, not only him, but Cara and Marta also, he became angrier with every mile he drove. Then he started visualizing something else. Although he knew that he shouldn't be thinking this way, he started imagining, not the face of the bully staring up blankly from the ground, but the face of the man who's office he had just left.

The next morning Jim put a good face on things in church. He affirmed and preached a positive message. Still, it had required a considerable effort, and by the time the family arrived at the restaurant, the worry lines on his face were more pronounced. Somewhere during the middle of the entrée, he said to Cara, "I didn't see Marta at church this morning." He had meant it as a casual remark, but it sounded more critical than he would have liked.

Cara returned his gaze. She clearly wanted to say something but remained silent, her coldness immediately discernable. Even Timefor Terror sensed the mood and quieted herself. Then Cara said, "Why *would* she come?"

Jim tried to stop himself but could not. "What are you talking about?" he demanded.

At this point, Cara became very un-Cara-like. "Up until now, Marta believed the church was a forgiving place. But I guess she was wrong."

Cara's mom immediately petitioned her husband, "Why don't we talk about this later, dear—maybe someplace more private?"

With a "Harrumph," Jim relented, not wanting the argument to end without having the last word.

So it was that Cara appeared in her father's basement study about an hour after they had spoken in the restaurant. There were no preliminaries. Jim said, "You have no idea what I've gone through for you and Marta."

"Why didn't you come to me in the first place?" Cara challenged.

"About what?"

"To see what should be done? If I had been your son, you would have consulted me. Wasn't I in charge of Friday night's event?"

"Cara, nothing you could have said would have made any difference."

"Are you sure?"

Now Jim doubted himself. He paused, and then released a long breath to calm himself. "What would you have told me?" he asked humbly.

"Dad, Marta was abused by her father. After her mother divorced him and remarried, Marta's stepbrother Johnny abused her for years. Dad, Marta is the victim here."

"If she was a victim, what was she doing in the laundry room with Denzel?"

"Dad, do you think this is the first time Denzel has been with a girl?"

"Cara, you can't know these things."

"Denzel is a sociopath! He's done more damage to more girls—"

"Cara, stop this right now."

"Listen, Dad. Marta just told me this isn't the first time he's been with her. Here's the setup he uses. He supposedly has this call to be a missionary. That's why

Cara's Call

Marta should trust him. Then he senses God's call on her life and says they have emotional oneness. And then she has to prove they have oneness."

"Cara, I don't feel comfortable talking with you about this."

"Afterward he tells her she is damaged goods. No one else will have her. Her only chance to be in ministry is to do everything he says. Dad, this is the same kind of control Johnny had on her. Friday night happened because Denzel forced her—"

"Cara, I can see now that there was more to it than I knew, but the fact is that Marta—"

"The fact is that the one man in the whole world she trusts is you. And she needs that man to love her no matter what she did. Dad, did you know Denzel called her last night after your meeting and said that you admitted to his father that she was loose as a goose. Denzel is still playing her, Dad. But now she has no one to protect her."

"Oh," was all Jim could say, deeply grieving. "I need to talk to that pastor about his son. When he finds these things out, if he won't discipline him, I'll take it up on a district level."

"Dad, I don't care two hoots about the district. But I do care about Marta. And you should, too."

Jim was stunned. "I do care about her, Cara."

"You have to apologize to her."

"No, I won't. I didn't say those things he accused me of."

"Doesn't matter. You didn't trust her. And you didn't stand up for her."

Jim thought about that for a minute, and then tears filled his eyes. "Will she even come back so I can—"

"She'll be there tonight."

"I'm so sorry, Cara. It's just that when I think of Shay coming into the laundry room and seeing what he saw I just—"

"You don't think Shay ever saw a naked girl before?"

"Cara! That's enough!"

"Dad, girls proposition guys all the time through texting. They send pictures of themselves naked or in sexy poses."

This was too much for Jim and he countered, "Cara, it's girls in church who text Shay."

"Like Denzel is in the church?"

"But you're accusing your brother of—"

"I'm not accusing him of anything. It's a statistical fact that a significant percentage of guys get sent pictures like I just told you about. As popular as Shay is, you can bet he's had his share of—"

"Cara, I'm not at all comfortable talking with you about—"

"Dad, listen to me. Kids are assaulted today by pornography. It's easy to get addicted. There's a better than fifty-fifty chance Shay struggles with pornography right now. I'm not accusing. Those are the stats. Maybe if you start accountability partners, at least—"

"We have a filter."

"And he has a phone," she countered. "Please, Dad, if you are not comfortable talking to me, then at least talk to him. He's your son and you owe him that."

"Cara, what is wrong with you!"

"Dad, when you see Marta tonight, make sure you use specific words. Tell her, 'I love you,' and tell her, 'I'm proud of you.'"

"Cara, I don't think—"

"And, Dad, make sure you hug her when you say it." With that, Cara fled from his study, went up to her bedroom, and sobbed for an hour.

That evening after service, when Cara saw her father embrace Marta and speak affirming words to her, Cara was happy and sad at the same time. For as pleased as she was for Marta, more than anything in the world, Cara wished it was she who was being embraced by her father.

Chapter 15

The end of the semester was a disaster. Cara's final exams were scheduled one right after another. Unhappily, the last exam would be the worst. It was scheduled for Wednesday morning. Forty percent of her psychology grade was riding on the outcome of an exam given by a professor who was very vague as to how to even prepare for the final.

"Amanda, I so need you more than you'll ever know. Can you do a huge favor for me?"

"Name it," Amanda responded into her phone at four-thirty on Tuesday afternoon.

"Can you drill me on concepts for my psychology final?"

"Sure. When?"

"Eleven o'clock tonight at Denny's."

"Okay, but why so late?"

"Long story, but I need you to help me so I can stay awake. I've only had eight hours of sleep in the last two days."

"Fine with me. But how am I supposed to drill you about a class I've never had? I don't even know what they've covered."

"I've got flash cards and concept blurbs. I'll show you."

Since the Denny's was in Salem, it took Amanda only five minutes to get there. She identified Cara's beat-up Mazda in the lot and easily located Cara at the booth in the back. Her table was covered with homemade flash cards, Cara's computer, and a pot of coffee front and center. The worry creases along Cara's forehead signaled to Amanda that they'd better get right to work.

"Okay, the card asks for the difference between Jung and Freud on the Freudian concept of the id."

Cara started talking, but Amanda stopped her, having turned the card over to find it blank. Cara quickly showed Amanda where she could find the concept blurbs on her computer and then continued to rattle off the information.

Because the answer seemed satisfactory, Amanda reached for the next card. She asked, "Why didn't you start on this review right after your final this afternoon?"

Cara's Call

"I've been getting together with this guy named Jerry on Tuesday nights, and he is just about ready to commit his life to the Lord. He is so pumped, but he leaves tomorrow morning for the summer. It's always been Tuesday nights at eight o'clock, and I didn't want to miss the last one."

"It couldn't wait one more day?"

"Jerry's driving home to Kansas for the summer. He's leaving tomorrow morning."

Amanda was about to protest Cara's scheduling but then thought better of it and got back to the review cards. By one in the morning, Amanda was pretty wrung out and tried to convince Cara to go home. "Come on, Cara, you know half of these really well."

"That's just it. I only know half of them," she sighed. "Thanks for coming. Go ahead and take off. I'll be right behind you."

At two o'clock, Molly, the friendly waitress, nudged Cara awake. Cara had just laid her head down to rest for a second. But that had been forty minutes earlier, and it was clear she could accomplish nothing more. Leaving five bucks as a tip, Cara gathered her belongings and staggered out the door. The night air was better than coffee at reviving her. She made her way to her car and threw her stuff into the back seat.

While Amanda lived only five minutes away, Cara's trip home required ten miles of two-lane highway. Perhaps it was the straight stretch of road that contributed to her eyelids getting heavy again; she fought back by turning up the music, rolling down the window, and slapping herself awake. Only when an oncoming truck sounded a long blast of its horn did she realize she had wandered into the wrong lane.

"Sorry," she said to no one in particular. Now she was wide awake and certainly shocked enough to make it the rest of the way home. As added insurance, Cara bit down hard on her lip, beating back that relentless fog that tried to overwhelm her. Cara was now confident she would make it the rest of the way home. She almost did.

The operator answered the phone: "Nine-one-one, what is your emergency?"

"Yeah," said a man's voice. I was driving east on Route 16—that's same as Brubaker Road, ma'am. I'm two miles east of Route 23 and it looks like there's been an accident. A car smashed pretty badly into a tree. There's smoke coming out from under the hood."

"Sir, is there someone in the vehicle?"

"I'm walking over to it now. Yeah, there is. A girl."

"Can you tell if she is—"

"She could be alive. But I'm not sure. You'd better get someone out here right away!"

From somewhere deep inside of her Cara could hear voices.

"You're going to have to cut that door open, Clyde," said one voice.

"Hurry up, now," said another. "We may not have much time." The speaking was at once garbled and hurried, fuzzy and intense. Then, there was nothing.

Cara became vaguely aware of a beeping noise that would not stop. After listening to it sounding again and again, she understood.

"Alarm clock!" she said to herself and attempted to rouse herself awake.

She somehow understood she was supposed to be somewhere important. Then she knew. She had overslept and was going to miss her final.

As Cara turned to disarm the odd-sounding alarm clock, her body screamed in protest. Her leg hurt, as did her arm. Her neck burned with pain. So did her stomach and her torso. Even her face hurt. Now upset and disoriented, Cara desperately took in her surroundings. Then she saw her mother's face looking down into hers.

"It's okay, Cara. You're going to be all right now. Everything's okay," said her mother soothingly.

"Mom, I have an eight o'clock final! I need to—"

"It's okay. Don't worry about it. You've missed your final, but that doesn't matter now."

"What time is it?"

"It's one-thirty in the afternoon. You've been in surgery, and you're just now waking up. We're in the recovery room. We're at the hospital, dear."

Cara looked down and saw that her left arm was wrapped in a cast. She also became aware of the little plastic tube that fed oxygen into her nose. And the beeping she was hearing came from some sort of monitor behind her.

Cara's mom was still talking. "You're going to be okay. They've put everything back together. The doctor doesn't think you will have any permanent damage, but they'll be monitoring things."

"What happened to my face?"

You have a broken nose. It's okay. The surgeon said you'll have bruises and two very black eyes; and you'll look like a raccoon for a while."

"And my arm?"

"Clean break. You'll be in a cast during the summer, which is too bad."

"Anything else?"

"Well, yes, quite a bit, actually. There are some internal injuries. That's mainly why you were in surgery. But like I said, the surgeon told us he believes you'll

Cara's Call

make a full recovery, and you won't have any permanent functional loss to any of the systems in your body."

Cara interjected, "And the car?"

"Totaled."

Cara tried to picture what she looked like. She saw herself at a costume ball in a raccoon mask. It was so embarrassing. And stupid. "I'm scheduled to work later on today, Mom."

"I don't think you'll be back at work anytime soon."

"Hey, honey, I love you," said a new voice. Cara looked behind her mom to see her dad, now moving toward her bed. His face registered deep distress. He clearly wanted to hug her but didn't know what was safe to touch.

Afterward, two things about how she woke up would always stay in Cara's mind. It wasn't the sharp pains caused by her sudden movements or the fact that she had totaled her car or even that she had missed her final. The first memory was imagining herself in a raccoon mask. The second thing was more important: her dad told her that he loved her. She knew it, of course. It was just that she couldn't remember the last time that he had spoken those words to her.

A nurse wearing a shower cap said they needed to move Cara. An orderly appeared. He was good looking, in his twenties. He would transport her. Cara felt vulnerable. She had no idea what she was wearing under that blanket or what her raccoon eyes actually looked like.

Fortunately, the orderly simply rolled Cara's whole bed out the door and down the hall, her mom and dad flanking the contraption. The guy was bent over, almost in her face. She could think of nothing but raccoons. Crowding into the elevator, no one uttered a word. The elevator either went up or down—Cara couldn't tell which—and finally, a bell signaled their arrival on the appropriate floor. The door opened, and Cara was ferried onto a hospital wing.

They wheeled her into a two-person room, but Cara couldn't see the other person since the privacy curtain was in place. Several hospital-type people appeared unbidden to manhandle her onto the regular hospital bed, but the transfer was over before Cara could hyperventilate with panic. She sighed in relief, though she now became aware of new aches and pains.

The orderlies left and another crowd appeared. Amanda was there, and Jerry, the friend who was supposed to have driven to Kansas. Cousin Fred clasped the string of some sort of funny balloon while Ron held a plant. Five other girls from the fellowship group tried to get through the door.

Suddenly, a rather formidable-looking nurse took command. "I'm sorry," she said, "but we have work to do here. Please wait down the hall in the visitors' lounge."

Because the group was too slow in leaving, the nurse raised her voice, startling everyone with the command, "Leave now!" If the nurse would have been a hundred pounds lighter and had a mustache, she could have passed for Adolf Hitler. Or perhaps Cara's imagination went in that direction more because of the nurse's actions than her visage.

After the room cleared, the nurse ominously said to no one in particular that she was required to take the patient's vitals. In short order, she strangled Cara's good arm in a blood pressure cuff and then proceeded to conduct other tests, poking and prodding without explanation. Three grunts and a groan by the nurse was the extent of the entire conversation. The nurse then vanished and could be heard taking charge of matters in the hall.

First to enter were Marta, Ron, and Amanda. Amanda blurted out, "I'm so sorry I didn't follow you home. If I had, this wouldn't have—"

"Amanda, you actually tried to get me to go home. This all happened because I haven't been taking care of myself and was careless enough to—"

"Hey, it was an accident," said Ron, defending Cara against herself. "This stuff happens. I remember this one time—"

Marta couldn't wait for her turn to say something and spontaneously leaned over the bed, kissing Cara on the cheek. "God was protecting you," she announced with certainty. "Because you're special to Him…and to us." It was such a spontaneous expression of love that the tears rolled down Cara's cheeks.

"Amanda, is my computer okay?"

"I'm afraid it went the way of the mean green machine."

"Oh no. It had all my notes from the semester and now I'll need another one."

A couple minutes later, Ron looked at his watch and announced to the other two that their time was up. As they left, Cara heard a voice booming down the hall: "Now I want you three to go in; remember, you may stay only five minutes." Cara smiled. Barn-Boss had evidently been deputized by Gestapo Nurse to oversee visitation and was now keeping things in good order.

After an hour and a half of musical chairs, Gestapo Nurse pronounced to one and all, "The patient is tired. No more visitors! Room 524 is now off limits." Although Cara had been reduced to a nameless patient in bed number one in a hospital room, she was actually glad to be shielded from those who meant well. She quickly dropped into a deep sleep.

Cara awoke to find her mom in the room, as well as Sandra and Shay. Shay looked frightened but worked to cover his fear, saying, "Hey, I'm really sorry you were in an accident, but the good news is Dad's letting us skip Bible study tonight to be here."

Her mother said, "Josh wanted to come. But he's in charge of youth service and he couldn't get out of it."

"Of course," said Cara, drifting back to sleep. For the next hour, she faded in and out of consciousness. About 8:30, the threesome tiptoed out.

At some point there must have been a shift change. Cara sensed that someone else was in charge. She kept hearing a voice that was so calming that, when Cara first opened her eyes and saw the lady in white, she thought it might be some kind of angelic presence. She said so, but the nurse assured her that she was quite human.

From the middle of a dream, Cara was startled by an odd noise. "Pssst," it said. Cara thought the patient on the other side of the room might be calling to her, but when she blinked open her eyes, Cara could see even through the dimmed hospital lights that the lady was sleeping soundly.

"Pssst," repeated the interruption, and this time Cara willed her eyes open. Someone quietly entered through the door. It was Josh.

"What are you doing here?" Cara whispered.

"I got here as soon as I could," he whispered back.

"How'd you get in here this time of night?"

"Family can come anytime, and that nurse is really nice. She said I could visit you if you were awake."

"But you're not family."

"I told her I was your fiancé."

"Josh!"

"Well, it's almost true. And besides, I needed to come up to tell you something else."

"What?"

Josh leaned down very close to her ear. "I love you!" he whispered, and then kissed her on her forehead.

Cara should have been glad. This was the first time she'd heard these words from him. And in a way she was glad. But nothing was simple anymore. This wasn't a date. In fact, Josh hadn't even called or texted her in the last two weeks, so she didn't know what to do with what he'd just said. Was this an "I'm sorry about the accident" kind of "I love you"? Was it an "I'm sorry I haven't had time for you lately" kind of apology? Was Josh, in fact, now making a commitment to her for the future? And now was Cara required to tell him the same, returning with an "I love you, too" kind of commitment? Although she could kick herself for thinking way too deeply about this, Cara was honestly confused. Tears coursed down her cheeks. Which, of course, upset Josh.

"Thank you for coming, Josh," she said way too blandly. "Can you come back tomorrow and we can talk some more?"

He said he sure would and seemed a little embarrassed. She said once more that his visit was very special and she would never forget it. As he made his way out of her room, she realized whatever that moment was supposed to be, it was gone now. Cara knew she had hopelessly dropped the ball. She berated herself for not doing the right thing, even though she didn't know what the right thing was.

Cara was certain she would lie awake all night reliving her awful indecision. And yet, four minutes after Josh left the room, Cara was asleep again and did not wake up until morning when a new nurse mumbled something about having to take her vitals.

Chapter 16

Cara walked unsteadily toward the bathroom. When she had seen herself in the mirror the previous night, she was surprised that her face did not look a lot worse. This morning it did. Sometime during the morning a doctor came in to introduce herself. She was Cara's primary physician, and although she spoke clearly, she had an Asian name that Cara didn't quite catch.

"How soon before I can get back to my regular schedule, doctor? I have to do children's church this Sunday."

"Hold on, young lady. When I do send you home, you're going home to rest. My understanding is that you've been burning the candle at both ends, and this behavior contributed to your accident."

Cara thought that a doctor, of all people, should be the last one to lecture her about being busy, but she tried to keep her attitude in check. It was one thing for Cara to willingly take the blame for the accident. It was another thing for this lady to give her a guilt trip. Yet, because Cara was adept at masking her feelings when she had to, she simply said, "I understand." Still, her mind raced ahead as to how she could accomplish important things while she recuperated. She began making mental lists. Her mom had confiscated her phone, but as soon as she could, Cara would have to check her messages and get things going.

"Well, how's our girl doing?' asked Bob.

"Better than you'd think if you had seen that car," said Jim. "The highway patrolman who came by later asked how many fatalities there were."

"By the grace of God..." said Bob, because he was worried and didn't know what else to say. "Did our flowers come?"

"Yeah, they're lovely. In fact, the room is full of flowers. I'm pretty amazed, actually. I didn't know she knew that many people. A number of pastors and churches in the area sent flowers, too."

"Aw, that's nice. I'm glad she's doing well. Say, you don't think it's all that preaching stuff that pushed her over the edge, do you?"

"No. I don't think so."

Cara's Call

"Jim, maybe she just needs to back off for a while. This might be a good time to make changes. Maybe give her a break from her fellowship group and children's church...that sort of thing. And another thing. This would also be a good time to get rid of that Marta. She's obviously a bad influence on Cara."

"Bob, I'll admit that Cara does have a lot of time invested in her fellowship group and she's teaching a couple of Bible studies. But I think it was more everything together—"

"Jim, I'm telling you, sometimes crises actually present opportunities for change. This deal with Marta is probably half the reason that—"

"You're not trying to say Marta had anything to do with the accident!"

"Well, I guess not. Only that Cara was worried about her, and beyond that, Cara had too many other things on her mind. But, I've got to tell you, Jim, Marta's not a good influence. If both Cara and Marta took a break from things, that would be for the best."

"I've got to admit, I'm confused. You may have a point, Bob."

"Cara, do you feel up to a talk?"

It was an odd request, so unlike her father. "Well, sure, Dad."

"Good, because I've been thinking a lot about things and—"

"Cara, Cara!" said Marta running into the room with genuine enthusiasm. She was trailed by Ron and two others from the fellowship group.

"Oh, I'm glad you both came. Marta, you and Ron will need to facilitate the group tomorrow night. Amanda came in earlier today and said she would do the lesson." Cara continued, "Marta, you have the script for the Muppets on Sunday, don't you?"

"Yes."

"Dad, I'll be able to teach a week from Sunday, but this week, I need someone else."

"Yes, well, I've been trying to talk to you about that."

"Marta would be able to teach. Or if you would prefer, Mom said she could do the main lesson and just have Marta expand the support role since she knows what is going on. Just tell us what you want done and we'll do it."

Jim looked at Marta's smiling face, saw that Ron had finally gotten a haircut, and thought of how sensible Amanda was. "Yeah, then."

"Yeah what, Dad?"

"Your mom. She can take the lesson on Sunday."

An hour later Josh appeared, and Cara's dad left to give them space.

"Then you weren't a dream," said Cara.

"Well if you want to dream about me, it's all good."

"It was sure nice of you to come," Cara said, a little too rushed.

There was an awkward silence before Josh said, "Hey, I know I haven't really been the most supportive lately. And you've been carrying way too much, and I want you to know that I'm sorry."

"Josh, you're not trying to take some sort of blame for the accident, are you, because it was totally—"

"No, that's not it. It's just that when I realized how close I came to losing you, I began to appreciate how special you are, and how much I really care for you."

"That means so much. But Josh, can you do me a favor? Let's wait until I get out of the hospital to talk about this. I'm kind of in emotional overload right now. Everyone looks at me with pity. Seven people told me they loved me, even my cousin Fred."

"If that's not a sign of the times, I don't know what is," said Josh.

"Josh, I do want to invest in our relationship," Cara continued, "but I think there are some things we're going to need to work through. And I want to talk to you about those things when I get out of here."

"Sure," said Josh. "I totally get that. But I want you to know that I meant what I said. And you're not obligated in any way by it."

Cara smiled and felt obligated.

That evening Amanda and Greg came. Also Kevin. Greg, whose countenance never told a lie, took one look at Cara and immediately scrunched up his face in horror.

"It looks worse than it is," said Cara in an attempt to calm him. "The doctor says these black eyes will fade in a week or so."

"Well, it doesn't matter to me," said Amanda, bending down to give her a real hug. But as she did, she suddenly held back. "I love you, Cara Shepherd," said Amanda. "I'm so glad you're going to be all right."

Then Greg spoke up, clearly trying to make up for how he had earlier winced at Cara's appearance. "Actually, that dark shading around the eyes is very fashionable; it's very Goth—sort of chic."

Cara gifted him with a smile, and then turning to Kevin, said, "Eight people told me they love me today. That's a new record for me." Cara wasn't sure why she was saying this. Maybe it was the drugs. "So, do you love me, too?" she asked.

Without hesitation, he said, "Cara Shepherd, I have always loved you."

Cara's Call

Cara suddenly remembered something important. "Amanda, they won't let me go to your graduation this Saturday."

"It's okay. Being a nurse is more important than being in a ceremony. Cara Shepherd, you will soon find out how good I am. Although my first official duties as an RN will be at senior youth camp, I'm going to take a little time caring for you, too, just as soon as I pick up my diploma."

"Nor will you get to see me graduate," said Kevin, who now seemed to need attention.

"What's this?"

"I'll be graduating tomorrow night."

"*Summa cum laude*," said Greg, bragging on his brother.

"And will you be teaching second grade?" asked Cara.

"Actually, I'll be starting my official teaching career in the fall by teaching third grade. But I'll get there."

"I have something else to show you," said Amanda.

"What is it?" Cara asked. Amanda held up a hand to display her engagement ring. "Oh, Amanda, why haven't you told me before now?"

"It just happened last night. I probably should have waited to tell you until you got out."

"Amanda, I am so happy for you! And you too, Greg!"

Just then, Shay barged in saying, "Mom said I needed to bring you up some mint ice cream. I told her I would but you have to share. I've tasted it and it's pretty good. Make sure to leave me some."

"That's so sweet of you," said Cara.

Cara spiked a high fever on Saturday morning. It happened so quickly and the fever went so high that unknown doctors hurried in and issued orders to scurrying nurses. But nothing they did was effective. By early afternoon, Cara became apathetic as her face flushed scarlet. In a couple more hours, she was only intermittently aware of her surroundings. At one point she opened her eyes briefly to see that her mom and dad were there, both of them with pained looks. This was the last thing she saw before she lost consciousness.

That night Cara roused in the ICU, and briefly remembered she had missed both Amanda and Kevin's graduations. Greg and Amanda had gotten engaged. Life was passing her by. Those were her last lucid thoughts. As day broke there was no change in her condition. She was unaware of any coming and going, of doctors, nurses, or the constant observation by those around her.

When she did awaken, it was sudden. A nurse witnessed it. One minute Cara's face was scarlet and she was mumbling irrationally.

The next minute she was aware of everything and fully conscious of her surroundings.

"Could I have some water?" Cara asked dryly, suddenly aware that her hospital gown was drenched in sweat. The nurse who brought the water confirmed it. Cara's fever had not merely broken. It was instantly gone. Cara had looked at the clock that evening when she awoke and noted that it was 6:07 p.m.

They kept Cara in ICU overnight for observation but transferred her to a regular room in the morning. Her mother was there and thrilled to see that Cara was better. When Shay came in that afternoon, he was almost euphoric, sharing, "Cara, when Dad said, 'I rebuke this fever in the name of Jesus,' it was like I was all tingly and stuff. I knew something good had happened."

"When was that? Morning or evening?"

"Evening, right at the beginning of service." Cara nodded and smiled appreciatively.

Despite the prayers and antibiotics, Cara was slow in recovering her strength. Not until Thursday were they confident enough to release her and only then with a promise from her parents that they would put a lid on her activities. Her mom and Marta held down children's church while Amanda and company took the lead with the fellowship meeting. The second Friday she was home, Cara was able to sit through part of the meeting.

A week later she met Josh at a local breakfast place. She didn't want anything date-like. Cara once again tried to set the stage to talk about her calling. "I've had these Bible studies with my father."

"What about?"

"I'm feeling a sense of call."

"Thank God. I've got to tell you. I didn't want to say anything before now, but I've prayed that God would specifically give me a wife who was called to be a minister's wife."

"Josh, maybe I should clarify."

"Okay."

"Well, it's just that God has spoken to me specifically about things; not just about being a helpmeet, though I want to be the best possible wife for the person I marry. It's something else." Josh was silent, anticipating that whatever followed wouldn't be good. "Josh, I believe God has called me to preach."

"Maybe you need to explain what you just said. You're not talking about, like, pulpit ministry, are you?"

Cara's Call

"Well, I wouldn't need a pulpit, but yes—speaking, leading, helping, overseeing. The whole deal."

"This sure doesn't sound like the Cara I know: someone who hates crowds, somebody who's not real fond of lots of people all in one place."

"Yeah, I know. It sounds crazy, doesn't it? I have no idea how I would do it, and I've got to tell you, it scares me to death."

"Cara, I hate to say it, but you've been a little schizo since I've known you. Think about all the different things you told me you were going to be. First a lawyer, then an English teacher, now a preacher. Maybe tomorrow the pendulum will swing back and you'll want to be a lawyer again."

Although Cara could not keep the tears from clouding her vision, she steeled herself and cautioned, "Be careful that you don't mock what God is speaking to me, Josh."

They looked at each other in silence.

Josh sighed. "I love you, Cara. You know that I do. But...I kind of have my own ministry. I wasn't looking for someone to be in competition with me."

"Which I wouldn't be. I could enhance your ministry. I really am proud of you, Josh."

"Cara, how in the world could you support me?"

"I would do it with the greatest pleasure. I could serve you and help you in every way that—"

"Two heads make a freak, Cara."

"What is that supposed to mean? How can you even say that?"

"Well, suppose God tells me something to do, and then what if you believe God is telling you something else. How would we even be able to function?"

"The same way it works in every family. We would pray for God to lead us. Josh, I know that I could trust your leadership."

"Cara, exactly what is it you feel called to do?"

She tried to tell him. It was a painful, tortuous half hour, and at the end of the conversation, they both committed to pray about things and that they would talk again. But when she left, something felt broken.

"Dad, I need to talk to you about a scripture."

"Okay, I'll do my best."

"What do you do with the Timothy text that says not to suffer a woman to teach or usurp authority over a man?"

"You sound pretty intense," he said. What he didn't say was that she looked like she'd been crying.

"Well, I just got off the phone with Josh, and we've been having some discussions."

"Cara, I know that you've read at least half a dozen books that deal with the verse. Why are you asking me?"

"You've got to admit I have a pretty vested interest in interpreting the text in a particular way. In fact, when I explained my understanding to Josh, he said I'm dead wrong. Maybe I am. Would you study it out and give me your honest answer? I promise I will be receptive as to how God is speaking to you and your interpretation."

Jim was stuck again. He was trying to be so careful. And yet, how he interpreted a particular passage of scripture would dictate his daughter's future; including, it would seem, the future between Josh and Cara.

Jim charged the ball that Bob had hit short. He returned it, but it went right back to Bob who easily sailed it past him. "Game," Jim conceded to Bob and grabbed for his keys from the back corner.

"Bit off your game, Jim. You weren't even able to make it close."

"Hey, who won three straight last week?" countered Jim, smiling easily.

"It's Cara, isn't it? Jim, I've been thinking of how to fix this. Just let her speak at a youth event. That's what I do. Let the teenage girls in my church speak five to ten minutes."

"Bob, what do you think of 'I suffer not a woman to teach'? I've been studying it out."

"It's not something I preach about. It's just there."

"Okay, but in the same place in the passage, it says that a woman will be saved in childbearing."

"I don't get you."

"Do you preach that women are saved in childbearing?"

"Well, they should be submissive and have children. Yes, I suppose."

"So that's what saves them?"

"I'm not following."

"That's the text."

"Are you saying it isn't there or what?"

"Not at all. I'm saying there is a context to the Timothy text. From what I have studied, Paul was addressing a local situation in Ephesus where women were following false prophets. These false prophets were women who rejected marriage and family because they thought themselves more spiritual. In the letter, Paul is addressing that issue, telling them not to teach their doctrine, and to get married, that sort of thing."

"Suffer not a woman to teach…it's right there in the text, Jim."

"So is childbearing. Does that mean that an unmarried woman can't be saved because she doesn't have children?"

"You start doing that context stuff and pretty soon you can strip away the meaning of the whole New Testament. Sure it has a context, but you've got to take the clear teaching of the text."

"I've got to admit that I struggle with that. Now, in the Greek—"

"Jim, you don't know anything about Greek."

"True, Bob. It's not me. It's just what the books say."

"Do they all say it?"

"Well, there are a few Baptist authors who argue against it."

"Well, I'll go with those guys then."

"It's on the Day of Pentecost, Bob. Your daughters will prophesy—"

"Fine. Let them prophesy. Just don't let them preach."

"Are you telling me that you've never had a girl come and tell you she was called to preach?"

"No."

"And what would you do if it happened?"

"I don't know. Tell her 'I suffer not a woman to teach,' 'women keep silence…' something like that."

"Really?"

At this point Bob put down the racquet and started talking very quietly, as if he were letting Jim in on private information. "Look, Jim, I've seen too many woman missionaries that were anointed to believe that those scriptures forbid women to minister."

"Then why have you been arguing with me about this?"

"Because I'm trying to keep you between the ditches. That's all. I don't want Cara to get hurt. I'm telling you that nothing but trouble will come of this, Jim. You mark my words."

"If I tell Cara that the scripture doesn't forbid it but I do, I will hurt her so deeply that—"

"Hurt! You take another position and you'll hurt her worse. Two things you need to think about. First, no one will accept her ministry. Second, from what you said, if you tell Cara what you're telling me, you can say goodbye to Josh. And it will be your fault, won't it?"

"I get your meaning. And I hate to say it, but I think I'm fried either way."

Chapter 17

"I've got a bit of a conflict with our Bible study tonight, honey," said Jim, which really wasn't a lie, because, indeed, he was conflicted all over the place with what to do about that verse in First Timothy, as well as his conflict with Bob, Cara's future, and Cara and Josh's future together.

"Okay," said Cara, clearly disappointed.

"But I was wondering if you could do me a favor?"

"Sure."

"Would you speak in service tomorrow night?"

"I thought you said it would upset Sister Pridgitt and Sister Brady."

"Well, I have a plan. Why don't you just testify for a really long time?"

Cara smiled, nodding that she would. As she left, Jim couldn't help thinking that it was a disappointed nod.

After the usher collected the offering, the regulars in the audience were expecting Jim to conduct his midweek study. Instead Jim announced, "Tonight, I am going to have my daughter Cara testify." There were twenty-six in attendance: ten from the fellowship group, because they had heard Cara was speaking. Sister Pridgitt was already pretty suspicious about the whole operation. She was whispering to the good sister next to her, apparently offering a prayer request.

Cara felt mixed up inside. She had no desire to talk to the normal people from church, and during prayer, the Lord had opened up some answers related to struggles that some in the fellowship group were having. One part of her was as nervous as she had ever been in her life, but, because she felt like she had something she needed to say, necessity drove her to overcome her nerves and speak. She stood behind the pulpit and opened her Bible. Sister Pridgitt scowled.

"I want to testify about the car wreck I was in," said Cara, settling Sister Pridgitt a little. Cara began, "The Lord has prompted a special scripture to my heart, and I would like to share it before I testify. First Peter chapter two, verse nine, says, 'But you are a chosen generation, a royal priesthood, a holy nation, His own special people, that you may proclaim the praises of Him who called you out of darkness into His marvelous light.'

"I praise the Lord for saving my life," Cara said. "I should have been dead. And something about knowing that you are gifted with life changes your priorities. I'm not saying that I didn't have purpose before. But I am now more aware than ever of incredible purpose, whether I live for a long time or for a short time.

"But it's not just me who has been gifted with purpose. Everyone here tonight has been given a commission to change their world. And not only that. You have been empowered to do it.

"Do you want to know what God's plan for revival is? It is to love one another. And as we love each other, others will see it and will be attracted to what we have.

"And another thing. When we have purpose, then everything about us becomes an advertisement for Jesus Christ. I was writing out my make-up final for psychology last week in the student lounge. Now, before the accident, I doubt I would have ever done what I did, but I've just been so thankful to be alive and to live out God's purpose that I think I'm changing some.

"Okay, so there's this girl I know. She's had classes with me all semester, and all semester long she's said nothing to me. For whatever reason, when she saw me there to take that test, she asked, 'Why do you have such long hair and always wear skirts?'

"She was sincere. So I took her on my journey. I said, 'Because I wanted you to ask.' She smiled and shrugged, so I went on. I said, 'You see, God has given me a special purpose, and He wants to change the world. As a girl made in God's image, I celebrate by wearing my long hair and by wearing clothing that reminds me how He made me. And do you know what else? Because I am okay with who I am, I don't need to wear a lot of extra stuff. He loves me as I am and delights in me.'

"She knew I wasn't putting her down. I could tell she was okay with what I said. So I went on. 'Do you know what else? I thought God had me here to take a test, but I see He had another reason. I believe God sent me here today to tell you something.' Her eyes got real big. 'I believe God has a special plan for your life. He is calling you to be a part of His own special chosen people who are going to change the world. I should have died a few weeks back. But God preserved my life. It was a miracle. And God wants to do miracles in your life today.'

"I don't know what God is going to do for this girl, but He does have a plan for her life. You see, God doesn't divide the world into people He loves and people He hates. He loves everybody. And God doesn't look at people as saints or sinners. It's not His will that anyone perishes. God sees people as those who are in covenant and those He is calling into covenant."

Then Cara told a couple of Bible stories. She ended by sharing the story of her healing—how that one minute she was in the hospital delirious with fever, and then, when her dad and the church prayed a prayer of faith, the fever was instantly gone.

Cara closed her message in an unusual way. She said, "All right now, let's celebrate. I want popcorn testimonies. In thirty seconds or less, I want you to name something God did for you. It could be big or small, but for you, it was a miracle. And then, after we're done sharing our testimonies, if you need anything, no matter what it is, I want you to come and stand up front, and my dad is going to lay hands on you and pray for you. And when he does, he'll pray in Jesus' name, and the Lord will answer your prayer. Now, he's pretty good at this prayer business, because he's been doing it awhile, so I'm going to want you to come in faith."

Cara held out the microphone for whoever might come forward. Ron was first. "Peter was on drugs and stuff. And we prayed and everything. And he has never used drugs again...." The congregation clapped. Ron continued, "Except for that one time he messed up. But anyway, he's going to be baptized; at least that's what he told me."

Marta got up. "If it wasn't for the Lord and this church I would have committed suicide. I know it. Thank you, Cara. And thank Jesus. I mean Jesus Christ. You know who I mean."

Peter got up. "Yeah, I did mess up that one time a month ago. But God is good. And so is Ron. And Cara. And Marta and Steve. I love you guys. And I mean it."

Then Karen Shepherd rose to testify, evidently hoping to signal that it was all right for people who were not part of the fellowship group to speak. She began, "I thank God that my baby girl is still alive and with me." Then she started to sob and couldn't say anything else.

At this point Jim grabbed the microphone and copied Cara's style. "So if anyone has a need, God is here to meet it." Every young person came forward. Peter received the Holy Ghost and a girl named Silsby was healed. Cara was trying to pray with people but Sister Pridgitt kept signaling her. She ignored her as long as she could, but finally went to where Sister Pridgitt stood when it was clear the woman wouldn't give up.

"Did you need something, Sister Pridgitt?" Cara asked.

"Yes, I need to talk to you."

"Can it wait until a little later?"

"This is important. I think there's a mistake in your Bible."

"What do you mean?"

"Well, you read it wrong."

"What do you mean?"

"You read 'his own special people.' The Bible says 'peculiar people.'"

"Oh," said Cara. "I read out of the *New King James Version*. It modernizes the words so people can understand them a little bit better."

"Well the Bible says 'peculiar.'"

"When that was translated in the seventeenth century, the word 'peculiar' actually meant 'special.' So now that the language has changed, the *New King James Version* offers the same meaning as the original translation, that we are God's 'special people.'"

"But the Bible says 'peculiar.'"

"Certainly, the *King James Version* says 'peculiar,' but—"

"Cara, listen to me. Don't change the Word. We are a peculiar people."

Cara was surprised at how carnal she suddenly felt, and although she later repented, her answer seemed right when she gave it. She said, "Sister Pridgitt, I am wrong and I apologize. You are peculiar. I will never say anything else about you."

"Thank you," said Sister Pridgitt, who was about to turn and walk away.

But then she was interrupted by Oscar, an older man in the church who needed to say something. "Cara, that was the best preaching I've heard in a long time."

Sister Pridgitt harrumphed and was about to leave as Cara corrected him. "I was testifying, Brother Oscar," she said.

"We both know what that was," he said. "Keep it up."

Josh said he wondered if Cara was available when he was coming through town on Saturday, though he didn't say why. Why he couldn't just say he was coming to see her, Cara did not know. She supposed he wanted to keep it casual. Josh declined to meet her at the house but rather chose to meet her at a coffee shop.

Cara got there by borrowing her mom's SUV, a white Dodge that she had dubbed "Roger Dodger, zero-to-sixty in under two minutes." It was her third time to borrow her mom's vehicle. Even though the cast on her arm didn't hinder Cara's driving, her mom warned her several times to be careful.

"So, how was service?" asked Josh, sipping his latte. "I heard you preached."

"Word travels fast. It went well, but 'testified' is the word we're using. But the altar call was good."

"So, have you prayed any more about this?" he asked with no further preliminaries.

"What do you mean?"

"Have you prayed about what sort of call it is you have exactly? I mean, can you give me a timeline of what you want to do and when?"

Part of her was surprised by Josh's demand, but then the other part of her had guessed Josh would increase the stakes. When he needed to be, he was one of the most focused people she knew.

"Well, Josh," she said cautiously, "I know when the Lord spoke to me. That's certain. And I know my dad gave me permission to proceed. And I know I've talked to you and Amanda. That's about as far as I've gotten."

"And you've started speaking."

"I've been speaking for some time now, although it has just been in the fellowship group. As you know, Wednesday was hardly the launch of my ministerial career, unless there is an opening on the evangelistic field for testifiers."

"You're saying you're going to evangelize?"

"No. It was a joke."

"But you don't know what you are going to do then, do you?"

"Josh, did you know everything about your call? Do you know now?"

"Careful, Cara. You're treading on thin ice. I'm pretty sensitive about people undermining my place in the kingdom."

"Josh, I would never want to question your role as a minister."

"But you've already started arguing with me. That's hardly submission, is it?"

"We're having a conversation. I'm giving my opinion. Josh, God doesn't want a woman to be a doormat or a dishrag. Yet, that doesn't mean I don't respect you or that I am not trying to complement what God is doing in your life. Isn't that why the Bible says two are better than one, so each can complement the other?"

"I'm not sure about that. What if what you call 'complementing' is really undermining my authority?"

"It's not. God gives people partners to bring together two perspectives. You agree that God speaks to both men and women, don't you?"

"So, what if it turns out God tells you to go to Japan and I'm supposed to go to Afghanistan or Norway or something? How would that work?"

"Josh, please."

"Cara, I wasn't going to say this, but I guess I need to spell it out for you. Do you know what young men are thinking about when a girl who looks like you stands behind a pulpit and starts talking about Jesus and life and everything?"

"What?"

"Again, I'm just saying this for your own good. They're thinking, 'That girl is hot.' So, I've got to ask you: how does that glorify God? Answer: It doesn't."

Josh thought he had finally gotten through to Cara, because she broke into tears. He was sorry she left without speaking further, but it was a confrontation that needed to happen. If there was a chance of saving her, he would.

"Dad, I have to talk to you about sex."

Jim looked worried. "Okay, what about it?"

"Specifically, mine." Jim's eyes now grew wider. Cara continued, "Josh basically says that I'm disqualified from being in ministry because I am sexual."

"Cara, he did not say that!"

"No."

"I didn't think so."

Cara hesitated just for a moment and then said, "What he actually said was that I was hot. And because I was so hot, nobody would get anything out of the message."

"Oh."

"Do you have a little time to talk about his comment?"

"You know, Cara, I never got back to you on the 'suffer not a woman' passage. So why don't we deal with them both, say, this coming Thursday night?"

"Okay," said Cara. She left, not altogether satisfied. When she walked out of his office, Jim broke into a cold sweat.

Later that day Josh texted to see what Cara thought about what he'd said. Cara replied that she and her dad were talking about it. He texted back that this was a bad idea. She replied that it was a good one. He asked if she used the word "hot." She replied that she had. He texted that this was foolish. She texted that he was the one who said it. He texted her that he wanted to see her on Monday. She texted to ask whether it was to talk about how hot she was. He did not text back.

On Monday, he had a latte. She had black coffee. He didn't take a drink. Neither did she. There were no preliminaries.

"Cara, we need to talk."

"Okay. About what?"

"About this. About us."

"What about us?"

Josh fell into the cadence of his prepared speech. Cara could anticipate almost every word. As soon as he began, Cara silently interpreted his real meaning. "Cara, you're a wonderful girl..." *Always offer a compliment before twisting the knife* "...and I meant every word that I said to you..." *so even though I said I love you and that I was almost your fiancé* "...this is not about you, it's about me..." *and here comes the clincher:* "I just need to get more focused on the Lord and on my ministry..."

Of course, there was nothing more to be said since God was on Josh's side. It was over. But then, out of nowhere Cara knew something—something she could hardly believe. She realized it was true even though she had never considered it before. She did not ask; she did not complain. She spoke evenly and matter-of-factly. "Josh, you've been seeing someone else."

"No, that's not what, uh, it's not really the way, um, no, it's not that, I--"

Cara interrupted him to say that she understood and then made a quick exit.

Chapter 18

"**B**ob, did you ever talk to your kids about sex?"

"Well, sure—with Fred. I used that Dobson book, *Preparing for Adolescence*. Took him on the weekend trip, the whole deal.

"How'd that go?"

"Rough. But I was glad I did it."

"But not the girls?"

"The girls? No, I let the wife do that. Say, Jim, you're a little late on Shay."

"Thanks. I'll bear that in mind."

"This has something to do with Cara, doesn't it?"

Jim was clearly embarrassed, but he plowed on with his question anyway. "Uh...Bob, if a good-looking girl was preaching, would you lose focus on what she was saying?"

"What is wrong with you, Jim!"

Jim shared the conversation that Cara had had with him, and before it was over, Bob was equally embarrassed. They sat and looked at each other for a while without speaking. Then they both laughed, probably because they felt foolish. Bob was the first to break the silence saying, "You know, I have friends who tell me things."

"Okay?"

"Well, last year, there was a buck-ugly pastor in the southern part of the state who became enamored with this beautiful lady in his church and was going to run off with her."

"Yeah?"

"So, Jim, why would any woman be attracted to him?"

"Nearsighted perhaps?"

"Do you know what she said the reason was?"

"What?"

"She was attracted to him because he was such a spiritually powerful man. That's why she was willing to leave her husband, who was also in the church,

Cara's Call

and why she went to meet him at the airport. But he wasn't there because he got cold feet."

"Wow."

"And do you know what he told her was the reason he was attracted to her?"

"Because she was pretty?"

"I'm sure that's an important point. But he told her that he was attracted to her because she was so focused on spiritual things and worshipped like no one else in the church."

Jim was a little dumbfounded by the turn of conversation. "Bob, I'm not sure whether I should even believe you on all of this or whether you should even be telling me this stuff."

"Just saying."

"Just saying what?"

"Sexuality is a part of everybody's identity, man or woman."

"And this helps me how in my discussion with Cara?"

"Not sure. I'm just here to offer background info."

"Thanks, Bob, I'll keep this in mind."

"Don't mention it. I'll see you next Tuesday."

As soon as Jim opened the front door and saw his wife was in the kitchen, he had a sudden inspiration. Without preliminaries, he said, "Karen, I've got some issues I can't seem to get a handle on." Karen was startled beyond words. He continued, "Karen, I need you to talk to Cara about sex."

A smile spread across her face. "I did, over ten years ago."

"Well, not that. Josh said he didn't want Cara to preach, because she was hot and any guy who heard her would be distracted by that."

Karen laughed out loud. "I can see why you are upset. You wouldn't be a good father if you didn't want to protect your daughter."

"Do you think Josh may have a point?"

"Are you asking for my opinion?"

"Yes. I am."

"Hmmm...would her preaching be any different than her teaching in her fellowship meeting?"

"You're saying she's already been involved in ministry, so what he's saying is irrelevant? You may be right, but I don't think I could handle it if people were thinking of Cara in that way."

"You know, Jim, I've always thought you were pretty hot when you preach."

Karen had crossed a line. They had never talked like this before. Jim was about to rebuke her until he realized that he had started it; he had opened the door in asking for her advice. "Well, uh…thank you…I guess," he said.

"Jim, in all seriousness, have you ever wondered why Sister Pridgitt never leaves our church, even though she gets so upset at things all the time?"

"Never thought of it."

"Because she has an incredible crush on you."

"That's ridiculous and you know it."

"When she complains, who gets the softballs thrown at him, and who gets the zingers?"

"I have no idea what you mean."

"It's the women in this family who bear the brunt of her anger. Me, Sandra, and especially Cara."

"Karen!"

Karen smiled but said nothing else. There was an awkward pause, and finally Jim said, "So what am I supposed to do with this information?"

"I don't know. But I know one thing. You'll have to talk to Cara. I would say the wrong thing." And with that, Karen walked from the kitchen into the living room. Jim would have followed, but he was too embarrassed.

Later, they were reading in the bedroom. Karen was about to turn out the light when Jim asked, "Karen, what if you and I talk to Cara together?"

Karen turned off the light. From the dark he heard, "No. I'm sure I'd say things differently than you would. Jim, I really would need to run things by you first before I said them. Otherwise, it just wouldn't work."

In the morning as they were eating their cereal, Jim suddenly said, "I trust you." Karen noticed that he had a desperate edge to his voice.

"Jim, I am not good at impromptu speaking. I can't do things that way. I kind of have to mull everything over a few times to think of what is best."

"We won't have time for that. Just say what comes to your mind, no matter whether or not it seems relevant or to the point or not."

"Please, Jim. You have no idea—"

"Do it for me, Karen."

"Here's the handout I made on the First Timothy text. I think you already understood that, Cara. But Mom and I are going to talk to you about sexuality."

Cara's dad was so serious and her mom looked so out of sorts that Cara had to bite her tongue to keep from smiling. This was clearly the strangest moment in her

Cara's Call

life. Her dad started out slowly, offering a verse about the Garden of Eden and two being one flesh. In an attempt to celebrate women in the Bible, he talked for almost ten minutes in generic terms. But they were no nearer to talking about the core issues by the end of his dissertation than they had been at the beginning.

Without warning, her dad stopped and looked at Cara's mom. Both Cara and her mom were surprised that she had been given such an abrupt cue. But Karen didn't beat around the bush. "Make sure you wear a longer dress when you have to stand on the platform, particularly higher platforms."

Apparently, this was just the sort of catalyst Jim needed, because he said, "What your mom's trying to say is that even if a woman is behind the pulpit, she is a sexual being."

Karen then tested her agreement with her husband, for a thought came to her. She continued, "Just as a man behind the pulpit is a sexual being." She paused to see if she was about to be rebuked. But Jim seemed happy for the support.

"And some people will look at women as sexual objects," said Jim.

"And some people will look at men as sex objects," said Karen. But this last statement was too much for Jim, and he asked Cara to excuse them. They moved over three feet to talk for reasons unknown to her. Yet, they certainly were talking loudly enough for her to hear every word.

"Karen, women don't have the same sort of lustful thoughts men have."

"What thoughts do women have?" asked Karen. "Are you telling me that if Joel Osteen wore a paper bag on his head, he'd have the same ratings?" Karen then softened her tone, but her voice was still audible. "Look, Jim, why don't I just go in the other room until—"

"No, I want you here."

"Okay, well, I'll just be quiet then, because—"

"No, you're doing good. I like it." Jim and Karen moved back over to Cara and Jim immediately went into high gear. "Cara, I'm trying to tell you that you have to be careful so that men don't view you as a sexual object when you minister."

Suddenly, Karen became so uncharacteristically animated that both Cara and her dad did a double take. She said, "Cara, every woman who ever ministers will be assessed as a sexual object by someone, so you shouldn't worry about it. All men have this biological thing where they can't help being attracted to a beautiful woman, even if they are married and they are faithful. Even pastors who would otherwise invite you to preach may not be able to take you seriously, because they don't understand their own sexuality. They think that because they are attracted to you then you can't possibly be a preacher."

As soon as Karen took a breath, Jim escorted her further away from Cara than their previous private conference, but they were still within earshot.

"Do you want me to leave now?" she whispered.

"No. No, you're good. I just don't think I agree with you."

"About what?"

"About...what you just said."

"Which part? That men have sexual thoughts?"

"No, not that."

"That when they see a beautiful woman, the fact that she is pretty won't color how they think of her?"

"Karen, it's just not as universal as you say. I mean, people didn't view Sister Freeman in the way you say."

"Not when she was older than Moses. After she had aged, they liked her because she was safe."

"Karen, they liked her because she could preach and get results. I'm just saying that you shouldn't generalize so much."

"You can't say Sister Freeman had no sexuality. That's silly. Have you ever seen pictures of her when she was younger? She was very good looking. If you don't think that made any difference in how she was received then—"

"Okay, okay," he said, apparently conceding he wouldn't solve anything now. They moved back to Cara. "Now, Cara, here's the most important thing: as a preacher in a church, you always need to be in submission to the pastor."

That one simple statement put forward by her father at once lifted Cara to new heights and at the same time cast a long shadow over her dreams. The good news, the really exciting thing, was that her father had called her "a preacher in a church." It was the first time he had used such language. It was accidental, of course. She should not make too much of it. But still, he had said it.

The second thing was more troubling. Cara had told her father about being called to preach but had said nothing about her sense that she was to pastor. She could now see that for her dad, there was a pretty wide gap between the two; maybe an impassible chasm. Perhaps if right then she would have talked more about her sense of calling, Cara could have avoided all the trouble that came later. But she did not. She chose a more cautious strategy. "Dad, is a pastor in submission to someone?"

"Yes. The district, fellow ministers, leaders in the church. That sort of thing. But my point about women—and this is my biggest problem with women in ministry—is that they have trouble with submission."

Karen immediately echoed, "And the biggest problem with men in ministry is their lack of submission. It's kind of a human problem, isn't it?"

This conversation was getting way too personal for Jim, so he retreated to safety by saying, "So you need to be careful in your mannerisms, dress and actions. No low necklines, tight outfits, gaudy dresses. Don't do anything that could be misconstrued or unseemly."

Cara thought these words might signal the end of the session, and when her dad nodded his head with authority, Cara knew she was now dismissed.

As soon as she got outside the door, she heard, "I'm sorry, dear. I shouldn't have even come—"

"No, dear, you were fine..."

Cara headed upstairs and missed whatever followed. She had to admit one thing to herself. She had just taken part in the most unusual conversation of her entire life.

"Cara, Greg and I had a big fight."

"What happened, Amanda?" replied Cara, for Amanda's distress was apparent even through a cell phone.

"Well, Greg said he would be a camp counselor, and we could spend time together at camp at the same time we were doing ministry. We were supposed to meet last night after service for a quiet talk, but he was nowhere to be found. When I finally got someone to track him down, he was playing basketball. He had forgotten all about us getting together. And that's only the tip of the iceberg. I guess I set myself up for disappointment."

"Did you talk to him about it?"

"I tried. But mostly I just cried. And Cara, it was all pretty public."

"Do you need me to come up to see you?"

"That'd be great. And Cara, there's something else I really need to talk to you about as well."

"What's that?"

"I'm going to have to tell you face to face."

"Okay."

Chapter 19

The camp wasn't on the map, of course, but Cara knew it was somewhere between Clinton and Heyworth on Highway 51. That's all she remembered. Then, just as she put the map down, the sign for the camp appeared, and she hit the brakes. Roger Dodger responded quickly enough for her to make the turn.

She turned onto the blacktop road, which eventually changed to gravel, and then finally to piping-hot dirt road that the wind made into dusty clouds. Even though the dirt road had been oiled to keep vehicles from kicking up too much dust, the effort was only partly effective. Yet, through the haze of dirt, Cara identified the line of campers snaking out the dining hall door—a solid indication that she had not missed lunch. Both the first and second campers Cara talked to had seen the camp nurse, so it wasn't long before Cara located Amanda. Presently, they both loaded up their trays, making sure to grab some home-grown vegetables fixed to perfection.

Cara lifted her fork and pronounced, "You go, Amanda—RN for youth camp! You are officially important!"

"Mostly, I just pass out Band-Aids and a little comfort."

From where Cara sat at the staff table, she had a clear view of a dozen teenagers encircling a ping pong table and cheering. Greg was right in the middle of that group. "Looks like he's in his element," said Cara. "What's he doing?"

When they cheered loudly, Amanda responded, "He is in the process of dethroning the youth camp's reigning ping ponger."

"Amanda, I can see those kids really like him. They're rooting for him!"

"Cara, they think he's some kind of hero. Greg arm-wrestled three guys at once and beat them all. That's all these kids can talk about."

Amanda then spied a dirty-faced youth at the back of the serving line. "Hey, Samuel," she yelled. "Where were you this morning?"

"Sorry. I forgot to come and see you," he yelled back. Cara was amazed. She had never in her whole life heard Amanda raise her voice.

Amanda continued to shout, "If you don't take those meds by one o'clock, you're not going to be doing yourself or me any favors. I don't want to be treating you full-time in the nurse's station. Now come with me." Whereupon Amanda simply got up and walked away.

Cara laughed as she reflected on how Greg and Amanda thought coming to camp would provide some "alone time" for them. Obviously, neither had read the job description.

The dining hall held good memories for Cara, and she had no need for anyone else to keep her company. Finishing her meal, she meandered outside to the snow cone stand where a bunch of guys stood with baseball mitts. She spotted her cousin Fred in the middle of the group, duded up in his Sunday best.

"What in the world!" Cara exclaimed.

"I got the day off work. So I came up to see what's happening."

"What do you mean?"

"You know, check the progress of the latest romances. Who's who, what's what, that sort of thing."

"You've lost your ability to text, then?"

"Sometimes you've just got to see how things are progressing firsthand to make the right assessment."

Cara smiled. "You're here on a mission?"

"It's hard work but somebody's got to do it. I never get any information from you," Fred teased. "Well, Greg and Amanda had a big fight on Monday."

"Oh?" Cara said, playing dumb.

"They're pretty much over it now. Jimmy and Rachel broke up. Rachel is now going with Salvatore and Jimmy is trying to get PJ to pay attention to him. Also, Josh and Stephanie are doing good and—"

"Josh and Stephanie?" Cara blurted out.

"Yes, there's rumor of a ring in the mix before too long."

Cara willed her voice to remain calm, throttling it down to a counseling voice. She repeated, "So, Josh and Stephanie are doing good, you say, and there's a rumor of a ring in the mix before too long?"

"Yes, Stephanie has been keeping me up on the whole thing."

"Stephanie's been talking to you about—"

"Not this week, of course. She hasn't had time because she and Josh are doing double duty as praise singers, counselors, and whatnot."

"Of course," said Cara. Stephanie had always hated camps and had never gone when they were younger. "That makes sense," Cara repeated dumbly.

"It all started at the spring youth convention."

"Uh huh..." said Cara almost inaudibly, but Fred no longer needed encouragement.

"Well, it was the last night of Illinois Youth Convention, and she got this call to be a minister's wife. And since you and Josh had already broken up earlier that year, she didn't mind going to him for counsel."

"So, it started at youth convention..." said Cara, numb with disbelief. She stared out across the hot field at nothing in particular, feeling as if she were a spectator in someone else's drama, hearing about some other Josh, a different Stephanie.

"Yes, one time they went to this really fancy restaurant on Route 18, and—"

"I'm familiar with the restaurant," Cara said, snapping out of her reverie. "Fred, I'm going to run over to see Amanda at the nurse's station."

Amanda, of course, was busier than she had let on earlier. When Cara arrived, two boys were waiting for her to give them medications. Further, because she had not yet been attended to, another patient named April complained to Cara, "I'm sick." Apparently, April thought her request for help would be effective to any adult in the area.

Amanda rescued Cara, steering the girl toward a chair. "Can you tell me what hurts?" she asked the girl.

"I hurt all over," said April.

Because April's health issues were not about to clear up anytime soon, Cara said, "Amanda, when you're done, come find me. I'll be over at the tabernacle. It sounds like they're having choir practice in there."

Cara walked over to the huge tabernacle and peeked in from the back door. When she did, Cara was surprised all over again. Up at the front, Stephanie and Josh were singing. They were apparently the featured duet. They stood in front of a hundred-voice choir, harmonizing on the verse of the choir song. But they weren't simply singing. They were performing. It looked remarkably staged. Like in a classic Broadway love duet, Josh and Stephanie gazed sweetly into each other's eyes. Then, as the verse progressed up to the high notes, each leaned in toward the other just a little more. Cara left.

The moment she exited the rear of the tabernacle, she saw Amanda hurrying toward her. "Why didn't you tell me?" cried Cara.

"I didn't know until this week. I didn't want to tell you over the phone. I am so sorry you had to find out before I could talk to you. It's all my fault."

"Nothing is your fault. I've just been so stupid!" she said as Amanda embraced her.

"Let me treat you to a snow cone," offered Amanda, even though Cara had just been there and had fled before she ordered. Actually, neither of them liked snow cones that much, but getting one seemed to be a good exit strategy. Amanda ordered the orange flavor, and Cara decided on cherry. They sat down at the picnic table and watched their snow cones melt in the hot Illinois sun. There was nothing to be said. Amanda didn't even try.

"Sister Amanda, Sister Amanda," said a little four-year-old boy with a dirty, striped shirt, layered dirt on his neck, and an echo of food around his mouth.

"Yes, dear," said Amanda.

"I need a Band-Aid," he pronounced, showing a fresh red scrape that went from his wrist to his elbow.

"One of the camp workers' kids," explained Amanda to Cara. "I'd better get him cleaned up." She took the little boy by the hand and started walking him toward the nurse's station.

After an obnoxious bell rang, a mob of kids fled from the tabernacle and rushed toward the snow cone stand. Taking this as her cue to leave, Cara rose from the picnic table, determined to get to her car and head home. She didn't get far before the crowd engulfed her. As the crowd separated into smaller clumps, amazingly, Stephanie and Josh emerged, laughing and giggling into each other's eyes. They saw Cara at the very moment she saw them. For an instant, time stood still. They were three people standing wide-eyed and frozen in place, no more than six feet from each other, three people all wishing they were someplace else, three people with nothing at all to say.

Stephanie was the first to recover. "Got any crusades lined up?" she mocked.

Josh, who was quick on his feet, fed off of Stephanie's remark. "Won't be anytime soon. Even her dad won't let her preach. But he will let her testify."

Stephanie snapped, "Even that's pretty dangerous. The apostle Paul said, 'Let your women keep silence in the church.'"

"That's Bible now-uh," repeated Josh to Stephanie, as if he were amening a conference speaker.

"But if you heard me," said Stephanie, turning googly-eyes to Josh, "that wouldn't be silence-uh."

"That'll preach," sounded Josh.

"But it shouldn't," laughed Stephanie.

"Silence now," said Josh in a singsong lilt.

"Shhh..." said Stephanie as they walked away arm in arm.

"Where are you?" said the voice into the phone.

"I'm going home."

"Fred said there was a scene at the snow cone stand."

Now it wasn't just tears but convulsions. Cara heaved in deep sighs and had to pull her mom's car over. Amanda could only listen as her friend struggled to recover. Cara finally managed to say, "I just want to go away and never be seen again. Ever."

"Where are you?"

"I'm on Route 51 going south. I just passed Clinton."

"You get yourself to the nearest McDonald's and call me. You hear me? There's a lady here who can cover for me. I need to see you."

Fifteen minutes later Cara and Amanda were drinking Cokes, and Cara was finishing the story. "They ridiculed me in front of forty kids; made me look like an idiot."

"It was guilt," said Amanda. "You've got to know that much. Josh felt guilty. And so did Stephanie. That's how they dealt with it. Their true character came out."

"But why did I have to be the brunt of all of it? It's just so wrong!"

No response was needed, so Amanda didn't offer one. But after a sip or two from their Cokes, she did say, "He wouldn't have been good for you, you know."

"Why?"

"Cara, I liked Josh at first, but then I started to see how controlling he was; how he could turn his smile on and off like a light switch. How he was trying to remake you. Then I didn't like him at all."

"Why didn't you say anything to me?"

"I would have supported you no matter what, even if you had married him. But I'm sure glad you didn't." More silence followed, along with the healing flavor of Coca-Cola.

"Amanda, I knew."

"What do you mean?"

"I didn't know who, but I knew Josh was seeing someone."

"Women's intuition?"

"No. It was more certain than that. It's like when God prompts me to say something specific when I'm praying for someone or like when He tells me something about someone just so I can pray for them in a better way. It was that kind of thing."

"I believe you. But why would God tell you that? And why wouldn't He tell you who it was?"

"I don't know. Maybe so I'll know He's still in charge. Maybe so I can move on from this. I have no idea. It doesn't take away the hurt, though. I feel like someone stomped on my chest."

After a long silence, Amanda suggested, "I think they deserve each other."

More silence ensued, and then from the storehouse of imaginations, each girl conjured up this and that scenario. Smiles crept unbidden to both of their faces as each girl was lost in her own private thoughts.

It wasn't SLU. That door hadn't opened back up for Cara. But it was Southern Illinois University. SIU was nothing to sneeze at, and Cara felt confident she was supposed to be there. The admissions counselor looked over his half glasses, showing Cara the schedule he had mocked up for her, and then, on another sheet, his three-year plan. "Orientation is August 13th, and you'll need to invest a whole week in—"

"There is something wrong with this schedule," said Cara. "It has me going three more years, and I already have enough credits to be a junior."

"Well, it's just that you switched your major from prelaw to English and are missing some prerequisites. So, you'll just have to come here a third year."

"But that's not possible," said Cara. "I just can't do it."

Dr. Jackson tried to be patient. "For one thing, you are missing a foreign language; you also lack English Lit. and another English course, so that's the issue. It puts you a year behind."

"Okay, but this is just not doable. There has to be another way we can work it. Time is just way too valuable."

"I can appreciate that your time is valuable, Cara," said Dr. Jackson with a little more emphasis in his voice. "As is mine. But there is nothing that can be done."

"No," she said evenly. "I won't be going three years here. Just two."

Dr. Jackson let out a breath. "All right, Cara. Please explain. How is it you are so certain that you won't be coming here three years?"

"Because God made me a deal that if I did this, if I committed my future to Him in this way, that it would only take two years."

Dr. Jackson once again peered over his half glasses and saw that the girl across from him was dead serious. He replied, "Well, apparently God forgot to inform someone at SIU."

But Cara did not give up. And ninety minutes later her schedule had been revised. She would have to take summer courses, and she wouldn't graduate until August. The big thing was that she would have to test out of two years of French and English Literature, but as she explained to the head of the guidance department, "That's a piece of cake for God to do." There were also two other courses they didn't count but that Cara was sure should be considered since they were equivalent to courses offered at SIU. Cara would challenge those in writing.

Chapter 20

"I quit my job at Office Depot," Cara informed her mom later that day.

"Oh?" said her mother. "Why?"

"Got to do a huge test for French and English Lit. within eight weeks."

"That's nice, Cara. I'm sure you'll do just fine. What are you going to do for money?"

That was a tough one. Since her parents didn't have that much money in the first place and since higher education wasn't higher on their priority list, these two factors created certain challenges. As soon as she was old enough to do so, Cara had always worked and bought her own things. It had been a matter of pride with her. But now Cara's status was that she had no car, no income, and no money. The insurance would not replace her car.

"Don't know," she said, still feeling bold after dueling with the guidance counselor. "God will provide."

While it was God who provided, He used Cara's mother to do it. She gave Cara free access to her SUV and her credit card. Whenever she could manage, she slipped her twenty bucks.

Cara journaled, "Took car to French tutor. Car was on empty. Filled it up with Mom's credit card. Lord, couldn't you supply my needs another way?"

Cara "testified" for the second time near the end of July. Bob asked Jim for the full report when they played racquetball.

"I hear you had a large attendance of young people Sunday night," Bob said.

"How is it possible for you to know everything?" asked Jim.

"Just what's important to know. So how'd Cara do?"

"Service was…uh…good," said Jim tentatively.

"But?" primed Bob, sensing that Jim had more to say and trying to get it to percolate to the surface.

"It's just that when she speaks…I don't know Bob, it's nothing like how I preach."

Cara's Call

Bob retorted, "You mean loud, fiery, and repeating the same point over and over until you can get the audience on its feet?"

"Well, I was actually going to use the word 'power.'"

"She's not loud enough for you, then?"

Jim continued, "She's almost conversational at times. There were a couple of times where she did get a bit loud and once she was almost yelling, but she lacks oomph, if you know what I mean."

"Frankly, Jim, I'm relieved. I would have been more worried had she sounded and acted like you."

"You're still not getting me, Bob. It's just there's no authority in her delivery."

Bob put down his racquet and used his shirt to wipe sweat from his brow. "Jim, you know that the idea of Cara preaching is not something I'm endorsing, but I need you to think about this for a minute. Jesus was a preacher. Do you think His style would be more like yours or like Cara's?" When Jim didn't answer, Bob asked, "Who do you think has more authority in their preaching—you or Jesus?"

They both laughed. Then Jim complained further, "It's not just that. I'm not sure I agree with some of her preaching."

"She messed up on the doctrine?"

"She's got the basics down great. It's just that there are some things on the edges that are not so good."

"Talk to her. That's what a pastor is for, Jim. You're supposed to guide people."

"Okay, I'll do it."

Jim waited until after Cara spoke once more so he could offer fresh critique.

"Cara, I need to talk to you about some things you're saying when you preach," he began.

"Good," she responded.

Jim was puzzled and his raised eyebrows said so.

Cara continued, "Dad, I've heard you preach hundreds of times, and I also know what you think of every visiting minister we've ever had. I count your 'amens' and watch for funny looks on your face."

Jim smiled despite himself.

Cara continued, "I'm getting less 'amens' per sermon than any visiting minister, and you get this pained look on your face. So, the sooner I know what I'm doing wrong, the sooner I can fix it."

"I wouldn't exactly say that you're doing anything wrong," said Jim. "You're doing good."

"But?" interjected Cara.

"But I have a few issues. That's all."

"Fire away," said Cara, and he did.

"The first strange thing is this: how can you say that caring for the environment is a holiness issue?"

"I wouldn't exactly use those words, but I do think the way we approach the environment should in some ways be like the way we approach other things. For example, we don't do drugs or smoke because we know God made us stewards of our bodies. In the same way, aren't we stewards of the world around us just like we are stewards of our bodies?"

"I just can't agree that the church should be joining forces with godless environmentalists."

"I'm not joining forces with anyone, but this question keeps coming up in the fellowship meeting, and the kids want to know the church's position on preserving the environment. That's the best I have been able to come up with so far."

"Cara, the church is called to be separate. Which leads to my second point. I do not think the true church of Jesus Christ should just go along with those who preach the social gospel."

"I'm not sure what you mean."

"When you call for the church to feed the poor and to be concerned about those who are impoverished around them, don't you see how this weakens the gospel?"

"Maybe you can help me see it, Dad."

"The Bible says if you don't work then you don't eat. The poor you have with you always…it's the kingdom that must be preached. If we feed their bodies but their souls are lost, they will still die without God."

"Does it have to be either/or?"

"And another thing. You need to get a little tougher on sin. I'm not sure you understand the depth of depravity in this culture."

"I'm pretty aware, Dad."

"Well, can't you just call sin what it is? This thing you keep saying, that God has two categories of people—those who are in covenant and those He is calling into covenant—you're pretty much giving away the store."

"Dad, every one of these kids knows that they have terrible faults and in their heart consider themselves to be pretty major failures. They are already ridden with guilt. They know they're sinners. What they have to work at believing is how someone can see them as worth loving unconditionally."

"Wrong approach, Cara. And another thing…"

Cara listened for the other thing. But as it turned out, there were three other things. Then, those three other things led them back to the first things they talked

Cara's Call

about, and before long, forty-five minutes had elapsed. The ironic thing was how much Cara really enjoyed every one of those forty-five minutes. For the first time in their relationship, her father was almost treating her as an adult. He let her give back almost as much as she took. At the end of their time, Cara felt that for the first time she had been heard by her father, at least in part.

"Can you come to St. Louis with me and my mother? We're going Saturday to pick out my wedding dress."

"I'd love to, Amanda, but I've got that CLEP test on Saturday."

"What's that?"

"It's a standardized test for college credit. I'm testing out of English Lit. I think I'm going to be able to do it. They have a pretty easy threshold to get credit. I've read on the subject until my eyes hurt."

"When do you do your challenge for French?"

"Amanda, I did it! I tested out of all four semesters. It helped that I had a little French in high school, so I did have something to build on."

"Wow! Did they accept your challenge on those classes you were appealing?"

"They took one but not the other. Which is not a big deal. With a summer class, I can still finish on time."

"Wish you could come with us, but I totally understand."

"Text me a picture of the dress."

"Bob, it wasn't pretty. It wasn't pretty at all," said Jim, putting some extra zing on the ball.

"Give me an example of what you argued about."

"Lots of stuff. Everything, really."

"Like?" said Bob. The discussion was working in Bob's favor, because Jim was hitting the ball way too hard now, which set him up for an easy return.

"It turns out I'm not preaching holiness if I don't include the environment."

"Now that is way off the beam."

"Yeah. But she didn't seem to want to back down on that."

"What did you do?"

"I told her that environmentalists were wackos and that Rush Limbaugh knew that a long time ago. Glenn Beck says they're really communists."

"What did she say to that?"

"Well, like I said, we didn't seem to be communicating on that point very well. Hey, Bob, did you know that there is a mass of garbage swirling around in the

Pacific Ocean the size of Australia? Cara thinks the church should have an opinion on it."

"No kidding. Well, I've got to admit, it's a bit odd, but it is hardly heretical. So, that's it? That's the only way that she's off?"

"She's afraid we're failing as a church."

"In what way?"

"She has this thing about the need to help the poor. Thinks that's an important part of the gospel."

"Wha'd you say?"

"I told her that I *was* helping the poor. I was doing it by going to work every morning, and this was also helping to feed the hungry, given that we now had enough food in the house."

"I'm guessing she wasn't impressed. Besides the sort of edgy ideas on poverty, you say she still believes the message, right?"

"She's got that down. She's saying stuff that I didn't teach that really backs up what we believe."

"So then, what are you going to do? Clip her wings somehow?"

"She's still learning, so I told her I was happy she was preaching and that I would use her more."

"But if she's going to be rebellious…"

"Well, I wouldn't say rebellious."

"Some guy who was talking five minutes ago said she was. And he sure looked a lot like you."

"Bob, she said if there was something—anything—that I don't want said, all I had to do was tell her."

"See, this is really my problem with women. They're too emotional. No offense, Jim, but they're suckers for pictures of starving babies in Africa and they cry mountains of tears to save the whales. Still, if you keep Cara on a short leash, you could cut the damage she does to a minimum. Are you are going to give her a list of subjects to stay away from?"

There was an uncanny silence as Bob stood at the door waiting for Jim to answer what was an easy question. Concerned, Bob pressed the point. "Jim?"

"I told her to follow God's leading, and if there were issues, we would settle them later between us."

"You know, Jim. They say this is how all these preachers start going liberal. They make allowances for their children. Hope that's not happening to you."

"I'm really needing you to come back to work," said Gary.

"I'm honored you ask, but I'm heading to SIU in two weeks. Maybe I could work some during Christmas break."

"But aren't you coming home during the semester?"

"I'll be coming home on weekends."

"Work for me on Saturdays, then. Come on, Cara, you know every department, and I'm losing all my summer help. Do it for me."

Cara liked Gary a lot and did enjoy working with him. She wasn't sure what the semester would bring and really shouldn't have agreed, but she just couldn't tell him no. Gary pressed his luck further. "So if you're not starting for two weeks, there's no reason why you couldn't give me a couple days next week, is there?"

The SIU campus in Carbondale was two hours and twenty minutes from Munson Heights. Less, if she needed it to be, because Cara could make good time on I-57. But things were less predictable when she got to those two-lane highways. On her way home from school the first weekend, Cara called Amanda. "So you're going to cover for me tonight?"

"I'll be there with bells on. I've got the lesson all ready."

"It's just for these first couple weeks. I'm having scheduling difficulties. And I'll be there tonight before you finish."

"Cara, I don't even know what you are driving. I know your insurance wouldn't give you anything for your old car. Are you still driving 'Roger Dodger?'"

"The same. On semi-permanent loan. And get this. When I left for SIU last Saturday, Dad slipped me a couple hundred dollars. He told me not to tell anyone. Amanda, he's really a softy underneath everything."

"No one will hear that from me. I promise."

Chapter 21

On her third weekend home, Cara had very little free time. She got home just in time for her fellowship meeting, then worked all the next day at Office Depot. During her work break, Cara was following up on texts when she came across a text from Elizabeth asking if they were still meeting. It was a good thing Elizabeth asked, for Cara had forgotten all about meeting her after work. She called Elizabeth to confirm.

"Are you doing all right?" asked Cara.

"I've got a boyfriend," she said at once.

"Well, you have a boyfriend then," Cara repeated in her counseling voice.

"Yeah. The bad news is that he's not really been too supportive of my calling to ministry, so I've got a couple of questions."

"Sure thing," said Cara. "See you soon."

It was Elizabeth's idea to meet at Denny's. She had just gotten her driver's license and wanted to try it out.

"How do you explain it?" asked Elizabeth as she was eating her salad.

"I explained the First Timothy text to you last time."

"No. From Corinthians, 'Let your women keep silence.' What do you do with that? Mark wants to know."

"Who's Mark?"

"The guy I told you about. My boyfriend."

"Right. Now let's look at the text," said Cara, opening her Bible to First Corinthians chapter fourteen. "It does say, 'Let your women keep silence in the church,' but it says this in a particular context. Remember, Paul had all sorts of associates who were women in ministry. And just three chapters prior to Paul's call for silence, he gave specific instructions to women who were ministering publicly. This is the chapter where Paul explains the importance of long hair."

"Well, then why does he talk about women keeping silent?" asked Elizabeth.

Cara had read several books on the verse, and there were varying opinions. She hadn't come to a final conclusion personally, because she thought that several scholars made equally strong explanations. She was just about ready to offer a

Cara's Call

book or symposium paper for Elizabeth to study, then thought better of it. Elizabeth needed quick answers. She needed pastoral advice. "Look," she said. "There were excesses in the Corinthian church and there were certain women who were speaking out of order. First Corinthians 14 is addressed to those women and the confusion they were causing."

"It's not against all women speaking?"

"Not at all."

"Okay. That's good, then."

Cara wanted to say more, but she was intuitive enough to know this was not the time. Elizabeth could study more about it when she was ready.

Elizabeth changed subjects. "How are things working out with your dad?" This was a fair question, since Cara had invited her into some of her struggles.

"I preached Sunday night. He didn't even say it was testifying."

"That's great!" said Elizabeth. "Did you stomp and snort?"

Cara laughed out loud. "So Elizabeth, do you want to stomp and snort when you preach?"

"I might," said Elizabeth with a smile. "If I really feel like it."

"Well, you don't strike me as the stomping and snorting type," Cara said with a grin. "Look, I'm no expert on ministry," Cara continued, "so I can only give you my opinion, one that could change. But I've been thinking that one of the things I need to celebrate when I preach is being feminine. That's how God made me, right?"

"I'm not sure what you mean."

"Let's think about it. Do you wear a necktie?"

"No."

"Why not?"

"That's a man thing."

"Where in the scripture does it say a man should wear a tie when he preaches on Sunday morning?"

"There's not a scripture. But it's not against scripture. And in our culture it is something men do."

"Granted," said Cara. "But what if a man decided to show his freedom in Christ by not wearing a necktie?"

"That would be okay."

"Elizabeth, would there be people in church who wouldn't listen to him because he didn't have a necktie on?"

"I guess so."

"So it would be better for him to do the things that are considered conventional for men to do, because what he has to say is so valuable that he doesn't want there to be distractions."

"Right, but I don't see what—"

"Here's the deal. In a lot of ways I am already at a disadvantage, because I am a woman who is called to preach, so I think the best thing to do is not to purposely do or say things or dress in ways that would prevent people from listening to me."

"You're saying I shouldn't raise my voice when I preach?"

"Elizabeth, I think its okay for women to be demonstrative in preaching. I'm not saying you have to preach calmly. Just be who you are. You don't have to change yourself into someone else to be a 'powerful preacher.'"

"So, no stomping and snorting then?"

"Well, if you want to," said Cara smiling, "I won't stop you."

"I don't think I will. I just thought I needed to be willing to do it."

"What'd we get for mail?" her mother asked Cara.

Cara had just arrived home from work and brought in the mail from the mailbox. As she began sorting through it, her eyes widened. What shocked her wasn't simply the wedding invitation addressed to the Shepherd family; it was the return address that specifically caught her attention. Cara tore open Stephanie's wedding invitation. She perused the particulars and cried out, "No! They can't do this!"

"What's the matter dear?"

"It's Josh and Stephanie. They set their wedding date the same day as Amanda's."

"Well, you weren't planning on going to their wedding anyway, were you?"

"It's not me, Mom. Don't you see? There may be fifty or sixty people who would like to be at Amanda's wedding who are now going to have to choose between the two! This is terrible!"

"Maybe Amanda could change her date."

"The invitations already went out."

"Are they at different times?"

"Three hours different, but that won't make any difference."

"Why?"

"Because Stephanie is getting married at Willeford's church in St. Louis and that's got to be a couple hours away."

"I thought Stephanie went to church in Herrick."

"She did. And she also went to Dupo, The Sanctuary in Hazelwood, and a couple other churches. She must have settled on Willeford's because she liked the building for the wedding."

Cara's Call

"Now, Cara."

"We're talking about Stephanie, Mom. You know how competitive she is. It's no accident that she picked this date either!"

"You don't know that!"

"I can find out," she said and hit speed dial. When Fred picked up, Cara complained, "Okay, Fred, what in the world is going on? How could she? How could Stephanie have her wedding the same day as Amanda and Greg's?"

"It's no problem, Cara. It's only an hour away so it works out just perfectly."

"It's more like two hours. I know that much."

"Still, it's not that far."

"Fred, be honest with me. Did Stephanie know Amanda was having her wedding that day?"

"I think when Amanda started talking about a Christmas wedding, Stephanie got caught up with the idea. But, Cara, I'm going to make both."

"Are you in Stephanie's bridal party?"

"Yes."

"What about pictures?"

"Oh. Hadn't thought of that."

"Fred, both Stephanie and Josh are high-profile people. If it comes down to a competition for guests, we both know where people will go." When Fred said nothing, Cara told him to go fish and hung up.

Since Cara could not bring herself to call Amanda, she phoned Amanda's mother instead. "Sister J," Cara asked, "did you hear the news?"

She had not. And while Amanda's mother did not complain about Stephanie, there was steel in her voice. "Well, then this decides it," she said.

"Decides what?" asked Cara.

"Amanda has always talked about what her perfect wedding would be. My husband and I have been exploring ways to make that happen. When you come over for your dress fitting next Saturday, I'll tell you more about it. But not a word to Amanda. Promise?"

"Sure," said Cara. The promise was easy enough to keep. She could hardly leak information she did not have.

Cara spoke in church that Sunday night. After the service, she pulled her dad aside and asked for an appointment. "When would you like to see me?" asked her father.

"Now," Cara replied, "if it works for you." Forty-five minutes after the dismissal prayer, Cara sat in front of her dad while he sat behind the desk.

Cara wasted no time. She simply said, "Dad, I want you to think about something. And it's important."

"Okay," replied Jim, his forehead creased in concern.

"I'll just say it, Dad. It might be better if you didn't have me speak anymore."

"Why's that?"

"You're going to lose people."

"Sister Pridgitt and her little group?"

"No, not them. They enjoy complaining about things too much to leave. Sister Grayson and her family."

"I don't think so. She's never complained to me."

"She's not a complainer. She's a doer. She'll talk with her feet."

"But she's submissive to her husband's wishes and he—"

"Dad, please."

Even he smiled at that. Then, he wondered at how casual Cara had become with him. In a way, he liked it. "Why do you think there will be a problem? She is a strong woman. Don't you think she would be happy that a woman is getting an opportunity to preach?"

"Not so much."

"Explain yourself."

"I don't know if I can. I'm not sure why, but I'm a threat to her. For whatever reason, she has set herself up to compete with me. She will leave. And before she does, there'll be an altercation with you. She will quit her position as church secretary and they will most certainly go to another church."

"Cara, honey. You can't know this. You're overreacting."

"Dad, a funny thing has happened to me since I started overseeing the fellowship group. I know things. Not about everyone. Not all the time. But things come to me and I know them—things mainly about the group that I oversee. Didn't that same thing happen to you when you became a pastor?"

If Cara had said that she levitated every morning, it could not have surprised Jim any more. It's not that she wasn't right. He knew things from God. About people in his church. About situations. He'd never tell anyone. He only prayed. But he thought this was his private secret, and he was the only one with whom God operated in this way. Now his daughter was speaking secret things out loud with no more caution than if she was ordering a sandwich at a corner deli.

"Dad, I think I was supposed to tell you. Now you have to decide what to do."

Cara's Call

Amanda had the bridal magazine open on the kitchen table and was pointing to the dress in the middle of the page. "It's going to be this one," she said. "Only they are going to add sleeves and raise the neckline."

"They'll do that for you?" asked Cara.

Suddenly Amanda's mom hurried in from the garage with a couple bags of groceries. "Amanda, please grab the rest of the groceries from the trunk while I take Cara in the other room to get her fitted."

Amanda had chosen two colors for the bridesmaids' dresses. As maid of honor, Cara would wear cherry blossom pink; the other girls would wear champagne. Cara's dress was long and sleek with three asymmetrical, horizontal tucks that formed classy flounces down one side. Cara loved it.

As Sister J was measuring and pinning, she whispered, "We found a carriage we can rent from Chicago."

"A carriage?"

"A Princess Carriage. Brother J can get a truck and a trailer, and there's a family in the church who raise beautiful horses, so at least my Cinderella will get her perfect wedding in one way."

Cara was beaming. "Mum's the word."

Sister J now had another request. "Cara, I'm not saying you have any direct influence on Stephanie, but could you maybe contact Fred and see if he can influence her in some way so she'll have the pictures taken before their wedding? A number of people in Stephanie's wedding party would like to come to ours too."

"I'll see what I can do."

Cara finally told Amanda what Stephanie had done. Masking her hurt, Amanda replied, "So maybe I won't have a Cinderella wedding, but at least I'm marrying my Prince Charming. And hey, my best friend is going to be my maid of honor, so I think I'm doing pretty well."

The semester flew by. Amanda's wedding rehearsal was the day after Cara's last final. She was happy for Amanda, of course, but as Cara drove over to Salem for the wedding rehearsal, two things bothered her. The first had to do with what was required of the maid of honor. If it were a Bible study or a sermon she would have been fine. But now she had to deliver a speech at the rehearsal dinner, and though the group was relatively small, a speech would be way out of Cara's comfort zone. She had thought of some funny stories to tell about things that had happened, but she was no good at telling jokes. Still, for Amanda, she would do her best.

The second problem had nothing to do with Amanda at all. It had to do with Elizabeth. Because Cara now felt responsible for her, and because there were things happening in Elizabeth's life that Cara didn't like, and because she was powerless to help, Cara looked for someplace to direct her anger. She didn't have trouble finding a target, deciding that if a certain youth leader would just do his job, Elizabeth would not be having these issues. Consequently, Cara determined to give Kevin a piece of her mind.

Although Kevin escorted her down the aisle during the rehearsal, they did not have time to talk. Cara tried to arrange to ride with him to the restaurant, but that didn't work out either. By the time she actually got to the restaurant, her maid-of-honor speech was now pressing so she was temporarily too busy to bother about Kevin. Throughout the meal, Cara kept glancing down at her prepared speech.

When Kevin raised his glass of Pepsi to toast his "little brother," friends and family snickered with delight, anticipating that Kevin would regale them with Greg's antics and accomplishments. Laughter filled the restaurant during Kevin's speech. If his narrative could be believed, Greg scarcely lived a day without adventure. At the table across from Cara, a proud mother beamed with pride in both her boys.

Now it was Cara's turn. As soon as she began telling the funny things that had happened with her and Amanda, she went off script and her nervousness evaporated. Heaping praise on Amanda was easy enough. But when she wouldn't quit, Amanda kept tugging on her sleeve until Cara finished with her ad libs.

Next, Amanda's father addressed the guests. "We are so happy that Amanda has found Greg. She calls him Prince Charming. And we think she's right. So, we have a surprise for Amanda and Greg. We want them to know how special they are to us." Brother J then directed the wedding party to look out the restaurant window where they saw a fairy tale carriage pulled by two white horses and driven by a coachman clad in tuxedo and top hat. Another spiffy coachman opened the door to the carriage and beckoned for the bridal couple. Neither coachman was dressed warmly enough for the weather that had dipped below freezing. But their smiles were genuine enough.

Everyone cheered while Greg said "cool" and investigated the horses, and Amanda embraced her father, tears of joy coursing down her cheeks. Soon Greg ran inside and said to Kevin, "Hey, you've got to see the inside of this! It's over the top!"

For whatever reason, Kevin grabbed Cara's hand and they followed Greg and Amanda to the coach. The cream-colored carriage had wooden wheels and intricate floral designs etched over the gilt finish. The horses were majestic, the carriage beautiful, and the leather cushions soft, but the open-air windows demonstrated that it was obviously made for summer excursions.

The coachman held the door of the carriage open, signaling for Amanda and Greg to get inside. "Kevin, you're coming too," said Greg. "There's a ton of room inside of this. Bring Cara."

They both protested but Greg would brook no arguments, easily shuffling them inside the carriage and into the seat opposite Amanda and himself. As soon as they were in, the coachman shut the door and signaled for the coach to be on its way.

Cara shivered a little, and Kevin put his arm around her to keep her warm. Kevin sat closer than Cara would have expected. Perhaps it was because she was uncomfortable with this or perhaps because she was already peeved with him that Cara started the conversation so abruptly.

"Kevin, I've got to talk to you about Elizabeth." It was odd conversation to be having in a Cinderella carriage, but the words just came out.

"Okay," he said, a little taken aback.

"I'm really worried about Elizabeth," she said more gently now.

"You're talking about Mark?"

"Yes. He wants life commitments at their age. He has the spiritual sensitivity of a rock. The kid is a spiritual black hole. This is just so wrong."

"True enough. I've probably got four or five wrong relationships going on right now in my youth group. It's more tangled than spaghetti."

"When Elizabeth sings and speaks, Mark pokes fun."

"Yeah, I know," he said, "but Cara, I make it a policy not to tell young people who to date. It's just too dangerous to get involved."

"I get that it's dangerous. But he wants to get married the day after they graduate from high school!"

"Listen to me, Cara. I'm trying to tell you something. Although it is my policy not to counsel young people in this way, this is one case that I made an exception. I told her to drop him.

"You did?"

"A girl has to be certain of one thing. If she is seriously considering a life partner, she should choose someone who will always accept her, someone who will not be jealous of her gifts—ever. He needs to love her for who she is."

Kevin's face was inches from hers when he said these words. Cara had a silly suspicion he might have stopped talking about Elizabeth and might have meant something more. She wasn't totally sure about it, but that didn't prevent her from blushing.

Chapter 22

Cara looked outside at the parking lot wishing for more people to come. Small piles of snow were clumped up on either end where a plow piled up the snow that had fallen earlier that week. There was plenty of room left for attendees who had not yet made an appearance. Nervously, Cara peeked into the auditorium. Amanda's wedding was going to start in five minutes and the sanctuary was only half-full. Cara grabbed her cell phone to call Fred. "Where are you guys?"

"We're halfway there."

"What's going on? You promised!"

"I know. But they were late getting started, and then we still had a couple of pictures we couldn't do before the wedding. I'm telling you, Cara, we skipped the reception! You owe me big time."

"Is it just you?"

"No, I've got some people with me."

"Are we talking seven or ten people or what?"

"Umm, I would say...close to fifty or sixty. We've got a caravan of cars and we're breaking the speed limit."

"Okay, I'll see what I can do about stalling." And though she did not want to parade back and forth in her dress, Cara passed through the church to find the pastor in the office behind the sanctuary. *The Nutcracker* suite played in the sanctuary. It would have to play awhile longer.

A half hour later, more than fifty young people swarmed into the building. Shortly thereafter Kevin escorted Cara down the aisle. Her vice-like grip on his arm could have brought a man to his knees. He leaned in to say softly, "You look very pretty." She smiled a thank you, but did not loosen her grip. She knew he was just trying to distract her from a panic attack she had told him she felt was coming on. Five pews down the aisle, Fred flashed Cara a thumbs-up. They made it to the front without incident and turned to face the audience.

Everyone stood and every head swiveled to watch Amanda as she came down the aisle on her father's arm. Loose ringlets framed the bride's face and her hair cascaded down her back. She wore a princess tiara and a glossy satin dress studded with seed pearls and draped with illusion. A long train flowed behind it, and she carried roses that echoed the pink and champagne colors of the bridesmaids' dresses. Cara knew the pictures would be perfect. As was Amanda. She shone.

Pastor Jean asked, "Who gives this woman to be married to this man?"

"Her mother and I do," replied a proud father. Amanda must have found five-inch heels, because now she stood only a few inches shorter than Greg. Both towered above her father.

Throughout the ceremony the flower girl waved at her mother, fidgeted, and dumped the rest of her rose petals on the carpet, so Cara tried to distract her by speaking softly about her aunt Amanda and her new uncle Greg. She adjusted Amanda's train and held the bridal bouquet at the appropriate times, and remained alert for anything else she could do to help. Fulfilling her maid of honor role kept her mind off her nervousness.

When each pastor pronounced a blessing on Greg and Amanda, Cara was genuinely proud that neither pastor had to lie about the young adults who stood before them. Greg grinned and kissed his bride. Up to now, everything about the wedding had felt just right.

But when the organ trumpeted the recessional and the wedding party turned to face the audience, Cara's heartbeat quickened and she felt dizzy. She had just taken a deep breath and willed herself to calm down when she spotted Justin, her Greek god, in the third row, sporting a tuxedo adorned with a deep red rose. The split second she made eye contact with him, he gave her a wink that shattered the last shred of Cara's composure. She could feel thousands of eyes staring at her, tens of thousands of assessments aimed at her, and millions of reasons why they all found her wanting.

The step down from the platform to the floor suddenly seemed like a ten-foot drop. She felt her brain fade, her forehead break out in sweat, and she quickly began to sway. "Hold me," she said, clutching Kevin's arm in a death grip.

Because Cara's face had blanched and she seemed frozen in place, Kevin braced her up with an arm around her back, practically supporting her entire weight. The whole audience seemed to hold its collective breath while Kevin helped her negotiate the step and move down the aisle. Heads turned, not wanting to miss the unfolding drama. As soon as they exited the auditorium, Kevin guided her to a quiet spot in the foyer and gently lowered her to one of the benches.

"You okay?" he asked.

"Not really," came the faint answer.

"Put your head down," he said.

When she did, color came back into her face—if nothing else—from embarrassment.

"The receiving line starts here," someone yelled, but Kevin did not leave her side. Long after she required it, he supported her, walking her slowly over to the receiving line and giving the guests one-handed greetings without loosening his hold on Cara. Once she started to tell him to ease his grip but then decided it felt good to be held.

She had just eased into a chair at the long reception table where the bridal party was seated when Justin leaned over the table and pushed his grinning face into her personal space. "Hey, doll."

"Hmmm. You look very wedding-ish," she said to him, ignoring the veiled compliment.

"Well, I was just as surprised as you when they asked me last week to be a groomsman for that other wedding, but it doesn't take that long to rent these things, you know."

"I suppose someone must have dropped out. I didn't know you were that close to Josh."

"I'm not. Actually, Stephanie asked me."

"Oh. But you must have left before the reception. What did they think about—"

"Couldn't be helped. I actually came to see you."

"About what?"

"About you going out with me. I've got tickets to a Christian concert in St. Louis in January."

He didn't expect to be refused. She could see that. "I don't know."

"It's a Saturday night. No school."

"Well, okay. Sounds great then."

Because Cara had been the keeper of the keys, she welcomed Amanda and Greg back to their apartment. Kevin, who had picked them up from the airport in St. Louis, followed them inside dragging Greg's monster suitcase. "Hey bro," he said to Greg, "I'm surprised you took your rock collection on your honeymoon. Don't the airlines charge you for every extra ounce now?"

"Well, a honeymoon only happens once, so I figure that—"

"Do you like my tan?" interrupted Amanda.

"Looks more like a burn," said Kevin.

"Oh, Cara, I love your coat. Is that the coat you got for the big date?" she asked.

"Well, not specifically for the date," Cara replied happily, "but you never know how January weather will be in St. Louis. I paid twice what I've paid for any coat in my life even though it was half price on winter clearance, but I love the leather."

"Me, too. That's a good color of brown for you."

"Did Amanda tell you that the teens from Charlestown are going?" said Kevin.

"Where?"

"To the concert."

"You've got to be kidding. Your whole group is going?"

"Yes," said Amanda. "It's really not that far over to St. Louis, and when I told Greg you were going, he told Kevin, and the long and short of it is that we will be at the family arena the same night you're there with Justin."

"Sounds nice," said Cara in a tone that hinted she meant the opposite. However, before Cara left the apartment she drew Amanda into one of the bedrooms and spoke more plainly. "Amanda, what in the world were you thinking to—"

"It wasn't me. I had no idea Kevin would get it into his head to crash your party. I'm so sorry." She brightened. "But it is open seating, so you can sit as far away from our group as you want."

Cara didn't want Justin coming inside, so as soon as his car turned into the driveway, she was out the front door calling out that she would be back later.

"Now, who did you say she's going out with?" asked Jim, looking up from the paper.

"His name's Justin," said Karen.

"Something wrong with him that I can't meet him?" Jim mentioned as he looked out the front window. "What in the world?" he said in shock. "That guy's driving a 'vette. And it's only two years old if I'm not mistaken."

"And how would you know that?"

"Just guessing. It looks like he's got a little bit of money."

"His parents do. His father got his start in construction and now owns a pretty significant business up near Chicago."

"Cara tell you all this?"

"No. Amanda's mom. She doesn't like him."

"Well, I wonder what he's doing with Cara. I don't know too many ministers with Corvettes. Does he plan to get into ministry?"

"I'm thinking ministry is the last thing on his mind."

"So I was wondering what it would be like kissing a minister," said Justin, backing out of the driveway.

Not a good start, thought Cara, and countered with "Amanda and Greg are coming to the concert."

"Oh," he said, obviously not liking the news.

"And there will be a few young people from church as well."

"What?" came the sudden, almost angry reply.

Cara was enjoying the exchange and dug deeper. "Yeah, I think about twenty-five or so, but the auditorium seats several thousand, and since there is open seating, we may not even see them."

Vette-Man, as she now began to think of him, revved up the car and started driving faster. He said he wanted to get to the concert early so they could get good seats. But once they arrived, good seats were the last thing from his mind. Instead, he directed Cara to the section farthest away from the stage; the darkest place in the arena.

Satisfied, he helped her out of her coat. As he did so, Vette-Man brushed his hand all the way down her back, touching her inappropriately. Cara spun away and turned to look at him, sure that he would apologize for accidentally touching her in that way. Instead, he served up a teasing smile. Then, he undressed her with his eyes. Cara excused herself to find the restroom. She didn't return until the first number had already begun.

At intermission, Amanda's phone was buzzing. Not just a text. A call. It was Cara.

"Meet me at the restroom to the left of the platform!" came the rushed appeal.

"Cara! What is wrong with you? Are you all right? Too many people? What!"

"Just come! Now!"

When Amanda entered the arena-sized restroom, twenty or thirty women were milling about. But no Cara. Amanda thought that perhaps she had the wrong restroom and was about to text her when she heard soft sobbing coming from behind the door of one of the stalls.

"Cara?"

The bolt unlocked itself and Cara came out, embracing Amanda but saying nothing. Her eyes were red. Yet, she was clearly in control of herself. After a few moments, she said, "Amanda, I don't know what I was thinking. This date with Justin was one big mistake." Amanda just listened—her silence inviting Cara to continue.

"I fought him off the whole first half and I will not take another minute of it. He is a total jerk!"

"Do you have your purse?" she said.

"Yes."

"Come sit with us. We have an extra seat."

"Can I ride with you and Greg back home?"
"Oh, Cara, we're staying in St. Louis, but I'll work something out."

Cara was already twenty minutes outside of St. Louis traveling east on I-64 when her phone rang. She said, "Hello," but had to plug one ear to really hear because of all the noise in the vehicle. "Sorry. What?" she said. "You'll have to speak up. The kids on the van are pretty pumped after the concert…what?" But it was simply too loud.

Finally, because he was apparently shouting into the phone, she was able to get most of what he said. She replied, "No, I won't be needing a ride…no…don't worry about it…yes, I'll be taken right to my house." And then, she replied once more, "No, you don't need to bring my coat to my house. In fact, you can keep the coat." Then she hung up.

Cara was sitting shotgun, the passenger side in the front seat of the van. There was so much racket that no one even heard the exchange. No one, that is, except Kevin, who was driving. He didn't say a word. Even after he dropped off all the kids and then drove another hour and a half to her house, he required nothing more. He simply let the music play and silence be his guide. She was never more grateful.

A week later, Kevin showed up at work. "I have this for you," he said, handing her the leather coat.

Cara's smile was wide and her eyes danced with delight and gratitude. As Kevin turned to head back out, she said, "Wait! Are you leaving?"

"Yes, I've got some things that—"

"Hey, you just can't leave like that. I want to take you to lunch."

"It's only eleven o'clock."

"Wait right there." Cara spoke to her manager and hurried back to speak to Kevin, "If you wait twenty minutes, I can take an early lunch."

"All right then, I'll be back in twenty minutes."

"Meet me over at Subway," she shouted to him as he went out the door. He evidently had heard, because he was waving and nodding his head as he got into his car.

Though she was a little embarrassed, Cara wore the leather coat over to Subway. It felt so good to have the expensive coat back again.

"Okay, is there a story here?" she asked, signaling for Kevin to stand in line with her to order.

"I wish I could come up with something lively, but I'm afraid there was no drama. I just asked him if he could drop your coat by the church when he was in the area and he did. I never even saw him."

"Your gallantry shall not go unrewarded. Anything on the menu and up to half my kingdom," she said.

She wanted him to act like a knight, speak with an old English accent and talk about her honor in a rather chivalrous way. But he just smiled at her. This was the downside of being with a guy who is of the "what you see is what you get" variety, yet she quickly recovered and realized she had something important to say to him.

"By the way, Kevin, I wanted to tell you that when I talked to Elizabeth the other day, my take is that she is doing much better. Still, she's really worrying about finding a guy who will be a good fit for her ministry. Almost to the point of obsessing."

"So I take it, you are telling her not to worry about it."

"Kevin, she's sixteen. Of course she is going to worry about it."

"But is Elizabeth's ministry contingent upon her finding the right person?"

"I'm not sure what you're really asking."

"Would she have a ministry even if she never marries? Or does she absolutely need a man to complete her?"

"Well, marriage is kind of a scriptural pattern, you know."

"But Cara, think of this emotional drain that she has all the time. Every day she is so anxious that she's not going to be able find the right guy that she is constantly distracted. So, how can we help her beat that?"

"Well, I've been telling her that she should discover her own gifts and make the most of them. She should be sensitive to God's voice, you know, walking though doors as God opens them." As Cara talked, she realized she had never noticed how nice looking Kevin was; how his eyes flashed when he spoke about things that mattered to him.

"Okay, you've said all that and it's not working. What next?" asked Kevin.

"Hey! Why is this my responsibility all of a sudden?"

"It's rhetorical. Because I think there is one more thing Elizabeth can do that will have incredible power."

"Okay, speak forth, oh mighty sage," said Cara teasingly.

Kevin did not play along. "Let me tell you what happened to me. I was in a pretty serious relationship with a girl. And it didn't work out. It was totally my fault, and she dropped me for good reasons."

Just as Cara was relishing the thought that Kevin was announcing himself available to her, he said something that at once made her hate him. He said, "And that's when I told God, 'Lord, I give you my future. If I marry or if I never marry, I release that to you.'"

Cara willed herself to maintain a poker face, though she did not feel it at all.

"Here's what happened, Cara. I felt a freedom I never thought that I could have. I have peace about the future, and I feel comfortable in my skin."

"How long ago was this?" asked Cara, evenly.

"It's been almost a year ago now."

"And you're saying that Elizabeth should do that?" she asked, not thinking at all about Elizabeth's issues but rather her own.

"I'm not telling you anything, Cara. I'm just sharing my experience. But in my heart of hearts, I believe it would help Elizabeth. I'm not saying you have to share this with her. But you could think about it."

Cara mentally said goodbye to Kevin as an option while verbally thanking him one more time for getting back her leather coat.

"Cara, I want to be there for you," he said, "and if there's anything I can ever do for you, I will."

Chapter 23

It was Tuesday. They were in the middle of the racquetball game when Bob said, "You'll never guess who visited our Sunday service. I would have called before but I knew I'd see you today.

"Was it the Graysons?" asked Jim.

"Yep."

"Well, I think they'll probably be coming your way."

"Man, you've depended on them since you started. She's been so loyal to you through all that mess with those people opposing you at the beginning. That's a big hit."

"Yeah."

"What happened?"

"Cara."

Bob said, "She's against women in ministry, isn't she? Jim, I told you this would lead to trouble."

"I don't think she's against women in ministry. Just one woman in particular. After I had Cara preach a week ago Sunday, she came to see me to tell me they would be transferring their membership someplace else."

"Bro—!"

They continued with the game. Nobody spoke. Ten minutes later Bob finally said, "Jim, I'm on your side, and I'm not one to say I told you so…"

But Jim would have none of it. "Say, Bob, didn't you lose a family when you put Fred in as your youth leader?"

"Two."

Nothing more was said for the rest of the game.

Kevin called her two weeks later. He started talking about Elizabeth but quickly turned the conversation in her direction. There was no pressure. He was a good listener. Before long, Cara had shared more than she intended about her struggles with her father.

Cara's Call

A week later, he called again. By the time he called the third week, he knew even more about Cara's struggles than Amanda did. Then, because Cara had met with Elizabeth the previous weekend, he asked her if she had talked to Elizabeth about releasing her rights to the Lord.

"No."

"Okay."

"See, Kevin, I'm not at all sure that I agree with you on this one."

"Okay. No pressure on my part then."

"I kind of think there is another way to approach this. I think Elizabeth should pray for the man she's going to marry. Pray for him every day. And pray that God will keep him and guide him and direct him so he matures in Christ and is ready when they marry."

"You told her that?"

"No. I didn't tell her anything. But that is just what I do—pray for the Lord to prepare my future husband."

"It's good with me," said Kevin. "I will not fault you."

Cara continued, "I have always been sure that God would bring the right person into my life."

"To complete you?"

"Well, not exactly that. But it's in the Bible after all that two will become one flesh. So you can't get rid of it. Kevin, I know what you're saying. I've studied Colossians 2 and what it teaches about us already being complete in Christ. I suppose that is what you were going for when you talked about being complete, isn't it?"

"That's what the Lord promises, doesn't He?"

"Okay, so part of me thinks you're right. That I'm okay. No, that I'm complete in Christ. That I don't need anyone else. I get that. But Kevin, there's a really big part of me that really would like to 'one flesh' with someone who is of a kindred spirit, so I'm not sure I can really buy where you end up going with this."

"Cara. I'm your biggest fan. I brag about you all the time. If you disagree, I'm totally fine with that. But I've got to tell you, my commitment to God has worked for me."

Cara switched cleaning nights with her mom because of homework, but the following Saturday night was her turn, and she was at the church vacuuming. As usual, the praise music blared over the church loudspeakers so she could hear it over the vacuum. For some reason, she was drawn to the altar area where a year earlier God had called her. Further, she was also drawn to Kevin's words, and she wondered what could actually be accomplished by the sort of commitment he suggested. Then she wondered what would happen if she didn't make such a commitment, whether, say, her not making such a commitment would come between her and God's precious promises to her. She doubted it. And she didn't really feel any conviction to do it.

"What a funny thing," she thought. "I gave everything to God, and now I find out there's something more I could give."

The music played and the vacuum roared, and Cara began to reflect on the very bumpy road that she had been walking since saying "yes" to God. Yet, thinking of the adventure she'd been on, she saw clearly that she would not have traded it for anything in the world. Despite Josh and Stephanie, there was Marta and Ron. There were also all their friends who were being affected by her call. Further, there was that incredible sense, an indescribable rush that she felt last Sunday night when she spoke. She was saying something for the Lord that would actually help change the world.

Cara simply let the vacuum run and went to the altar, intent on saying a sentence or two of commitment. "God, I want to give You this part of my life. In a way, I already have. Because I never again want to date someone who is not consecrated. Nor will I marry anyone outside Your will. So, I think that's enough."

Cara started to get up but then lingered. How long she knelt there she could not say. Eventually, she offered, "Lord, let me try again. I don't think I was putting conditions on You, but just in case, here's the deal. I release my right to get married, for you to find me a husband...Prince Charming or whoever. And if it is Your will, I will serve You as a single woman. And I will be the best—whatever it is you're making me—that I can possibly be. And, I...praise You that I am single."

She did cry—but not as much as she thought she would. She thought she would feel something, but there was nothing. Nothing good or bad. Not until she was driving home did she did feel a little lighter, a little freer. She would never be able to explain the feeling to anyone. She and God had had the talk. It was no one's business but hers. Not her mom or dad's. Not Amanda's. And certainly not Kevin's. She wasn't telling anyone a thing.

But of course, habits of thinking require that commitments be made more than once. And the truth of the matter is that Cara would have to make that same commitment three more times in the next six weeks. When she journaled about it, she asked, "Is this a commitment I would recommend to others?" She thought the question would be easy to answer, but when she put the pen to the paper, she wrote nothing; then, after a little while, she wrote, "I'll have to think about it."

Kevin called once a week. He almost always talked forty-five minutes. Cara wondered if he timed their conversations. She wondered if he had several people he did phone ministry with, and if they each got forty-five minutes of his time. But, of course, she never asked him.

Kevin had an intuitive gift to draw her out, to set the stage for her to share and for him to listen. Cara couldn't exactly explain how he did it. Further, because he seldom forced an issue, when he did bring up something disagreeable, she wasn't put off. Like during the conversation they'd had the night before when he revisited her calling.

"Let me get this straight, Cara. You are called to pastor, right?"

"Yes. You and Amanda are the only ones I've shared that vision with, or whatever it was."

"Okay, good enough. I'm really happy for you. But here's my question: have you ever actually explained this to your dad?"

"I've talked to him, yes. He knows about my call."

"Oh, good. I'm glad. What does he think of the idea of you pastoring?"

"Well, he knows about my call to preach."

"Oh," he said, pausing for her to continue.

"But I wouldn't exactly say he knows about the pastoring part."

"Okay."

"Kevin, you have no idea what I'm going through here. My father really can't go that far. Not yet, anyway."

"Okay.

"I did tell him about my calling. That's something."

"Yes, you did, Cara. You trusted the Lord and honored your father by giving him that information."

"I don't like the way you just put that. You're not implying that I'm not trusting the Lord or honoring my father by not talking about this other, are you? Because I'm just using wisdom, Kevin."

"I understand."

"No, Kevin. I don't think you do. It was great talking with you tonight, but I've got some homework I need to do."

Four weeks into the second semester the crisis came unexpectedly for both Cara and her father. He had asked Cara to think about taking the position of the church secretary, the one now vacant because of the family who had left the church. Cara had absolutely no desire to take the position, but she couldn't bring herself to say no because she felt it was on account of her that the secretary had left the church.

"Dad, I'm not sure I have the time," she said when he pressed her about it.

"It won't take that much time," he countered.

"Dad, if you really need me to do this, then I will do it. But I have to be honest. I don't want to. And frankly, I am wondering if I should not be concentrating on other things."

"Nonsense. You are called into ministry. This is the next step. The Lord called you, Cara. It is up to you to do what He called you to do."

"But I'm pretty sure that being a church secretary isn't the direction the Lord wants me to go."

"Well, what is it that you believe the Lord called you to do?"

"Dad, I need you to pray about something with me."

"Sure, honey."

"You remember I talked to you about how I sometimes have a sense of knowing things…you know, how God is talking to me?"

"Yes," he said, sounding more apprehensive than he meant.

"Well, it's about my future. When God called me to preach, it was to do more than just preaching."

"And this church secretary position would be more than just preaching."

"That's true, Dad. And I really appreciate you thinking of me. It's just that I'm talking about something else. Dad, I can't explain it totally, but I saw myself shepherding people, and they were all different ethnic groups, and I was helping them to—"

"Are you saying God's called you to be a missionary?"

Cara knew that whatever she said next would likely change everything, but she still did not hold back. "No, Dad, God called me to be a pastor."

Cara wasn't sure what she expected her father to say. Perhaps maybe a warning that she should be careful and cautious and to really pray about such a thing. Cara had prepared for something else as well—she thought her father might rebuke her, tell her that the Lord didn't speak to her. But she never could have anticipated the silence. After many long seconds had passed, her father said he needed to go do something and simply walked away. The conversation's abrupt ending unnerved her.

She didn't wait for Kevin to call but phoned him to explain what had happened.

"I am so sorry," he repeated several times.

For twenty minutes she rehashed the scene over and over. He gave no advice—only listened. Finally, she ended with, "So I don't know where that leaves me."

"Do you mean, in your relationship with your father?"

"I mean with my father, with church, with preaching, with my fellowship group, with my future. I am so totally confused and without direction. Kevin, where does that leave me?"

He had earned the right to speak, because he had listened. But she still didn't like his response—not at all.

"Where does that leave you? Dependent on the Lord. And that's not always such a bad thing, is it?"

"Kevin, I hate to say it, but that sounds pretty canned."

"Cara, there is no way I could know what you're feeling right now. I admit that. I apologize if I'm sounding trite. I don't mean to. But I do know a little bit about pain. Mine is not the same as yours. I get that. But almost all my growing up years I've lived without having a father who was there for me. I've done my share of hurting and being empty and praying and wondering why God allowed it."

"I'm sorry, Kevin. Sometimes I act like I'm the center of the universe."

"Cara, I'm not rebuking you. You honor me by sharing your feelings."

"Here's my problem, Kevin. I don't know what to do next. Do I assume that I can still keep doing the same things in church? Should I give up the idea of pastoring because my father doesn't approve?"

"Yeah, it's tough. I don't know. Maybe just keep doing the kinds of things you are doing. Journal about your dreams. Keep them alive that way. Maybe journal about what you think an ideal church would be like. Think about your pastoral gifts and how you envision yourself in leadership."

"I could do that. But it might just be too discouraging. I mean, will I ever have any use for the information once I write it down?"

"I don't know. But if you come up with something, I'd love for you to share it with me."

"And that's not being rebellious or getting ahead of God?"

"I suppose it might be. I'm a little confused on it myself. But for now, why don't we just think of it as a way for you to act in faith, believing that God will ultimately fulfill what he said He would do through you."

Chapter 24

Jim was hurting. Not so much for himself but for Cara. When she first said she was called, he went along with that. He let her preach. She wasn't that good at it. He offered helpful suggestions. She didn't receive them too well. But now this! Now, she was called to pastor, although the facts were plain. Why, just standing in front of an audience gave her a panic attack. Called to pastor, indeed! He just needed wisdom on how to let her down easily.

Jim tried to imagine Cara attempting to pastor someone like Sandra, and he laughed out loud. The only thing that prevented him from just telling her—the only thing—was what his wife had said to him that night. That if he crushed their daughter, she would never speak to him again. Of course, she hadn't meant it. But Jim couldn't get the words out of his mind. So, because he couldn't think of anything to say to Cara that would not crush her, he hadn't spoken to her at all for about three weeks.

What he needed was for Karen to be on his side. That might not be easy. She would likely bring up how good Cara was in Sunday school and how she oversaw a minimum of fifteen young adults that came every Friday night to the fellowship meeting.

That was another thing. Up until now, he hadn't really thought that much about what it was Cara did on Friday night. The more he considered it, the more he realized she must not really be leading the group. It would be impossible. Not with her phobias. Still, if she wasn't leading the group, then who was?

It wasn't as if he was looking for ammunition to talk to his wife. Nor was it exactly true that Jim was trying to eavesdrop. While it would be accurate to say that up until now he had never used his office to study during the fellowship meeting, this didn't mean he could not be in there while the meeting was taking place. Part of their original agreement was that he could use his office if he wanted to do so. Further, he really did need to study for his Sunday morning message.

Jim could hear Marta tuning her guitar. Like every other Friday, they came downstairs joking and laughing. They came in all shapes and sizes and in every kind of getup. It amazed Jim how young adults, who barely believed in God, sang

Cara's Call

along and even prayed, laughed, and talked. He could hear Cara superintending things, but there were also other voices that she must have brought into leadership. He recognized Ron's voice, and there were some other voices he didn't recognize.

After a couple of choruses, Cara led the group in prayer, although there was quite a bit of back-and-forth discussion with it. After two or three gave advice about some girl's issues, Cara stopped the discussion and said, "Okay, Christina, that's a special problem. I get it. Nothing about it is easy. Let's bind this thing in Jesus' name."

And they did. Believer and nonbeliever alike, as easily as if she had asked them to check a box about whether or not they liked french fries. Several in the group apparently laid hands on Christina, but nothing about it seemed forced.

He heard someone say, "Johnny is really flipped out on drugs again. He'd gotten into some trouble, but he's been out now for a couple of months. He's calling me, trying to intimidate me sexually."

How can they talk about stuff so easily? thought Jim. Then he heard Cara's voice. "Let's pray for protection for Marta." This must have been that same stepbrother who came for Marta's baptism.

After they prayed, Cara taught a lesson of sorts. Actually, what she did was to read a scripture in Matthew, give a biblical principle, and then ask some convoluted question, challenging them to come up with answers. Small groups discussed the question for ten minutes. Then, she called on first one and then another. She was clearly steering the discussion in an attempt to reinforce the principle she was teaching. Yet, when someone charged God with not being fair, she didn't react. She replied, "So okay, that's a good question. And I sometimes wonder about that myself. Any responses?"

Ron told about how his life had been messed up, and how he blamed God, and how everything changed in one night, and how he was now changing the world. He wasn't preaching, he wasn't bragging, he wasn't even trying. But when he ended, it sounded as if he was choking on tears.

A holy hush fell on the group. Jim could feel it.

"Okay, God is here," he heard Cara say quietly. "I know that sometimes I don't think I deserve God's blessing or that He's not really concerned about my struggles. But then I realize there is no problem too big or small for Him. Right now, all you've got to do is ask. And God will hear your prayer."

Unbidden, several people stood and started laying hands on each other. The sounds of prayer would sometimes crescendo, then soften in intensity. The ebb and flow didn't seem to bother anyone and went on for quite awhile.

David S. Norris

Jim cracked the door to see out of his office. He wasn't comfortable with the fact that one girl was hugging a guy and crying. Cara didn't seem to be on top of that. Gradually, things got quieter, and then the group transitioned into a chorus.

When the talking began again, one guy, who was apparently new, said icily, "If all the churches were sold, we could feed the hungry in Africa."

Cara didn't punt; she asked for no one's help or support. She said, "You make a good point, Edmond. I appreciate that we need to do more for the poor. Thank you. And I've thought a lot about church buildings. So let me tell you what I've been thinking.

"Let's say that I have a chair I use every day from which I read my Bible and pray, where I talk to the Lord and listen to Him. Further, what if I reserve that chair for that purpose only? Would that be a special chair?"

"Sure."

"The Bible has a word for things that are set aside in that way. Because these things are dedicated to God and His purposes, we call them holy."

"I get that," said someone else.

"All right, then. Let's suppose a number of people got together, and covenanted that they would pray for one another and love one another, and that they would learn how to renew that commitment by working together. Then, what if they decided to meet in a building and dedicate the building for that same purpose? See, that's what we call the church. And it's holy. Not in a magical way. But because we have dedicated that space for that purpose."

"Yeah, but why do churches have to be so ornate?" asked Edmond.

"Good question," said Cara. "And I have to admit, there are some pretty fancy-schmancy churches. But from my experience, most churches aren't that way. In fact, in the places where Christianity is making the biggest impact in terms of growth, meeting places are often very simple.

"We should not be quick to condemn others, because buildings serve a genuine purpose. And another thing. I have never heard anyone ask that we sell hundred-million dollar football stadiums to feed the hungry—or art museums, or symphony halls. So, pardon me if I'm a little suspicious of the motive behind at least some people's critique."

Questions went back and forth. Comments and testimonies got sprinkled together. Yet, Edmond apparently wasn't finished, and after a while he asked, "So what about it, Cara? Am I going to hell if I don't believe in your version of Christianity? Do you insist that I say everything you say and do everything you do or be lost?"

Cara's Call

Cara responded, "Thanks for that question. But I wonder if the question might be better if it were framed differently. Christianity isn't about a list of rules or boxes you check when you've accomplished certain things. It is about relationship. When people ask me 'Is this a heaven or hell issue?' it makes me think that they may have mistakenly reduced Christianity to accomplishing certain tasks when in fact Christianity is so much more than that. Let me give you an example. What if, when my mom asked my dad to go to the store for a loaf of bread, he responded, 'Is that a divorce or marriage issue?' While marriage is not the same as Christianity, what I'm trying to say is that marriage, like Christianity, cannot be reduced to rules. It is a relationship."

Edmond was still not finished. "It seems that you are in charge here, Cara, and I have to tell you I think you might be ignoring people who have legitimate opinions. Does that sort of attitude demonstrate the love of Christ? It might be better if we just talked 'Jesus' at Starbucks rather than having your version of Christian values imputed on us."

Cara answered the challenge in kind, countering, "Edmond, let's suppose you were hired to teach a kindergarten class. Would you be imposing your values on them if you organized the class?"

"No, but—"

"And in fact, could a kindergarten class exist without someone in charge?"

"Well, no."

"Here's the neat thing about God. He has given gifts to those who have covenanted together to serve Him. In Ephesians 4:11, the Bible says He has given the gift of leaders."

Jim leaned closer to the door. She was talking about the five-fold ministry.

Cara continued. "I didn't ask God to do it. In fact, I have run from it. But He has made me a leader, not for my good, but for the good of the church. So here's the deal, Edmond. If you get five people together at Starbucks, within ten minutes time, someone will have emerged as a leader. You can't help it. It happens in every group. That person may not have a title, but he or she is looked to because of their personality or gifts or whatever.

"And I have another problem with just talking about Jesus at Starbucks. That sort of fellowship gets pretty thin. Because if people are really going to be in relationship with God and each other, then there is another word that has to kick in: commitment. And unless I am willing to give everything I can for you, Edmond, then I've got to say, I am not committed to you.

"Being a Christian is being a part of a community of people who have covenanted with each other on the deepest level. And that blows any discussion at

Starbucks all to pieces. In fact, this is what it means to be a Christian. It consumes my whole life."

Edmond didn't like being bested and notched up the intensity once again. "Okay, but I'm talking about the external things you seem to be imposing on people, Cara. The long hair, the dress, all of it. I've got to tell you, it strikes me as bondage and hypocrisy."

Cara was equal to the challenge. She said sternly, "Edmond, we've never told anyone how to dress for this meeting. You can wear a dress or loin cloth for all I care. But I will not be mocked in my commitments to Jesus. I wear long hair because it is biblical. I wear skirts because it is my genuine expression and celebration of who I am as a woman in Christ. And nobody is going to 'hypocratize' or 'bondagize' me out of what I do out of genuine celebration of how God made me and the fact that He saved me."

A brief silence ensued; then Marta announced that she had a song. They sang, and afterward, Ron prayed a blessing on everyone. Then they started milling up the stairs. Jim stayed in his office to think.

As the voices died down, Jim began working on the Sunday morning message. A half hour passed. Hurried footsteps on the floor above broke his concentration. Then the urgent sound of someone racing down the basement stairs. Suddenly, Cara burst unbidden into his office.

"Dad, you've got to come with me right now. Johnny's got a knife and he's threatening Marta."

Jim leaped to his feet and hurried to the garage. As the garage door was rolling up, he thought, "And that's why it's a man's job to pastor. Situations like this."

Cara had her phone on speaker. It rang twice before a voice answered. "Nine-one-one, what is your emergency?"

Cara replied, "There is a man with a knife threatening his stepsister. He is high on drugs and is not at all rational."

"Do you have an address and are you present at the scene?"

Cara rattled off the apartment number, explaining, "We are en route. But you'd better hurry. He's pounding on the door to her apartment, threatening to break it down."

"We're on our way. Please do not approach the man yourself."

"Ma'am, he will do physical harm and will sexually assault his stepsister if the police do not arrive before he breaks down that door."

"We're on our way, ma'am. Now if you could stay on the line so I could get some more details, I will take care of this…"

Cara's Call

By the time Cara and Jim arrived, the police had Johnny in handcuffs and were stuffing him into the back of their squad car.

"Dad, you've got to go embrace Marta. Don't say anything. Just hold her. Okay?"

Jim felt like a schoolchild being told what to do, but he obeyed. Marta sobbed and sobbed.

Cara stood nearby talking to one of the officers who was writing notes for the police report. Jim continued to hold the sobbing girl. Then Ron drove up, grabbed a baseball bat from the seat, and got out of the car. Cara caught sight of him and discreetly shook her head. He put the bat back in his car.

As Marta continued to cry, Jim realized she must not have been able to bring herself to call the police on her stepbrother. Probably because she knew he would go back to jail. But she had called Ron. And he had called Cara. Cara did not hesitate to call the police.

When it was all over, Cara left Ron in the apartment with Marta. Jim didn't think that was a good idea, but he didn't seem to be in charge of things. He and Cara walked out to the car. Jim felt stupid and unneeded. But then, he turned to see tears streaming down Cara's face. She walked over to him, and like she did when she was a little girl she said, "Hold me, Daddy." He did and she wept—wept like she was five years old.

"No," he decided silently, "women shouldn't pastor. They just don't have the emotional makeup for it."

"No, Dad," argued Sandra. "It's not the most sacrilegious thing ever. Texting in church is the same thing as passing notes used to be." It was the Shepherd family's weekly meal and argument at Ruby Tuesday.

"But they need to carve out some time for the Word of God. They're not putting Christ first. Like this morning—it's an affront to God if they text during the preaching!"

"Dad, I hate to say it, but they're addicted. They can't help themselves, yet if a preacher engages them, they will listen."

"Preachers shouldn't be held hostage to whether or not—"

"Cara doesn't have to work at it during her fellowship meeting. She's not out inviting the masses to come. Do they text during her deal? No!"

"They talk is what they do. How much learning can be—"

"A whole lot, Dad."

"And they argue."

"You don't know. You've never gone."

"No. But Friday, I was studying in my office—" began Jim.

"You were snooping!" retorted Sandra.

"I overheard," he said defensively. "I have a right as a pastor and father to know what is going on, don't I?"

Sandra was about to score big on this one. She said, "Why do I get the feeling that someone was eavesdropping on the—"

"Sandra, that is enough."

Having had the last word, Sandra took a different tack. "And you're saying it was just a bunch of arguing?"

Cara looked at him, and Jim could see a pained expression. He couldn't press the point, even if it might help win his argument. "Well, no. It was actually very good. But there was that one guy who was giving Cara a hard time. Some sinner criticizing the church."

The conversation stopped and all eyes were on Cara. It was clear that she didn't want to talk. But when the pause continued, she offered, "Actually, I don't have trouble with kids who are sinners. This was a church kid I was trying to help. He's been struggling a lot. I know I said I wouldn't take any more of them, but he hasn't been going to church and he's been working through a lot of issues.

"Dad, I would have talked to you about it," she continued, and was ready to explain that she couldn't because he had stopped talking to her, but instead said, "except that you've been pretty busy lately."

"What's his name?" asked Sandra.

"Edmond."

"Edmond Johnson!" exclaimed Sandra. "That guy got a girl pregnant and made her get an abortion. He should be shot."

Shay looked up from his texting, now that the conversation had gotten interesting. Karen suddenly said, "You know what? I heard that Edmond's sister just got married. She married that nice boy from Kankakee."

Jim could see that Sandra was about to unload some more about Edmond. He mused to himself, *That's why women should never pastor. They just tell way too much.*

Of course, Sandra obliged him. "I'm telling you that the kid is bad news. And then he has the gall to show his face and cause problems," she said, launching a seven-minute monologue.

Jim couldn't help notice that Cara was red with embarrassment but said nothing more. *Another reason why women should not be allowed to pastor*, he thought to himself. *They can't keep women quiet who talk too much.*

Chapter 25

Later that afternoon, Jim said to his wife, "You know Cara talked to me about having a call to pastor, didn't you?"

Karen, who was sitting on the couch, didn't even look over to her husband in the recliner. Nor did she put down the Sunday paper she was reading.

"She didn't talk to me about it," neither confirming nor denying her knowledge of Cara's belief that she should pastor.

"You also know how I feel about these things," he said.

Karen nodded ever so slightly. She was clearly not going to argue. So that was good. He allowed the silence to hang in limbo awhile before adding, "Pastoring is part of the five-fold ministry. Definitely not something a woman is equipped to handle emotionally." Karen continued reading the paper, not replying.

"What do you think about it?" he insisted.

"What do I think about what, dear?"

"What do you think about what I said?"

"You mean…about pastoring?"

"Yes."

There was a pause; Karen was clearly choosing her words carefully. "Well, what is it exactly that a pastor does, Jim?"

"You know good and well, Karen. A pastor has a church, and he is the undershepherd of the sheep."

Karen nodded, agreeing. She paused so long that he thought she had finished speaking. Then she asked, "So, if a pastor didn't have a church building, he wouldn't be a pastor?"

"He would still be a pastor."

"Oh."

Karen paused again, and for the second time, Jim thought the discussion was over. But then she asked, "And if he had a church building but no people, would he be a pastor?"

He hesitated momentarily before replying, "No, I suppose not."

She paused for effect, then asked, "Do all the people in your church listen to you equally?"

"No, of course not."

"Then you're more of a pastor to some than to others."

"I would say there are some people in my church who don't listen to me at all. And some, not so much."

"And are there people outside your congregation who take your spiritual advice?"

"Absolutely. People call me. Some ministers. Sometimes business people. You know, they just need advice."

"It is really your leadership gifting that is pretty key, then? Something you have naturally as well as spiritually?"

Jim sensed where she was heading with the conversation, so he cut her off. "No. The key is authority, dear. And authority comes from the Lord."

"I believe that," she said. "I agree with you one hundred percent." Then, Karen purposefully put down her paper, got up, and left the room.

They were on their way home from church that night when Jim decided to continue their conversation. Even though it was late February, the weather had been surprisingly warm during the day. Yet, when the sun set, there was a freezing chill in the air. Big messy drops of rain sploshed onto the Shepherds as they got into their car. He turned the key and flipped on the wipers as they pulled out of the parking lot. It was just the two of them as Cara had gone back to SIU, and Shay had gone out to eat with the young people.

Jim said rather abruptly, "You know, Cara almost outright fainted at Amanda's wedding."

"Yes, I know."

"And do you know why that happened?"

"Yes, I'm aware."

"Well, then you see what I mean."

Silence greeted his remark. Jim pressed the point. "If someone is afraid of people looking at them, you can understand how that could be a hindrance in pastoring."

"I see what you're saying," said Karen, noncommittally.

"And that night, after the whole deal with Marta, Cara just collapsed in my arms. 'Hold me, Daddy,' she said. Women weren't meant to carry some things."

"It can be difficult to carry loads," came the measured response.

"And you can see how emotional difficulties and an inability to be in front of crowds would be a hindrance in pastoring, then, can't you?"

"Absolutely," came her flat-toned reply.

"Well, then?" came the voice of an insistent husband responding to the lack of enthusiasm from the other side of the car.

After another pause, she asked, "Well, what?"

"Well, what do you think?"

"Are you asking for my opinion?"

"Yes. Yes, I'm asking for your opinion."

She let the moment of thoughtful silence linger before saying, "Being afraid of crowds and being emotionally vulnerable certainly are things that could hinder people who pastor. Are there other things that could be a hindrance as well?"

"I'm not sure what you're asking."

"Well, Jim, do any of your pastor friends ever struggle with depression, or anger, or bitterness, or maybe just wanting to give up at times?"

"I suppose so."

"How about other things? Do you have any friends who struggle with pride, say, or who have blind spots?"

"Yes, dear, but that is a horse of a different color, isn't it?"

While another long pause suspended the conversation, Jim reflected on Cara's ability to ask just the right questions. She came by that gift honestly.

Because his sparring with Karen had done him no good, he asked, "How does she do it?"

"Sorry, dear. How does who do what?"

"How does Cara, who has a phobia of groups, lead her fellowship group?"

"I asked her about that one time," said Karen.

"Well…"

"You may not like the answer."

"Try me."

"It has to do with poopy diapers, dear."

"What?"

"Poopy diapers."

"How could it have anything to do with poopy diapers?"

"Well, dear, one of little Angel's diapers needed to be changed, and Sandra had Cara change it. The diaper was loaded, and it was the messy kind. Then, because Angel was throwing a tantrum and got her hands in it, she was covered from head to toe. The changing table was a mess. It was so smelly that Cara started to gag. She called Sandra in from the other room. Sandra rescued her and changed the diaper.

"Well, when Cara asked Sandra how she was able to change that diaper without gagging, Sandra said, 'You can do a lot of things you don't think you can if

Cara's Call

you're doing it for people you love.' Cara says this is the only way she can speak to groups of people. She's called to do it. And she loves them."

While Jim felt defeated in part, he rallied, saying, "But this crying thing. You can't be a leader and sob over everything."

A long silence filled the front seat. Rain began to fall more heavily, so Jim turned the wipers to high. Only the rhythmic cha-chunka of the wipers sweeping back and forth on the windshield interrupted the quiet. Although Jim supposed that this was the end of the discussion, he heard a small voice say quietly, "Sometimes I cry." Then, after a few cha-chunkas of the wipers, the voice said, "I cry about things that really hurt. Things I wish I could fix but can't." As the wipers continued to swish back and forth on the windshield, Jim glanced over to see soft, quiet, tears rolling down Karen's cheeks.

Jim reached over and stroked her neck tenderly. "I need your support on this," he said. "We need to stand together. I think Cara would have a hard time pastoring with all these issues she has."

The only response was the patter of rain and the stroke of the wiper blades. Finally, Karen responded. She spoke so softly that Jim had to lean in to catch her words. "Jim, you are right. Cara does have a lot of issues that weigh against her being successful. On the other hand, I think we've got to ask what it means that God called her. Still, I know that a calling is not enough."

Jim smiled. It seemed that, after all, they would be in agreement. Then Karen continued. "Cara needs something beyond her call. She needs a blessing. Yet, since she's not going to get it, I guess we'll never know. Will we?"

"Know what?"

"Jim, Cara is not rebellious. She will not do anything without the support of those who love her most."

"Karen, what are you saying?"

"I'm saying that perhaps eventually Cara might have found out she wasn't gifted enough to pastor; on the other hand, although she wouldn't have pastored like you do, maybe she would have been awfully good at it. I guess we'll never know, will we?"

It was the "we'll never know, will we?" that bothered Jim the most. He thought about those words sometimes when he studied. He thought about them sometimes when Cara's fellowship group members started ringing the doorbell. But most of all, he thought about it on Sunday nights when his second oldest daughter was amening him from the audience.

Jim even leafed through a couple of books that were remnants of their failed Bible study, reading here and there. He decided to float some of the information by Bob, just to see what he thought.

"I was reading this book about Eva Hunt," he said during a break in their racquetball action. They were even at seven apiece and were trying to figure out if they had time to finish the game.

"Who's Eva Hunt?" asked Bob.

"She's really well known here in Illinois," said Jim.

"I never heard of her," Bob said, sounding surprised.

"Well, she's not alive anymore. But she was a woman church planter and pastor. She probably did more than anyone else ever did in starting and building churches in the state. You know that huge church in Herrick?"

"Yeah?"

"One that she pastored. And she rescued churches that were started but not really thriving. She planted, helped, and turned around more churches than you can shake a stick at."

"No kidding," said Bob, clearly losing interest.

"Yeah. Say, Bob, did you know in the early twentieth century somewhere around a third of all Pentecostal ministers were women? A lot of them pastors."

"You don't say," said Bob. "I'm glad men have stepped up to the plate. I heard some of those women were pretty bossy."

"Yeah," said Jim. "Do you know any women pastors?"

"No," said Bob. "I've seen a few of them voting at district conference. They look kind of bossy."

"Yeah, I've heard that same thing, too," said Jim deciding to drop the conversation.

When they met the next week, he decided to take a different angle. Jim began, "I've been reading a couple of books about the early church."

"Any good preaching material in them?" Bob asked.

"Some stuff," said Jim. "Anyway, did you know they didn't have church buildings back then?"

"I don't suppose I knew that," said Bob.

"Yeah, they were mostly house churches."

"Yeah," said Bob. "Like Paul is always greeting the church that is in somebody's house."

"Yeah, that's what I mean. Well, anyway, I've been reading how that worked and sometimes it was a man who was in charge and sometimes it was a ministry team, like a husband and wife."

"Oh, yeah?"

Cara's Call

"Yeah, like Priscilla and Aquila."

"Yeah?" said Bob, interested now.

"Well, I know that I don't know any Greek or anything, but they say, because of her being mentioned first and other factors, that Priscilla was a lot more prominent and capable than Aquila."

"Too bad for him," said Bob.

"And there were a number of house churches that had women over them," Jim continued.

"No pastor?"

"Well, apparently, the women were the pastors."

"No fooling," said Bob. "Glad they grew out of that."

"Yeah," said Jim. "Guess you're right."

Green grass was now peaking out here and there, trees were budding, and random shoots were popping up unbidden from dormant gardens. It was a Sunday afternoon, and as they were entering the house after their Sunday afternoon dinner, Cara's dad asked her if she would preach for him next Sunday night.

"What does that mean?" she asked, thoughtfully.

"It means that I'm asking you to preach."

"Well, Dad, there was this gap of time after our last discussion when I didn't become church secretary. And I told you about what I thought God had for me. And then, we didn't talk. And also, you didn't ask me to preach. When you didn't ask me to preach anymore, I thought this probably meant something. But I wasn't sure. And now, we still haven't talked, but you're asking me to preach. I don't want to read too much or too little into this invitation. Yes, I will preach. I just didn't know if there was something else you wanted to say or not."

"There's not. I just want you to preach."

"I'd be glad to, Dad. And I'm honored. Thank you for asking."

At the next racquetball game, Bob anticipated Jim's desire to continue their discussion and immediately nipped it in the bud. "Jim, I have already conceded that women have moved me to tears and that they have a place in the body of Christ. But read my lips. They have no place in the five-fold ministry. Nada. None."

"Well, that's what I thought too. But I've been rereading this stuff and it looks like maybe they did. There was this apostle named Junia—a woman—and there were these prophets who were women. I'm just wondering if, in fact, every single one of the fivefold ministry was, at some point, filled by women," said Jim.

"Do you realize how stupid you sound right now?"

"Bob, I'm still not sure if any of this works today."

"Jim, if you start letting every woman who says she has a call get behind your pulpit—"

"Bob, I'm just saying it might be scriptural. That doesn't open my pulpit to every woman who says she has a call any more than it opens up your pulpit to every man who says he has a call."

"Jim, we both know this is about Cara. I'm trying to be kind. I'm warning you, though. Do not encourage her. She's your daughter and all, but Jim, think this through. What if it's not from God?"

"I get that. And I'm scared to death of making a mistake. But on the other hand, what if her call really is from God?"

"Trust me on this, Jim. It's not."

Chapter 26

"Could you bring me a glass of iced tea?" Jim asked his wife. He was working through his Sunday evening service in the recliner.

"Absolutely," said Karen. The trouble started as she was handing him the glass. "It's been ten weeks now, hasn't it, Jim?" she said. Then she sat down and acted as if she was about to read the paper.

"I'm not sure what you mean," Jim said. And while this wasn't altogether untruthful, he had a pretty good guess as to where the conversation was headed.

"First of all, I want you to know that I haven't talked to Cara, nor is she complaining, nor does she have a bad attitude."

Jim could smell a confrontation brewing. His wife usually made appeals by telling stories, coming in the back door, asking him to think about something. Her current statement did not sound at all like she was about to make that sort of appeal.

"Okay," was the only thing that Jim could think of that would certainly be safe.

"Cara talked to you toward the end of January, and it's April. If you have decided Cara shouldn't pastor, don't you owe it to her to talk to her?"

There it was. His wife had thrown down the gauntlet. Now it was up to him to say something. To be a father. To be a pastor. To be wise. To have answers and not have doubts. The problem was, of course, that there seemed to be no clear course of action. As much as he had prayed, he could not seem to find God's will. He knew, though, where his wife ultimately stood; she stood with her daughter.

"I'll talk to her tonight after church," he said, not because he had received sudden inspiration but because his wife was right. He had waited too long and needed to have some sort of conversation with Cara.

All through the service, he wondered what he would say. Even afterward, as Cara stepped into his office, he was still at a loss for direction.

He didn't even sit down to make the meeting official. As soon as she appeared in the doorway, he said with uncharacteristic urgency, "Cara, I know you've been waiting for me to talk to you about your sense of call to pastor. And I apologize for not having this conversation until now."

Cara's Call

"I'm glad you're talking to me now, Dad."

"Cara, I've been studying this out. And there sure are a lot of things to consider."

"Yes."

"And I don't have it all worked out, yet."

"Okay."

"But I do want you to proceed."

He said those words as if he offered an answer, as if Cara was supposed to understand. She waited for him to continue and give more information. But after a few moments passed, and it became clear to her that he intended to end the conversation on that note, she said, "Dad, I need you to maybe offer a little more clarity on what you just said. Could you?"

"See, that's the problem. I'm not sure what I'm saying. Some of the books talk about house churches in the early church. And that women were over them. I guess I can see that."

Because he stopped talking once again, Cara felt she had to speak. "Okay. Do you want to study this out together some more? I'm not trying to be difficult. You said I should proceed. I'm just not sure what that means—when you say I should proceed."

"Well, I am thinking maybe you should cautiously consider what works in our culture. I think that in Bible times, God used women to minister in various ways. And I see that at the start of the modern-day Pentecostal Movement women played an important role. I think they have had a place."

"All right…"

At that point any hope of clear direction ceased. Cara remained silent, so Jim felt compelled to add, "I do not want to be a hindrance in how God is working in your life."

"Okay. Dad, what are you asking me to do?"

"I honestly don't know. Why don't you find some women, who are involved in ministry, and see how ministry works in their lives. Then figure out how it should work in your life. Does that sound doable?"

"Dad, as I understand you, you are saying I have your blessing to move forward in what I believe is a call on my life to pastor?"

"I'm still not sure how I feel about everything, but I give my blessing for you to work through it in your own way. And I'll keep working on things in my way."

"What does that mean, Dad?"

"I don't know, honey. I don't know."

It was only then that any real progress on the subject was made, not so much because of Jim's words, but by the fact that he took Cara into his arms and held her close.

Cara saw the tears in her father's eyes and wondered if that were half the reason for the embrace, so she wouldn't see him crying. But it didn't matter. He hugged her tightly, saying, "I just know that I don't want to do anything wrong."

"What's that supposed to mean?" Cara said to Kevin on the phone. "Talk about a mixed signal."

"Cara, I would take this conversation with your dad as an important green light. And from what you told me about your previous conversations, I would also take it as a miracle."

"Yeah, but there was no 'I'm proud of you' or 'I'm in your corner' or 'Attah girl!' Why couldn't I get that?"

"I don't know, Cara. I'm not sure. Your dad has not been a pastor all that long, and he's still working on figuring stuff out. He gave you all he could. From what you said, he's balancing a fear of being wrong with another fear. He doesn't want to hurt you."

"What does he think he's been doing to me these last three months?"

"Be careful, Cara," Kevin cautioned. But he said it kindly and let her cry on the phone until she was ready to talk again.

"Kevin, what do you think is the real issue? Why is he so afraid? Does he think I'll suddenly run off and do something stupid? That people will talk about me or that I'll be isolated from others? I'm not some frail little thing. I mean, you don't worry about me in that way, do you, Kevin?"

She was surprised by the pause on the other end of the line, and surprised further when Kevin finally admitted, "More than you know. If someone really cares about someone else, he can't help but have concerns."

That comment didn't seem to come from Kevin the counselor but Kevin the something else. She did not know what to make of it. Then, just as quickly, Kevin switched back to advice mode.

"Why don't you start on this new search the same place you initially started? Talk to someone at the seminary."

"Like a professor?"

"Maybe. But maybe not. Maybe there is someone who could steer you to women in ministry, to women who could give you their story. I'm sure someone at the seminary could give you names of people."

"I'll give them a call."

The following Saturday, her boss Gary pulled her aside. Lately, he hadn't been treating Cara as a regular employee at Office Depot but as something more.

"Cara, I've got a problem, and I don't know what to do."

"Okay?"

"Well, you know how you've been helping me train those new employees?"

"Sure."

"Well, it's about Vincent."

"I really like him. What's wrong?"

"He called me up and quit this morning. I hate to lose him. Could you phone him to see if you can tease out what the issues are for him? And if you can solve whatever they are, I'm forever in your debt."

Later in the day, Gary asked if she'd gotten in touch with him.

"He'll be available next week. Just give him a call."

"What's the deal?"

"Well, I called him. At first he didn't want to tell me, but then it all came out. Gary, you know how brusque Harriet can be. Vincent thought she was mocking him. I got him to see that the problem was with her and not him. Try not to schedule them both at the same time until I get a chance to talk to her."

"Cara, you're the greatest. Can you help me with Billy? He keeps coming in late."

"Nope."

"If you could just talk to him—"

"He's sleeping in. You can't fix that, Gary. The Book of Proverbs is pretty clear about that kind of employee."

"Are you telling me to fire him?"

"I'm only telling you I can't help him."

"Well, thanks then. Have you thought any more about officially becoming my assistant manager this summer?"

"I'm still thinking about it."

"Hey, Kevin," Cara began. "Getting information about women in ministry was a whole lot easier than I thought it would be."

"What do you mean?"

"I talked to the president of the student body at the graduate school."

"What did he say?"

"Not 'he', but 'she.' She's done a ton of research on women who minister. She's called women all over North America, compiling information and stuff."

"Sounds good."

"It even turns out that one of the professors, who is over the counseling program, pastors with her husband. And actually, most of the women going to school are pretty active in ministry as well. And there's something else, too."

"What's that?"

"It seems like there's more interest than ever in women who minister. Crystal—she's the student body president—did a seminar in Michigan for any young lady who felt a call on their lives. She had forty show up!"

"Sounds great!"

"Guess what else? She gave me a whole list of women to call so I can get some questions answered. But she said it would be best if I could visit as many as possible. That way, I could see for myself how God is working."

"Sounds like a great idea."

"Yeah, I'd really love to do it this summer, but I'm afraid it's not going to happen."

"Why do you say that?"

"No mun…no fun."

"I get that. You're probably right. But what if going on the trip is meant to be an act of faith?"

"I doubt it." She sounded so final that he immediately dropped it. But the seed was planted in her mind, and the more Cara thought about it—and as crazy as the idea sounded—the more Cara wanted to go on this trip.

With only two weeks before summer vacation, Gary was getting anxious for a decision. "So, are you going to be my assistant manager?" he asked Cara.

"I'd love to, Gary, and maybe sometime in the future, I will. But right now I can't."

"Cara, it's just for the summer. I'm not asking you to quit school."

"I know, but I decided to load up on some summer classes and do one more thing."

"What's that?"

"I'm going on a three-week trip across the United States and Canada."

"See the sights?"

"Nope. Visit women who are active in ministry."

"That's wonderful. But it sounds expensive. What are you going to do for money?"

Cara laughed. "You know, Gary, I don't have the slightest idea."

When Gary saw that she was serious, he said, "Well, then, I'm going to pass the hat at the store."

"Cara, I need to talk to you about Ron."

"Okay, Marta, what about Ron?"

"Well, he asked me out on a date, and I told him yes, but I'm having second thoughts now."

"Why?"

"Because you told me you had committed your future to the Lord and you were never going to get married, so I was wondering if I should do that, too."

"Marta, I didn't say I would never get married, only that if I never got married, I would be okay with it—that I had given up all my rights to the Lord, including my future."

"Do you think I should give up Ron for the Lord?"

"Marta, what I think is that you should ask the Lord about His will for you and Ron. Okay? One more thing. It's even more important now that you don't have Ron over to your apartment anymore."

"We never did anything wrong!"

"I know that. But if you really start liking him, then there might be some temptations that would be really strong."

"Yeah, I see what you mean."

"Marta, I need you to do something for me. I'm going to be gone for three weeks on a trip. You know that new curriculum I got for fellowship meeting? I need you and Ron to work through it. I'll help you, but I think you could handle the main lesson, and Ron could assist you. Okay?"

"You mean you want us to do it without you being there? How could we? And where are you going? Are you going by yourself? When are you leaving?"

"My friend Elizabeth and I will be traveling together. We're leaving a week from Monday."

"Where?"

"All over the country. Particularly to churches where women are ministering. I need to find out how they do things."

"But you already know how to do things."

"You're very kind."

"Cara, you won't forget us, will you?"

"How can you say that?"

"Well, what if someone asks you to pastor a church or something while you're away or what if we have an emergency while you're gone or what if—"

"Marta, you're going to be just fine."

Chapter 27

"Cara, my mom said I shouldn't drive in big cities."

"Don't worry about it, Elizabeth. We've already talked about it. I'll drive when we get around larger towns."

"She also says that I am to pay for all my own food. I've got money so you don't have to—"

"Yes, I know, Elizabeth. You told me twice and I certainly will honor—"

"Speaking of which, do you see anything coming up?"

"Still looking for a good exit. The interstate is pretty well marked, so we'll probably see something come up pretty soon."

"Just a second, Cara. Got a call coming in—Hey, Kevin."

"Hey, Elizabeth, I heard you guys were leaving today. Are you on the road yet?"

"Left right after breakfast. Say Kev, you've got to talk to her for me. Cara's trying to starve me. It's almost two o'clock and we haven't eaten yet. Kevin, we went clean through the southern part of Illinois, we cut across the boot hill of Missouri, and now we're on Interstate 55 halfway through Arkansas, and we still haven't stopped for lunch! Whenever I ask about it, Cara keeps acting like she's looking for a good exit."

"Watch it there," said Cara, smiling.

"Where are you ladies heading to tonight?"

Elizabeth checked the itinerary—the same one Cara had given her parents—complete with home, office, and cell phone numbers. "It says we're going to meet with Sister Jackson. She's a pastor in Marvell, Arkansas."

"Is she related to the Jacksons who pastor in Wood River, Illinois?"

"I'll ask. Hey, Cara, Kevin wants to know if Sister Jackson is related to the Jacksons pastoring in Wood River."

"Could be, but I doubt it. She's African American."

"Uh, Kev, that would be a no."

"Well, let me talk to the driver then."

Cara's Call

Elizabeth handed over the phone, whereupon Kevin offered an excited monologue as to how he would be praying and asked Cara to email him an itinerary. Then, he finally got around to the question he wanted to ask all along. "Cara, I don't want to get too personal, and you don't have to tell me, but how are you managing to pay for everything?"

"I saved some. Friends gave me money. And something else. I can tell you but you are sworn to secrecy."

"My lips are sealed."

"My dad."

"So, like what? He just gave you a roll of bills and told you not to tell anyone?"

"Something like that. Then, right before I left, Mom gave me a couple hundred dollars."

"So, she probably told you the same thing, right? Do not tell a soul?"

"Actually, she just told me not to tell Dad."

"Cara, I love your family."

Three days later Kevin called Elizabeth again.

"So how's the world traveler?"

"I am totally pumped, Kevin."

"And what exactly are you so pumped about?"

"We stopped at Sister Jackson's house, and it was like Grand Central Station. She's not co-pastoring with her husband or anything. She is the pastor. She's doing so many things and helping so many people, Kevin. But she took time for us."

"I'm glad for that. That's awesome!"

"Kevin, what a story she has! It was impossible for them to build their church. But then God so totally did the miraculous."

"Cool."

"And then, for Sunday morning service, we went to this church in Dallas. And they have women ministers who actually sit on the platform and do ministry just like 'regular' people. And we got to talk to them."

"What? The fact that they're sitting on the platform didn't hinder the service?" Kevin teased.

"And then, Kevin, get this. We're, like, walking out, right? And the parking lot is as big as Disney World, right? And guess what?"

"No idea."

"The ministers park all the way to the back, at the farthest point in the parking lot. Is that mind-blowing or what! Don't you think Jesus would park on the other side of the parking lot?"

"Don't know. What does Jesus drive?"

"And then we went to see this one lady named Mary Ellis. And she has done, like, everything in ministry!"

"Fantastic. Let me talk to Cara."

She handed over the phone. "Elizabeth's not driving you crazy, is she?"

"Kevin, you didn't let her finish the story. It's a good one. We just came from visiting with Sister Ellis, and I could totally identify. She told us how the Lord would wake her up in the middle of the night and give her messages to speak, how she would pray for hours. Kevin, that's happened to me."

"Is her husband a pastor?"

"No. A businessman. But he encourages her. And her pastor encouraged her to get her license. She says that when God opened doors, she just walked through them. That's what I want to do."

If it were possible, Cara sounded even more hyped than Elizabeth, which prompted Kevin to ask, "You're not driving Elizabeth crazy, are you?"

"You're just jealous you couldn't come with us. Elizabeth is incredible. I love her."

"And I love you both."

After they left the Dallas metro area, Elizabeth took the wheel. She was fine driving on Interstate 30 and did so until almost all the way to the big city of Shreveport, Louisiana. When they got the outskirts of the city, Elizabeth took an exit, drove into the parking lot of a restaurant, and pronounced, "Lunchtime!"

"It's only eleven-thirty!" exclaimed Cara. "We've got to make good time today!"

"We'll make good time after lunch," said Elizabeth. "You can drive the next couple of hours." Elizabeth smiled sweetly and headed toward the door of the restaurant. Cara had no choice but to follow.

When lunch was over, Cara took the wheel and headed south on I-49. After a couple hours they entered Alexandria city limits. "Turn at the next corner," said Elizabeth, directing their final approach.

After a quick phone call from Cara, Melani met them at the church door. She was a pretty lady in her forties—very perky. She welcomed them with a friendly smile, asked them about their trip, and if they needed anything—all in thirty seconds. Having dispensed with pleasantries, she launched into the tasks at hand: showing them the building and answering questions about the ministries of the church. Although Elizabeth was impressed by the huge auditorium, the maze of facilities, and the many programs that Cara was asking Melani about, the longer they progressed, the more weary and less enthusiastic Elizabeth became.

They finally wound their way into Melani's office where Elizabeth could sit down. When the girls followed her into her office, they saw pictures and artifacts scattered around on walls, tables, and bookshelves. They saw pictures of faraway lands and people, stacks of reference books around the walls, and boxes and bins that hinted at projects in the making.

Because Elizabeth had been zoning in and out during the tour, she hadn't quite gotten who was who and what was what. To clarify, she asked, "Now, who are these Anthony and Mickey people and how do they fit in?"

Melani answered politely, "Anthony is the senior pastor of the church. My husband, Terry, is associate pastor. And although Mickey and I choose not to share their titles, we are still very much a part of the team."

"Okay," said Elizabeth, now relaxed in her chair. Then, because Cara hadn't ever stopped her from asking questions before, she simply plowed forward, asking Melani, "Okay, so what exactly do you do?"

Melani smiled patiently, offering, "A lot of different things. Whatever needs to be done. Sometimes its things I'm really passionate about...and sometimes it things I do because there is a need."

Elizabeth nodded and responded, "Actually, I came with Cara on this trip mostly to find out about preaching."

Melani smiled but responded good-naturedly, "Ah, Elizabeth. I see that we're going to have a very interesting visit! And I'm glad you have a heart for preaching. But maybe we should back up a little."

"The first thing you need to understand is that 'preaching' is only a very small percentage of what pastoring involves. There are one hundred sixty-eight hours in every week. Although the minister spends more hours in preparation, preaching itself only takes up about two or three of those hours. The other one hundred sixty-five hours involve real life. Hurting, laughing, learning, loving, anger, giving, taking, working, helping people—kingdom people—live out their lives in a carnal world that is diametrically opposed to kingdom principles.

"People have to pray consistently and live in the Word in order to live life God's way in that kind of world. And it takes more than two sermons a week to help them maintain that consistency."

Apparently, Elizabeth wasn't quite getting it. She said, "Okay, so you aren't really a preacher after all, are you? I was sort of wanting to talk to people who were called, not just preacher's wives."

Melani did not take offense and was patient with her. "I was fourteen years old when the Lord called me."

Elizabeth countered, "But how could you..."

Melani continued. "Sister Nona Freeman spoke one night at this very church, and as a fourteen-year-old girl, I knelt and told God that wherever He wanted me to go and whatever He wanted me to do, I would give it one hundred percent. I was positive that it would be in a faraway, exotic, adventurous place with beautiful weather and gorgeous scenery, but God has a sense of humor. He decided to leave me right here where I was born."

Elizabeth wrinkled her brow, now clearly perplexed. "But I don't understand," she said. "You say you were called. Yet, from what you said, all you do is help your husband create processes and systems that help disciple people. Don't you think that if God called you, you should do something, like…bigger?"

"Oh, Elizabeth! How mistaken you are!" Melani wasn't scolding her, she simply spoke from the overflow of her own heart. "We are never limited when we totally surrender to God's call!"

And then, if it were possible, Melani spoke with even more passion. "I do what I do simply because I'm called to do it, not merely because I'm married to my husband. We've often talked about the fact that if he were to be taken from me, I would still continue with my personal ministry exactly as I operate now. God called me before I ever met my husband, and I was developing my personal call before I met him. What I do complements his ministry, but it's not because of his ministry."

Elizabeth nodded and was now suddenly taken aback by pictures of lands she had never seen, asking, "So, all these places on the wall, that's places where you've gone and stuff?"

"Elizabeth, I'm not limited because I've found when I follow the voice of God He uses me to meet needs, not only here in this small town, but around the world! From my place here, I'm involved with missionaries in Africa and Asia and Europe and several other global endeavors. I'm presently spearheading the development of a discipleship program that can be adapted to every age level."

Finally, Elizabeth was getting excited and offered spontaneously, "Wow! That's incredible. I want to be just like you! So, how do I get this global ministry?"

What Elizabeth lacked in tact, she made up for in enthusiasm. Melani smiled, offering, "My father-in-law used to say that 'if you'll deepen, God will broaden.' I'm thankful I realized early on that to be called to minister did not necessarily mean I had to define it in the traditional boundaries of the pulpit. I don't mind speaking behind a pulpit occasionally when God asks that of me, but I realize my ministry is so much more than that. I wouldn't trade the adventure of not knowing what, when, or where I will be used next for anything in the world!"

The next day they were driving northeast on Interstate 20 with Elizabeth at the wheel. She was still trying to absorb all that she had learned. She was happily talking with Cara when a flashing red light appeared in her rearview mirror.

Elizabeth meekly pulled over to the shoulder. The state trooper wasn't smiling as he walked up to their car. He had one hand on his gun. He spoke softly but with a lot of authority, "Could I see your driver's license and registration, miss?" Cara handed the registration over to Elizabeth who then included it with her driver's license. The policeman looked at the license, looked at Elizabeth, then back at the license again. "Do you know how fast you were going?"

"No sir. I didn't really look at the speedometer that much."

"I clocked you at seventy-nine miles per hour. Where are you going in such a hurry, young lady?"

"Well, officer," Elizabeth said. Cara tried to signal Elizabeth not to say anything more, but Elizabeth was oblivious. When Elizabeth got a little nervous, she tended to talk very fast and say whatever popped into her head. "...my friend Cara never stops to eat and she said I could drive for two hours and it's past supper time and she doesn't care, but I do. So I was trying to get to a good exit before she took over driving and starved me to death."

Cara was certain the man would yell at Elizabeth and give her the maximum fine. Instead, he did a strange thing. He laughed so hard that tears ran down his face. Then he said, "There's a Cracker Barrel eight miles up at the next exit. They've got good food." Then he poked his head in the window and, with a repressed smile, charged Cara, "And I want you to stop making your friend speed so much, okay?"

Cara nodded seriously as the officer handed Elizabeth's license back to her along with the registration and walked back to his vehicle. "What was that!" said Cara. "You speed, and I get yelled at!"

Chapter 28

Several days later, Kevin called Elizabeth again. "Are you still down south?"

"Not so much. Guess what! We've stayed at two pastors' homes and I've gotten to speak once and Cara twice. And last night we stayed in a 'roach' motel, but we didn't know that until we'd already taken the room. Cara got ten dollars taken off the bill, but she said it should have been more."

Kevin laughed. "Next time, check the room before paying. Let me talk to Cara." She handed Cara the phone. "I wasn't getting any answers about geography from Elizabeth. If you are not down south, where exactly are you?"

"We're in Delaware right now, and I'm on a country road. Maybe we can talk a little bit later."

"Where are you going?" asked Kevin.

"We are going to meet Janet Trout," said Cara.

"Bear right here," commanded Elizabeth who was meticulously following the directions in her hand.

"Why did you pick her?" Kevin asked.

Cara replied, "I talked first to one man and then to a woman who went to the Bible college that she ran, and they recommended I contact her."

"They didn't mind that the school was run by a woman?"

"They told me they were proud to have gone to Kent Christian College."

"Was it a school to produce women preachers?"

"No. I didn't get that impression at all. But what convinced me to meet her was when I asked those former students about it, they said that their schooling taught them by example that being a woman in ministry is normal. No one even thought twice about it."

"Are you going to meet her at the house?"

"I feel like I've already met her," said Cara. "Elizabeth ordered a half dozen books she wrote and can't stop talking about her."

"Turn here," said Elizabeth, "right across from the Amish schoolhouse."

Cara's Call

Cara turned into the long, paved driveway, saying, "Gotta go, Kev. Even though she won't be home for an hour or two, there is this other lady who's meeting us who will get us settled. We're staying with her tonight."

"Wow," said Elizabeth when she saw the house, and "Wow," she offered again when they were led into the front room. They had been settled into the guest room for an hour or so when Sister Trout arrived and offered them coffee and a snack in the family room. She was older than Elizabeth thought she would be. But Elizabeth was not surprised how nicely she was dressed, given what she had read about her.

"Thank you, ma'am," said Elizabeth, after she took a cookie from a plate. Cara was completely floored. Cara didn't realize that "ma'am" held any sort of place at all in the vocabulary of this sixteen-year-old. Not only did she say "ma'am" but she kept stroking her cloth napkin in an attempt to keep it straight and proper.

Janet Trout narrated her story in easy fashion. How she followed God's call as a young person, first, on the mission field and then as an evangelist. She then told of the churches that she and her husband had started, the Bible college that she began, and her vision for the future.

Elizabeth sat wide-eyed, drinking it in, saying not a word. Only when talk turned to Janet's doctoral dissertation, did Elizabeth zone out. Words like *excellence*, *priorities*, *interdependence* and *synergy* all ran together nonstop and became tangled in her thinking. Elizabeth responded in the only way that made sense, by asking for another cookie.

At one point, Cara interrupted to ask if she could take a few things down on her laptop. She wrote it all down exactly as she heard it. She even read aloud two important sentences to make sure she understood them correctly. Janet nodded and continued, "I seek to conduct myself in ways that are honest, authentic and beneficial to the children of God. I want my life to be a testimony of the goodness of God to those who do not know Him. I envision myself as dynamic and capable, fair and unwavering, simple and complex, powerful but meek. I value myself because He called me."

When it was close to midnight, their host was not at all tiring, but because Elizabeth was nodding off, Cara said, "Thank you for giving of your time and for your hospitality. Maybe we should—"

"I was thinking," Elizabeth interrupted, now suddenly awake. She had apparently been waiting to ask a question, but seeing the evening coming to an end, she determined to speak up. "Do you mind if I ask you why you haven't retired yet?"

Janet Trout, who was in her seventies, did not take offense. She said, "I'm not done yet. Just as I want my life to be a testimony of the goodness of God, I also have a deep burden to serve as a catalyst for change for those who need direction. Elizabeth, I've got more to do."

"More to do?" repeated Elizabeth.

"God called me when I was very young, and I've been faithful to that call for all these years. Yet, there are a few more things to start, a few more things to finish, a little bit more to write. There's simply more that I must do." She continued, "I will not die with it all inside."

Elizabeth and Cara left the next morning, heading north on Route 13. Because the signs were a little confusing as they neared Wilmington, they had trouble crossing into New Jersey. "Turn right up here," said Elizabeth.

"No!" insisted Cara. "It's this other lane." But of course, it was not, although they still did not know the right way. Cara circled around once more until she begrudgingly followed Elizabeth's directions, which turned out to be wrong as well.

Elizabeth's phone rang. "Hey, Elizabeth," came Kevin's friendly voice.

"It's for you..." growled Elizabeth, fumbling with the map. Cara shook her head, indicating she was not in any mood to talk. But Elizabeth handed her the phone despite her protests. Cara was mildly annoyed. "Kevin, we're in the middle of something right now." This was a first, but Kevin accepted it in good grace and quickly offered a good-bye.

Twenty minutes later, they finally found the correct exit, though tension in the car hardly eased. Only when they got to the church an hour later did both girls lighten up a little. They were scheduled to visit Cindy Miller. According to Cara's notes, Cindy not only co-pastored with her husband but also was a national speaker. And she flew to St. Louis on a regular basis to teach counseling at the graduate school.

Sister Miller was friendly, but distracted. She no sooner greeted them than she asked them to wait for a couple of minutes in her office. She directed someone that was in the other part of the church to do something. She made one call on her cell and one on the office phone. "A couple of emergencies that couldn't wait," she explained. Then she sat down with them, turning off her cell.

When Cindy sat down, things changed. She now seemed totally relaxed, as if she had all day, when in reality Cara knew that their appointment was only scheduled for an hour. "Tell me about your travels," she said, at once totally focused on her visitors. It was interesting to Cara that this was the first woman who had actually asked about other places she'd been. Cara started explaining, but faltered a little under the direct gaze that seemed to be looking for something deeper than mere social chitchat.

Cara's Call

"Cara, you have certainly put a great deal of effort into being here with me. What would you like to ask me?"

Cara shifted in her chair and responded with one of her prepared questions, "What has your experience in ministry been like?"

Cindy responded by asking Cara to be more specific.

Cara then added, "Well, it seems that many people I've talked to about my particular calling to pastor feel that, as a woman, I will never receive the same sort of respect or opportunities as men in ministry."

Cindy replied, "It's true. You won't. What's more is that I've found such lack of respect is not just limited to gender. Age, race, level of experience and even marital status could disqualify you in some people's eyes from pastoring. I guess my questions for you would be, 'Whose respect do you need? What kind of respect are you looking for?'"

Cara's eyes shifted back and forth, not sure how to answer. "I feel like I have my father's respect, but I know that there are some who don't understand or agree with his support. In some ways that affects how he acts toward me."

Cindy smiled, "Wouldn't it be nice if everyone agreed with our decisions and supported our efforts?"

Cara smiled and replied tentatively, "Yes, it would."

"But life isn't that simple, is it? What is it like when you think about pursuing your calling without everyone's support or approval?"

The questions went back and forth. It was both exhausting and exhilarating for Cara to begin exploring her thoughts and feelings so deeply. It was a unique combination of tears and laughter, heart searching and moments of personal awareness.

The hour passed quickly, and soon Cindy began closing the conversation with some final questions for Cara to consider. She said, "I know you came to me because I am also a woman in ministry. I want to leave you with some thoughts to ponder as you continue your travels. Do not make gender the focus of your calling or a default excuse when things do not go your way.

"If you believe that God has called you, then you understand that God called a woman, and you should conduct yourself and minister out of that context. Be yourself. What is it about you that God wants to use? Be careful not to approach ministry on the defensive. Don't make assumptions on how people will respond to your ministry. You cannot change other people's opinions or convictions. Be true to God at work in you and through you.

"Every decision comes at a price. If you choose to pursue your calling, what will it cost you? And, if you choose not to, what do you think that price tag will look like? Don't try to answer that now, but you will need to answer these questions before long."

Cindy stood up, signaling their time was up, and walked them to the door. Hugging Cara, she reminded her to stay in touch and call her if she needed to talk. Laughing, she reached over to hug Elizabeth and said, "Next time we will talk about you." Elizabeth gave a nervous chuckle and hugged her back.

As soon as they were out the door, Elizabeth said, "She's scary, isn't she?"

"Yeah," said Cara, "but a good kind of scary."

The next morning they drove north on the New Jersey Turnpike, intending to skirt wide of New York City. Both girls had studied the map extensively, and Elizabeth worked hard to continually interpret the map and spit out directions, but the further they went, the less sense the map made to her.

They were not supposed to be going into the downtown area, but the skyscrapers kept getting closer and closer. At a toll booth, Cara asked, "Are we on the Garden State Parkway?"

The heavy set guy in the blue jacket shook his head. Very loudly he offered in words hard to understand, "You aah so faa away from the entrance to the Gaden State Pakway that it is laughable." He continued, "As soon as you cross the G.W. here, you'll be in Noo Yaak." Indeed, the majestic George Washington Bridge loomed behind him.

"What's the fastest way to Connecticut?" asked Cara.

He simply shrugged, as if to say, *Not my problem, honey. You're holding up traffic.* "That'll be eight bucks."

"But I didn't mean to—you mean, this is New York already. Can you tell me which way to—"

"C'mon. There's a thousand cars behind you. I haven't got all day."

A half hour later, Cara called the lady in Connecticut she was going to see to tell them they wouldn't be there for lunch. "We're not going to make it," she said with a small cry in her throat.

Perhaps it was because Cara sounded so miserable that Crystal, the lady they were meeting, was so nice. "Whenever you get here will be just fine," she replied.

At five minutes after three, Cara finally arrived in Manchester, Connecticut, but it was 3:20 before they arrived at the church. The pastor's wife, Crystal, didn't seem stressed at all that they were late.

When Elizabeth got out of the car, she at once forgot the trauma of New York City, taking in everything at the church. She was clearly impressed during their tour. It was great, she kept repeating. The church, the pastor, and his vision for

Cara's Call

ministry, were all great. Elizabeth was particularly taken with Crystal Elliott, the pastor's wife.

After a short tour, Crystal took them to a very nice restaurant. Elizabeth watched her all during the meal, and she could not help staring. Perhaps the thing that impressed her most was how young she looked. She and her teenage daughter could pass for sisters.

Cara was asking Crystal most of the questions, with Elizabeth soaking up the answers, when suddenly she burst out, "I've decided that I want to be a preacher just like you!"

Crystal smiled and then offered, "Actually, I don't think that's such a good idea, Elizabeth."

"Why?"

She put her napkin down and then said emphatically, "God is more interested in originals than copies. Elizabeth, you really don't want to be like me or anybody else. I promise. Do you want to know how you can accomplish anything God called you to do? Just be the Elizabeth He's created you to be. That's enough."

Elizabeth nodded, but didn't seem to be listening too closely. "Yeah, but I'm pretty sure I'll be everything I'm supposed to be only if I look more like you, had a new church building, and some good-looking kids—that sort of thing. See, I think I'm supposed to minister in music and also preach."

Elizabeth's frank, wide-eyed sharing made Crystal laugh. Then Crystal tried once again. "Elizabeth, there is no single pattern for what God calls people to do. I'm just trying to do what God called *me* to do. I do some speaking, but I don't think of myself as a preacher."

"If you speak, then you're a preacher."

Crystal paused but then shared, "I've met women who call themselves preachers. I don't mean to be critical; but some are way too masculine in both their approach and appearance for me to be able to identify with them. I just have to be me."

Elizabeth said, "Okay, so I know I shouldn't stomp and snort. But I do want to be thin like you and have nice clothes and preach and be in charge of stuff. Your husband's a really good-looking guy, too. I had this one boyfriend named Mark, and he was pretty hot, if you know what I mean. But he made fun of me when I sang and preached."

"So you dated this loser because?"

"Well, Jesus could heal a withered hand; so how hard would it be for Him to change someone's attitude. I mean…really?"

"Elizabeth, without your husband's support—someone who truly believes in you—you are going to be really limited. Without my husband believing in me, I would not be who I am. I cannot stress enough the importance of seeking God before you date anyone!"

"Okay. I promise; no more fixer-uppers."

"Elizabeth, you're great. But I've just got to tell you that working for God doesn't come cheaply. One of my best friends, Barbara Willoughby, once told me that anointing comes through suffering. Since the beginning of time, whenever God has chosen and used people to accomplish great things, it has come with a price."

"Yeah, we've been learning that on this trip. But whatever price you're paying, that's what I want to pay. So, what's the best way to get thinner?"

Crystal thought for a moment, and then seemed to decide something. She said, "Elizabeth, I need you to know a couple of things, okay?" Elizabeth nodded her head like a puppy dog while Crystal continued. "Look, my life is hardly perfect. Throughout the past ten years, I've suffered the loss of twins, my son was born sixteen weeks premature, there's been incredible financial pressure from building a new facility, deep disappointment from people whom I counted on for support, not to mention health issues.

"There have even been days when I've tendered my resignation to both God and my husband. Neither one has ever accepted it, but there have been times when it would have been much easier to quit. Having a call to be a minister is the easy part. If you are willing to have a lifetime of 'nevertheless' moments, where you submit to allowing God's will, you can accomplish anything God called you to do."

"Wow. Well, then, maybe I don't want to be like you. But what diet would you recommend?"

"Elizabeth, God called me to work for Him as a young person. I'm not trying to paint a negative picture of ministry, just a realistic one. While there is nothing more painful than watching others turn their back on God, there is nothing more rewarding than seeing a new convert deepen their relationship with God."

"Do you really think I could do it?" Elizabeth asked.

"Be thinner? Or succeed in ministry?"

Elizabeth thought for a second, then settled on "Ministry, I guess."

"Of course you can succeed," said Crystal. "I believe in you. But you must make your calling sure and settle in your mind that no matter what the cost you will never give up!"

Cara's Call

Bob was feeling good about winning the first game and offhandedly asked, "So what's this I hear about Cara?"

"What about Cara?"

"I hear she's on some kind of road trip or something."

"Yes, she is, in fact," said Jim cautiously. "She has a week and a half to go."

"Is it true that she's visiting women ministers?"

"Yeah. She's met some pretty interesting people. She called me last night to talk about it."

"Jim, what were you thinking letting her go on this sort of crazy trip?"

"What do you mean?"

"Who do you think she's going to be talking to when she goes from place to place? What would attract her attention? What sort of women?"

"I'm not following you, Bob."

"She's an idealist, Jim. She'll be attracted to women who are doing extreme things, ones who are not the norm."

"I'm not sure that the people she's—"

"Jim, Jim, Jim. You mark my words. She's going to come back from this trip with all kinds of crazy plans. You'll regret the day you ever let this happen."

Jim felt uneasy. He wondered if he had failed as a father and a pastor.

Chapter 29

"Elizabeth, when are you guys coming home?" Kevin asked.

"Four days from now, but first we have to visit Michigan and after that head to Chicago. Right now, we're driving through Toledo, and we'll hit Michigan within the hour, unless I can talk Cara into stopping for a snack. This lady is ruthless when it comes to a time schedule!"

"You say you have four stops left?"

"Yep. Today we see a pastor's wife, tomorrow a lady pastor, and the next day a student pastor. And that pretty much wipes out Michigan."

"Wow, you're wiping out the whole state pretty quickly!"

"Hey, Kev, when you're good, you're good."

"Let me talk to the driver."

As Elizabeth passed over the phone and Cara answered, Kevin asked, "Where are you heading to now?"

"I'm trying to get through Detroit before rush hour if little miss-stop-for-snack-lady will hold her horses till we have an early dinner."

"Glad that's all working for you, then," said Kevin laughing. "So now that things are coming to an end, are you starting to look forward to getting home?"

"I'm looking forward to getting to Chicago," she said, and because she said no more, he didn't press it.

They found the exit in Troy, and turned right to get to the church. Claudette was waiting for them there. She was tall and stately with dark hair. She looked to be about sixty. Shaking her hand, Cara felt like this woman truly cared for her—like she had known her a long time. She gave Cara her full focus.

When they got to the restaurant and ordered, Cara glanced at her notes and sought to confirm them. She said, "Sister Walker, they said you weren't just a pastor's wife, that you also minister all around the country and even around the world. Does your husband travel with you?"

Cara's Call

While Claudette seemed comfortable talking about herself, she had something on her mind; something that she needed to say. She sidestepped Cara's interests and got right to the point, saying, "Cara, I'm so glad you came to visit me. I prayed for you and Elizabeth this morning."

"But you don't even know me."

"Yes, but the Lord knows you. And Cara, there are a couple of specific things the Lord spoke to me. I am to share them with you. Would you like to hear them?"

"Well, sure."

"Let me ask you something first. Is it true that people very important to you have rejected your calling, and this has hurt you very deeply? Cara, you're wondering how God could have allowed this hurt if you were really called, aren't you?"

Cara said nothing, but tears coursed down her cheeks. She didn't have to say anything—this woman had looked through a window into her soul.

Claudette went on, "Cara, as hard as it may be for you to receive, I feel compelled to share this with you. I believe you need to thank God for your present lack of understanding. This rejection is forcing you to go back and revisit your calling."

Cara replied by sharing something she had written in her journal, something she'd determined never to share because it would prove that she wasn't brave. She said, "I've been crushed again and again," but that was all she could get out.

Claudette stroked her hand and spoke softly to her. "I know, dear. I know. Cara, your brokenness is causing you to weep at the feet of our Lord who called you to preach His word. Cara, I have learned that we can kiss the wave that crashes us against the Rock of Ages."

"I've been trying to figure out how to do that," Cara said. "But sometimes it seems like I'll never find my way."

Claudette was comfortable with silence. After a while she said, "Let me offer you some practical things that will help you. I would advise you to fast unto the Lord to empty yourself of any confusion, doubt, or resentment that you might be feeling at this time. The fast will quiet your spirit so you can more clearly hear God's voice." Then she said, "Do you journal?"

"I do. I've been using it as a prayer journal."

"That's good. But don't forget to write out the entire story of your call. Relive it. Believe it. Trust His voice. I will be your prayer partner and agree with you for God to confirm His call to you through a spiritual voice you trust. Let me know when it happens."

"Will God really speak to me again…I mean…in the same way that He called me?"

Claudette continued, "God doesn't always speak the same way. But yes, He will confirm your calling."

"Did He do that for you?"

"Yes. My Dad was president at Gateway College, and I had joined the Gateway students for a very late-night prayer meeting. I knew that the Lord had called me to preach when I was seventeen years old in Tupelo, Mississippi where my dad was over the children's mansion. But six years had passed, and I was intimidated to step out by faith. I needed a confirmation."

"So, God gave you a confirmation?"

"Oh, so clearly His voice came to me that night at a late-night prayer meeting. Cara, God spoke through the gifts of tongues and interpretation of tongues. The Lord said to me in the Gateway chapel, 'I will give you a burden, a purpose, and a vision. Just go in my name!' That was thirty-eight years ago, and He has never left me."

Elizabeth, who had been a spectator during the entire exchange, watched closely as Claudette embraced Cara and prayed a blessing into her ear.

Even though she felt stupid for saying it, Elizabeth did not want to be left out. Craving a blessing, she asked, "Do you have anything for me?"

"Yes, Elizabeth," said Claudette smiling. "Jesus gave me a verse for you early this morning. It's First Thessalonians chapter five, verse twenty-four, in the *Amplified Bible*: 'Faithful is he who is calling you to himself and utterly trustworthy and he also will do it. He will fulfill His call by hallowing and keeping you.'"

Then Claudette leaned over and prayed a blessing into Elizabeth's ear, ending with, "Elizabeth, I love you. I'm praying for you. I believe in you, and I believe in God's call on your life. I'm always your friend."

Two days later, they pulled in to Paw Paw, Michigan, and were met at the church by Angela who immediately invited them to her apartment. "You can stay with me tonight and we'll have a lot of fun. I'm calling in the pizza now, so what would you like on it?"

"Anchovies make me gag. Other than that, I'm good," said Elizabeth. Cara agreed.

Angela was pretty, had smooth brown hair, and wore fashionable glasses. She looked to be a few years older than Cara. She was easy to be with, apparently very comfortable with who she was.

"Are you from Paw Paw?" said Elizabeth, apparently energized by the thought of pizza.

"No. I'm from Ontario. But I've known the pastor and his family for a while, and when the door opened for me to come here and be the student pastor, everything just seemed to work out. I'll probably work a part-time job, but most of my time will be invested in ministry."

Elizabeth suddenly had another thought. "You're a minister, right? Because you seem like a regular person. Are you sure you're a minister?"

Angela laughed. "Guilty on both charges. Minister and regular person."

"How could that happen?" asked Elizabeth. "How can you be a minister?"

Angela laughed again, clearly having a good time with Elizabeth's questions. "Well, I was raised in New Brunswick, and someplace in my heart I felt the call of God on my life. At the time, I didn't know any women who were ministers, and I was so up and down as a teenager I felt unworthy of God's call. I took an interest in Bible college and received the Sheaves for Christ scholarship. Although I didn't have clear direction from God during my first year at ABI, His plan for my life continued to unfold over time.

"A lady named Sister Ann took an interest and believed in me. Then, in different ways, the Lord confirmed His calling to me while I was at school. You see, when you first start out in ministry, you have all these exciting dreams and things that God whispers. But they are not always fulfilled right away. Yet, God knows right where we are and He continues to speak to us."

"What do you mean?" asked Elizabeth.

"Well, let me tell you a story," said Angela. "One of the most significant times in my life was when I went to Jamaica with six friends for a short-term missions trip."

"Cool. Did He speak to you when you were preaching?"

"Actually, before I ever left. My flight from Buffalo, New York, was delayed for hours due to stormy weather. As I was boarding my flight, I sat down at my requested window seat and looked at my reflection in the window. Looking at myself, tears began to flow down my cheeks. I couldn't hold in the feeling of failure any longer, despite all the people surrounding me.

"I told God, 'This is how I feel right now. I feel like my ministry has been delayed. I was overwhelmed by the clouds and thick darkness around me, and I felt like my tears were going to drown me in defeat.'

"As the plane lifted off the ground, I felt like there wasn't any hope for me. Then, we passed through the turbulence of the storm, rising above the clouds. I saw the most beautiful horizon. Beautiful colors cascaded the sky, from the brightest orange to a colorful pink. I looked below the plane and there were dark, stormy clouds, but as I looked ahead, there was light."

"God spoke to me in that moment. He said, 'Just as the plane rose above the clouds, you will rise above your storm. There are new horizons for you to reach.

Look over the horizon; your eyes cannot see the end of the sky, neither is there an end to My mercy or a limit to My grace. My grace is sufficient for thee: for my strength is made perfect in weakness.'

"From that moment, somewhere in the sky during the summer of my first year at Bible college, God has continued to open doors for me and deepen my burden for ministry."

"But how did you get your minister's license?" asked Elizabeth.

"My dad was starting a daughter work in Elliot Lake, Ontario. I moved home after graduating from ABI to help in the church. God opened doors right away; He's so faithful. He opened doors for me to teach abstinence in the high school, and I sat on a youth committee with the mayor of my city. I moved to Elliot Lake with the intention to fill in any gap. My dad involved me in music, youth ministry, Sunday school, and speaking in church from time to time. He encouraged me to get my license. I resisted at first, because I didn't deem it necessary to minister. However, when I prayed about it, I felt it was an important commitment to the Lord in acknowledging how He is working in my life."

"Were there other women ministers who helped you?"

"Well, when I first started out, I attended my district conference and as I looked around the church, I realized I was the only woman in the service at that time. Feeling overwhelmed, I walked outside and sat on the curb and cried until there were no more tears. Then, I felt God strengthen me in that moment, and when I finally regained my composure, I walked back inside.

Elizabeth asked, "How'd it go when you went back inside?"

Angela said, "Better than I thought. Everyone seemed so encouraging and accepting. They made room for me. Of course, there are always a few who don't believe in women ministers, but that's okay."

The next day they headed west on I-94 steering south toward Wheaton, Illinois. After what had happened in New York, Elizabeth was pretty nervous about traveling through another big city, even though Cara assured her they wouldn't actually have to go through Chicago. After driving an hour and a half, Interstate 94 dumped them onto I-294. Elizabeth thought that traffic was bad then, but it was nothing compared to what happened when I-294 spilled them onto I-80. They no sooner got onto I-80 than three trucks roared passed, one on the left and two on the right, and then they seemed to be locked into wall-to-wall congestion, more semi-trucks than a person could count. What amazed Elizabeth was how closely the trucks followed each other. The cab of the truck beside them almost touched the trailer of the truck in front. Elizabeth proclaimed, "Man alive, this has to be the busiest road in the world!"

"Actually, I think that this stretch of road sees more traffic than anywhere else! Incredible, isn't it?" Elizabeth had another word for it, but she kept it to herself and was not at all sure what was getting into Cara. There was certainly nothing to be happy about being in the middle of all this traffic.

Cara's phone rang, and because she checked the caller ID, she didn't even say hello. "So, Ashley, we're on I-80 just crossing into Illinois," she said excitedly. "How soon before we get there?"

"All depends on traffic. Call me when you are close," Ashley answered and hung up.

"If that's the lady we're staying with, I think we're in trouble," Elizabeth commented.

"Why's that?"

"Well, if she's got so little to say, this could be a big waste of time."

Cara laughed. "Ashley has more to say and can say it faster than anyone I know. You'll love her. We already know each other. I've been in contact with her for months."

"I take it she's not old, then?" said Elizabeth.

"Just a little older than I am."

When they arrived, Elizabeth got a little attitude, at least for a while. She had come to think that it was only she and Cara who shared confidences, and she thought of this trip with Cara as her special trip. But now, Ashley and Cara were chatting energetically about their trip, Chicago, or whatever else came to mind. Elizabeth felt like leftover Limburger cheese.

Finally, over Cokes, Elizabeth was able to get out of her funk and conduct her regular interview with the woman minister. "So, when did you know you were called?" she said without preamble.

Ashley's eyes lit up and everything about her became energized. "My dad pastors in Georgia, and as a child, I always remember wanting to 'be used by God,' though I'm not sure how much I really understood about what that meant. When I was twelve, God spoke into my life."

"What happened?" asked Elizabeth.

Ashley excitedly continued with her testimony. "It wasn't just that I got a wonderful touch from the Lord. There was an evangelist at our church who prayed for me. It was an incredible moment. He took my own hand and placed it on my stomach. He then began to prophesy. He said that I would feel the pains of spiritual childbirth and that through me God would birth children.

"Obviously, at age twelve, this was quite overwhelming, and I couldn't have really understood its whole meaning, but I was sure that I was called to ministry and that my calling would be unique."

Cara then interrupted Elizabeth's interview, inquiring about something she had been mulling over for the last few days. "Ashley, God confirmed His plan along the way, didn't He?"

"Oh, yes," said Ashley. "I remember a time when I was sixteen that Chester Wright prophesied to me. He confirmed that God has a unique calling on my life and I would never again be able to be comfortable being normal. He spoke to me that everything would be different—even my relationships and friendships—because there was something unique God wanted me to do.

"Then when I was nineteen, God confirmed His call once again to me at a general conference during my sophomore year of college. Then, at the age of twenty at a Mantle Conference in Kansas City, I felt confirmation that pulpit ministry would be a huge part of my calling into ministry."

"It must have helped having all that support at Bible college," said Elizabeth.

"Well, I did have support," said Ashley, "but some things about it were a challenge."

"What do you mean?"

"I was the only girl. It was the guys and Ashley; whether it was speech, theology, or classes on pastoral studies. It was just me."

"Did you a snag a boyfriend out of all those guys?" Elizabeth asked, now trying to figure out what she could expect.

"I dated a couple of different guys in Bible college. But in the end, neither worked out. I really wasn't on the same page."

"Tell me about it," said Cara with a smile. Cara was relaxed around Ashley.

"What did you do after Bible college?" Elizabeth asked.

"Yes. After Bible college, I went back home to Georgia to help my dad with music and ministry."

"And you have your minister's license?" Elizabeth asked.

Ashley nodded, "God called me. He deserves my full commitment."

Elizabeth continued, "What does your dad think about it?"

"My dad and mom both believe in me. They're absolutely great!"

"If they're so great, why did you leave them?" asked Elizabeth.

"Well, about the same time I got my license, Brother Vito LaCascio called my dad to see if he minded if he contacted me. I'd met their family before. When

Dad talked to me, I explained that I'd had a burden for Chicago for some time. He agreed that I could go, trusting my judgment. I came up to help with their church in Wheaton. I planned to stay for about six months."

"Has it been six months yet?"

"Elizabeth, Cara knows this already. We talked about it a few weeks back. The day that forever changed my life was Tuesday, September 21 during early morning prayer. I remember telling God that I was tired of not feeling good and I was in desperate need of direction from Him!

"Then, I felt His gentle presence, wooing me. He knew I was frustrated, but He tenderly summoned me: 'Trust Me' was His invitation. I wanted to trust Him, and I got up from where I was and began to walk along the side of the couch in the basement, truly wanting to hear from the Lord."

"Did the Lord tell you not to go back home?" asked Elizabeth, clearly caught up in the story.

"The next thing that happened literally rocked my world and will forever change my life. In the clearest voice I have ever heard God speak to me, He said these words to me: 'I have called you to plant churches!'"

"Wow!" said Elizabeth."

Ashley continued, "I remember the impact of these words almost knocking me over! Is He kidding!? But even in the midst of the shock, in that moment, it was like my life suddenly fell into place. I knew immediately that Chicago was exactly where I was supposed to be. I had this overwhelming sense of trust toward the Lord, knowing that every step I take, He will order."

Elizabeth asked, "So, like, God just asked you to start churches? Like out of the blue?"

Ashley continued, "Well, that's the funny thing. A few hours later, God brought back to my memory a situation that had happened at Gateway. I remembered the last day of Pentecostal History with Brother Johnston; he spent the entire class time admonishing us that the future of Pentecost was in our hands. He looked around the room with passion in his eyes and challenged us that we could plant churches and we could see revival. I remember raising my hand with frustration in my heart and saying, 'Brother J, but I'm a girl! What does that look like for me!? I can't just walk into a city and plant a church!'

"I will never forget his response. He looked straight into my eyes, pointed his finger at me and said, 'Ashley, YOU can plant churches!'"

Elizabeth interjected, "By yourself? I mean, you can't go alone? Can you?"

"I don't know all the details. I don't have a timeline. There are still days when I wonder what the next step is, if I will have someone to partner with in planting churches or will God send me out as a single woman. However, the thing I no longer struggle with is trusting Him for my future. While sometimes, yes, I wonder what He has planned, I have an overwhelming trust that my life is truly in His hands and He will clearly direct me in His perfect timing!"

Chapter 30

The next morning they were going home. Elizabeth was now looking forward to it, ready to sleep in her own bed. The good news was that they got the car packed up the car pretty quickly. The bad news was that they were leaving very, very, early.

Elizabeth wasn't sure whose idea that had been, but Ashley and Cara had somehow decided to take a little trip into Chicago. Because she and Cara would be leaving for home from there, Elizabeth had no choice but to tag along.

They followed Ashley's car, for she apparently knew where to go. Elizabeth, who had not at all been seized by the same spirit of adventure that Cara had, said, "You know, the sun won't be up for an hour!" Cara didn't respond, but after forty-five minutes, both cars pulled over and everybody got out.

Elizabeth wasn't sure what they were supposed to see. Ashley and Cara left her standing by the car and walked out onto a bridge where they were apparently intent on watching thousands of headlights from the oncoming traffic driving into the city. That's about all there was to see, for the skyline of Chicago was barely visible. Elizabeth thought that there must have been better scenery someplace else, but since nobody was asking for suggestions, she just kept quiet.

From where they stood on the overpass, Cara and Ashley continued to stare out into traffic. Finally, Elizabeth thought that Cara might be getting as cold as she was and walked out to complain. When she saw both of their lips moving, she realized they were praying.

Elizabeth turned away and then tried to pray herself, but she wasn't even sure that God was up this early. After a reasonable amount of time had passed, she went back out onto the bridge to complain that they should get back to their cars so they could all get warm. But Elizabeth thought better of saying something when she saw tears on both their cheeks. She then contented herself to stand next to them, saying nothing.

"I've been thinking of how I could do this," Cara blurted out. "Train young people who have a burden!" Ashley was surprised at her friend's sudden outburst. Cara continued, "See, we could issue a call for young people who want to change

Cara's Call

the world; then we'll train them in local churches. It'd be easy to get groups of young people to come to Chicago."

Ashley raised a skeptical eyebrow. While she didn't want to discourage Cara, this plan didn't sound too practical. "Just how would you train them in local churches?"

"Well, we could combine youth groups and have different classes in different churches. You know, teach some about evangelism, teach some on doctrine, and some on church planting. Then, we could have this conference for girls who feel a call. Or maybe we could have one for all young people, because young men—"

Ashley probed, "You're going to have conferences, and then you're going to have training. Pastors will just send their young people to these things and then happily ship them off to Chicago to start churches."

"Absolutely! Now, you've got the concept."

Ashley smiled knowingly. "I appreciate your vision. But nothing happens unless there is some, you know, influential person with a lot of clout who can see beyond what already exists; someone who wants to change the world and try innovative ways to do it. Someone people trust. So, Cara, who do you know like that?"

It was a fair question. Cara was stumped, and to stall for time she asked, "Excuse me, could you repeat that?"

"Who do you know with clout?"

There was a short pause. Then Cara simply said, "God." It was the only answer she could think of. She hoped it would be good enough.

A half hour later, they were heading out of Chicago.

"Hey, Kev," Elizabeth said, picking up the phone.

"Hey, Elizabeth. Let me talk to Cara."

It was funny how things had developed on that trip. During the first part of their trip, Kevin had spent the majority of the time talking to Elizabeth, calling every few days. But then, as the trip progressed, he began to call more often. Then, the amount of time he talked to Elizabeth grew shorter while the time he talked to Cara grew longer. The last week had been mostly just protracted conversations with Cara. Elizabeth didn't say anything. Nor did she act jealous.

"You designed the whole trip to end in Chicago, right?" he asked, trying to get a handle on things.

"Yes. A girl named Ashley lives there, and I wanted to spend some time with her."

"But I gathered earlier that there's something significant about Chicago."

Cara paused, debating whether or not to say something. Then she blurted out, "Kevin, I've been thinking a lot about how to change the world."

"Okay," he said encouragingly.

"Kevin, as I see it, I have two problems with reaching the world."

"Only two?"

"Work with me on this Kevin."

"Sorry. I'm all ears. Two problems. What are they?"

"Well, the first is that we live down here in the cornfields, and it's pretty hard to reach the world from here."

"Well, there are people here, too."

"Think about what they did in the Bible to reach their world. First, they went to major cities, and then they used those locations as bases to evangelize other areas. So that's what the church should do. We have to go to major cities like, Chicago, say, and branch out from there."

"Okay. So a person goes to Chicago." said Kevin.

"Not a person. The apostles started churches with groups. And we should do the same. We just need to find young men and women to answer a call and then train them. Kevin, you know that if young people have purpose, they can do anything."

"Okay, so, specifically, who is going to Chicago to start churches?"

"Anybody. Everybody. I mean, who wouldn't? It's such an opportunity."

"I can think of lots of people who wouldn't go."

"Well, I would. I would go."

"You would or you will?"

"What do you mean?"

"What I mean is that Cara Shepherd doesn't make stuff up. Yes, she's got a vivid imagination and is one of the most creative girls I've ever known, but in her heart of hearts she is a literalist."

"And what is that supposed to mean, Mr. I-Have-All-The-Answers?"

"What I'm saying is that it sounds like God is dealing with you about Chicago. He has already spoken to you about it, hasn't He?"

"I don't want to talk about this right now, okay?"

Cara was two hours from home when the phone rang. "Amanda!" exclaimed Cara. "It is so good to hear from you!"

"Well, phones go two directions," said her friend. Her friend's comment puzzled Cara because Amanda never complained. "Sorry for not calling," she said.

"Yeah, so for whatever reason, I have to get my information from Greg who is getting his information from Kevin, who seems to have a lot of it."

"I said I'm sorry, Amanda. What do you want to know?"

"For starters, I want to know how you and Kevin are doing. It looks like good stuff is happening between you."

"What are you talking about, Amanda?"

"I mean, he seems to really like you, Cara."

"Oh, Amanda, it's not like that. Before this trip, Kevin called me once a week for forty-five minutes just to support me. And he's been a great support this whole trip. Because he's not teaching in the summer, he has more time to call."

"Oh, I see," said Amanda, who didn't seem to be seeing at all. "You don't like him, then?"

"Of course I like him. But we're just friends. Amanda, remember that thing I told you? My commitment to the Lord? That I would be content being single?"

"Yes?"

"Well, I am. And we just talk, that's all. He's supporting me."

"He's never flirted with you."

"No. It's not like that, Amanda."

"Cara, there's more than one way to flirt. So how often is he calling?"

"Every day. Well, lately it could be more than once a day."

"And how long are you on the phone?"

"Amanda, it's not like that! This is so unlike you. Why are you even pushing this?"

"Well, the truth is, Cara, Greg made me call you about this."

"Greg! What does he have to do with anything?"

"I can explain more to you later, but I really need to do it in person. When are you going to make time for me? Can we have a girl's day out when you get back?"

"Unfortunately, as soon as I get back I have two six-week intensive classes. It's kind of an overload, because I should be just taking one class, and there will be homework every night."

"Okay, but let me know when you're free. I really miss my best friend."

Saturday night the Shepherd family went out to eat, and afterward Jim asked to see Cara in his office. He was nervous but determined not to show it. After willing himself to engage in fifteen minutes of general stories about her trip, Jim finally got around to asking the questions he had saved up, questions prompted by his friend's suspicion that she would be influenced by radical elements. His first question was general, a kind of invitation.

"So, Cara, what did you take away from the trip?"

Although she didn't have a ready answer, Cara was genuinely glad her dad had asked this question.

"I've been journaling the whole trip," she said, "and I've met a lot of people with diverse ministries, so it's probably going to take some time to really think about."

"I suppose some of the ministries were more extreme than others?"

Cara gave him a puzzled look, not sure what to say.

Feeling like he needed to press further, he added, "Were some of the women you visited radical?" As soon as it came out of his mouth, he realized that he had not led up to the question appropriately, but it was too late to take it back.

Cara's eyes rolled right in deep reflection, mentally sorting through the various stops. After several seconds she said, "I could identify with some of the women more than others because they had ministries more like what I would like mine to be, but to ask whether some were radical or not is something I hadn't considered. But yes, I would say two or three of them were radical. Probably I would call Sister Jackson and Sister Trout radical. Maybe one or two more. The rest were more concerned about not being associated with a particular group.

"What do you mean?"

Cara spoke thoughtfully, considering her words. "They all said it in different ways, but they meant the same thing. Some of them repeated over and over that they were not into telling men what to do. Others assured me they were not loud, say, or brusque, or bossy, or whatever. However, what was consistent is that they didn't want to be included in that group."

Jim was confused and asked the obvious question: "What group is that, Cara?"

Cara began softly. "The group that men hate."

Her words now came slowly and were full of emotion. She spoke deliberately, hardly conscious of her father in the room. She spoke words that surprised her, words that issued from some unbidden place, from some deep hurt inside of her. "I think it's because they get talked about so much. They're not trying to be controversial, they're just trying to please God. Dad, they just don't want anything to get in the way of fulfilling what God has called them to do."

Cara talked while blinking away tears. Jim thought he should say something to help, to offer some comforting words. But he had a problem. Anything he said could be misunderstood. He might be deemed to be supporting radicals. He may well be affirming those who would usurp his influence with his daughter, those who were out of bounds or out of order.

Despite his fear, twice he almost broke the tearful silence. He almost told her that it was all right, that he trusted her, that he knew she was on the right track. He only hesitated for fear of being misunderstood. Finally, when he could take no more, he decided to throw caution to the wind and offer words of consolation. Unfortunately, her crying stopped abruptly and it was too late.

Cara's Call

Now he chose safer words. "So, you'd put Sister Jackson and Sister Trout in the radical camp?"

Cara stared ahead blankly, offering, "Yes. They're both pioneers. I get the impression they don't believe they'll be accepted no matter what. Although it may be for different reasons, it seems to me that they've resigned themselves to the fact that they won't be accepted by some people no matter what they do."

"So, they've gotten radical, then," repeated Jim.

"Yes," said Cara, nodding. "Radical in their faith. And Daddy, they remind me of someone."

Jim finally felt peace. His daughter had called him "Daddy," what she called him when she was most needy. He hadn't lost his influence.

"Who do they remind you of?"

"Daddy, they remind me of you."

Her words took his breath away. It was only because he had already planned his follow-up question that it came out easily enough. It was a question intended to see what damage the trip had caused Cara. "So, honey, what is it you want to do differently now that you've been on this trip?"

If Cara suspected the question was some sort of challenge to her, she gave no indication. She replied easily, "I'm still working on some things I want to share with you. But one thing I know for sure is I want to help other girls by giving them this same experience that Elizabeth and I had."

Jim was apprehensive. "The same experience?"

"Yes," said Cara. "There are a number of girls with whom Elizabeth and her friends have put me in contact. They're teenagers, and, because it would be impossible to take them on that kind of trip, I was thinking maybe we could get together at church and talk about our experiences. Some of the ladies I visited could come here, and they could speak into these girls' lives."

"Oh," said Jim. "That would be very expensive. Just to promote it would be cost-prohibitive."

"That's the good news," replied Cara. "We'd just promote it on Facebook. So there wouldn't be any expense. Just word of mouth. I'll put out the call—"

"But the cost of the speakers!"

"That's also good news. Several said that if we had something like this, they would come at their own expense."

"Cara, this sounds bigger than a local church. I'm not sure, but the district may have to approve…"

"Could you find out for me, Daddy? Could you get approval?"

"I'll pray about it, Cara."

Two days after she had rolled into town from her trip, Cara sat in an early morning class two hours away from home. She would be chained to her chair for the next four hours. Although she had a break until her three-hour block class that evening, the workload of both classes required that Cara spend the afternoon in the library.

About three o'clock, Cara looked up and was shocked to see Kevin standing in front of her. "Kevin, you are three hours from Charlestown! What are you doing here?" she asked.

"Just needed to see that you were actually back, that you were more than just a voice on the telephone."

"What a nice surprise!"

Over coffee, he shared, "The youth group has been going well this summer, and Greg and Amanda are really coming along. I think they could handle the kids well enough on their own."

Cara found herself thinking how Kevin's words sounded; so different from the way he usually talked to her. She asked, "So, if you don't work with the youth, what would you do?"

"I don't know. I'm thinking of reaching the world."

"Okay," said Cara, confused. "What is it you want to do? Sometimes I feel really stupid. You are always helping me, and I guess I've never really asked what it was you want to do. Kevin, what are your goals?"

Then Kevin asked a very odd question. He said, "Do you like hockey?"

Cara smiled. "I've seen it once or twice, but I don't understand it."

"Well, you know how in baseball, you have statistics that tell how well the player is batting or pitching, say?"

"Yeah."

"Well in hockey, if players score goals, they get credit. But they also get credit another way."

"How?"

"If they assist someone. If they feed the puck to other players who then get the goal. I kind of see myself in that way."

"So you assist people to fulfill their dreams."

"Yes."

"And that's enough?"

"More than enough."

"Kevin, I know you help all the kids in your youth group and you help your second grade students. When we talk, and when you assist me, am I like...in that same category?"

"What are you asking?"

"Do you see me as... uh... in the same category?"

"Of course not. You are... my friend...and you are special to me."

At that moment, Cara hated Amanda. She had turned what had been an easy relationship into something markedly more complicated. The stakes were increased and Cara didn't like it. Not at all.

Kevin paused, and Cara, who had demanded nothing from Kevin up to this point, said, "I'll have to think about what you're saying. Hey... look, Kevin, I've got to go get some reading done before my class tonight."

Chapter 31

Cara decided it was time to cool things with Kevin for awhile. She was able to do that for the six weeks of her classes. But when her classes were over, Kevin insisted that they celebrate. He asked that she drive over to Charlestown for one of their after-service, Friday night pizza get-togethers. She only went out of guilt. But once she got there, she realized how glad she was to see him.

He asked her to keep him company while he took the kids home. Conversation came easily enough, and everything went well until the kids were all dropped off. Then he started talking in that odd way he'd been talking lately. "Okay, so let's just say that one of us has been missing the other one pretty badly the past few weeks, given that the other party didn't have time to talk."

"Can you be more specific? Who, exactly, has been missing who?" asked Cara pointedly.

"It's 'whom,' actually," he corrected, clearly stalling.

"Well?"

"Okay. Let's just say a certain guy, who likes to be in control of everything and be the helper in every situation, is starting to think really hard about a particular relationship."

"Theoretically speaking of course," said Cara, enjoying the moment.

"Right," said Kevin. "Now you're getting it. Well, suppose that this certain guy started reflecting about one particular relationship that started by trying to help out things. And then it turned into an important friendship. That sort of deal."

Cara was not going to help him anymore. Nor would she let him live in this theoretical world. She merely raised an eyebrow indicating that he'd better get to his point.

"Okay," continued Kevin. "I don't know when it happened," he said, and then paused nervously, fumbling for words. "Probably sooner than I let on. But for some time now, I've liked you more than just as a friend."

There was silence. Cara waited for him to say more, and she got a little angry when he didn't. Though her response could have sounded reassuring at any other

Cara's Call

time, instead, she issued a clipped response that sounded more like a challenge than anything else: "And I like you more than just as a friend."

Kevin clearly did not like her tone. There was another pause, and then he said tentatively, "Well, I think we should reflect about what that means exactly."

Cara sighed, disappointed. "Sounds like an awful lot of thinking and reflecting to me," she said. "You're probably going to have to do better than that." But for whatever reason, he couldn't. There was a long silence, and then tension, and finally, she decided they should probably talk less on the phone. Still, this was a commitment she found hard to keep.

"Could we meet today?" Amanda insisted.

"No." It was the middle of September, and Cara didn't really have time to meet.

"Tomorrow?"

"Tomorrow afternoon at four would work. What is it about?"

"We'll have plenty of time to talk about it when we're together."

"I don't have much time."

"I'll need an hour."

As soon as they had ordered their food, Amanda started in on her friend.

"Cara, do you remember what that Stuart Green guy said about not being needy in relationships?"

"Yes."

"And that sometimes, the more unavailable you are to a person, the more attractive you become, because you are a whole person who knows what you want?"

"Vaguely, yes."

"Well, I want to talk to you about your conversations with Kevin."

"What about them?" asked Cara defensively.

"Well, since you and Kevin both said you are going to become monks—"

"Amanda, how dare you talk like that!"

"Well, didn't you say you'd given up the idea of being married?"

"No. You've missed the point altogether. I don't know what Kevin said. But what I said was that I would give up my right to be married. That I would gladly be married, but that my future was up to God, and I would be content in Him."

"Whatever. My question is this: if you and Kevin are so content with the will of God in your lives, reaching the masses or whatever, then why are you both wasting so much time talking to each other?"

"Amanda, are you jealous?"

"Cara, you've totally missed my point. I'm not jealous at all. I think I'm happy for it, but I have to ask what 'it' is."

"What 'what' is?"

"Fourteen hours a week of telephone time."

"We don't spend over ten. And it's usually a lot less."

"Yeah. I thought so. I was just guessing, but I didn't miss it by much. So, Cara, is it normal for two people to counsel with each other about the will of God in this way?"

"Of course it is."

"For ten hours a week? Just because you are friends?"

"Yes, good friends." Cara replied a little more tentatively.

"Purely platonic?"

"Well, I don't know how Plato got involved here," she said, sidestepping.

But Amanda didn't even crack a smile. Instead, she asked, "Do you talk with your brother that much?"

"Of course not."

"And how about your best friend, Amanda? How much time do you spend talking to her?"

"So you *are* jealous!"

"Cara, I really need to tell you something. Do you know why Kevin's fiancée broke up with him?"

There was a pause and then a worried, "No."

"Read my lips. It's because he's such a slow mover. He can talk about commitment, but he just has no follow-through. Cara, they were talking about marriage for two years, but he would never get any closer to it at the end of two years."

"And this should worry me because?"

"Maybe it shouldn't worry you at all. But if you secretly hope that this is the guy for you, then you'd better have some sort of strategy. Have you been out on a date with him?"

There was silence. Finally, she said, "I told you we were just friends."

"Okay, Cara, have you ever heard of triage?"

This was an odd turn in the discussion. "Triage? Doesn't that have something to do with the emergency room?" she asked.

"Well, it can refer to more than one thing, but on the battlefield it has a very specific meaning. Because the medic has limited time and resources, he has to make choices as to whom to treat first, particularly if there are a lot of wounded. So, he divides them into three different categories."

"Hence, triage," said Cara.

"Right. The first group may include those who, though they may be in terrible pain, are going to live without assistance. The medic passes them by. Then there are those who are going to die no matter what he does. Even though he hates to see them suffer, he has very little time for them. But then there's the third group: the ones who can recover if they get help."

"Amanda, make your point!"

"Greg insisted that we do an intervention. He called it triage. He thinks it's possible for your relationship to survive and even thrive. So, he sent me over to talk to you, and he's talking to Kevin."

"You've got to be kidding me!"

"Cara, in this platonic relationship that you two have, what will be the indicators that you have moved to something else—I know, supposing it's God's will and all. Remember. One of the things that makes you attractive to Kevin is that you're not anxious. But there is going to be a downside to that, particularly because we're talking about Kevin. If you keep acting like you're acting, then you may well be keeping him from doing what he is supposed to do in a relationship."

Cara just stared down into her plate, not sure how to respond.

"Cara, I'm not telling you what to do to fix this relationship. It's your deal. But I do know that what you're doing now isn't working. And whatever it's going to take to bring change, you're not helping the situation."

An hour later, Cara called Kevin. She didn't even say hello.

"Hey, Amanda had a talk with me this afternoon."

"Greg and Amanda are double-teaming us."

"What did you think about the conversation that you had with Greg?" asked Cara. "I mean, did the word 'commitment' come up at all?"

"The big 'C' word came up several times. Greg thinks that I need to step up."

Then Kevin, who was never far from offering helpful ideas to others, seemed to struggle with what to say next. Finally, he said, "I told him we had something really special that was developing. That we were focused and had made commitments to each other."

"That's funny, Kevin, because I don't really remember any of those commitments."

"I mean, we talked about how cool it would be if our goals would come together and if there was a possibility of us working side by side in ministry."

"Are you sure that was me you were talking to, because I sure don't remember that conversation, Kevin."

"Well, maybe I didn't state it in those exact words. But that is what I meant."

"Okay. Well, I've got a homework assignment I have to finish, so I'm going to catch up with you tomorrow," she said testily.

Cara's anger contributed to her questions as to who the real Kevin actually was. That confident helper, who could tackle any question in the world, or this weak and spineless jellyfish, who couldn't seem to make up his mind about the greater issues of life.

Cara didn't do much homework that night. What she did do was journal. And pray. And cry. The truth was that, up until now, she had been so focused on all her other issues that she hadn't really worried too much about Kevin. However, life would no longer allow such a luxury.

Kevin opted out of his youth group's Friday night pizza run and drove over to Denny's to meet Cara after her fellowship meeting. The waitress at Denny's poured them coffee. It was already eleven o'clock. Kevin ordered bacon and eggs, pancakes, hash browns, and orange juice, as if he was ready to settle in for a long talk. However, when his food came, he didn't touch it but rather served up an entrée of complaints.

"Okay, I don't know why Greg and Amanda had to create a crisis. Why did they have to formulate labels or some sort of artificial standards about us and our relationship? We know what we have."

"What do we have?" asked Cara.

"Cara, you know that I love you and I am proud of you."

"Yes, but you love pepperoni pizza and you tell all the kids in your youth group that you are proud of them. Which one is closer to our relationship: am I more like a kid in your youth group or more like pepperoni pizza?"

"Cara, that is so unfair."

"I was praying about our issues, and I think I have some insight. You can tell me to go fish if I'm off," she said.

"Okay."

"This has to do with your father, doesn't it?" she asked.

There was anger in his voice. "Go fish," he said too abruptly.

"He walked out on your mom and you."

"Cara, why don't we leave my father out of this?"

"Don't you see? That's what you're afraid of. You're afraid that you're going to walk out on me. That we'll get married and you'll do just what your father did."

"Cara, you are crossing a line here. I don't want to talk about this anymore."

"Fine," said Cara. "I get that. I'll tell you what. I think we'd better put a hold on our relationship, or whatever it is, until you figure out what it is you do want to talk about."

Cara had provoked him. She took a risk, but it was a calculated risk. She knew that girls had an emotional advantage in fights like this. She also knew she was right about what she had said.

Sure enough, about two in the morning, her phone rang. Not just a text—it was an actual phone call. But she was up.

"So, I called to say that I think you were right," said Kevin.

Cara was not about to let him off the hook so easily.

"So, then, you called to say I was right?" she repeated, slipping into her counselor tone.

Kevin hated that voice. He would have called her on using it on him except that he was hardly in a position to negotiate. He continued, "So… I've got to admit that my father walking out on the family colors a whole lot of what I do."

"You're saying that you are aware that your past affects your actions right now?" she asked.

"And I want you to forgive me for not acknowledging it."

"Which I do, Kevin. Is there anything else you want to say?"

"Only that I'm aware of it. And that I'm hoping it will affect me less in the future… and I'm hoping you'll have patience with me."

"Okay and thank you so much for that, Kevin. But I don't."

"Excuse me?"

"Kevin, do you remember when you talked to me about committing my future to the Lord? That I needed to give up my right to be married?"

"Of course."

"Well, I did that, Kevin. And it has changed my life. But I would say there might be a 'part two' to that sort of commitment."

"What are you saying, Cara?"

"Kevin, just like you committed to God your right to be married, I think you have to make another sort of commitment."

"Like what?"

"You have to give up your right to be single."

"I've never heard of such a thing."

"Obviously."

"What would that do? I mean, what does that even mean?"

"It means that singleness is no more a right than being married is. And if God is big enough to direct you as a single person, He is big enough to keep a marriage intact. Kevin, I'm talking about an act of faith, one that you have to make."

"Here's the bottom line, Kevin. Your problem is really not with your father. And your problem is not with me. Your problem is with the Lord. You don't believe He is bigger than other people's past failures. You don't trust Him to give you the wisdom and power to do what is right in a marriage. You have a spiritual problem."

Cara sensed that zinger hit Kevin square in the face. Kevin looked as if he had been slapped in the face. Certainly, she could have said it a different way. She wasn't even sure she was right. But it felt right. And if it wasn't, it was up to Kevin to tell her how it wasn't right and what his issues really were.

"So... you want me to like... do this... right now?"

She hadn't intended to say what she said next. But it changed everything. She couldn't say it was from the Lord. In a way, it was a roll of the dice for her future. But she said it anyway.

"Take as long as you want," she said. "I'm in no hurry. But we're not going to talk again until it happens."

After she had hung up, she realized that she'd lied. She said, "I'm in no hurry." She should have said something else. Maybe, "There is no hurry." Because, the truth was, she did not want to wait another day.

Two weeks later on a Friday morning, Kevin called.

"Hey, Cara, I need to talk."

"I'm just about to step into class, Kevin. I don't have much time."

"But I need to tell you something important."

"Okay, but if you wait until later, then I would have more time to talk."

"This can't wait."

"All right then," said Cara.

"Okay, so I did it," he said.

Cara smiled a frustrated smile. This was so like Kevin. "I think I know what you're saying, but just for the record, remind me one more time what it is you did," she replied.

"I told the Lord I would trust Him to help me make long-term commitments. And that I would trust Him for the future. You were right! That really was my problem. I couldn't trust God for my future, no matter how much I tried to talk to others about it."

"How is that going for you then?" she asked flatly.

"Well, I'm not sure. I just did it this morning."

Cara was now a little bit angry. "Kevin, you're like the alcoholic who hasn't had a drink in an hour and is telling me his whole life is changed," she said.

"That is so unfair."

"All I'm asking is what real difference that decision is going to make in your attitude, actions, and habits of thinking."

"Cara, I just called to tell you, because I thought you'd celebrate with me."

Now Cara smiled genuinely, in spite of her steeled attempt not to let this guy into her heart without a stronger commitment. "Well, I love you, Kevin O'Reilly, and I want you to know I am proud of you. And also, I want to say we'll talk more when you sort through the practical implications of your decision."

Chapter 32

Cara got Kevin's second call that afternoon. "Will you speak in youth service for me tonight?" he asked.

"Kev, you know I have fellowship meeting at the house."

"What's the matter? You don't trust the leaders you've been training?"

"You're asking me to speak in your youth service tonight?"

"Yes, I am. I figured you had to work tomorrow, and I didn't want to make it a late night or anything, and I thought we could talk."

"I'll be there," said Cara, hoping for the best.

Before the service, Kevin said, "Greg and Amanda are going to take the kids to Pizza Hut. There's a little hamburger stand—"

"Sure."

The food came, and after they said grace, Cara put some ketchup on her fries. Kevin was as nervous as a cat. "Okay, so I'm thinking we should talk about getting married at some point."

Cara looked at him, incredulous. "Just like that? Just like we should talk about going to Pizza Hut or a hamburger joint?"

"Cara, I'm trying to have a serious conversation here."

"Be that as it may, I do have some issues."

"What?"

"We haven't exactly had what you might call a normal sort of dating experience. Kevin, I actually have two problems."

"Okay, what are they?"

"First of all, where's the leadership on your part? You know, why don't you create an actual plan so we can talk about it?"

"And the second thing?"

"Well... I don't know how to say it, but Kevin, where's the romance?"

"What? You want a romantic, candle-lit dinner or something? Maybe I could also hire a violinist while I'm at it."

"See, Kevin, that is what you do! You diminish what a girl wants by joking your way out of it. Do I need to ask for flowers? Would you ever think about taking me out officially on a date? You haven't even kissed me, yet!"

"Well," he said. "I see your point now. And as to the kissing, we can take care of that right now, if that's what you want."

"Kevin, do you call that romance? Sometimes you act like an idiot!"

"All right then," he offered. "I will draw up a plan, I'll get romantic, and then we'll start planning the future."

"You don't have too good of a record on this."

"What do you mean?"

"Weren't you in this same planning stage for two years in your previous relationship?"

"Okay. I see what you mean. I'll have specific dates set up for the commitments."

Only half-teasing, Cara said, "This isn't a ten-year plan, is it?"

After work on Saturday, Kevin picked Cara up from Office Depot. He said he had planned something for her. They went to Denny's, which wasn't too original, but apparently the meal wasn't the important part. Kevin carried what looked like a rolled-up blueprint in his hand, and while they were waiting for the food, he unrolled the document.

"Who did this for you?" asked Cara, when she saw that the title of the document consisted of large flowing letters written in calligraphy. It read, "Kevin's Commitments to Cara."

"Ah," he said, "I possess knowledge about which you've only begun to scratch the surface." His bragging was very un-Kevin-like.

Cara laughed. "No, really?"

"My friend Randy," he admitted.

She paused to read through the flowing script noticing that it sounded like an attempt at Old English legalese. From a literary perspective, it was terrible. But that didn't matter. Kevin had done something; something that demonstrated that he was, indeed, willing to make serious changes.

The body of the document began, "Kevin O'Reilly, the party of the first part, promises to make the following commitments on the following schedule to Cara Shepherd, the party of the second part." Kevin then went on to explain in detail what would happen on their first, second, and subsequent dates. Their first date was planned out in considerable detail. He would provide the flowers, romance, and appropriate kissing. After reading this, Cara responded, "Kevin, this is so cheesy."

The document went on to say that in February, on or before the fifteenth, he would talk to her dad about approval for their marriage and the official surprise engagement would be the last Saturday night in March at a very romantic dinner. After she graduated in August, they would make final preparations for the wedding to be held in October.

"Kevin, do you really think that you can do all this by these deadlines? I don't mean to be critical. It's just that you have this incredible fear of everything you say in here, and I'm sure that you'll find some excuse to—"

Apparently to prove that he would follow through, Kevin interrupted her by leaning in close and kissing her.

"I'll follow through on or before the dates in the contract," he said.

"You're making a believer out of me," she said. "And I'm really happy about it. But are you sure you're not overestimating your power of persuasion with my father."

"Cara," he said. "Are you kidding me? I put my life into the hands of thirty second-graders every day. How hard can this be?"

"We'll see." she replied, hoping for the best.

The Saturday before their first officially scheduled date, Kevin and Greg were driving back from a paint ball tournament in rural Illinois. Greg said, "Say, bro—, congratulations on your plans and everything, but don't you think you'd better meet Cara's dad before you ask him to give you his daughter's hand in marriage?"

Kevin said that it was a good idea, because he thought his brother was talking in general terms. But Greg was not. He said, "Well, Kev, it's only twenty minutes to stop at Munson Heights. It's on the way back. Perfect timing."

"Greg, I'm dressed in paintball clothes and I could use a shower."

"Yeah, but isn't Cara's dad kind of a macho guy? Who knows, you might impress him!"

A phone call later, it became official that he and Greg would be stopping by the Shepherd home. Pastor Shepherd answered the door. He looked right over Kevin's head and said, "Greg, man, good to see you!" Both Kevin and Greg were ushered in as Cara was coming down the stairs.

"You remember my brother, Kevin, from the wedding, don't you?" asked Greg.

Jim looked closer at the shorter visitor. "Oh, I do now. He was a little cleaner back then. So, Greg, did you get anything when you guys went bow hunting? Didn't you hunt in old farmer Willard's back forty?"

"Yeah, we set up a stand, but I could only go two days. Got nothing. Say, my brother Kevin came over to see Cara."

Jim turned to Kevin. "Oh, are you going to join her leadership training group? I think it's important."

"Probably not that but—"

"You should, you know. It makes a big difference." Then, searching for common ground, he asked, "So, Kevin, do you live with your parents?"

"No."

Jim, not much of conversationalist, thought of another question. "Are you going to school?"

"No.

"You should go. That's where the future is. But who am I to talk? I didn't have much schooling."

"Well, I actually have already—"

Cara joined in. "Dad, Kevin is the youth leader in Charlestown. He and I have been talking—"

"Oh yeah. The skit for the rally next month. Are you pretty good at skits, Kevin?"

"Well, I'm not much of an actor."

"Too bad. Maybe Cara will put you on props then. Say, Greg, who's your pick in the wild-card game next Saturday? And don't say Chicago…"

Ten awkward minutes later, Greg and Kevin were en route to Charlestown again. "I think that went well," said Kevin as they backed out of the driveway. Then they both laughed until the tears came.

When they caught their breath, Greg admitted, "Yeah… well, maybe not my best idea, Kev."

Sunday evening after church, Cara's mom and dad were in bed. He was marking up F. B. Meyer's biography of Peter.

"Dear, Cara talked to me about that Kevin," she said.

"Kevin who?" he asked.

"You know. Greg's brother. Youth leader in Charlestown?"

"Oh, yeah. He was by here yesterday afternoon practicing for a skit, but the kid can't act."

"I think Cara is dating him."

"Not possible!"

"Why do you say that?"

"He has to be seventeen years old."

"He just looks young."

"And he's short. Did you see them walk down the aisle together in Greg's wedding? She towered over him."

"That's because the only heels she could find to go with the dress had four-inch stilettos. Really, he's as tall as Cara."

"No way."

"Well, a half-inch shorter, maybe. Probably the same height when she's not wearing shoes."

"Maybe we could get her to go barefoot then."

"He is really nice."

"He's a bum. Why can't these kids dress up a bit more? He doesn't strike me as a serious prospect. He doesn't even go to school."

"Well, actually I think that—"

"I don't want to talk about this right now. Maybe if it gets more serious, I'll talk to him. I wish Cara would have stayed with Josh. Hey, whatever happened to that guy with the Corvette?"

"I don't know, dear."

"She leaves the guys who could support her and goes out with bums."

Kevin stopped by the following Saturday. He said hello to Cara's dad and then he and Cara went out for coffee. It was Cara's idea.

The second week of February, Kevin stopped by his brother's apartment. "So," said Greg, "Have you tamed the savage beast?"

"I've had to strategize as to how to cross paths with him. I've talked with him six different times since December, but I'm still waiting for the chemistry to kick in."

"He hasn't warmed up to you, then?"

"Well.... No, not at all. And the schedule says I'm to ask him for his daughter's hand within a week, based on the commitment I made to Cara."

"Don't do it, bro—"

"Got to. I promised Cara to stay on track with this schedule. And I need to do it."

"How long have you been dating?"

"Do you mean formally?"

"I didn't know there was more than one kind."

"Well, we've been talking for a year."

"I've been talking to my mailman for five years."

"I mean, I've been seeing her for well over half a year."

"I don't even know what that means. How long have you been dating? When was your first date?"

"You mean, like where I picked her up to go out to a restaurant? That sort of thing?"

"Is that a difficult question, Kevin?"

"Well, officially, December."

"All right, why don't you come back in a year and maybe we can talk." But Kevin didn't move. He simply smiled, patiently.

"Do you have a job?"

"Yes."

"So what do you do?"

"I'm a teacher."

"How old are you?"

"I'm twenty-five."

"Really. That's hard to believe. So, you teach high school?"

"Second grade."

"Hmmpph."

More frustrated than he'd been in some time, Kevin recalculated a way to disengage without being totally defeated.

"I'll tell you what, Brother Shepherd," he said, "I realize that this is rather sudden. I'm really sorry for springing everything on you so abruptly. So, why don't we take some time to process this? And maybe in about three weeks or so, you'll have some more questions for me that I can try to answer."

That satisfied Jim and he consented.

When Cara heard about their conversation, she thought it was Kevin at his best. There might be hope after all.

"What kind of crazy deal is that?" asked Jim.

Karen knew when to let him vent, so she didn't even bother to respond.

"A kid shows up and demands my daughter's hand in marriage. She's still in school, Karen. Did he actually think of that?"

Only now did Karen look up, timing her response perfectly.

"Are you asking me what they have planned, dear?"

"Do you know?" he asked.

"Well, Cara has run a couple of ideas by me. But, of course, they're just ideas. Nothing settled or anything."

"Well?"

"You remember that Cara graduates in August, right?"

"This year?"

"Yes, August of this year."

"And?"

"Well, Cara has always talked about an October wedding. Not that it has to be in October. This is all negotiable. Of course, nothing would happen without your approval."

"Who will be in charge of all this planning? Cara or Kevin?"

"I don't know, dear. My guess is they'll probably do it together."

Jim noticed Karen's extreme interest in her magazine, apparently signaling that she'd had enough discussion about Cara and Kevin for the night.

Jim humiliated Bob on the racquetball court with a score of fifteen to three; there was no question that Jim had issues. He was huffing and puffing and could hardly talk. But he was so upset he couldn't stop himself.

"Bob, what would you do if a kid shows up on your door and has been dating your daughter for two months and wants to marry her? Answer me that! What would you do?"

Bob replied, "Depends who the kid is, I suppose."

"Kevin O'Reilly from Charlestown."

"Sure. I know of him."

"Then spill the beans. What do you know?"

"From Charlestown. Teacher. Solid guy."

"How do you know?"

"Well, my brother-in-law's nephew is in the youth group. Kevin's the youth pastor. You know, they say it is the best youth group in the section. Started with nothing and they've got between forty and fifty kids that come every Friday."

"You're kidding me, right? He strikes me as a bit wimpy. I thought Greg was the youth leader."

"No. Ralph—that kid I told you about who is in the youth group—he says that Greg follows Kevin around like a puppy dog."

"Greg's no one's puppy dog, Bob. How does a little guy like that get so much authority?"

"Beats me. He's older than Greg. And Jim, some people wear their authority a little easier than others."

"Bob, they haven't been dating all that long. I can't give my approval until they go out a lot more."

"How did that dating thing work out for Sandra?" This was Bob's shorthand for a lot of things. None of them good.

Jim only smiled, admitting defeat on that point.

"Who's in charge in that relationship? You've got to admit, Cara's pretty stubborn about certain things."

"From what I hear about the crazy way they do their youth service, Kevin's got a lot of strange ideas himself. So who can say? But it would be worth looking into, finding out who is going to be in charge. You wouldn't want Cara getting stuck with a wimp."

"Lot to think about, Bob," said Jim, picking up the ball. Bob could see that Jim would probably cream him during their second game as well.

"Karen, did you know that Cara feels a call to Chicago to start a church?" asked Jim.

"Yes, dear, she's talked to me about it. She told me that you and she had discussed it last fall."

"She didn't really discuss it. She simply told me. She said she didn't require words of affirmation, but if I didn't approve, I should let her know."

"So did you let her know?"

"Not so far. But here's my question. Are they planning to go up to Chicago and start a church as soon as they're married? Because I don't think they're ready."

"That's a good question, dear. Maybe you could ask Kevin. So, then, is that a different issue than whether you'll give them permission to be married?"

"Karen, I want to know something. How could any fellow let Cara drag him around based on her calling? What kind of spineless person would allow for that?"

"That's another good question, dear. Maybe you should talk to Kevin about it."

"See, Karen, kids don't think about these things, do they? They're just in a hurry to run off and get married. And they're not ready. They're too young."

"To get married or to start a church?"

"Both!"

"That could be, dear. How old were we when we married?"

"That's beside the point. These are different times, Karen. Kids need to wait a little bit longer now."

"I understand, dear."

"What do we even know about him? He could secretly be an axe murderer for all we know."

"I suppose we could check the trunk of his car to see if he's hiding anything."

"Be honest, Karen. We don't know him."

"I understand, dear. Amanda's mom knows Kevin, and she told me that she thinks he has excellent character. Of course, she is only one person, and I really can't say that I know him that well myself. Did you know he's already started his master's program in education?"

"They have no ministerial experience. They have nothing."

"Dear, how much furniture did we have when we got married?"

Jim smiled. "We had a kitchen table and a bed, so we had the main things covered."

"Is it really possible to have all the answers when you get married?"

"Karen, I'm just trying to fulfill my responsibility as a father and a pastor."

"I know, dear. And that's why they need your approval for their marriage without too many strings attached, don't you agree?" This complaint was as strong as any Karen was likely to lodge with her husband, and she knew there was a chance it could make him angry.

Chapter 33

"Who's going to wear the pants in the family?" asked Jim.

Kevin smiled. "That would be me. I don't think Cara owns any pants."

Jim didn't laugh. He didn't so much as crack a smile. "When would you plan to get married?" he asked.

"Well, we're still working on the details. It would have to be after Cara graduates."

"Possibly in the fall, huh? Have you talked to her about this?"

"Well, we have talked about it informally. But I was kind of getting my ducks in a row before I officially propose."

"You know, Cara has some ministry issues. So I need to come back to this question, because it troubles me. Who's going to be calling the shots?"

Hopefully, God will."

"I'm talking between you and Cara."

"If you're asking if I will be a good leader for your daughter, I believe that I will."

"That didn't sound too confident."

"Pastor Shepherd, I want to ask you as confidently as I can right now," he began with a twinkle in his eye, "for your permission to proceed."

Jim did not hesitate. "You have my permission to proceed under one condition."

"What would that be?"

"Let's talk more about timing and ministry."

"Are you saying you might rescind your permission if I offer the wrong answer to those questions?"

"The wife likes you. Bob says you're a good man. And Cara obviously loves you. You have my blessing. The other thing is just working out details—important details, mind you—but nothing I would hold over your head."

"Would it work out to talk through our plans, say, a week from Friday?" asked Kevin, sensing that time was on his side and realizing that getting Pastor Shepherd to take things in bite-sized pieces would likely work in his favor.

"Sure. A week from Friday would be fine," Pastor Shepherd agreed.

Cara's Call

An hour later, Kevin and Cara sat at Denny's drinking coffee and strategizing about what to do next. A text suddenly appeared on Cara's phone. She looked at it and exclaimed, "Oh no!"

"What is it?" asked Kevin.

"It looks like Fred texted everybody on his phone list."

"What's it say?"

"'pastorshepherdsaysyes!'"

"How did Fred get this information?" Cara asked. "You only told your brother and I only told Amanda."

Kevin smiled and said, "Leave it to Fred."

In the next two minutes, twenty texts appeared on Cara's phone—texts of congratulations, questions, and well-wishing.

"Well, at least, that's over with," said Cara.

"If that were only true. I have no idea how to bridge the gap on what I have to ask for at my next meeting with your dad, but at least I've got a few days to think about how to approach him."

Seeing the set of Pastor Shepherd's jaw gave Kevin pause. His future father-in-law began the conversation by rehearsing his concerns.

"You're aware Cara wants to be a minister and that, in fact, she wants to be a pastor?"

"Absolutely."

"And does that sit well with you?"

"She has the call of God on her life."

"Are you a minister?"

"No."

"Do you want to be one?"

"Well, I want to be whatever God has for me to be, but up until this point in my life, I really haven't felt any specific call in that direction."

"Where do you think Cara wants to pastor?"

"Chicago."

"She told you this?"

"We decided this together. It's something we both feel to do."

"But it is Cara's calling. To Chicago."

"Yes."

"She's prepared to start a church up there?"

"Well, I would say she is 'preparing.' No one ever quite feels prepared."

"And this is something you both feel prepared to do?" Jim asked, not giving up the use of the word "prepared."

"Well, ministry is nothing you can ever do on your own. And no matter how much we work toward this goal, we will still be entirely dependent on God's leading and provision. When we first get married, we need to spend quite a bit of time in just getting to know each other as a married couple and working together in ministry before we move to Chicago. But we want to go there sooner rather than later."

"What does 'sooner rather than later' actually mean?"

"We're thinking of possibly a year, maybe two, after we get married."

"And what sort of preparation are you talking about?"

"Well, a number of things. Cara wants to get started in some course work at the seminary as a distance learner. Also, I think it is important for Cara to get her license this year."

"You think, or she thinks."

"Actually, this is something I'm insisting on for her. She's pretty laid back about it."

"And you wouldn't get yours?"

"Not at this time. I would get it if I felt God was leading me in that direction. And I am certainly open to what God wants to do in my life."

"So you say. But it sounds to me like you've pretty much got this worked out."

"Trying to… sir," he added, because it was feeling like that sort of conversation.

"How can you insist she get her license? What kind of talk is that?"

"Pastor Shepherd, in your opinion, has Cara demonstrated an ability to teach, speak, lead, and counsel those under her direction?" Kevin asked.

"She certainly has done that for a while. But she doesn't need a license to do those things, now does she?"

"Pastor Shepherd, any minister is just as called with or without their ministerial license. And Cara believes she could do all these things without being licensed but—forgive me for asking—couldn't you or any other pastor minister without a license? The truth is that it is important for the faith community to publicly and officially recognize those who are called to lead them."

Jim thought about it and nodded his head ever so slightly. But, because he didn't know what he was conceding, he challenged something Kevin had said, "What kind of language is that anyway: 'faith community'?"

Kevin tried to figure out how to dance around what was at best a peripheral issue. "Of course, the district would have to approve," he finally said, "and even before that, those to whom she is closest would have to approve."

"You're saying this isn't something she'd run off and do."

"A pastor has to sign and give his approval so that everything can proceed."

"And you're saying she'd take my advice on this."

"Has she ever not submitted to you?"

"Has she ever agreed with me about anything on ministry?" Pastor Shepherd countered.

"That's a different question, isn't it?"

"What if I would say no?"

"Brother Shepherd, we need a pastor's blessing. I'm trying to figure out what church we're going to go to once we get married."

Later, Kevin decided he should have chosen those last words a little more carefully. Somehow, he had not managed to establish what he'd intended to say first, which was that he thought Pastor Shepherd was a wonderful man, a good father, and an able pastor, and that he was really hoping to sit under his ministry. But now, he would never get to make any of those points because, after Kevin said what he did, there was no opportunity to say another word.

A torrent of words gushed forth from the man who would be his father-in-law: the word "submission" recycled at least five or six times, as was the charge, "usurping authority." At one time even the phrase "stealing my daughter" was uttered. While some might not have called it a tirade, whatever it was, it lasted ten minutes, and when it was over, Kevin was excused without comment.

Karen read from Philippians chapter four in her morning devotion. She needed it. She said the words aloud. "Be anxious for nothing, but in everything by prayer and supplication, with thanksgiving, let your requests be made known to God."

Karen leaned back in her chair and repeated the verse again and again. She then began to say her prayer request over and over again, all the while praising God for how He had helped and would continue to help.

Her husband was a wonderful man. But he was competitive. He never said whether he beat Bob in racquetball. He didn't have to. The score practically shone out of his eyes.

Jim had another challenge as well. Karen had seen Jim that morning and knew that, once again, the deep melancholy that sometimes gripped him was back for the vacant look in his eyes had betrayed him. She had no training in these things but thought perhaps it was his fierce need to be right that bore some blame, or perhaps not.

The melancholia had happened a couple times earlier in their marriage. It had happened once more when they had taken the church and there was that big mess to work through. The last time it happened was when Cara told him she was called to preach. Now it was back. It seemed there was nothing she could do to help. Nothing but pray—and that is exactly what she did.

"We're going to tell no one," insisted Cara. "Not even your brother. I don't want this getting out on Facebook or being gossiped about."

Kevin nodded. "Total agreement. For now, anyway, this stays between you and me, and maybe we can keep Fred at bay."

"I'm looking at some apartments on the south side of Munson Heights," Cara noted.

"That's nice. But don't get your hopes up on anything just yet."

"Aren't you the one who told me that you thought that it was God's will for us to be here?"

"Of course. But it's possible for someone to thwart God's purpose by making the wrong choices."

"And it is possible for God to turn things around. Kevin, we've got to agree on this. We've got to bind this thing in Jesus' name."

"Cara, I get that we need to pray, but there is a very short window of time."

"What do you mean?"

"I have to decide whether to keep my current position or put in for teaching jobs in school districts near Munson Heights."

"Kevin, this is what you should do. Apply over here, but keep your options open as long as possible. We'll wait until the very last possible minute before we tell them yes or no."

Kevin thought about this plan for a moment and seemed to be filled with a new confidence. "We can do this, Cara. I'll hit the internet and start fishing."

Cara now looked glum. "Welcome to my world, Kevin. Are you sorry you ever—"

"Now, Cara, you talked me into praying. That prayer's going to work. So don't try to talk me out of it."

"How's the new son-in-law coming along?" teased Bob.

"Good, good," said Jim flatly.

"From what you've said, it doesn't sound too good."

"He's a bit more stubborn than I expected him to be."

"Jim, you should hear yourself talk."

"What do you mean?"

"First, you worry he's going to be a wimp. Now you're worried he's too stubborn. Which is it, Jim?"

Jim laughed in spite of himself. "Well, why not a wimpy, stubborn guy?"

Cara's Call

"You know what they say, Jim. Nobody really ever likes their son-in-law. It's not jealousy, just normal fatherly concern. But at least you're not losing Cara. I mean, you are actually getting a little extra help out of the deal at your church. Look at it that way."

"Let me ask you something, Bob. It's about Cara. Okay, so she's getting married. Once the knot is tied, who is she primarily responsible to get her guidance from, her father, who is also her pastor, or her new husband?"

"Well, that's a tough one, Jim. I'm never one to diminish the role of a pastor or a father, but you know, the Bible does say 'leave and cleave,' doesn't it? So, I'm afraid that if push came to shove, he just might be first. But, hey, the good news is, if he moves to Munson Heights, you'll still be a voice in both their lives."

"Yeah," said Jim. "That's something to think about."

Even though Kevin hated to mess up the calligraphy, he had crossed out the old dates of commitment that he had already missed because of the delay of several weeks due to Cara's father. Still, he was not far off in his planning and was able to highlight the adjusted dates by using blue rather than black ink.

"So, the next event comes up next Saturday," he said.

"What's next Saturday?" asked Cara, wanting him to say it out loud. She didn't want to be a project.

"That's when I'm officially taking you to a nice restaurant and surprising you by proposing and sneakily offering you that ring we already had sized for your finger."

"Kevin, you are such a nerd."

For whatever reason, Kevin showed up for their fellowship meeting on Friday night. This was highly unusual because it was his youth night, and he never missed. He explained that he just wanted to get a first-hand look at how Cara did things. As usual, the group was spread out all over the basement. Some were in chairs, some on the floor, and some on the old sofa.

Marta led in songs. Peter did the prayer requests. Ron taught the lesson and oversaw the small group discussion. Cara led only the closing prayer, but throughout the meeting, Ron and Marta kept looking at her for direction or affirmation.

"So, remember," said Cara, "we want to pray for Chelsea and Ron for their upcoming midterm exams. And we need to remember Jerry's brother for healing. Any other requests before we pray?"

"I have one," said Kevin.

"Okay?" said Cara.

Kevin moved from the wall where he stood and walked over to where Cara was standing. It seemed that he wanted to share his request with the whole group, so Cara took a step sideways. Then unexpectedly, Kevin knelt down awkwardly in front of her, and asked, loud enough for all to hear, "Cara Shepherd, will you marry me?"

For once in their relationship, Cara was totally and completely surprised. Her face diffused with color. It was an awkward moment. No longer feeling in charge, she was left only with the sense that people were staring at her. Here she was, standing in front of the group, and there was Kevin, on a knee. He had the box with the ring in it. He wanted an answer. He was still waiting and the group was clapping, but Cara simply had no voice. She would kill him for doing this in public!

When Cara nodded yes, Kevin took her into his arms. "Why now?" she whispered into his ear.

"They deserve to see." And when she saw his tears of genuine delight, she forgave Kevin and loved him even more. Then Kevin said, "And you deserved to see them see."

"We need chairs," announced Ron, suddenly in charge. He made the happy couple sit in the chairs and announced that the group was going to be praying a blessing on the newly engaged couple.

"I thought you were supposed to surprise me at a romantic dinner tomorrow night," whispered Cara as the ruckus was going on.

"Oh. About that. I need the ring back so the chef can put it in the dessert."

"You're not serious!"

"Dead serious. Cara, I'm going to prove to you that I will keep my commitments. All of them."

Ron began, "We call down your blessing in Jesus' name…" A roar of additional blessings and prayers echoed his. The prayer went on for what seemed like a long time, maybe three minutes or more. Afterwards, there were more tears mixed with smiles and a couple of high fives.

Kevin said he now had another announcement and stood to address the group.

"When I was little, my father abandoned my family. I haven't seen him much since then." Tears came to his eyes, but he continued, "He calls me once in a blue moon, usually when he's drunk. He usually wants something from me. Most of the time it's money." Some of the young people nodded as if they knew by experience what Kevin was talking about.

"Anyway, I've got to admit that, in the past, I choked on commitment issues because I honestly was afraid of the future. I was afraid that I would drink. Or that I would abandon my family. Or that I wouldn't be able to tell my kids how important

Cara's Call

they were to me. That I would be unfaithful to my wife and turn into some sort of needy character."

Everyone's eyes were glued on Kevin. "I believe in you!" shouted Ron suddenly from the back of the room.

"Thanks," said Kevin to the unexpected interruption. "Your support really means a lot. And I also believe that God will help me keep commitments. I want to make a commitment right now in front of all of you. I want to publicly pledge my unconditional love to Cara."

Kevin paused momentarily, apparently trying to think of what to say next. Then he continued, "So, anyway, I have a song that I want to be my song of commitment to you, Cara."

Then, in a voice that cracked and with a melody that only vaguely resembled the original, Kevin started singing a Steven Curtis Chapman song. "Tomorrow morning if you wake up, and the future is unclear, I will be here--"

"Kevin, stop!" said Cara loudly.

"What's wrong? It's my commitment that I will never, ever leave you. I want that to be our song."

"It can be our song. But only if you're not the one singing it. Kevin, you're tone deaf."

"I'm crushed," he said, but he was smiling.

"I'll tell you what. Why don't we let Marta be the one who sings it at our wedding?" She kissed him as Marta swooped up her guitar to rescue Kevin.

CHAPTER 34

The last days of the spring semester came quickly, and Cara turned in her last paper. She now only had to survive three days of finals and she would be through with her program—except for summer school. After she had studied for her final as completely as her brain would allow, she picked up her cell and called Kevin.

He picked up on the third ring, but he was really groggy. "What time is it?" he asked.

"Only one-thirty," said Cara. "I was brain-dead and just needed to talk."

"Some of us go to bed before midnight."

"Sorry."

"Cara, are you a night person or a morning person?"

"Duh!"

"Cara, from your experience, do you think that I'm a night or a morning person?"

"I never really thought about it."

"Lately, I've been thinking a lot about this one lady I know."

"Careful, Kevin. You don't want to get me jealous."

"She's in her late sixties. She's a professional psychologist and does a lot of premarital counseling. I've checked with her to see if she will do some sessions with us."

"She's a Christian?"

"Yeah, of some stripe or another. I've sent a couple of people from the youth group to her, and I've heard really good things about their sessions. Anyway, I believe we could get some good advice. My pastor doesn't do premarital counseling. And as you well know, counseling is not your dad's strongest gift."

"Well, because Dad is marrying us, he'll need to do two sessions."

"No issue with that. Glad for them, and I wouldn't want anyone else to marry us. I was just thinking a little bit of extra help would be good."

"I'm in. What exactly does she do at the premarital counseling?"

"Helps us define our roles. To think about the preconceptions that both of us will be bringing into our marriage. As well as help us find out who's a morning person and who's a night person and what time they should be calling each other. That sort of thing."

"Good night, Kevin. I love you."

The nameplate on the psychologist's office door read "Dr. Katherine Fielder," but she insisted they call her Kathy. The walls of her office were pastel green, adorned with framed landscapes and floral arrangements. The large office had what appeared to be two small breakout rooms adjoining.

Plenty of questions came up during their first session, as it was a sort of "get to know you" meeting. In addition, Kevin and Cara both had to fill out extensive questionnaires about their likes, preferences, values, goals, family history, and current relationships. After the session, they were to do homework assignments together. They were to discuss a number of things that came up in their first session. Fairly standard procedure. However, toward the end of the second session things actually got interesting.

"Now, Kevin and Cara, I want to ask you some questions. But if you ever feel I'm crossing a line, violating your core principles or values that are important to your tradition, please stop me."

"Okay."

"You keep on talking about Cara's call. But what confuses me is that every Christian has some sort of call. Every Christian has some sort of ministry. Wouldn't you agree with me?"

Kevin leaned back on the couch where he and Cara sat, and looked evenly at Kathy who sat across from them. "Good point. But Cara's sense of calling is different. Just like everyone receives and gives advice, say, but not everyone is a licensed counselor."

"Fair enough. But shouldn't everyone feel called to a vocation? For instance, Kevin, do you feel called to be a schoolteacher?"

"I do, actually."

"Okay, then, what makes Cara's calling any better than yours?"

"I wouldn't say that it is. It's just that it requires something more of a couple and a family than does mine. I can leave my classroom at the end of the day, and it would not necessarily affect what happens in my home. But, because she's a preacher, say, or a pastor, her calling in large part determines where we'll live, our priorities, and how we spend our time. And it makes every other vocational calling secondary. So, if Cara were to support herself by being a plumber, say, or an astronaut, her primary focus in life would still be linked to her calling."

Kathy was writing all of this down, letting Kevin take his time as he spoke.

"Accepting a call as a preacher invites God to speak to you in a special way," Kevin said. "This is lived out in Cara's life. The Lord does speak to her. And this doesn't happen just when she prepares to preach but at other times as well. Sometimes it is just an impression. Sometimes it is a specific direction on what to teach." Kevin went on to explain a few instances where God made things known to Cara.

"This all sounds a bit mystical," said Kathy.

"Not at all," said Kevin. "Every Christian experiences this to a greater or lesser degree. Think about it. Hasn't the Lord ever spoken to you when you read the Bible?"

Kathy ignored the question, so Kevin continued. "Cara doesn't make a big deal about it. But it enables her to pray more specifically about a specific situation, or she may speak something God gives her to speak. She doesn't really talk about it a lot. It's private, just like she wouldn't talk about things I say to her privately; you know, the sweet nothings I whisper into her ear."

Kathy challenged Cara. "Is what Kevin just said really true?"

"All but that bit about sweet nothings. Kevin, you have never whispered sweet nothings into my ear."

"I have, too."

"When?"

"When we went to Denny's that one time."

"Oh. That. You were just whispering nonsense syllables into my ear."

"Yes, but didn't I say it sweetly? There you go, then. Sweet nothings."

"Oh, brother."

Kathy laughed despite herself. Her change of posture, although subtle, let Cara know that Kevin had won her over.

"So, Cara," Kathy began, "you would really like to stay in Munson Heights to continue your ministry there, but, from what I understand, you can't because your father has refused to give his full approval to your future plans. Particularly with regard to you're becoming licensed as a minister."

"It's something Kevin feels strongly about. And I respect his judgment."

Kathy said, "For what it's worth, I think Kevin is right, but I've been thinking about this and about your father. I wonder if this really has to be a closed door. You and Kevin should pray about this more, and maybe you'll get some insight about how to make a second attempt."

Kevin and Cara looked at each other mischievously, feeling that somehow God was confirming a promise to them through her advice.

"I just have to explore one more area so I can begin to get some clarity, and it may be a bit sensitive."

Cara's Call

"We're ready," said Kevin.

"In conversation, you've used the word submission several times in a way unfamiliar to me. Here's what I think you mean: the wife submits to the husband, and everybody submits to the pastor. Is that about right?"

Kevin smiled. "It's a bit more subtle than that."

"Okay, but if Cara submits to you, and then you submit to Cara... do you see what I'm asking?"

"Oh," said Kevin. "I get your question. The way Cara and I figure it, submission relates in different ways to different spheres of authority. The home is different, say, than the church. As an analogy, I carry a certain authority as a teacher. I am in charge of the classroom. But that doesn't mean I am automatically in charge of everyone I meet. Or, say, if Cara were a policewoman and gave out tickets, she wouldn't submit those tickets to me as her husband to see if I approved. It's a different sphere of authority."

Kathy replied, "I'll have to think about this. Cara, is this just as clear for you?"

Cara responded, "That's why we're here to see you, so you can help us sort this out. Do you think there will be confusion in our family about roles?"

"I'm sure there will. Just as there is confusion in every family about roles. See, even in your family, where it ought to be abundantly clear that everyone submits to your father about everything, my guess is that it's a lot more complicated than that."

Cara thought about it and nodded. "A lot goes on behind the scenes. I know my mom can influence things, but that doesn't mean she is not submitted."

Cara chose a quiet time to talk to her mother. She stated simply, "I have to tell you something, Mom. It looks like Kevin and I are going to move to Charlestown when we get married."

"Oh?" responded Karen, disappointment clearly displayed on her face. "I thought it would be nice if you stayed here."

"It would be nice."

"Well, why don't you?"

"In preparation for Chicago, Kevin thinks that during the next year or so I need to be working toward getting my ministerial license."

"Oh, I see now," she said knowingly. "He talked to Dad about it and..."

"Yeah. Dad didn't want to be pigeonholed. He didn't say no, but he felt like Kevin was too demanding, and he said a lot of pretty blistering things to him. We're still open to living here and praying that God will open a door, but things don't look good right now."

"But Cara, I think in the end your dad would have—"

"Mom, I'm a little scared. If Dad doesn't believe I can pastor or that Kevin and I can start a church, then I really wonder if maybe I'm missing something. Maybe I'm getting ahead of myself."

"Oh Cara," her mom said, embracing her.

"Mom, do you believe in me?" Cara whispered.

"More than you'll ever know."

"Cara, I've been practicing that song that Kevin couldn't sing very well."

"Wonderful, Marta. So, you'll be singing in the wedding?"

"I know it's in October, but you'll need to give me the exact date. Say, Cara, how soon is he moving over to Munson Heights?"

Cara grew wide-eyed, but only momentarily. "Well, there's a lot to consider. We're still working out all the details."

Marta erupted, "Just… you don't leave us! You hear?"

"Dear, I was wondering if the Salem church would be a good place for the wedding."

"Good a place as any," Jim said noncommittally to his wife.

"I suppose I could suggest it to Cara. That would save us from having to rent a hall or using a restaurant for the reception. I mean, if they would do it."

"Do they have a date, yet?"

"I get the impression that they want to do it in October, but Kevin won't set the date until he officially asks you to perform the ceremony."

"Strange kid… that Kevin… isn't he?"

"I wouldn't know. He seemed nice the couple times that I've talked with him. Do you find him strange?"

"Yeah. Do you know what he did? He pretty much demanded that I commit to signing Cara's application for her ministerial license or they wouldn't live here."

"Hmmpph," said Karen, nodding sympathetically at her husband.

"Not much submission on his part, is there?"

"He's rebellious, then?"

"Well, he certainly didn't show much respect the way he talked to me. And he's wimpy, Karen. How could a guy have any self-respect at all if his wife were a pastor and he was just a… well, whatever he is."

"Okay, then, you think he's weak?"

"Absolutely."

"Jim...I wonder then how he could have talked to you about Cara's ministerial license and about asking to marry Cara, being that he's so weak and all?"

Karen called their meeting tea time, and asked Cara to carve out an hour or so for wedding preparation. When their tea arrived, she opened her notebook to show that she had already been busy.

"Pastor Jean okayed the use of the Salem church, dear, and Amanda's mom will coordinate. I'll be helping her. You need to pick the colors, and do it soon."

"Mom, I've thought about this since I was ten years old. Let me tell you what I want. You know I've wanted October to symbolize the change of the seasons in my life. I'm thinking earth tones to celebrate the creation. The altar would have a canopy of sheer fabric, and lace entwined with branches and bronze ribbon. The bridesmaids should wear chocolate brown and a dark mint green."

"Well, whatever you and Amanda's mom decide," said Karen. She did have something else she wanted to say, but it had nothing to do with wedding decorations.

"Cara, I have something to tell you, and it is important."

"Okay," said Cara, a little fearful of the sudden turn in the conversation and at her mom being so un-mom-like.

"Cara, I don't want you to repeat this."

"Okay, Mom."

"He would never say so, of course. And he loves Sandra, and Shay is his pride and joy. But you are your father's favorite. His eyes light up when he talks to you. Have you never noticed?"

Cara shook her head, laughing. "If I'm the favorite, he has a funny way of showing it."

"But it's true. Who does he turn to when he wants something done? Who is the child who is safe never to talk back to him or ever disobey him?"

"Mom, I wonder if that's still true."

"Of course it is."

"I don't know if I'm safe anymore. I wonder if he can accept me if I'm more than just his little girl. I wonder if he's lost to me."

"Do you trust me?"

"Of course I do."

"I have a good feeling about things. It's going to be okay, honey."

Chapter 35

Jim was in the recliner going over his sermon for that evening. Music played in the background, and Karen was reading the Sunday paper. She looked up and said, "That was a good message this morning."

"Thank you," he said, only half listening.

"And I really enjoyed hearing Bob last Sunday night," she continued.

"Yeah, he is refreshing."

"And, of course, it was good to hear from some young people, too. It was great to have Joey over from Salem."

By now Jim had a suspicion that there was more to what Karen was saying than a mere catalogue of recent speakers and services. Sure enough, her real intent became clear as she said, "I've noticed, though, that you haven't asked Cara to speak lately."

"Oh?" he said absently.

"I could be mistaken, but I think it's been a couple months now."

"You don't say."

"Maybe it just seems like it's been that long. Like I said, I could be wrong, but it seems like it's been since Kevin talked to you that she's not done much of anything in service."

"Is she complaining to you?" asked Jim.

"No, not at all." Jim went back to his notes until he heard her say, "It's just that, when I passed her bedroom late last night, I heard her crying. In any case, her crying is probably not related at all to her not speaking. You know, she's got final exams before too long, and then her summer classes. And there are just so many things related to that, or it could be something about her wedding. Who knows?"

Now Jim became thoughtful. Noticing he was mulling things over, Karen continued, "Probably just an irrational fear on my part. I guess I was just worried that you were withdrawing from her. Really stupid of me, I guess."

At that moment, something happened on the inside for Jim Shepherd. The change was not loud or pronounced. In fact, it had been gradually happening for many weeks now. Indeed, it was so gradual that if someone had told him he had

Cara's Call

made a turn, he would have argued that he had always held the same position. And though there was change, it was not without hiccups.

"Cara," said Jim when she came in the door from church that night.
"Yes, Dad."
"You'll be speaking next Sunday night."
His tone of voice made it clear there would be no discussion about this, so she simply said "Okay," and went up to her room.

Monday morning, Jim put in a call to the district superintendent of Illinois, a first for Jim.
"Say, Brother Coltharp, I need to ask you about something."
"Sure, what can I help you with?"
"Well, my daughter has an idea about sponsoring a conference for young ladies who have a call to minister. Anyway, I told her that I would check to see if we needed permission from the district. Quite a bit of time has passed, and I just haven't called."
"Are you wanting to make it a district event?"
"No, just something that we would advertize and do locally."
"Well, you certainly don't need my permission for that. But I do have to say that I think it is a good idea."
"That's great."
"And it's your daughter?"
"My second daughter, Cara. I'm sure you don't know her. She doesn't really stand out in a crowd or anything. She's pretty quiet."
"That's better than you know."
"What do you mean?"
"Well, it's a funny thing about women in ministry. We put the bar so high that it's hard for women to find the courage to fulfill their calling. Consequently, only those who are bold and challenging even try. And then, we usually complain that women who are in ministry are too bold and bossy."
"Never thought of it that way."
"But it's not just women in ministry where our organization is struggling. Young men also feel as if there is no room for them in ministry. Like young ladies, they want to be in ministry, but they just don't see a path. It's not because God is not speaking that more young people are not entering ministry. He's doing His part."
"God always does His part," Jim murmured noncommittally.

"Pastor Shepherd, I've got to tell you that I'm really encouraged. I believe that I'm seeing a lot more zeal now by young people who want to work for the Lord than I have in quite some time. Our challenge is to carve out a space for them, create a road to ministry that seems possible for them. I'm afraid unless we start thinking creatively, we may not be able to take advantage of what God is doing."

"I never thought of it that way."

"So when's the date of the conference?"

"I don't know. I'm not even sure if it's going to happen. Cara's getting married. She may be moving away, so it's all very tentative."

"I hope it works out. Say, you may want to contact the district superintendent of Missouri. His daughter has a call to preach. I'm sure she'd be a great resource."

"Yeah, well, sure. I'll really think about that."

"Pastor Shepherd, what you are doing is important. It is the local church that winds up being the gatekeeper for young people entering ministry. You have no idea the potential of what you are proposing. You're going to make a big difference."

"Thanks. That means a lot."

Bob reared back to zing his strongest serve so it would fall dead in the rear corner on the left. Although there was very little bounce, Jim scooped it out easily and with a mastery of his racket, he offered a solid return.

"Say, Jim," Bob said, "I hope you're not suffering too badly with that future son-in-law of yours. I'm thinking that maybe I steered in you in the wrong direction."

"Actually, I like him a whole lot better now. I think he has some depth that wasn't readily apparent to me at the beginning."

"Yeah, but do you know what I heard?" asked Bob. "I hear that Kevin and Cara are already going to a marriage counselor."

"Where'd you hear that?"

"Well, remember the kid in the youth group I told you about? Apparently Greg was on the phone with his brother Kevin, and they were talking about it in front of Larissa, who's in the youth group. She told my cousin. So, it's practically public knowledge."

"I had no idea."

He was about to mention the whole counseling mess to Karen when she brought up issues of her own.

"Jim, I get the impression that the kids would really like to stay here after they get married," she said.

He didn't ask how she knew about it—where she had gotten that information. He just stared blankly ahead. Then he said, "Well, that's good, then. They should come to see me."

Karen was encouraged but was hardly finished with what she had just begun.

"Jim, do you remember when you went out and visited the Johnsons after they decided to stop coming to church?"

"Yeah."

"What was it they said to you after you went out there?"

"Well, they thanked me. And they said the fact that I extended myself proved to them how much I cared. I've really been able to rely on them since then."

"Jim, I think Cara is getting ready to leave. But I don't think it has to be that way."

"Well, like I said, she should talk to me."

"I'm probably talking out of school, and forgive me if I am. Probably Cara shouldn't have talked to me. But my understanding is that your last conversation with Kevin was about twelve weeks ago, and there was some indication that you thought that he lacked submission and that he was stealing your daughter."

Jim said nothing but looked very sad.

Karen continued, "I may be wrong, dear, but I was just thinking that maybe if there was even the teensiest indicator that there was an open door to talk to you about it, they probably would."

That night Cara knocked on the door of her father's study. "Dad, Kevin wanted to me to check with you to see if August fourth was a good day to meet for premarital counseling. We can wait until closer to the wedding if you want. I know August is a few months away, but he just wanted to make sure we had the date nailed down."

"Sure, Cara. That's fine."

"And thank you for being so kind about this wedding. Dad, I thank you for all your support in my life. I know that you've gone a long way for me. And I will never forget what you've done for me."

"Well, I only did what was right."

"I need to tell you about my group, what's going to happen. Because things are happening really quickly and we haven't talked yet about how to transition things before I leave. So, I thought it might be important."

"Okay, well, then…what are your ideas?"

"The group is probably going to lose a few people after I leave, but that is to be expected. Just like when you took this church and a family or two left. People have to figure out who they're going to follow, and it's not something you can legislate."

"What's that supposed to mean?"

"Dad," she said, in a tone that sounded prophetic, "the group will drop from about twenty-five to maybe half of that. Some of the strongest leaders will not stay. I will not contact them until after they stop coming to church. But then I will get them to move to Charlestown and later up to Chicago with us. You'll need to pick a leader for the group before I leave, though, or they will all be lost."

"Who do you think?" he asked weakly.

"Who do you think?

"Peter is bright enough. He seems to be the most sensible."

"He will not listen to you. He will take the whole group out of the church."

"Who then?"

"Marta. I want to tell you something else. Shay can help even though he's only seventeen. He will grow into a strong leader for that group in three years."

"But Cara, I don't know about Marta."

"Think about it, Dad."

"But Cara, Marta is a girl!"

Cara looked evenly at her dad and tried to hold his gaze, but she could not prevent the hurt from showing in her eyes. As Jim realized how stupid his remark was, he stood to his feet, got up from behind his desk and embraced Cara. "I'm sorry," he said.

They continued embracing. Jim could count on one hand the times he had hugged Cara like this after she had reached her teens. But it was a real hug this time, a genuine show of affection.

Then, ever so softly, he said, "Cara, I don't want you to go. I want you and Kevin to stay here this year...before you go to Chicago."

"All you had to do was ask," said Cara. Then pulling back but still holding his arms, she said, "But...Dad, I need your blessing."

He pursed his lips, thought, waited, and then said, "I trust you." She looked at him, willing him to say more. He offered, "And...uh, we can work everything else out. I'm sure of it." It wasn't what Cara wanted, not what she hoped for. It didn't stop the hurt nor eliminate all the questions for the future, but it was enough. Just barely, but it was enough.

She leaned into her father and said softly, "We'll stay then, Dad."

After a few moments, her Dad held her at arm's length once again and said, "But don't you think you and Kevin need to talk a bit more about this? You can't be making decisions for him. It's just not right."

"Dad, Kevin sent me in to talk to you."

"You know, Cara," he said with concern, "I really want you here, but wouldn't Kevin have to drive all the way over to Charlestown to teach?"

"He has an offer to teach in Salem. He needs to let them know by tomorrow whether he's taking it."

At two o'clock in the morning Cara heard her mom's gentle voice outside her bedroom door. "Cara?"

"Hey, Mom, come on in," she said as she opened the door.

That's when Cara caught the fragrance of food and saw that her mom was carrying a grilled cheese sandwich on a plate in one hand and a glass of iced tea in the other.

"You're the best," Cara said.

Her mom didn't leave but sat in one of the chairs. She was so quiet that at first Cara didn't realize she was still in the room.

"Cara, can I talk to you?"

"Sure, Mom."

"It's about you and Kevin."

"Okay, what about us?

"Well, Dad is concerned about you two going to a marriage counselor. He wonders if you're having problems already, and frankly he's concerned."

Cara smiled. "You know, Mom. It's pretty normal for engaged couples to get extended counseling nowadays. It really helps their marriages. I didn't say anything to you, because we didn't want to offend Dad."

"That's what I figured," said her mother. "It's just that he was worried about it and asked if I would talk to you."

Karen noticed the bewildered look on her daughter's face, and asked, "What's wrong, Cara?"

"Mom, I'm twenty-two years old. As long as I've lived, Dad has never sent you to talk to me about any real concerns of his. He simply issues commands."

"Hmmm," said Karen. "Things are changing. My guess is that he doesn't want to hurt you. We've had some pretty rocky times here lately, and I think he's trying to get beyond them."

If her mother had offered that explanation to comfort her, it wasn't at all effective. In fact, it had the opposite effect on Cara, who said sharply, "And is it my fault that we are having rocky times?"

Her mother was gentle. "No, honey, it's not. I've been wanting to talk to you some about this whole thing, but it seems you're always so busy. Maybe this is not a good time. I know you have studying to do."

"There's nothing in the world I would rather talk about than this."

"Can I tell you a story?"

"I'm listening, Mom."

"I was raised in a little town in Texas," Karen began. "Your Poppy was pastoring back then, so I was brought up in a preacher's home. I guess the church was doing all right. It's hard to remember, really. But then, there must have been some kind of church split, because one day there was just a handful of us left in church. I'm not really sure what happened, because Poppy never talked to me about it."

Cara nodded, but didn't speak.

"That was pretty hard for me as a teenager. Then I met someone who swept me off my feet. Your father was quite a wild and flashy character in our community. I had never really dated, and I was just thrilled that he gave me attention. I had no problem leaving church. There wasn't much to leave."

"Mom, you've never told me this before."

"Well, anyway, I think it's time I told you." She paused, then continued, "We were so young, and all that partying led to some pretty bad scenes for us as a young couple. Things happened that were so terrible I would never speak of them. Just when it looked like our marriage was lost, your father decided he needed God. So, ironically enough, we went back to Poppy's church. That's where Dad got saved.

"We were zealous for God. I was like a new convert and your dad was a wild man for Jesus. I know you might find this hard to believe, but there was a big revival among the young people in our community. Your dad was so well known in that area, and the change was so great, that it had quite an impact on everyone. And the church grew.

"I have to admit I thought that my dad and mom were really behind the times. I had more education. I knew more of the current songs. Better ways of doing things in church. And we were learning new evangelistic techniques, things my dad wouldn't have even considered. It was all so refreshing and wonderful. I didn't realize how much pride I had. Just being young, you know. You don't see yourself as clearly as you can see others. It was normal. It's generational pride."

Cara could see where this was headed. "When did you understand that you had generational pride, Mama?"

"Not until this last year, Cara… not until this last year."

"Are you saying that I have pride, Mama? Generational pride?"

"Cara, your father's father never told your dad that he loved him. And my dad, your Poppy, who was your dad's mentor, was as tough as nails. He always thought it would destroy a person if he told him that he was proud of him. And all your dad's other mentors were very strict men and were very certain about things. So, throughout his whole ministry, the examples that your father has followed have been men who understood that a minister needs to be man's man."

However noble her mother's intentions, Cara was having a hard time with this explanation. She erupted in protest, "He wouldn't talk to me, Mama. For months he wouldn't talk to me…"

Unbidden tears flowed down Cara's cheeks. Then came the sobs. Deep painful sobs. Karen got up from her chair, pulled Cara to her feet, and held her like she was a small child. As Karen held her tightly, Cara heaved as her tears poured from her, tears representing months and months of hurt. Karen held her daughter until the crying eased, then she pulled her close and whispered into Cara's ear, "Honey, you've grown so much in the last year. And it has cost you a lot. But you'll never know what it has cost your father."

Just as softly, Cara whispered back to her mother, "What do you mean, Mama?"

"Like I said, your father has always been taught that if he really were a man of God, he needed to live in certainty, to stand boldly, to know answers all the time. You know, Cara, at least in part, he gave that up for you."

"I need him to tell me, Mom…I need Dad to say—"

"Hush, Cara. Think about someone other than yourself now. Think about how far your dad has come. He's read books that have intimidated him. He's had to work through figuring out what part of those things his heroes have taught him are really in the Bible. And being right—being certain—that's so important to your father. This has been a real crisis for him."

"But what about me, Mama…what about me… What has it cost me?"

"I know honey… I know. And you've done so well. And you've grown. But you didn't have to change so much from who you've always been. You've only had to move inches. Your dad's had to move miles. And he's not through moving yet. The journey is still going to be pretty painful."

"I hear what you're saying, Mom, but I don't like it. It hurts so much."

"I know Cara…I know," she said, stroking her daughter's hair.

Chapter 36

The August sun beat down on the audience seated in the bleachers as Cara, with the golden cords of an honor student draped across the front of her gown, walked up to receive her diploma. Shortly thereafter, mortarboards flew into the air, followed by the pandemonium of families getting together for pictures. Friends and well-wishers stood by as Sandra organized their family for a photo-op. "Okay, Shay, you switch to the other side."

Cara's phone buzzed. She fished it out of her purse and answered it, even though she didn't recognize the number. Abruptly, she heard a male voice uttering a string of profanities. He ended with, "You will die, whore!"

Cara quickly walked over to Marta. "Is Johnny out of jail now?"

"Yeah, last week. We've got that restraining order so he can't come near me, but I think I saw him following me in a car."

"Does he have your new cell number?"

"Not yet."

"But he has mine, right?"

"I think so, yeah. I'm pretty sure. He had it before."

"Okay, I'm going to call the police. Johnny just called me, so we need to think about how we're going to keep you safe."

"Cara, I'm not the only one who should be concerned. Johnny is very angry at you. He says you took me away from him."

"It's going to be okay. We'll tell people who are close to us. Not only will we get a network of support to help each other, but we're also going to be praying."

"Let's pray right now!" said Marta, surprising Cara with her strength.

Despite the fact that they were in the university parking lot and Sandra was waiting for Cara to get back in line for the picture, Marta laid her hands on Cara and launched into a prayer. When Ron saw it, he came over and started praying as well, as did others from the fellowship group.

"Father," Marta said, "we pray a network of protection around Cara and me. Help Johnny to turn to you. Protect him from himself. And help the police get to him before someone is hurt. I pray in the name of Jesus and trust you for the answer! Amen."

"What's going on?" Jim asked Karen.

"Oh, you know those kids. It's just how they do things."

Cara chose to wait until they got to the restaurant to explain the situation to Kevin. They sat at a long table with twenty others who were loud and laughing, so it was easy for her to be private in outlining the circumstances. After sharing the details, Cara asked, "Should Marta be staying at her apartment?"

"She has to live her life," was his even reply.

"Maybe I should go stay with her."

"Over my dead body!" Kevin said more loudly than he ought. A few heads turned and looked in their direction, but they were polite enough to return to their meal without further consideration.

In a biting whisper, Cara leaned in and challenged her fiancé: "Kevin, you don't own me."

Kevin paused, took a deep breath, and in as calm a voice as he could muster said, "Cara, you might be putting yourself into harm's way."

Cara replied with the same calm firmness. If others had been close enough to them, they would have been privy to their very quiet fight, but as a whole, the group was largely oblivious.

"You were the one who didn't seem to think Marta was in harm's way. And now, you say that if I'm with her that I could be putting myself in danger? You can't have it both ways, Kevin."

"Settle down, Cara. Let's think this through rationally."

But Cara was in no rational mood. "How's that going to work if we go to Chicago? Do you keep me in the apartment all day long so I'll be safe? Is that it? Ministry requires a certain amount of risk, Kevin."

"Okay. New idea. Let's bring this to the counselor tomorrow night. This is a good test case. We have to decide if this is a ministry issue or a family issue."

As the food was served, Cara became upset with herself. Cara simply did not fight with others; yet, she had just vented her anger on the one she loved the most. Worse, this day was supposed to be one of the happiest of her life.

"Kevin, are you sorry you ever got involved with me?" she asked.

"How can you say that?" he said loudly. And then even more loudly and proudly, he said for the benefit of everyone at the table, "I love you, Cara Shepherd. And I am so proud of you!"

"This is the first big fight?" asked Kathy with a twinkle in her eye.

"It's more like a tiff," said Cara, embarrassed.

"Well, if it is really just a tiff," said Kathy, "you should be able to solve this without my help. I'll tell you what; I'll give you five minutes to do it. You go in that other room and come back when you've got it figured out."

The side room had two chairs that could readily be seen though glass doors. Cara did most of the talking. Even including their time for kissing and praying together, it took less than three minutes before they were back out in the larger room.

"Let me guess," said Kathy to Cara. "Marta's going to stay at your house." Cara colored immediately and nodded. Kathy now turned her attention away from Cara and said, "Kevin, I want to explore with you why this fight happened; why you responded differently than you normally would have."

"Okay," he said soberly. "I didn't know that I did."

"Sure you did. Normally, you explore options, give people choices, and affirm what others have to say. But you didn't do that. Now, let's cut to the chase and talk about what you don't like to talk about. Kevin, your mom's an alcoholic. She has been for a long time. You only knew your dad when you were little. And I have here, 'Things were very rocky.' Did I get that right?"

"Yes, you did."

"Did your father beat your mother?"

"Well, sometimes when he was drunk he would."

"You were what? Five years old maybe? Probably younger. So, these are some of your first memories, Kevin. Now, what did you do when the violence was going on? Did you try to protect Greg?"

Kevin, who wasn't startled by much, was in awe of her insight. "Sometimes we would hide in the closet."

"And, Kevin, after your dad left, you felt it was your job to continue to protect your mother, didn't you? To shield her from difficult things."

"Well, yes, I guess I tried to play that role."

"Right. That explains your early maturity. And it also explains something else. Kevin, don't you think the relationship you have with your brother is a bit odd?"

"We have a great relationship!"

"That's what I mean. You don't know how abnormal it is for two male siblings two years apart not to compete. But you have no memory of fighting with Greg, striving with him. Only helping him."

"Well, he helps me, too."

"True. But when you were five years old, you didn't know that your brother would turn out to be the size of a professional wrestler, did you? You were the older

Cara's Call

brother who saw that it was your duty to protect and guide. You set yourself up as the surrogate father. My point is that these relationships are default relationships. They tend to define how you see life and how you approach conflict. Your default relationship is to protect, and in the case of conflict, you generally flee from it. Isn't that about right?"

Kevin was now very uncomfortable. "I think I've moved beyond that in some ways…"

"Granted. For what you've been through, you are very well adjusted. But when you don't consciously think about it, something inside tells you not to make waves; that you only have value when you are helping and that you should avoid taking the lead. Yet, in an emergency you will make an exception."

"Well, I don't know…"

"Kevin, I'm trying to help you here. The reason that you got into a fight with Cara is that something kicked in from your childhood. You were worried about her safety. That is perfectly legitimate. My only point is that you were layering your past onto that fight. I just need to make that visible. Cara is not your mother. She's not a younger sibling who needs to hide. She has incredible instincts in a crisis. You have to trust her. You have to believe in her."

"Okay, you got me," said Kevin. He turned to Cara. "Would you forgive me for not trusting you?"

"Yes, Kevin," Cara eagerly replied.

"And you, young lady…" began Kathy in a voice that sounded angry. "I've got a couple of things to say to you. First of all, if Kevin ever has a concern that you are in danger, you must listen to him immediately. You hear me?"

"But I was only trying to—"

"No. I know exactly what you were trying to do. You're worried about the future. You're concerned about your calling. Your fear is that you won't be able to do it. So you projected onto Kevin your father's doubts in you. Another thing, Cara. Just because you may well wind up in Chicago does not mean that you are going to be working in skid row. Get a life, girl. If you ever consciously put yourself in danger to prove your ministry, I'll call you up and thrash you myself."

Cara was beet-red. "I get that. But—"

"See, that's the problem with you, Cara. You are in conflict with your father, but you have more of your father in you than you care to admit."

"Excuse me?"

"Cara, if I understand your father correctly, he is a man of principle. And he will live by that principle, no matter what. And when it comes to doing what he believes is right, he will not relent, come hell or high water."

"That's true."

"Cara, look in the mirror. Let me tell you something that neither you nor your father wants to admit. You *are* your father."

"No way! I don't operate like my father—"

"Sure you do. You just proved it. And Cara, you also have the same leadership skills as your mother."

"Excuse me, but I don't think my mother really has what you would call—"

"Cara, wake up and smell the coffee. Your mother has been leading your household. Now, in your family dynamics she has to drive the car from the back seat. She has to plant suggestions, bide her time, be selective in her battles, that sort of thing. But the successes of your church and family probably have more to do with your mother's insight than your father's boldness. And you have those same skills. You are your mother."

Cara started crying. "I'm a mess," she sobbed. Kathy let her cry for a little while before continuing.

"Cara, take a Kleenex and breathe." She did. Kathy continued, "As I already noted, I happen to think that you and Kevin are some of the most well-adjusted young adults that I know. You are both mature beyond your years. But I've got to tell you, you haven't had the most normal relationship. First, he's counseling you about your life and issues, and then you're counseling him about his issues. You haven't really given yourself time to enjoy what I would describe as a really normal guy-girl relationship.

"And do you know what? It doesn't matter, because this is working for you. So it's okay. But that is the reason for the fight. You are just at the beginning stages of negotiating what it means to be in a normal relationship as peers. And believe me, it is going to be painful when neither of you gets to play the God-card."

Cara started crying again. "Our children are going to be a mess."

"Stop your crying, Cara, and look at me," said Kathy. "Why will your children be a mess?"

"Because I'm Mrs. Bossy Pants and Sister Grand Poobah Pastor and I won't submit and I have to be in charge. It's just so—"

"Cara, stop. This is very healthy for you to verbalize your fears. Thank you for trusting me with your deepest concerns. And it is good that you are thinking about the future in terms of others. But slow down. Let me ask you something. Who is most likely to have the most well-adjusted children? Those who are trying to live out someone else's idea of how they are supposed to construct their family and their ministry, or those who are sincerely following God's plan for them to the best of their ability?"

Cara's Call

Kevin and Cara looked at each other and smiled. For the first time that night, they felt like they were doing something right.

As they headed toward the car, Kevin said, "Now, that was painful! I feel like I've been pounded to a pulp."

"Me, too. But I feel good about it. Maybe we should do what she says: visit her a couple of times during our first year of marriage. She's right. We might have missed a couple of stepping stones in the way our relationship developed."

"I'm game. Still, I do feel black and blue. Next time, I'm wearing shin guards."

"Jim, I'm sure you remember that Marta will be moving in to the house tomorrow night," said Karen. "She so appreciates you making room for her. Would you prefer she stay in the basement or in Cara's room?"

Jim, who had been sitting in the recliner reading the paper, was now distracted. It wasn't just that Marta was coming. It was everything that all this represented. He got up, went to the closet, and started rustling around on the top shelf for his shotgun.

"And to think that Johnny threatened Cara, too. Do you know where those shells are for this thing?" he asked, holding up the shotgun.

Karen ignored his request in an effort to settle the question at hand. "If she stays in the basement, that might get in the way of your studying."

"Wherever she stays will be just fine," he said as he searched through the corner cabinet in the kitchen. Cara walked into the kitchen just as her dad said, "Do you think I left that box of shells in the garage?" She saw the shotgun and wondered what was going on. Mumbling, Jim walked by Karen for the third time in his desperate search for ammo.

When he walked through the kitchen yet one more time with the shotgun, Cara said, "What's—" but her mother shook her head while saying softly, "No more talk about Johnny."

Jim went into the garage, threw this and that box aside, and then came back in the house, first slamming one door and then another. Apparently, he wasn't having much success, for they heard him back in the garage yelling, "Dear, I've got to run to the store... If I get my hands on that punk, he'll wish he'd never..."

After he was gone, her mother said to Cara, "You know, I'm thinking that the less we say about Johnny the better."

"I think I understand, Mom."

Chapter 37

Before graduation, Cara had sent out her résumé. Although Gary had offered her the assistant manager position at Office Depot, she was keeping her options open. Consequently, when the first of September rolled around, Cara was busy making callbacks to see if the positions she applied for were still options. Unhappily, she was having very little success with her efforts. Because she had only one last place to check, she'd almost resigned herself to staying at Office Depot.

"Munson Heights *Daily Herald* personnel office, Pam speaking."

"Yes, this is Cara Shepherd. I sent in my résumé about three weeks ago for the copy editor position."

"I'm sorry, what did you say your name is?"

"Cara Shepherd, and I—"

Pam ignored Cara and shouted to someone else in the office. "Delores, you are not going to believe this. I've got Cara Shepherd on the phone... Yes!" Then there was a click, and Cara thought Pam had hung up on her.

After thirty seconds of nothingness Cara was just about to give up when a different voice came on the line.

"Hello," said the female voice.

"Yes, this is Cara Shepherd. I think I lost the woman I was speaking with and—"

"Sorry about that, Cara. Pam was transferring you to me. My name is Delores."

"Yes, Delores. I was just calling about the copy editor position to see if that job had been filled."

"I'm so sorry, but we have filled that position. Still, an interesting thing happened in the process. When John Casey saw your résumé and the special commendations you have received, he called your store manager. So, anyway, Mr. Casey wonders when you can come in."

"I'm sorry. I thought you said the copy editor position had been filled."

"That's true."

"Ma'am. I'm just trying to understand—"

Cara's Call

"John Casey runs this paper. He is looking for an executive secretary. I'd like to schedule you for an interview with him if that is possible."

"Sure. Just let me know when to come in."

Cara was about to enter the *Daily Herald* building when she sensed that someone was following her. She turned in time to see someone duck behind a building. She immediately stepped inside the lobby of the building and called Marta. "Marta, what color did you say Johnny's car was?"

"Red. It's a little Chevy. Why?"

"It may be nothing, but there's a red Chevy parked down the street from where I am."

"I'll be praying."

Cara went upstairs and at once met Delores who quickly ushered her into an inner office for her interview. Although he was in the middle of a phone conversation, John Casey signaled Delores to direct Cara to the chair in front of his desk. "Yes, dear. No, I think about five o'clock. Love you, too."

Casey then hit a button, evidently getting back to someone else on hold. "James, just get the replacement part then. I'll trust your judgment. No, whatever you think. Yes, goodbye."

Mr. Casey was a distinguished man who looked to be sixty. He seemed comfortable behind the large executive desk that backed up to a full-length window. He addressed another caller. "Tom, if you have to give them ten or even fifteen percent more to get them to sign on annually for their advertisement, do it. No. Whatever you think... Goodbye."

"Uh yes, now...you are Cara," he said, looking at her intently.

"Cara Shepherd, sir."

"And why should I hire you?" he asked bluntly.

"I don't know that you should. That's something you'll probably have to sort through in this interview. Don't you think?"

"I like you already. Now, what can you do for me?"

Listening to the phone calls, Cara knew she liked this man, and she shot up a quick prayer for wisdom.

"Mr. Casey—"

"John, please."

"John, you are someone who is interested in the big picture, and you don't want to worry about details. You need someone who can anticipate what you need and finish what you start. Right now, I'm guessing you don't have that kind of person. Perhaps I can be of service."

"Well spoken," he said. "But I've had ten other people in here who said the same sort of thing."

"John, I believe my life has purpose. But not jut my life. Your life, as well as those of your employees, has incredible significance. You have a reason for leading this newspaper company that goes well beyond making money. I want to find out what your mission is and help you fulfill it."

Now smiling, Mr. Casey leaned back in his chair and said, "Gary is my nephew. He wants to hire you at Office Depot as an assistant manager, but he told me I should snag you if I can. He said you're good. And he's right."

Mr. Casey then scribbled an amount on a notepad and slid it across the desk. John Casey seemed to be a man who made quick decisions and apparently had just made one. "How does that figure look for an annual salary?"

The salary was twice what she would have made at Office Depot and it took her breath away. He mistook her hesitation and said, "Of course, that figure doesn't include benefits. We have a good benefit package. But I need you to drop everything you're doing and start next Monday."

"Well, if I take the job, I need to give Gary a two-week notice. And if possible, it would be nice if I could get a few days off for a honeymoon in October."

"Of course. And Cara, can you make a long-term commitment to me? I mean, if you're interested in the mission of this company, I would like to see you here for a long time."

"Oh, I'm so sorry. Maybe I'm not the right person, then. I'm not really sure what the future holds."

"What are you talking about?"

"I have commitments that could possibly cause me to move. I may be leaving the area in as short a time as a year or two."

"What sort of commitments?"

"Ministry."

"You're marrying a minister?"

"No, he's a teacher."

"You're becoming a minister?"

"Something like that."

"Good. Then just be a minister here on the side. Use your skills to make my company successful."

"It could be that I'd be required to move to Chicago to fulfill obligations in ministry."

"Just tell them no."

"John, can I ask you something? Was that your wife you were talking to earlier?"

Cara's Call

"Yes."

"I like it that you told your wife that you love her in front of me. It makes me want to work for you. Now, what would you do if your wife asked you to pick up a loaf of bread on the way home?" Cara wasn't sure he'd be amused by her questioning, but she had to try to explain herself.

"I'd pick it up."

"Why?"

John was clearly less patient than before. "Well, because I love her. And because she asked me to."

"Same thing for me. That's why we'll be going to Chicago."

"My wife is sending you to Chicago?"

"Someone I love the most," she said, pointing up.

"How about I hire you and pray against that, then?"

"Can I let you know tomorrow?"

"This needs more prayer?"

"I just need to run your job offer by my fiancé."

Cara shook hands with everyone in the office and then made her way to the street-level entrance. Only then did she recall that Johnny might be waiting for her outside. She reached into her purse for her cell phone, looked out the doorway and surveyed the street, ready to call nine-one-one if she saw anything suspicious. The street was deserted and the red Chevy was gone.

"So, Jim, what did you ever find out about that marriage counselor?"

"Yeah. Well, Bob, it turns out the kids just wanted a few extra sessions, you know, to make sure they were ready for marriage."

"But was the guy even a Christian?"

"It was a lady. I guess she was."

"Could be trouble, Jim. All this secular stuff. Did you actually get a chance to explain the biblical concepts of marriage to them to, you know, make sure they stay straight on this?"

"We had one session. I kind of went over it. I'm thinking we're pretty good. Our next session is to go over plans for the wedding. You're still going to be able to help aren't you?"

"I've got my line down pat: 'Who gives this woman to be married to this man?' I can handle it. Say, you are going to have some Word at the wedding aren't you?"

"Well, we haven't met yet, but I'm doing the wedding, so I suppose I'll have some discretion."

"Tremendous! It's going to work out for you to live in Munson Heights," said Kathy. "I'm so glad. Now Cara, explain what this means to you."

"I think I can answer that," said Kevin.

"I already have your answer," challenged Kathy. "You appreciate the stability of the family, Cara's ministry, ease of relocation for a new job, and familiar surroundings. It's all in my notes. Got it. But my question is not to you. It is to Cara. Why do you want to stay?"

"What do you want me to say?" asked Cara.

"Talk about what it means to you personally."

"Well, the fellowship group needs me. That's one thing."

"Cara, your relationship with your father is pretty complex, isn't it?"

Cara smiled. "You've got that right."

"And you haven't done anything without his approval?"

"True."

"And he has been pretty grudging at giving you his approval at times?"

"I wouldn't use—"

"Cara, isn't it true that he has kind of dangled his blessing out there like a carrot on a stick?"

"I wouldn't be pursuing ministry without—"

"—and you really want, you really need his blessing."

Cara replied, "His blessing would make a difference."

"Okay. I'm just trying to help you see reality, to help you prepare. It seems to me that so much depends on his full blessing. What if you don't get it?"

Cara thought for a moment. "I guess, I just keep thinking it's going to happen."

Kathy changed course, asking, "So Cara, what will make this a perfect wedding?"

"I don't need a horse and carriage. Kevin is what makes it perfect."

"That's beautiful. But Cara, is that all?"

"What do you mean?"

"Your father is marrying you, right?"

"He and Kevin's pastor."

"What you're not saying, but what I think is true, is that you need your father's blessing during the ceremony."

"Well, sure."

"Cara, you may have to strategize to help your father out on this. Whatever you do in your family dynamic to get messages through to your dad, you will probably need to employ every means possible."

Now established in her new job at the newspaper office, Cara was leaving for the day to go to the church to meet Kevin and her dad for their second counseling session. As she pulled out of the parking lot, she saw a red car behind her making the same turns as she was. When she pulled into the church parking lot, the car slowed down and then cruised down the road.

"Dad, before we get started, I just want to let you know that Kevin and I have been going over the vows, and we are wondering if we could make a little change?"

"Going to drop out 'submit'?" he said, only half kidding.

"Actually, we want to add in the phrase that we will love each other unconditionally. It's Kevin's idea, but I think it's great!"

"Oh."

"And we've been talking. We wanted to keep things pretty short. Kevin asked his pastor to just offer recollections about him and then to pray a prayer of blessing on him. I was wondering if you could do the same, reflections and then pray a prayer of blessing."

"You still want me to conduct the ceremony, don't you?"

"Yes, absolutely."

"And as a minister doing the wedding, you would expect me to find the mind of the Lord on this, wouldn't you?"

"Of course, certainly, Dad. Absolutely."

Two days later, Cara called Amanda to give her some bad news. When she heard, Amanda was profoundly upset.

"You didn't! You wimp. You told me it would be over your dead body."

"She's my only sister. And she begged me."

Despite Cara's intention to avoid bringing it up, the issue arose when Sandra asked, "Are you going to use Sissy as a flower girl?" Cara immediately knew where this was heading and thought of all the ways she could say no. But, of course, she could not.

Amanda continued to argue, "Cara, she's not just Time for Terror. She's gotten worse. That little girl is TIME FOR TERROR in all caps. You'll live to regret this."

"Maybe I can get a tranquilizer gun. Besides, I don't know what my little cousin from Texas is going to be like, but Mom asked if he could be the ring bearer. I'm taking a chance on him, aren't I?"

"I would say that it's the difference between inviting an unknown person and inviting a terrorist intent on blowing up the church."

"Now, I do my part right before you preach, right?" Bob asked, trying to confirm when he was supposed to say his line in the wedding ceremony.

"It's more toward the beginning, and I may not be preaching, Bob. They want it pretty short."

"You mean that the Word of God will not go forth? What kind of wedding is that?" Bob said insistently.

"It's what they asked for."

"Jim. Come on. No scriptural principles?"

"I don't know."

"You should speak on God's divine order in marriage. They need it."

"Well, I want it to be right," said Jim, "so, if that's what it takes."

That night, as they were reading in bed, Karen said, "I've been thinking a lot about this. Do you remember when we went to that wedding up in Chicago?"

"Jimmy 'what's his face' and Allison?" he replied.

"Yes, dear. I really loved it when the pastor told stories about his daughter and how proud he was of her."

"Oh, I remember that wedding now. That was that sappy ceremony where the bride and groom sang to each other."

Karen ignored the remark. "You know, Jim, Cara is really unique. Not too many young people have dedicated their lives to the Lord and to ministry the way she has--"

"Yeah. That would be something good for Amanda to bring up at the reception when she makes her remarks."

"I want you to come with me, Dad," said Cara. "I think you will really like the apartment. I know I do."

Her dad backed his truck down the driveway and ten minutes later, they were at Woodview Apartments. Just as they turned into the parking lot, Cara saw a red Chevy pull in on the other side of the lot.

Her dad's shotgun was under the seat, and it was loaded. Part of her wanted him to bring the gun with them into the apartment. Then, she made her decision and said nothing as they got out. She hoped it was a decision she wouldn't regret.

Kevin was waiting for them and opened the door to show them in. "It could use a feminine touch," Kevin explained, which was clearly an understatement. Although he had lived in the apartment three weeks now, no pictures hung on the walls. Further, there was very little that could be detected in the way of furniture.

"Could you use that couch from the basement?" Jim offered spontaneously.

Cara's Call

They could. Neither Cara nor Kevin would accrue debt. They didn't want their dreams mortgaged by "stuff."

"And I think we've still got those old drapes," her dad added. "They're somewhere in the attic. They may not be good, and even if they are, they might have to be altered. I don't even remember what size they are."

Cara couldn't believe how talkative her father was all of a sudden. She showed an interest in the drapes, although in truth, the color she remembered wouldn't go at all with the carpet. Actually they wouldn't go with anything. But she didn't want to appear to be ungrateful. Twenty minutes later, her dad's talking spurt was over. He was beginning to show signs of boredom, so Cara and her dad said their goodbyes to Kevin and made their way to the front lobby.

As they started to walk out into the parking lot, Cara kept her cell phone in hand, ready to call the police if necessary. But she saw nothing. They walked over to the truck without incident. Cara spotted the red car heading out of the parking lot as she was getting into the passenger side of the truck, but now that the danger had passed, she said nothing to her father.

Chapter 38

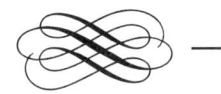

During the Sunday afternoon meal the week before the wedding, Sandra asked, "Do you want me to go up a key on the bridal march the second time I play it?"

"Yes," said Cara.

"Now I just want to confirm," Sandra pronounced, that we're not talking about a long ceremony."

"Less than half an hour," Cara replied.

"Good," said Sandra. "Because at my wedding, Dad spoke on the proper role for a wife for over ninety minutes."

"I did not," Jim said defensively.

"I'm glad you're just going with the blessing by the pastors," said Sandra.

"I might offer a scripture or two," said Jim.

"Please, Dad!" Sandra said. "Help us out here."

At the wedding rehearsal, Sister J had everything under control. She provided an agenda for Cara and for anyone else who was doing anything in the ceremony. Still, while she was organized, she was no match for Sandra. As Sandra scooped up her list and started toward the keyboard, Sister J asked, "Who's going to supervise Sissy until she walks up the aisle?"

"No big deal," said Sandra. "I'll be busy on the keyboard. Maybe you could do it, or if Cara's not doing anything, that'd work, too."

Overhearing the exchange, Cara was not really too surprised by her sister's presumption. Cara, of course, could not be expected to watch the child, so what Sandra intended was pretty clear. On top of everything else, Sister J was stuck with supervising Sissy. But Cara had been around her sister too long not to have anticipated some sort of glitch. "Elizabeth," she called out, and a head turned in her direction. "Elizabeth, I want you to get some more help on the guestbook. You'll still be in charge of it, but I've got something else I need you to help me with as well."

"Absolutely!" said Elizabeth.

"Sissy," said Sister J, "you're going to walk down the aisle when I tell you. Okay? And this is your nice cousin Brett. No Sissy, don't hit Brett. Be nice to him."

Uncle Bob was at the rehearsal so he could practice asking, "Who gives this woman to be married to this man?" Cara wasn't sure how it happened that Uncle Bob had a part in their wedding ceremony, but clearly now wasn't the time to make waves.

Although they were a half-hour late getting started, the rehearsal went according to plan. Sister J cued the four groomsmen and helped each of them stay in step with their assigned bridal attendant. Ron and Marta looked nice walking down the aisle together. Shay was not excited about being paired with his cousin, whom he said looked like a geek in her glasses, but there wasn't much he could do about it. As the maid of honor, Amanda kept asking Cara if there was anything she needed.

Cara received the text during the rehearsal dinner, and, because she thought it was no doubt some last-minute need, she checked her phone. The text read, "Have a nice wedding!"

Cara's face paled. Attached to the text was a picture of a knife with blood on it. "What is it?" asked Kevin, instinctively reaching for the phone when he saw the shocked look on his fiancée's face.

"Johnny!" he exclaimed.

"Kevin, you know I've been trying not to worry my dad about this too much. But I think we'd better inform him and make some sort of plan. It looks like we're going to have trouble tomorrow."

After all the speeches were made and gifts distributed to the bridal party, Kevin and Cara pulled her father aside to ask what they ought to do. When there hadn't been a focus for his concern, Jim had been pretty distracted. Now that there was a clearly defined objective, he was certainly up to the task.

"Well, of course, we will put the police on notice," her dad said. "We can have some of our own people on alert as well. Why don't we have Greg oversee them? I know he'll be pretty busy during the ceremony, but he's our best man. Safety's our greatest concern."

"Time to go," said Sister J, releasing Time for Terror's hand. While the lady who launched her held her breath, Sandra's daughter was perfect, spreading the mixture of autumn leaves and flower petals that Cara had chosen. Brett, the ring bearer, ignored his partner as he marched stoically ahead.

"So, are you ready?" Jim asked his daughter as they stood waiting in the foyer.

It didn't sound like the adult Cara who now spoke. "Daddy, I don't think I'll get faint. But if I do…"

"I know, Cara—hold you up. You can count on me."

The police, of course, had been warned to look for a specific red Chevy. They cruised the parking lot several times and even went down the side streets. Up until now, Johnny had never strayed far from that vehicle. The ushers were told to be on the lookout for a greasy-looking character, though no one had thought to give them a picture of Johnny. That is why no one noticed a relatively clean-cut young man in a suit seated in the third to last row on the end.

Johnny nervously felt for the leather sheath attached to his belt under his suit coat and fiddled with the smooth bone handle of the hunting knife he had brought with him. So far, everything was going according to plan.

Jim looked at his daughter and marveled at the swiftness of time. It seemed like just last week she had been born, yesterday she was having her sixth birthday, and only minutes ago she was graduating from high school. How was it possible, he wondered, that he was about to walk her down the aisle and give her away in marriage?

"Cara," he said admiringly, "You're beautiful."

And she was. Cara had chosen the dress. Amanda had proclaimed it "simple but elegant." Sister J had noticed how its A-line design and fitted bodice flattered Cara's beautiful figure. The white, satin dress had an embroidered lace mandarin collar, with a short, elegant V-neckline in front. Sleeves made of the same embroidered lace extended gracefully to her wrists. The satin bodice was embroidered in an intricate floral pattern which ended at the waistline. The dress then gradually flared into a flow of pure-white satin that was interrupted about ten inches from the hem by the same floral embroidery pattern on the bodice.

Johnny turned his head toward the foyer doors, anticipating the bride's entry. While drugs weren't entirely responsible for Johnny's disconnect from reality, they were certainly the catalyst for much of his delusional behavior. Johnny truly believed that if Cara were gone, and if her demise were to take place in a very public setting where Marta and everyone else could witness the act, then Marta would respect him and listen to him again.

Cara's father kissed her on the forehead and then asked Sister J to straighten her veil. "Your hair glistens," she said as she adjusted the sheer, elbow-length veil that adorned Cara's chestnut hair, swept up in curls for the occasion.

Suddenly, the chord for the bridal procession sounded, and the auditorium doors opened dramatically. Jim offered Cara his arm. As they stepped into the au-

Cara's Call

ditorium, she saw her mother eagerly rise from her seat on the front row and turn to face them. The rest of the audience followed suit.

"Radiant... radiant... be radiant..." Cara repeated under her breath. As she smiled, she mentally focused on drowning out the nervous thoughts that assailed her as she slowly made her way down the aisle.

Jim walked proudly, arm in arm with his little girl. He would make sure that she made it to the altar without incident. He glanced at her face to ensure she wasn't about to swoon or that she wasn't afraid like when she had nightmares as a child.

Flashes from cameras dazzled her; they seemed to snap, crackle, and pop all around. People leaned this way and that to ooh and ah over Cara's dress and whisper to one another approvingly. The chapel train flowed gracefully behind her as she, on her father's arm, gradually relaxed and enjoyed the wonder of the moment.

Meanwhile, her father mentally protested the whole ceremony. *She can't be a bride,* he thought to himself, *because she's my baby girl. Didn't she called me Daddy moments ago and ask me to hold her up in case she starts to faint? No, I'm not ready to give her away. It simply isn't possible.*

He glanced over at her again, this time noticing how the deep green in the arrangement of autumn flowers she carried matched the green of her lovely eyes. He also noticed his daughter's poise, how elegantly she carried herself. And it suddenly dawned on him that his little girl had grown up.

Bob discreetly walked up the side steps to the back of the platform, readying himself for his bit part in the ceremony. He had made sure before the wedding that Jim had brought his fifteen points on "God's Divine Order in the Family." Jim had dutifully obeyed, as he almost always did when it came to Bob.

When he saw Bob standing on the platform while he escorted his adult daughter down the aisle, a revelation came to Jim. He had continually deferred to Bob for one very good reason. It wasn't simply because Bob had good arguments. Mostly, it was because he sensed that Bob understood his true concerns—that Bob was motivated by his same genuine desire to protect his daughter from all the bad things that could happen to her.

Then he began to reflect on his own lack of trust. He could honestly say that he didn't trust how others would treat her. As painful as it was to admit, in some small measure, he didn't quite trust Cara's abilities. But now, walking down the aisle, he saw the real truth of it. Arm in arm, walking his daughter down that aisle, he saw it as clear as anything he had ever seen in his life. Sadly, the real issue was that Jim did not trust God. His wife had been trying to communicate that fact to him for the last two years. He didn't have confidence that God would lead and guide Cara, that He would hold her up, that He would protect her.

Those who saw that single tear run down Jim's cheek might have guessed at the emotions that had spawned it. But of course, they would have been wrong. No one but Jim knew the godly sorrow he felt at that moment, and no one but Jim knew that he determined at once to do something to demonstrate his absolute trust in God. Jim searched his mind for some specific thing he could do to show his confidence in God and in Cara. Then, it came to him: it was specific, public, and affirming. He wasn't sure what would happen when he did it, but that didn't matter. It would be an act of faith.

As he and Cara neared the altar area, he gently guided her to the foot of the stairs, and then they stood still. He could feel her hand resting lightly on his arm as the music transitioned to a close. She was now in full view of the audience. The bride, adorned in white satin and lace, the center of everyone's admiration and attention.

"Who gives this woman to be married to this man?" boomed Uncle Bob with pride.

"Her mother and I do," Jim announced, equally as loud. Bob winked at his friend as Jim placed his daughter's hand into Kevin's. Jim then leaned over to Kevin and whispered into his ear.

Kevin wasn't sure he had heard Jim's words quite right. He thought Jim said, "I love you, son," but after thinking about it a second, he was sure it couldn't have been that.

Jim's conversation with the groom caught Bob off-guard. He was further surprised when Jim left Cara and Kevin, walked over to Karen and whispered something into her ear as well. For her part, Karen wasn't sure why Jim had said what he'd said, but she kissed him, something for which the audience showed immediate approval. Well, most of the audience anyway. While his wife was left trying to figure out what had prompted Jim's request for forgiveness, it hardly mattered. Jim had made an important decision, and she was sure it was a good one.

Bob was now very anxious that he might do something wrong. They had practiced this quite a bit differently than it was now playing out. He was supposed to say "You may be seated" to the audience when Jim gave the bride away. Now, although Jim seemed to have given Cara away quite adequately, he did not do the next prescribed thing—that is, go to his proper place on the platform as planned. Instead, Jim was now talking to the bride. "Things are clearly not going according to protocol," Bob mused to himself impatiently.

"I just didn't want you to get hurt," Cara's father whispered into her ear. "Would you forgive me?"

Cara nodded and tightly embraced her father. Only after an extended hug did he completely release Cara to Kevin's care and walk up to the platform.

"If I faint..." whispered Cara.

"I know," said Kevin, "hold you up."

Because the chandeliers had been dimmed, and because no one in the audience expected an intruder at a wedding, no one noticed the man at the end of the third pew from the back, slip to the floor on his hands and knees. No one saw him unsheath the hunting knife and clench the blade sideways between his teeth.

Marta stepped back from the line of bridesmaids to her acoustic guitar, all tuned and ready to go. She slipped the strap over her head and around her arm and moved into the microphone as Bob pronounced, "You may be seated."

Marta's first chord was complemented by the sound of strings from the keyboard. On the chorus, Jim would add the bass guitar and Shay the drums. She looked out over the audience and began singing. "Tomorrow morning if you wake up and the sun does not appear, I will be here..." and then, abruptly, she paused and gasped. There could be no mistaking it. It was her stepbrother. Marta quickly recovered and nervously began singing again, just as Cara turned to catch a glimpse of a man with a knife in his teeth crouching by the wall and looking over a pew toward the platform.

Greg had seen him too, and into his cell phone he said, "Yes, send a squad car right away."

Marta continued singing, "Tomorrow morning if you wake up and the future is unclear, I will be here..." Greg slipped to the side of the platform and headed down the aisle. Four other men acknowledged Greg's action by heading in the same direction.

Marta was singing, "When the laughter turns to crying..." as Johnny, crawling on all fours, encountered the unforeseen difficulty of a man standing in his way. He wasn't sure why the man was standing in the side aisle during the middle of the ceremony, but Johnny easily adjusted and crawled to the left to get around him. Sadly, the man also moved to the left. So, to compensate, he moved all the way to the right as Marta was singing "...through the winning, losing, and trying, we'll be together, 'Cause, I will be here."

The man reappeared yet once more, blocking Johnny's way. Marta sang, "...when the mirror tells us we're older, I will hold you, and I will be here..." Johnny then realized that the man's shoes were not facing toward the ceremony in front but were pointing directly at him instead.

Johnny looked up and saw a giant looming over him. His mouth dropped open in surprise, causing the knife to clatter to the floor. He immediately lunged for the weapon, but the giant put his foot on it. Giving up for the moment, Johnny decided he'd better try for a quick exit. He stood up and turned to run only to encounter another obstacle. Several tall figures stood behind him, blocking his way. At once, Johnny felt himself being grabbed from both sides, and presently, the small crowd of men ushered him down the aisle, out the door, and into the waiting police car.

Crisis over, Marta beamed as she sang the last line of the song, "...our lifetimes are made for years...so I, I will be here...I, I will be here." There was spontaneous applause from the audience, during which Greg snuck back up to the platform and Marta took her place once again among the other bridal attendants.

As the applause ended, Kevin's pastor began his remarks. His assignment was to reflect about Kevin and pray a blessing on him, something he had no difficulty doing. He shared stories that illuminated how incredibly proud he was of Kevin and his brother. Of what an asset they were to the church in Charlestown and the difference they were making in lots of lives. Kevin's mom beamed from the front row. She had made a special effort to remain sober for the occasion and couldn't have been happier.

Jim then stepped to the microphone, and as Cara had feared, he pulled out the several pages that contained his typewritten charge to his daughter. The silence was palpable as he adjusted his reading glasses. Despite Jim's last minute apparent change of heart, Cara still feared he would be reading every word of his prepared sermon. She dreaded the empty feeling of a shattered dream if she did not receive her blessing.

Jim began, "I had planned on reading a piece that I worked out for the wedding on God's divine order for marriage." When a hearty amen erupted from the front row, Karen turned her face fully in Bob's direction and stared at him disapprovingly. Bob didn't seem to notice.

"I discovered something today, something about myself... and others. I guess what I'm trying to say is, I don't need to read fifteen points on the divine order for marriage, because I am looking at a young couple who are making God their foundation and building their future on His plans." Jim took the papers and ripped them in half.

Bob was aghast. But Jim was not yet done. He took his time, tearing it again and again, dropping the shredded bits to the floor.

Cara's Call

Then Jim said, "Cara, Cara… you look…uh, beautiful today. And I want you to know…"

"Say it," willed Karen from the front pew.

"Come on, Dad," whispered Sandra from the keyboard.

In the drum cage, Shay rolled his eyes.

"Cara," Jim continued, "I want you to know that I'm proud of you."

Tears rolled down Karen's cheeks. Sandra bit her lip, wishing it was she who was being blessed. Shay lowered his head, wishing he was part of some other family. There was a brief pause, but it was clear that Pastor Shepherd had more to say.

"Not everyone's going to know what I'm talking about and that's okay. Right now, I'm talking to you, Cara. Until this day I thought what I wanted was best for you. I thought my motives were right. And for the most part they were. I wanted to be biblical. I wanted to do what the church wanted. I wanted to do what a good father should do."

Cara did not know what her father would say next, but already tears were forming in her eyes.

"Today, as I walked you down the aisle, I realized that I had another motive, one that I hadn't acknowledged to myself until that moment. It was fear. Fear that I couldn't protect you. That people might think about you inappropriately, or that they might talk about you or reject you and that I couldn't keep you from being hurt. In short, I didn't believe you really had what it takes without me protecting you. As sad as that sounds, I discovered a problem that was even worse. I didn't believe God knew what He was doing either. I wouldn't accept that He knows what is best. So, I want to say to you, Cara," he glanced up, "and to You, Lord, that I'm so sorry." Jim was trying to say more but couldn't form the words due to his tears. He took out a handkerchief and wiped his eyes.

Finally, after he was able to regain his emotional footing, he said, "I want to pray a blessing on your life." Though Cara was the object of her father's focus, Kevin listened intently, grasping his bride's hand.

"Father, God who creates and redeems, I thank you for my daughter." Jim paused, apparently struggling as to how he would proceed. And then he said, "I thank you for the call you have placed upon Cara's life… and for… uh…Your promise to use her in ministry…"

As Jim began his prayer, several things happened in quick succession. First, Marta stepped forward to join in the prayer of blessing. Because she saw no real distinction between a wedding and their night fellowship meeting, she too laid her hands on Cara's back. Second, Ron, seeing that he was missing out, left his place among the groomsmen and laid hands on Kevin. Third, Greg joined in, and this was the key to everything that happened next, because it brought the whole bridal party up to participate in the impromptu blessings.

"And I pray your blessing on Cara's ministry and on this marriage..." There were, of course, about twenty or so in the audience from the fellowship group, some more regular than others. It only took the first one to step out of his pew and head toward the platform before it was like a dam bursting. And from across the audience in this or that pew, first one and then another came unbidden to the platform to add their blessing to the mix.

Then, people who were not part of the fellowship meeting realized that whoever wanted to could go to the platform to pray. So, although there was not room for them all, they poured out onto the floor and got as close to the platform as possible. Still, they came. And they prayed.

Jim continued, "and that You will protect them in every circumstance..."

Flashing lights from an incoming squad car could be seen through the stained glass. They were quickly extinguished, no doubt reminded by someone that there was a wedding going on and that the danger was now over. "...and that You will bind this wonderful couple together for Your purpose and plan. In Jesus' name, amen."

When Jim opened his eyes, it appeared as if the entire audience had invaded the platform. Of course, this was not the case, but he made a point of saying, "You may all be seated," with an emphasis on the "all." Only as everyone cleared out could he see Bob still on the front row shaking his head in silent protest, but Jim no longer cared.

After the vows, another song, and the unity candle, Pastor Shepherd said to Kevin, "You may kiss your bride." Hoots and howls attended the rather lengthy kiss. Shay temporarily forgot his embarrassment long enough for a drum roll and cymbal crash. Bob shook his head some more. Jim announced, "I now present to you Mr. and Mrs. Kevin O'Reilly."

After the kiss, Cara thought about how, ever since she'd been a small girl, she'd envisioned what her wedding would be like. At first that vision contained a golden carriage, but she had thrown out that idea long ago. She no longer cared that Prince Charming had never materialized. Then, in more recent months, Cara had begun to replace those fantasies with more concrete plans as to what would happen and who would be participating. Yet, in all of her imaginings, she never could have envisioned the reality of what had happened on her wedding day.

Those extraordinary happenings kept Cara from fainting amid the flash and flutter of the recessional. Despite everything and against all odds, two significant things she had prayed for so earnestly had actually happened. First, Cara's father blessed their marriage and her ministry. Second, the man whose name she took and to whom she promised her life was truly a man who kept his commitments. He would love and support her no matter what lay ahead.

As Cara really considered these blessings, she realized one more thing: This was the perfect day.

Acknowledgments

The narrative of *Cara's Call* grew out of a short drama presented at general conference and at the symposium. A number of people contributed to the script. Shauna Hord was instrumental as director; Jordan Wright was very helpful in writing the script; others who helped include Meagan Dunn, Amanda Hershberger, Shenae Huba, and Chris Green. Thanks as well to Claudette Walker and Mary Ellis for their contributions and for their guest appearances in the play.

Special thanks to Shauna Hord, under whose superb direction each character came to life. While Maegan Dunn's masterful performance of Cara in some way influenced my writing of the book, it was those characters about which I was most uncertain that were aided by the two performances of the play. Specifically, Evan Zenobia's interpretation of "Josh" and Jordan Wright's interpretation of "Stephanie" offered a foundation upon which I could build in the novel.

I especially want to thank the ones who offered their time in both writing and editing the chapters involving the narrative of Cara's travels. Those who contributed include but are not limited to Melani Shock, Janet Trout, Cindy Miller, Claudette Walker, Angela Harwood, and Ashley Stewart. Thanks as well to Brent Coltharp.

The lion's share of editing was done by my first and second readers: Lisa Taylor and Pat Bollmann. Everett Gossard also invested considerable time, offering initial direction and considerable help in finishing up. Lee Ann Alexander served as a copy editor. Thanks as well to Michelle Wire, Jessica Crawford, Kate Estreich, Maegan Dunn, all who collectively worked to expunge words and phrases that would have demonstrated that I was actually too old to write this book. Both Amy Landaw and Claudette Walker polished off errors that almost slipped onto the printed page. Gwen Oakes also honored me by reviewing the manuscript.

Details of Amanda's wedding are drawn from Amanda Hershberger's "ideal wedding" with additions from Pat Bollmann. Details of Cara's wedding are derived from the imagination of Maegan Dunn with additional work by Lisa Taylor.

In addition, special thanks to Kent Elliott and Faithworks for designing the cover, Laura Jurek, who laid out the book, and to Andrew McCay from Believers Press for printing.

A Word about the Accuracy of *Cara's Call:*

Because it is the author's intent for *Cara's Call* to be as authentic as possible, references to district and general officials depict people now in office. The theological position of the professors at the graduate school reflects the current reality. The youth convention, youth camp, the rallies, and the events that take place at the church in Salem are depicted as accurately as possible. Those ministries with which Cara comes into contact in her travels attempt to accurately depict current ministries. Words offered by those in ministry who meet Cara were primarily written by and/or in collaboration with those individuals to whom the words are ascribed.

Munson Heights, Bloomingtown, and Charlestown are all fictitious towns, respectively located geographically in Illinois where one would find Omega, Bloomington, and Charlestown, Illinois. All the people associated with those towns are fictitious, including Cara, her family, her friends and those with whom she is associated. Again, not only is Jim Shepherd, Cara's father, fictitious, but so are his associates in ministry, Bob, Pastor Gulliver, and Pastor Broadberry. It is the author's intent that the reader not associate fictitious characters or their words with any actual person, past or present.

Annotated Bibliography

In addition to the sources cited below, you can find additional resources at carascall.com. For example, you may access research papers by David K. Bernard, David S. Norris, and UGST graduate students. Additional bibliography is offered on the website from Professor of Church History, Steven J. Beardsley, who teaches a course on "Women within the Pauline Community," and by Prof. Cindy Miller, whose research for her doctoral dissertation was related to this subject. The website also features testimonies of women who minister.

Alexander, Estrelda. *The Women of Azusa Street,* Cleveland, Ohio: Pilgrim Press, 2005.
Alexander teaches at Regent University and has a long-standing interest in women in ministry. This volume chronicles nineteen women who played a part in the Azusa story. It serves as an introduction to the significant role women played in the seminal Pentecostal revival. It includes a bibliography for more in-depth research.
Prof. Robin Johnston

Beck, James L. and Craig L. Blomberg, eds., in *Two Views on Women in Ministry.* Grand Rapids, MI: Zondervan, 2001.
In the book, Craig S. Keener and Linda Belleville espouse the "egalitarian" view of women in ministry while Thomas Schreiner and Ann L. Bowman espouse a "complementarian" view of women in ministry.
Prof. David S. Norris

Belleville, Linda L. *Women Leaders and the Church.* Grand Rapids, MI: Baker Book House, 2000.

Although Belleville acknowledges various perspectives that would restrict women in ministry, she comes down squarely defending the biblical right of women in ministry. Lisa (Nance) Reddy utilizes this work as an important source in her research paper entitled "Exploring the Glass Ceiling…" Access her paper through carascall.com.

Prof. David S. Norris

Benvenuti, Sherilyn. "Anointed, Gifted and Called: Pentecostal Women in Ministry," *Pneuma* **vol. 17, (No. 2), Fall, 1995: 229-235.**

Benvenuti not only offers a strong presentation celebrating women in ministry in the early twentieth century, but also she writes with passion about the loss of place that women have generally experienced among Pentecostals. Good historical information, although it is not focused on a Oneness Pentecostal demographic.

Prof. David S. Norris

Bilezikian, Gilbert. *Beyond Sex Roles: What the Bible Says About a Woman's Place in Church and Family.* 2nd ed. Grand Rapids, MI: Baker Book House, 1985.

Beginning at the beginning—God's creation design—Bilezikian examines the full range of biblical texts related, as the subtitle says, to "a woman's place in church and family." He concludes, correctly, I believe, that no ministry in the church is prohibited on the basis of a person's gender. In addition to treating carefully all of the relevant scriptures, he includes ten wise, practical guidelines for working through difficult questions. In an appendix, Bilezikian responds to Wayne Grudem's treatment of *kephalē* (sometimes translated 'head') in ancient Greek texts, concluding that the word is never used in the New Testament with the meaning 'authority.' Early twentieth-century Pentecostal sentiments opened wide the doors for the powerful ministry of Spirit-filled women. *Beyond Sex Roles* is an excellent resource to show that the opening of these doors was biblical indeed.

Prof. Daniel L. Segraves

Blumhofer, Edith L. *Aimee Semple McPherson: Everybody's Sister,* **Grand Rapids, MI: Eerdmans Publishing, 1993.**

Aimee Semple McPherson was the iconic female Pentecostal preacher of the twentieth century. Blumhofer's biography is a readable account of this lady who refused to be restricted on almost any front. Given her prominence, a number of books about Aimee are available as well as her autobiography.

Prof. Robin Johnston

Butler, Anther D. *Women in the Church of God in Christ: Making a Sanctified World,* **Chapel Hill, NC: University of North Carolina Press, 2007.**

Butler tells the story of how women gained influence in the patriarchal world of the Church of God in Christ, the largest Pentecostal denomination in the United States. This is a study of how women in COGIC challenged gender roles and carved out influence in their church.

Prof. Robin Johnston

Clouse, Bonidell, and Robert G. Clouse. *Four Views of Women in Ministry.* **Downers Grove, IL: Intervarsity Press, 1989.**

The four views included in the text are all views held by Evangelicals, though a large segment of Evangelicals have historically been in opposition to women in ministry. Robert Culver holds to what the book terms a "traditional view," forbidding women from ministry; Susan Foh allows for more inclusion of women in ministry so long as they are squarely under male leadership; Walter L. Liefeld's approach moves further in allowing women to be a part of what amounts to be a plurality of leadership; Alvera Mickelson holds to an egalitarian understanding of men and women in ministry. The book is in part dated, but it gives clarity to several different perspectives.

Prof. David S. Norris

Fee, Gordon D. *Listening to the Spirit in the Text.* **Grand Rapids, MI: Eerdmans, 2000.**

While the book consists of a miscellaneous compilation of Fee's works, his chapter entitled "Gender Issues: Reflections on the Perspective of the Apostle Paul," is worth the price of the book. Fee offers anthropological clarity on how house churches operated and offers clarity to the way in which women pastored house churches.

Prof. David S. Norris

Goff, James R. Jr, and Grant Wacker, eds. *Portraits of a Generation: Early Pentecostal Leaders,* **Fayetteville, AR: University of Arkansas Press, 2002.**

This is an edited volume of brief biographies of early Pentecostal leaders. Seven of the twenty chapters are about women.

Prof. Robin Johnston

Goss, Ethel. *The Winds of God.* **Hazelwood, MO: Word Aflame Press. (1958) 1985.**

This book offers an incredible look at what normative ministry looked like in the early days of modern day Pentecostalism. Goss is not promoting women in ministry. The reader will simply see how normative it actually was.

Prof. David S. Norris

Hull, Gretchen Gaebelein. *Equal to Serve: Women and Men Working Together Revealing the Gospel.* **Grand Rapids, Mich.: Baker, 1998.**

Have you ever noticed how people on both sides of the women's leadership issue quote from Paul's writings? Paul tells women to be quiet, and he tells them how to have their head covered while actually leading in prayer and prophesying in the church. How can these positions be reconciled? Hull's book examines the biblical record without shying from the so-called difficult passages. In addition to her strong biblical scholarship, Hull's primary contribution to the discussion is the shift away from a 'rights' perspective to the opportunity to respond to God's call to serve. Apostolic readers need to add the critical reality of all God's people being filled with the Spirit—a reality that points to the empowerment to do what is impossible by human efforts alone.

Prof. James L. Littles

Keener, Craig S. *Paul, Women and Wives; Marriage and Women's Ministry in the Letters of Paul.* **Peabody, MA: Hendrickson, 1992.**

Keener's work should be a standard academic reference for any serious student of scripture when it comes to the subject of the place of women in the New Testament. Keener blends sound exegesis with serious historical inquiry.

Prof. David S. Norris

Mathes, Michael. *Lady Moses: The Life and Ministry of Reverend Eva Hunt.* **Vanity Press: Herrick, IL. 1980.**

Written to celebrate an important Oneness Pentecostal minister, the book offers a celebratory yet honest look at the challenges and accomplishments of a gifted woman. This book was the primary source for a biographical paper written by Chris Anderson on Eva Hunt. This paper may be accessed at carascall.com.

Prof. David S. Norris

Palmer, Phoebe *The Promise of the Father. n.d. n.p.*

Palmer's book, which can be difficult to get, is an early defense for women in ministry. She was a vital part of the nineteenth century Holiness movement that was a precursor to the modern Pentecostal movement. Her writings on women in ministry continued to be influential in the early Pentecostal movement. A number of biographies of Palmer are also available.

Prof. Robin Johnston

Stanley, Susie C. *Holy Boldness, Women Preachers' Autobiographies and the Sanctified Self.* **Knoxville: Univ. of TN Press, 2002.**

This is a really helpful read to understand the nineteenth-century climate that framed both a practical and theological launching opportunity for Pentecostal women in the twentieth century. Because the Holiness Movement was the soil out of which Pentecostalism grew, an understanding of Stanley's claims goes a long way toward understanding Pentecostalism's unique beginnings.

Prof. David S. Norris

Thetus Tenney. "The Ministry of Women in the Oneness Movement," in *Symposium on Oneness Pentecostalism: 1988 and 1990.* **Hazelwood, MO: Word Aflame Press, 1990.**

In her symposium paper, Thetus Tenney goes beyond some of the books written and edited by Mary Wallace who featured women in ministry but on a more popular level. Originally offered as a symposium paper, the research is helpful, as is her emphasis.

Prof. David S. Norris

Wacker, Grant. *Heaven Below: Early Pentecostals and American Culture.* **Cambridge, MA: Harvard University Press, 2003.**

Women earned the right to vote in the United States on August 26, 1920. This ended a 72-year push for the right to vote since the historical Seneca Falls Women's Rights Convention in 1848. Women were providing Spirit-inaugurated leadership in the Pentecostal movement before they had the right to vote! Reading Wacker's excellent work on the early years of the Pentecostal movement will illustrate the many ways women were involved in those early years. The book should raise questions of why the movement has trended away from this Spirit-led revolution while secular society was finally beginning to realize the justice and wisdom in including women in public discourse. Is it possible the Apostolic church could see a re-restoration of women's inclusion in leadership 100 years later?

Prof. James L. Littles

Warner, Wayne. *Maria Woodworth-Etter: For Such a Time as This,* **Plainfield, NJ: Bridge-Logos, 2005.**

Warner's biography on Woodworth-Etter is a readable account of the most outstanding female preacher who spanned the Holiness and Pentecostal movements. In addition to Warner's work, a large number of books by Woodworth-Etter are available.

Prof. Robin Johnston

Webb, William J. *Slaves, Women & Homosexuals: Exploring the Hermeneutics of Cultural Analysis.* **Downers Grove, Ill.: IVP, 2001.**

Fortunately, scripture was written within a historical context. The alternative is to deny God's incarnational nature as seen from Genesis through Revelation. Reading scripture is also from a historical context. Webb explores some of the more technical issues of hermeneutics in this book. While few Apostolics would call for a restoration of slavery as seen in various forms in scripture, many still hold to a limited view of women's place in participating in God's mission in the world today. Some fear granting women the 'right' to lead would be followed by acceptance of a similar position for homosexuals. Webb proposes biblically conservative ways to address these questions in an honest, transparent way.

Prof. Robin Johnston

W. T. Witherspoon, *Women's Place in the New Testament Church,* Columbus, OH: Modern Printing, n.d.

In the past, the premise of the book has had considerable influence through those whom Witherspoon influenced, both directly and indirectly. While both Frank Bartleman and G. T. Haywood could offer asides about women, this booklet offers a specific and organized approach against women, even when they were clearly chosen by God. For example, with regard to Deborah's position as a judge, Witherspoon would counter, "Yes, God used the woman as a leader when a God-appointed leader was too weak and cowardly to take his place alone at the head of God's people, refusing to go unless the woman went with him" (p. 9).

Prof. David S. Norris